The Marriage Menders

Patricia Wendorf has always been fascinated by the way that family secrets are passed down through the generations. In her latest novel she combines the excitement of a detective thriller with a subtle and perceptive analysis of marriage and family life. Patricia Wendorf married a German POW in 1948 and this was the basis for her first novel, *Peacefully in Berlin,* which was runner-up for the *Guardian* Fiction Prize. Since then she has written a number of well-reviewed novels, including the *Sunday Times* bestseller, *Larksleve.*

Her compelling novels *One of Us is Lying* and *The Toll House* are also available from Coronet.

Praise for Patricia Wendorf:

'Beguilingly understated … an Aga-saga with attitude'
Sunday Telegraph

'A novel of real quality'   *The Times*

'Highly charged, lots of drama'   *Mail on Sunday*

The Marriage Menders

Patricia Wendorf

CORONET BOOKS
Hodder & Stoughton

First published in Great Britain in 1999
by Hodder and Stoughton
First published in paperback in 1999
by Hodder and Stoughton
A division of Hodder Headline

A Coronet Paperback

10 9 8 7 6 5 4 3 2 1

A CIP catalogue record for this title is available
from the British Library.

ISBN 0 340 70830 1

Printed and bound in Great Britain by
Mackays of Chatham PLC, Chatham, Kent

Hodder and Stoughton
A division of Hodder Headline
338 Euston Road
London NW1 3BH

FOR MARGARET INGALL

GLOSSARY OF ROMANY WORDS

GORGIO	NON-GYPSY
DIDDECOI	DEROGATORY TERM FOR GYPSY
ATCHINTAN	GYPSY ENCAMPMENT
DINELO	FOOL
GAVVERS	POLICE
LUBBENY	HARLOT
TATCHI ROMANES	GENUINE GYPSY

Imogen

Funny, isn't it? The assumptions we make about our parents.
I would have sworn that my mother and father had lived
lives so ordinary, so dull, that nothing of interest could ever
possibly have happened to them; when all the time there was
this seething Hitchcock-type drama in their past about which I
knew nothing; an old crime that had never been resolved but
which I now see had spoiled all our lives.

The story broke last August. At a time of the year when
newspapers are short of dramatic copy, the events in the village
of Ashkeepers made inch-high headlines. The suicide of an
elderly widow would not normally have been reported in the
London papers, but when linked to an unsolved fifty-year-old
case of infant kidnap, well, I don't need to draw a picture for
you, do I?

You must have read about us in your Sunday papers. Even
if you were propping up a bar in Alicante or Torremolinos at
the time, you will not have managed to escape our little drama.
I am reliably informed that we appeared repeatedly on several
foreign newscasts in that week when my Aunt Dinah was found
hanging from a beam in her kitchen.

You may also have noticed how, in subsequent media
productions other family members had only walk-on parts. The
way my mother told it, she was the only one who suffered.

After half a century of total silence on the subject of her
first child's kidnap, there she was, bursting into print, chatting

confidently into furry microphones, appearing on breakfast television. But speaking always from her own point of view. Of course!

My daughter Francesca says she understands her grandmother's feelings, and thinks the publicity will in the long run be healing and therapeutic.

Niall dismisses the whole thing as a nine-days wonder. He and I disagree about what he calls my lack of compassion. To hear him talk you would think Nina was his dearest friend. 'You are not supposed to take sides against your wife,' I told him. 'Most men loathe their mother-in-law. Why can't you be normal?'

My mother thinks I have forgiven her the long years of coldness and deception. Well, she would, wouldn't she? That's the way she is. Always has been. She expects life to be predictable. Assumptions come as naturally to her as breathing.

After a long night of listening to her admissions and excuses, with wads of sodden Kleenex littering her carpet, even as we slumped exhausted in our chairs, I could see her filing me confidently away in her mind, as she does with other supposedly solved problems.

I come under I for Imogen.

'Only surviving offspring. The one who wasn't kidnapped. The one who, when told of the sad events of nineteen forty-seven, was naturally sympathetic and understanding. All is now right between us.'

But it isn't right, Mother. It never will be.

My trouble is that even now, filled as I am with resolution and anger, still I lack the courage to be truthful with her. I smile. I am agreeable and nice. I connive at this game we have always played in which she is right and I am hopelessly mistaken.

I can't believe I was born a hypocrite. Hypocrisy has not yet to my knowledge been listed as a genetic disorder. But I learned early on in life that a wise child in a family like mine is obliged to play the dangerous game of 'let's pretend that everything is normal', in order to survive. Even then I was aware that Nina was semi-detached in her feelings for me. By the time I was eight years old I had recognised that my father and I were in a conspiracy of two, dedicated to the cause of keeping my mother if not happy, at least reasonably contented.

I grew up, and nothing changed. My father died, and there was I, although a wife and mother, still tiptoeing around Nina, making her world a more bearable place in which to live. Until last summer.

I remember the exact moment when my life changed. Six months ago I would have said that instant conversions do not happen. I distrust these overly dramatic statements when made by others. Especially my clients.

I work with dysfunctional families. Need I say more? My moment of truth was delivered in a cheap brown envelope. Written on a sheet of grey lined paper, spelled out in shaky capitals, the message read, 'YOUR SISTER WAS MURDERED AND YOUR MOTHER DID IT'.

I would like to be able to say that I did not for one moment give credit to a word of this. But I cannot. I was an only child. I could never imagine my mother being capable of murder, and yet my reaction to the spiteful little note was strangely one of resignation rather than horror. It was as if I had always known subconsciously that my parents' oh-so-perfect façade was a sham. Incredible, wasn't it, that with a single shift in certain brain cells I was able to see my life as it really was, and not as I had been schooled to believe. There is no smoke without fire.

It seemed as if from one second to the next I ceased to be gullible and acquiescent and became critical and questioning.

My advice to a client who found herself in a similar situation would have been to destroy the anonymous letter and forget about it. Instead, I folded it back into its single crease and replaced it gently into the type of envelope which usually contains a final demand for prompt payment. And in a way it was a bill; one which only my mother could settle.

It took some courage to approach her. Believe me!

Ironic, wasn't it. Here was I, the trained counsellor, the one who was supposed to know all about feelings of betrayal and inadequacy, admitting finally to myself that my whole life had been a lie, and what was worse, that I was and always had been frightened of my mother.

Now, I am good at what I do. I am considered to be responsible and caring, serious and concerned yet also impartial. Sometimes I doubt that I am any of these things, even though I carry a briefcase and wear black with touches of white. As a card-carrying hypocrite I find it always helps to look the part.

But with Nina appearances mean absolutely nothing, although even at her age she can, when she chooses, look absolutely stunning. She does not often choose, preferring to go about in a builder's labourer's cast-off duffel jacket and baggy-kneed trousers. Her more eccentric behaviour had been reserved mainly for her family, until the day she decided to go public and reveal the most private details and best kept secrets of her life.

For her TV appearance she was as regal as the Queen and looked a good deal more fashionable.

Knowing the truth about the past can only be beneficial. To know all is to forgive all. How often have I trotted out these blatant lies, these sickening platitudes, to my troubled clients.

How dare I! What did I know about anything? What right had I to pontificate?

Yet in spite of my anger and changed life, still I was unable to march straight away into my mother's house, wave that nasty little note under her nose, and demand an explanation.

I arranged a treat, an outing. A cinema visit, which she loves. I drove her home after the performance, and with the voice of Madonna singing 'Don't cry for me Argentina' still ringing in our ears, I presented Nina with the letter which accused her of murdering a sister of whose existence I had never been told.

The shock, I now realise, might have caused a stroke or even death in a less tough and resilient woman of advanced age. But, being Nina, she rallied swiftly with the help of a cold compress to the forehead and a snifter of brandy. With her back now hard up against the wall and nowhere else to go, she talked into the early morning hours.

With many halts and bitter tears I was told the whole fantastic story. I learned for the first time about my father's family and her own. The grandparents, aunts and uncles, whose names had never been spoken in half a century of silence. It was too much to take in all at once. I keep waiting for normality to return, but it now seems unlikely. I left my mother's house and drove to one of those scruffy roadside tea-bars which lurk in the country lay-bys. I sat with the car door opened wide to the cold air of early morning and watched the sun come up golden in a pink-flushed sky. I drank bitter gritty coffee from a plastic cup, and pulled out a pen and pad from the glove compartment.

I began automatically to make notes, and then realised that I was now in the peculiar position of being my own client, and with no notion of how I should proceed. To complicate matters even further, I had been foolish enough to agree that I should be the one to tell the whole sorry tale to Francesca, my daughter.

So you can see, can't you, that in spite of enlightenment and resolution and my changed life, I am still dancing to some degree to my mother's tune.

The decision to move down to Taunton was mine, and since I am the principal wage-earner, and the payment of all bills, especially the mortgage, devolves upon me, I feel that I have a moral right to make such judgements.

And let's be honest about it. Niall can be happy anywhere as long as he has a few pounds in his pocket and no responsibility for anything at all.

He is your original, prototype con man.

He has this unique ability to look busy and important when, in fact, other people are doing the real work.

The cosy little myth that he buys derelict cottages, renovates, and then resells them at a profit was invented by me to save my face rather than his.

Niall has no pride. Left to himself he would degenerate into the sort of man whose spiritual if not actual home was in the Red Lion or the Queen's Arms, with regular visits to Ladbrokes and various West-Country racecourses thrown in, to ease the monotony of his idle days.

As it is, I make it my business to find him the occasional rundown cottage to tinker with, if only to support the fiction that he is still capable of gainful employment. When my mother insisted on buying the Toll House in Ashkeepers, and gave Niall the job of making it habitable, his consternation was a pleasure to behold. But ever true to form he proved he can still move fast when the situation demands. A few minutes on his mobile phone and he had employed two young, strong men who would do the dirty and manual work, while his own contribution to the project consisted of issuing orders to his employees, visits to the local planning authority and the ferrying of materials from builders' and plumbers' yards. The job, quite predictably, took twice as long as necessary.

Meanwhile, my mother was forced to move into a small hotel while waiting. It was late autumn; winter had set in earlier than usual, and with all her warm clothing locked away with her furniture in a city storage unit, Nina was obliged, or so she said, to borrow the young builder's stained and shabby duffel jacket. A garment which, by the way, she has never given back, and still wears at times when she knows it will cause me the maximum embarrassment.

Nina, quite predictably, is convinced that the sun shines out of Niall's nether region. A belief which I have never attempted to discourage. I discovered long ago how impossible it is to fight a mutual admiration society of two.

House-hunting in a strange town in midwinter is a daunting experience. The heavy rain fell out of low skies on that January morning when Niall and I saw Taunton for the first time. The windscreen wipers groaned and shuddered at the downpour, while we argued as to whether we should stay overnight in a bed-and-breakfast, or make the uncomfortable drive home later on that evening. Trivialities of that sort make up at least eighty per cent of our total conversation, while the important issues which we should be discussing remain unspoken. We lack the courage to admit that our marriage is over. If Niall was being truthful he would tell you that he has more in common with Nina, his mother-in-law, than with Imogen, his wife of many years. If I was telling the truth I would say – but why go into all that? We both know the marriage will not end, cannot end. It is held together by Niall's dependence on me, and by the sheer force of Nina's considerable willpower. Impossible, you think?

You should just hear her on the subject of the sanctity of wedlock. You would believe that Satanic rites, cannibalism, and the disembowelment of infants came lower on her list of crimes than divorce. She might well have invented the phrase, 'Let no man put asunder . . .'

I swivelled my gaze from the streaming windscreen to Niall's chiselled profile. Considered dispassionately, he is still a desperately attractive man. I had noticed this aspect of him only lately when he accompanied Nina on her visit to breakfast television. He sat beside her on that dreadful salmon-pink sofa with the clashing arrangements of purple and yellow flowers rearing up behind their heads, while the pneumatic blonde who conducted the interview crossed and recrossed her legs so often that her minimal skirt rode up to the region of her navel. She giggled and simpered and fluttered her mascara so blatantly in Niall's direction that my mother noticed and became exasperated. Even an adored son-in-law could not be allowed to upstage Nina Franklin.

I have a video recording of that hilarious few minutes. As I have said, it was only when viewing my husband on camera that I was struck by his charm and distinctive looks. He is the type of whom film directors say, 'The camera loves him,' and I wondered why I had taken so long to realise it.

I can't imagine how he manages to look so healthy.

He is a regular and devoted drinker and yet he has the same trim waistline and flat stomach that he had when we married. He drives the pickup the full one hundred yards to our newsagent's shop when he fetches his daily forty Dunhills. He has a bad back/knee/shoulder whenever the lawn needs mowing.

And yet! His thick brown hair is glossy; the only lines in his face are due to laughter. He is long-legged, broad-shouldered, deep-chested. His manner is polite and pleasant, his smile shy. He has been recently told, so he informed me, that he might be suitable to appear in magazine advertisements and TV commercials.

Told by whom? I wondered, but did not ask. Could it be possible that female TV presenters also have 'casting couches', and if so, do I give a toss? Thinking about it, it could be a good thing for both of us if Niall was able to cash in on his only talent. He will never be remembered for any skill beyond the bedroom. I can see him now in a TV studio, artificially tanned, windswept with the aid of an out-of-vision fan, craggy in his open-necked shirt, advocating health farms, cornflakes, cough mixtures, romantic weekend breaks. Especially the weekend breaks.

You get my drift? Of course you do if you are also a deceived wife. How else, other than by extra-marital sexual gymnastics, could a six-foot-four, fifty-year-old man who smokes, drinks and eats a cholesterol-loaded diet, keep his weight at a steady eleven stone and two pounds?

At this point you will either be finding my story an echo of your own plight, or you will have decided that I am a very unpleasant person, an ungrateful daughter and a shrewish wife.

Well, that's fine by me. Think what you want to! No skin off my nose! But just allow me to suggest that if you had met me *before* last August, you might have taken a different view. Why, you might even have approved of the old-style grovelling and pathetic Imogen who believed her task in life was to make the world a pleasanter place for those around her. You might have described me as 'sweet', or 'kindly', the perfect wife and daughter. But may I also point out that if you do find yourself approving of such hypocrites, women who fool themselves that they really, really do not mind when they are used as doormats, then perhaps you should be taking a long and searching look at your own life? Just pause a few minutes now, and think about it.

But if you have the stomach to stay with me, I promise you now that my tale will be, at times, a rough and tough exploration of the human condition, but honest. I am telling it for the benefit of all those miserable wives and daughters who over the years have sat in my office, and wept their tears and were given bland and useless advice by a counsellor who was quite unable to sort out her own husband and her own problems.

In the time it took to find a car park and a pub, the rain had ceased and weak sunshine shone on Taunton. The wine bar was furnished with white wrought-iron chairs and tables. I passed the time by drinking pineapple juice, reading the advertisements for Blackthorn Cider, and studying the sepia photographs of Old Taunton which hung around the walls. No coherent or sensible conversation could be expected from Niall until he had sunk his first double whisky.

I said, as he set down the almost empty glass, 'I'm told the house agents' offices are found mostly in High Street.'

'Whatever,' he said in the flat tone which meant it would take a second drink to get him on his feet and moving.

With another whisky in his hand he made a visible effort. 'So what are we looking for?' he asked. 'Out of town? In town? Large or small?'

I unfolded a street map of Taunton and laid it on the table. 'What do you think?'

He shrugged, drank up, and looked hopefully towards the bar. 'Time to go,' I said firmly, folding up the map. 'High Street is just around the corner.'

Niall remained seated, as if he had grown roots around the white wrought iron. 'You don't have to do this, Imogen.'

'Do what?'

'Move house and job. Disrupt everybody's life. Especially your own.'

I began to look at him more closely. Two double whiskies should have calmed him, made him as near normal as he was likely to be. He should by now have been smiling, amenable, but he was not. I said, spacing each word so that he could not mistake my meaning, 'I have to do this, Niall. I have to set some miles between myself and Ashkeepers.' I spoke quietly, reasonably. 'I have tried to put out of my mind what happened there last August, and I can't.'

He said, 'It was much worse for Nina, and now, when you should be supporting her, you're running away.' It was the most positive and passionate statement he had made in years, but instead of reassuring me that he was still capable of connected thought, it made me angry and incautious.

I leaned back in my chair; every separate whorl and kink in that intricate pattern of wrought iron was now pressing hard against my spine. I studied his rugged, almost-handsome features. When I spoke I hardly recognised my voice. I was no longer in my 'counsellor's' mode. Gone was the modulated tone, the carefully thought-out observations. For years I had coped with, tolerated Niall, by deliberately treating him as yet another needy client; as a not-quite alcoholic; a workshy but charming rogue. But since the day of the anonymous letter, when my whole life changed, I had taken a keener look at him and I did not like what I saw. It was his noble championing of Nina which finally released me.

'You bastard,' I shouted. 'You stupid, brainless, bloody bastard. How dare you compare me with my mother. This image you have of Nina as a victim of fate really has its comic aspect! You might as well see Maggie Thatcher as a poor defenceless downtrodden woman. I'll tell you about my mother, Niall. She is sarcastic, opinionated, and downright bloody-minded, and as for me supporting her, why should I? All she has ever done is find fault with *me* and sing *your* praises.'

His eyes opened wide; the alcoholic glaze almost disappeared and he was nearly alert. 'Stop it,' he muttered. 'People will hear you. What's happened to you, Imogen? I've never heard you use that sort of language.'

The barman was polishing glasses, listening but with his head averted. I breathed deeply and rubbed my sweaty palms across my expensive skirt. I looked at Niall and realised that he was genuinely outraged. It was then I really lost it.

'Niall,' I said, not lowering my tone. 'Have you ever thought there might be something kinky in the way you cuddle up to my aged mother? I wonder what the law has to say about a son-in-law who—?'

'Shut up!' He was wide awake now, as I intended he should be. The blood came up underneath those photogenic features. His gaze was focused. 'If you mean what I think you mean,' he stuttered, 'then you are disgusting. Why are you doing this to me? I don't deserve it. And why now?'

But even as he spoke, his hand was reaching for the tumbler, his head was turned towards the bar. I saw the desperation in his face and wondered how long it had been since he'd needed three doubles before lunch to get him moving.

Suddenly weary, sick of him and of myself, I said, 'Go on then. Sink yet another if you must. Be quick about it, we haven't found High Street yet.'

But once inside the estate agents' office it was Niall who asked the questions and displayed enthusiasm. Perhaps he had some rural image of himself, modelling Barbour jackets and green wellies, promoting fishing weekends on Channel Four. He asked the sales negotiator, 'Have you any reasonably priced country properties, fairly secluded?'

We were handed a dozen printed sheets, photos attached, of chocolate-box cottages in immaculate condition, and way beyond our price range. I waited to be consulted but it seemed that the third double whisky had stiffened his backbone.

It was as we turned to go that the young woman said, 'There is something else, but you may not be interested in renting?'

Niall returned to her desk with an alacrity which roused all my suspicions. We had just sold our town house to my daughter and her husband. I thought of the sizeable cheque deposited only yesterday in our bank account. I was anxious to have that cash anchored firmly to another mortgage. The thought of so much money, so easily available to Niall, brought a weakness to my knees. But by the time I had gathered my wits sufficiently to argue we were on our way back to the car, carrying photographs and information about a distant farmhouse, and with an appointment to view at three o'clock that afternoon.

The hills of the West Country are beautiful.

Even in winter, with a bitter wind sending scudding grey clouds up from Devon into Somerset, every turn of the road brought a vista that was like an unframed masterpiece done in oils. As we penetrated deeper into the country the lanes became narrower, their banks steeper, with sharp unexpected bends. Driving required all my concentration. I depended on Niall for navigation. I risked a sideways glance at him and was surprised at the animation in his face. I had never asked him if he was happy living in the city, and he had never said that he was not. He rarely spoke about his early life. I had a vague recollection of stories he had told Francesca when she was little, which involved a rural childhood, a small farm. The map of the area supplied by the house agent lay folded on the dashboard. We drove through small, attractive villages and on into rolling farmland, broken only by the occasional house and outbuildings. I wanted to ask him if he knew where we were going, to demand that he at least consult the map. But the fall-out from the acrimonious scene in the wine bar was strong between us; and perhaps I still hoped that a change of location, of lifestyle, might make a difference. I remembered how he had taken the initiative in the estate agents' office. But then reality broke through. The cynical bit of my mind was saying that it was too late for him to change.

There had been too many whisky-inspired new beginnings.

It was the sort of place which is featured in longshot on touristy postcards promoting the West Country. The house stood on rising ground, flanked by stone-built farm buildings, backed by a stand of beech trees and fronted by a meadow which sloped down to a shallow stream. Pale winter sunshine and a decent distance had romanticised the thatched roof and pink-washed plaster of the walls and chimneys. I turned in at an open five-barred gate from which several spars were missing, into a farmyard ringed by heaps of rotted manure and rusted machinery which would surely disintegrate if moved. I switched off the engine and wound down the window. The air was cold and clear. The rain had left puddles the size of miniature lakes. Now I could see the alarming sag of the thatch and the broad cracks that crazed the old plaster of the walls. I stepped out of the car, still staring at the house, and swore as my black courts filled with water. Niall walked ahead taking long strides and avoiding conversation. I caught up with him in the front porch. I stood teetering on the frayed doormat and poured water from my shoes.

I said, 'If you'd told me what you had in mind, I could have worn gumboots.'

'If I'd told you,' he said, 'you would have vetoed the whole idea. Anyway, I didn't know the place was vacant, did I, until an hour ago.'

I didn't believe him, but when he unlocked the door of Sad Acre Farm, I followed him in.

Niall

'You do realise, don't you,' she said, 'that if we decide to live here, I shall have a round trip of twenty miles every day to my Taunton office?'

'Twenty-two,' he corrected, 'if you start counting from the centre of town.' He continued to wrestle with a window frame which rattled in the wind but refused to open, while she struggled with a door which stood open but refused to close. It had been the same in all the rooms. Layer on layer of paint on every surface, so old and thick as to make the outer doors and windows virtually burglar-proof, while the interior had been unintentionally rendered open-plan.

He smiled at the thought, keeping his head averted so that she would not see and be upset at his inappropriate amusement. Imogen was a serious person.

She abandoned the door and moved to the fireplace. She sat on the bench inside the inglenook, crossed her legs and let her foot swing. He thought how good her legs looked in black nylon, the ankles slim, her narrow feet elegant in high heels. She wore her dark heavy hair in a French pleat, pinned with a butterfly ornament in filigree silver. Tiny silver butterflies nestled in her earlobes, and she wore an ornate silver ring on her left index finger. She had dressed that morning in the style she considered suitable for the viewing of trim little houses which had fully-fitted kitchens and bathrooms with bidets. Had she been forewarned of this foray into the countryside, it would have been designer jeans and a genuine hand-knit Arran sweater in place of the dark skirt and pale grey cashmere jacket. A part of her present irritation was to do with the fact that because of his deception, she was unsuitably dressed for the location.

He had known for some time that Sad Acre Farm was available to rent. The lie had been told more from habit than actual need; it was a game he played, a secret amusement, to see how many tall tales she would swallow without a confrontation. Driving up here had required all her concentration. He had been able to relax into his own thoughts and feelings, a rare escape when in her company.

That last double whisky had been a mistake.

He had not really needed it. The ordering and drinking of it had been to show her that he could still do anything he wanted, if and when he chose.

The barman had heard every word of her disgusting outburst against Nina and himself. It shouldn't matter that a stranger, who regularly heard far worse language and insults in his line of work, had been a witness to Niall's shame. But it *did* matter, and he could not put it from his mind. Since last year's drama in Ashkeepers, Imogen had undergone a change of character and mood that was increasingly difficult to live with. He wondered if she might be menopausal. He had heard that even quite nice, hitherto cheerful women became shrewish and depressed in their late forties. He wanted to ask her about it, but as yet had lacked the courage to put the outright question.

As it turned out, it had been her anger, her loss of control in the wine bar, which had finally decided him on his course of action. Until then he had tried to convince himself that he hardly cared where they lived, or how. As far as he was concerned, the most important features in this town of Taunton were the twin joys of its cricket-ground and racecourse. He had come down here some weeks ago, secretly, and made his own study of estate agents' windows. The faded notice which offered Sad Acre Farm for rent had caught his attention. If the sales negotiator had forgotten their arrangement that she should mention the farm just as he and Imogen were leaving the office, he would have been forced into enquiring about it. It gave him a disproportional satisfaction now to have his wife believe that their viewing of Sad Acre was down to pure chance. He felt he was beating her at a game she hadn't even recognised that she was playing. He experienced a rush of affection for her; misled and deceived as she was, she had managed, he conceded, to keep her looks and her figure. She had never been tempted on to sun-beds and beaches until her skin was baked to the texture of old leather; or overdosed on aerobics until she was all stringy sinew. Obsessive-compulsive by nature, yet Imogen was a womanly woman. But his admiration of her looks was purely academic. The same thoughts crossed his mind when looking at any attractive female. Although he and Imogen shared a luxurious king-sized bed, very little save sleeping ever occurred there.

It had been a slow, insidious cooling. They had married young, and Francesca had been born within the year. From the beginning he had felt that more was expected of him as a lover, as a husband and father, than he could ever deliver.

But for his mother-in-law's understanding of his problems with her daughter, her championing of him, Niall believed he would have thrown his hand in long ago.

He gave the paint-clogged window one last ineffectual push, and concluded it would never open. Without turning her head, his wife said, 'You'd better do something about that window before summer comes. About all the windows.'

He said, 'Don't worry about it. We can leave the doors open if we need fresh air.'

'Niall,' she said, 'it may have escaped your skilled professional notice, but it's only the front door that closes at all in this crazy house.'

Her sarcasm bounced off him. She spoke as if her mind was already made up. He could hardly believe his own luck.

Without protracted argument, without her extracting promises from him that they both knew he would never honour, she was in effect if not in actual words indicating her willingness to stay.

Imogen

I must be crazy; either that or pre-menopausal.

I could at least have made him plead, grovel, get down on his knees and beg. Instead I have meekly agreed to live here with him, in a house that lacks running water, electricity and gas, and has only the most unthinkable means of sanitation. I suspect by conceding the first round I have already lost the whole fight.

Oh, but how badly he wants to stay here! His need is so great he seems to reverberate with it. I can hear it in his voice, see it in the way his fingers move gently over that old carved newel-post in the staircase, the cracked panes in the windows; those dangerously loose boards of polished pine in the sloping floors.

He is like a lover who meets an old flame after years of absence, and willingly forgives her the odd blemish that has come with time.

He followed me from room to room, anxious and trying not to show it. He said, in answer to my unasked question, 'Well, we were warned, you know, that the place was in a rundown condition. The rent has been adjusted accordingly to take care of that.'

I bit back the sour little answer that anyone stupid enough to live here should be allowed to do so rent-free.

There was no point, was there?

The house was everything that I abhor. Dirty, shabby, mouse-ridden, and spoiled by half-hearted attempts made at

some stage to modernise it, on what must have been a shoe-
string budget.

And yet, I had stood at those gummed-up windows and
looked out across the green sweep of valley, the smudge
of blue horizon, and the widest skies I had ever seen, and
found myself pulled into a dream which was not my own,
but which seemed to belong to my feckless liar of a husband.

'Ground rules,' I said. 'If I agree to live here, albeit temporarily, certain things will have to be understood.'

He nodded. 'Well, of course, I can see that. Whatever
you say.'

'First of all, the money from the house sale. It must go into
a separate high-interest account, one which requires both our
signatures before a withdrawal can be made.'

He shook his head and put on a hurt expression. 'You don't
trust me, do you?'

'Absolutely right. Full marks for comprehension. I do not
trust you. There is also,' I went on, 'the matter of living
expenses. This move to the Taunton office is a promotion
for me, but the increase in salary will soon be swallowed up
by the cost of extra travelling. I shall also need a newer, more
reliable car; and as for this old barn of a house, we shall need to
spend a few hundred pounds of our own money, just to make
it habitable for the next six months.'

'Ah yes.' He turned back to the window and ran his fingers
nervously across the yellowing paintwork. 'That's something
else we need to talk about.' He paused. 'The lease is for five
years. Nothing less will be accepted.'

'Niall,' I said, speaking very quietly, 'how do you know
this, about the lease?'

'It's in the prospectus. Small print.'

'No it isn't. I looked especially.'

'Are you sure?'

'Quite sure. I wondered why it wasn't mentioned. When
renting, a period of three or six months guarantee of tenure
is usual.' I halted, just long enough to allow a line of sweat to

break out across his hairline. 'You knew about this place, didn't you? It was no accident we came here today.'

'I'd heard a rumour it was vacant. The house and five acres of pasture.'

I said, 'Forget the pasture. We shan't need it. Unless you are planning to buy a helicopter?'

'Cows,' he said. 'I am planning to buy cows.'

I stood up very slowly and moved to join him at the window. I looked out at the slopes of grass which ended at the river. 'Have you completely lost your mind? You know damn-all about most things; about cows you know absolutely nothing.'

'No,' he said. 'You are the one who knows nothing about cows. I was born and brought up on a dairy farm. Had you forgotten?'

I looked up into his face and realised that he was stone-cold sober. Any Dutch courage he might have gained from that third whisky had been lost to anxiety, and the need to tell the whole truth.

I said, 'I remember those stories you used to tell Francesca. I thought you were making it all up. You never struck me as having ever been a country sort of person.'

'And how would you recognise a "country sort of person" if you met one? And why,' he went on, 'would you think I needed to invent a childhood?' His shoulders sagged and a bitter line thinned his mouth. In a matter of seconds he looked ten years older.

'You were never interested when I tried to tell you about my home and family. You seemed to think that my life began on the day I met you, and that anything before that time was an irrelevance. I suppose you'll say now that you can never come to live here. That five years in a rented property is too great a commitment?'

I said, 'Do I have a choice? You seem to have set your heart on the place. If I refuse to go along with what you want, you'll do what you've always done. You'll go running to Nina. And let's face it, you can't begin to afford to stay here without me, and that's for sure.'

'Ah,' he murmured, 'as a matter of fact, I can manage quite comfortably if I have to. I've already worked out that I can put up two years' rent in advance. You remember that film work I told you about? I turned out to be quite good at it after all. It pays extremely well, and I've been promised more if I want it.'

He began to walk away towards the kitchen. He said across his shoulder, 'I shall be moving in here next weekend.' There was something in his voice which told me he was speaking nothing but the truth.

I said, 'You didn't tell me about this filming. What else haven't you told me? And why all the hurry? This is something we should talk about.'

'Next weekend,' he repeated. 'I need time to repair that little cattle shelter over there in a corner of the field, and sort out the fencing.'

There was a pride in his face and voice that had not been present since Francesca's birth. 'I take delivery,' he said, 'of the first four cows two weeks from today.'

I followed the direction of his pointing finger. The shelter he spoke of was minus its roof, and as for fencing, all I could see was a few frail and leaning posts linked together by barbed wire.

I pointed out that he might have problems hiring labour in this isolated place.

He said, 'I don't intend to use any labour but my own.'

I followed him into the kitchen. There was something over-assured about the way he stood, straight-backed and alert beside the window, making plans and surveying a farm he had not yet leased – or had he?

I remembered the estate agents' office, the girl who had called us back, oh so casually, just as we were leaving.

'There is something else,' she had said, 'but you may not be interested in renting?'

The kitchen windowsill had become a final resting place for deceased flies. A green stain in the old stone sink was the exact shape of the map of Ireland. That charade had been for my benefit. The awkward wife who needed careful handling. He had probably taken the girl for a drink, sat with her in that bloody awful wine bar and rehearsed her in what she should say when I appeared in her office; while all the time the signed lease for Sad Acre Farm was in his jacket pocket. For the first time in years, perhaps for the first time ever, I found myself wondering what really went on in Niall's mind. I controlled my usual impulse to confront him with his latest deception. I had tried so many times to understand his compulsive need to lie.

I said, 'I can't possibly be ready to move by next weekend. You'll just have to postpone these cows. It will take us at least four weeks to pack our furniture and get this house cleaned up and even halfway fit to live in.'

The drive home was made slowly and in uneasy silence.

Slowly, because I was bone weary, and in silence because there was nothing left to say.

So after years of dithering ineptitude, Niall had made a decision. Several decisions in fact, if his account of his new career was to be believed.

I negotiated the twisting lanes as dusk was falling and thought, light-headedly, how similar they were to the tortuous channels of his mind.

I tried to imagine him, living in that isolated spot, miles from the sort of low-life bars he loved to frequent, and having to come clean at last about the extent of his addictions. No more the daily visits to the corner-shop and off-licence. Once installed on Sad Acre Farm he would be forced to lay in his Dunhills in packs of five hundred; to stock his whisky by the crate. And then there was commitment, responsibility, qualities he had never possessed. Cows were living creatures, dependent on their owners. It would not be enough to turn them loose into a meadow and expect them to organise their own survival.

As for that house! Niall liked his creature comforts, hot showers, heat and light at the touch of a switch, four-minute meals from the microwave oven.

I allowed myself a secret little smirk. When I had asked him about cooking facilities he had led me proudly to a cast-iron monstrosity set into the rear wall of the kitchen. He explained its function.

'You light your fire in the firegrate and it heats the room; it also heats the water and cooks the most superb meals you have ever tasted.'

There was a little brass tap fixed to the rusty iron. Niall gave it a sharp turn and a trickle of brown water dripped on to the hearthstone. Looking at what must have been, in its day, a Victorian version of the modern Aga, I could not believe that mastering its moods would be all that easy.

A circular piece of fretted iron was hooked on to the bars of the firegrate to hold the huge, soot-caked kettle used, said Niall, to provide boiling water for tea and coffee. I lifted the kettle, and found that even when empty, its weight was considerable.

Absent-mindedly, I wiped my sooty fingers on my new skirt. 'Calor gas,' I said firmly. 'It's transportable. Comes in cylinders. Campers use it all the time for cooking and lighting.'

'But we shan't be camping,' he said. 'We shall be here for at least five years. Longer, if I can get the lease extended.'

'Then our need of some quick clean fuel will be all the greater, won't it.'

We were in the city suburbs when Niall spoke again. 'Do you realise we haven't eaten since breakfast?'

'How time flies,' I said, 'when you're having fun.'

At the drive-in McDonald's we bought burgers and a brew of coffee that would strip the old paint from those stuckfast windows.

Niall liked onions with his burger. The car would smell awful in the morning.

I don't usually permit smoking in my car. I have a printed notice on the dashboard which saves me the embarrassment of actually having to say so. But when Niall, reeking of fried onions, lit up a Dunhill without even opening a window, I found myself accepting his new assertiveness without a murmur. I put my weakness down to tiredness, and the shocks the day had brought.

Anyway, I told myself, I could afford to allow him a bit of leeway now and then.

After all, this new remodelled Niall wasn't likely to be long-lasting, was he?

It was only January; there was a lot of winter still to come. I imagined those lonely hills under snow, or in gale conditions; that draughty inhospitable house, and Niall deprived of his mornings in a smoke-filled bar, his afternoons spent watching the television screens in a Ladbrokes betting office.

As I garaged the car and locked it, I watched him walk away towards the house, irresponsible and carefree, whistling softly to himself, hands in pockets while he waited in the porch for me to unlock the front door and let him in.

Just for a moment then I had a rare sense of empathy with him. He was treading on clouds that night, his head filled with visions of grazing cows in summer meadows, and the sumptuous meals that would never be cooked on that rusty old firegrate.

And for the first time in our marriage, I felt a pang of what might have been anguish for him, and for all the broken dreams that he would be bound to suffer.

In the following week he made himself unusually available and useful. He cleaned out the loft, the garden shed and garage. He packed his tools and personal belongings, the clothes he would need for country living.

The house at Sad Acre was partially furnished. I made lists of what we would take with us, and which items could be left for Fran and Mitch.

After seven days of the dust raised by this galvanised Niall, I waved him off with some relief. I stood at the door and watched the winking red rear light of the overloaded pickup as he negotiated the driveway for the final time. He had not yet had a drink that morning, and I wondered how far he could drive before he would need to nip at his hip flask.

I turned back into the hall and caught a glimpse of my droopy dispirited self in the mirror.

Niall was on his own now, about to face problems and situations which were entirely of his own manufacture. I struggled with a sneaky admiration for him that almost bordered on respect. I walked through the silent house, pad and pen in hand, and noted all the jobs which needed to be done before I too could make my escape. I had intended, while in Taunton, to take a look at my new office, but there had not been time.

I made a large pot of tea and drank it slowly. This move, this new beginning, which had until last week been well within my own control, had suffered a landslip so that now the whole project was being dictated by Niall, and I was relegated to the role of camp follower. If I wasn't very careful I would find the shift of power was absolute, and that I was surplus to requirements. Like my state-of-the-art electric kettle and toaster, my combination washing machine and tumble dryer, my split-level ceramic hob and fan-assisted electric oven; my vacuum cleaner and hair dryer, my efficient central heating system. I tried to think positively about Calor gas, but all I could see was that barn of a kitchen, the stained sink and fringe of dead flies; the manure-littered yard and sagging fences. Just as I thought I had plumbed the depths of absolute despair, the telephone rang and my mother's brisk and confident tones boomed in my ear.

'Imogen. This is your mother. I haven't heard from you for several days. I was getting a bit anxious—?'

There was a time, before our alleged *rapprochement*, when she would have cut off her right hand before admitting to any anxiety about me. If worrying was to be done, it was not Nina's role to be that self-indulgent.

'Mother,' I said, 'you know how things are here. Surely Niall told you when he came over?'

'Oh yes! And I'm so pleased for you both. It all sounds idyllic. That beautiful farmhouse, in such a peaceful setting. All those empty bedrooms. As Niall said, a lick of paint here and there is all that's needed. I can't wait to see it.'

So now we were getting to it: *all those empty bedrooms!*

What promises had Niall made her?

With my free hand I reached for the teapot, and poured myself a cup of the mahogany-coloured liquid. Its scalding bitterness helped to put acid on my tongue. Just for once I refused to play her game of eulogising Niall.

'The place is a tip,' I told her. 'Niall is out of his mind taking on such a liability. We're not buying, you know, only leasing. The house alone needs thousands spending on it, just to make it weather-proof and habitable.'

'But Imogen, repairing old buildings is Niall's speciality. Just look at the wonderful job he did here in the Toll House.'

I couldn't bring myself to point out that without the help and skills of the Waynes and Darrens, the Kevins and the Jasons, Niall would not fix a single loose roof tile, or a worm-infested floorboard. In any case, she would never have believed me.

I could hear the capitulation creeping into my voice.

I said, 'It's just such a lot of heavy work to be done by one person. I shall be fully occupied with my new job. It will stretch me to my limits. I shall be heading up a completely separate department—'

'And all his plans for herds of rare breed sheep and cattle,' she interrupted. 'Such a good idea for him to begin with the Dexter cows and calves over winter, and to buy in some Jacob sheep in springtime. If he decides to develop and add to his stock, and set up a theme park, it could be very successful. He would need a licence of course, and an injection of capital, but I told him not to worry on either count.' She continued to prattle, but I didn't listen. Oh God! What promises had Nina made to Niall?

I came back to full awareness when she said, 'Have to go now. Primrose is dropping in for coffee. We're busy planning Ashley's wedding. It's to be a grand affair. Probably in Bath Abbey.'

I retracted the aerial and slapped the mobile down on to the table. As usual, my mother knew more about Niall's future intentions than I did.

As for poor Ashley Martindale, my newly discovered nephew, now caught between both grandmothers, God help him!

Niall

He decided to travel on the back roads.

With the pickup loaded to danger point, and last night's intake of Glenlivet still steaming round his system, to risk a spell on the motorway would be foolhardy and unnecessary.

For there was no hurry. Even when driving at his very slowest he would still arrive at the farm before midday. It was Imogen who had insisted on the early start. He could not recall the last time he had driven at this uncivilised hour. He was vaguely surprised at the quiet of the urban streets, deserted but for the pavement cleaners and the occasional heavily clad figure of some poor devil, hurrying through the icy morning to clock on in some dreary factory.

Once clear of the city the tension eased behind his eyes.

He began to enjoy the twists and turns, the uphill-downhill nature of his progress from one village to the next. Somebody had once written, Imogen would know the exact quotation, that it was the rolling English drunkard who had made the rolling English road. Some good old Somerset cider-drinkers had certainly been the first to tread this one. As he crested an especially steep slope he felt the ominous shift of the load behind him. He coasted cautiously downhill, and his hand of its own volition reached back to the pocket which held the hip flask.

He resisted the temptation; he tried to concentrate his thoughts on forward planning. He lit a cigarette, and pulled smoke deep into his lungs. Great thing, forward planning!

But Imogen's great thing; not his.

He was more your impulsive, spur-of-the-moment, easy-going sort of bloke. And blokeishness was his style. Not that he ever categorised himself in that or any other way. But he saw himself vaguely as one who always stood his round at the bar. Who accepted his betting losses without whining. Who loved his family without feeling the need to say so. Niall operated on instinct, and regular small doses of medicinal whisky and Dunhills Kingsize, which were safer and more enjoyable than any doctors' tranquillisers. In-depth self-analysis was something else he left to Imogen. Only when absolutely sober was he forced to face that other Niall. The bungler, the incompetent; the one who muddled through, patching and cobbling up his life, doing only what he was absolutely forced to. But a good sort nevertheless. Harmless and decent; and seldom absolutely sober.

Imogen was his problem.

He could picture her now, alone in the house and yet filling every corner of it with her energy and drive. Making her endless lists, selecting and rejecting; phoning Fran and Nina. Well – perhaps not Nina. Something wrong there. Always had been. But more than ever lately. He had come close to asking Imogen about it when they were in the Taunton wine bar, but she had been so shockingly fierce at his mild championing of her mother, so openly hostile, that he had thought it better to back off. There were certain things it was wiser not to probe too closely into.

On a one-to-one basis, Niall believed that he got on very well with women. Wives didn't count, of course. Marriage by its very nature was an unnatural state and doomed to fail. His greatest successes in love were with the wives of other men.

It was women in the plural who really terrified him, and within his immediate family Niall felt beset by some of the females he most feared.

The sky grew light as he came into Taunton. He recognised the

Tone bridge; he remembered the morning he had come here with Imogen, the scene in the wine bar, her unseemly language and his terror that at this crucial stage something would happen to ruin his manipulation of her.

He could, he told himself, have managed very well on his own. With the lease of Sad Acre Farm in his jacket pocket, and the beginnings of a Dexter herd already selected and soon to be delivered, he was, for the first time in his life, independent, freewheeling, unencumbered.

So why had her compliance with his plans been so essential?

Oh, he had considered dumping her; taking his half of the cash from the house sale, and returning to the bachelor state. Except that he could not really remember what that state was. Twenty-eight years of life lived with the same woman, in the same house, scored a deep groove in the mind. Certain ways of thinking and acting became habitual and hard to break.

If he ever became a millionaire, a lottery winner, he suspected that Imogen would still be his most valuable asset.

As he came on to the uphill roads that would take him to Sad Acre the pickup's engine shuddered, coughed, and then gathered strength for the climb ahead. The eastern skies were streaked a duck-egg blue and silver; hoar frost lay thick and white on hedge and field. He wound down a window and the sharp air struck his face and head with the force of a fist blow, clearing the whisky stupor from his brain, and the stink of cigarette smoke from the cabin. Memories came at him like arrows, each one finding its target. All those times, those people he had thought were long behind him. As he came closer to the farm he believed he could still smell the burning diesel from the Allis-Chalmers as his father fought with clutch and choke to start the ancient tractor. The tawny rumps of just-milked South Devons swayed gently across Niall's inner vision as they ambled from shed into crew yard, their breath pluming sweet and white in the crisp air.

'Oh shit!' he muttered, and again 'Shit,' as the tears welled out of his eyes to lie cold and static on his cheeks. He swung in through the ruined gateway and the misty house seemed to rise on its foundations and move out towards him. He killed the engine, closed the window, and reached for the hip flask. He lay back in his seat and waited for the spirit to reach his nerve ends. When the shudders in his stomach had eased to a gentle flutter Niall opened his eyes, thrust the flask into the glove compartment, and slammed it shut. It was then he remembered there was no longer a need for concealment. He thought about the crates of Becks, the boxed Glenlivet, the cartons of Dunhills hidden at the bottom of the pickup, underneath the tools, and Imogen packing ashtrays and the fire-extinguisher they had never yet had to use.

'Just in case you get careless,' she had said. 'We don't want you to burn the place down, do we, and that leasehold already half paid for?'

Coming here alone would be good for him. Good for Imogen too. She was always just that little bit too pleased with herself, sure of herself; knowing what was best for him, for everybody.

It was that damned job. What else could you expect from a woman who spent her days arranging and rearranging other people's lives. But there was, he suspected, another side to her, inadvertently revealed in curious ways. He thought about her briefcase, her single exotic possession, dark red snakeskin with gold-plated locks and fittings. She had bought it in a Spanish market. On her return to England she had abandoned forever her sober respectable case of dull black leather. He still wondered what else she might have abandoned on that solitary trip? The crimson snakeskin had a lush and decadent sheen that seemed to intensify as it swung against her thigh; that thigh slender in black nylon beneath the smoothness of her skirt.

A man could fantasise about such things.

That choice of briefcase made a statement about his wife which, when followed to its logical conclusion, was deeply disturbing, since it meant that she was not the woman he needed her to be. He reopened the glove compartment, grabbed the hip flask and drained it. He pushed at the pickup door, hesitated, then stepped out into the blue and silver morning.

Coming to the house with Imogen had meant nothing to him. He had walked through the downstairs rooms, seeing all of it with her eyes, the shabbiness, the dirt, the sloping floors, the cracked and crooked walls. Now he had returned walking in his own skin, living inside his own head, thinking his own thoughts. He pushed at the warped and heavy front door which was difficult to close, and made a mental note to do something about it. He began to move slowly through the rooms, touching, stroking, loving with his very soul the skills, the care, which had gone into the raising of this house. Walls that were fourteen inches thick; timbers which had hardly moved in over three hundred years, floors which had been laid down by his grandfather's grandfathers. Niall knew about building. Knew about it in his blood and finger-ends. All right, so Imogen thought, had said on occasion, that he was an idle, worthless bastard. She never recognised that *when* he worked, that work was *good*. Nina knew. His mother-in-law had acknowledged skill when she saw it. He had made a bloody good job of that old Toll House. He sat on the inglenook settle, stroking the rich mahogany, which looked and felt like satin. In his mother's day, bright woollen-tapestry cushions had lain in its corners. He remembered a time when his short legs swung several inches above the floor, and his mother, crouched before the fire, had made piles of golden toast, the home-baked bread impaled on an old wire toasting fork, and he eating voraciously, the pale farm butter dripping from his chin, famished after long hours spent with his father in the winter fields. He tried to remember his father within the house, but nothing came. All his images were outside: Dadda ploughing, mowing, riding the hunters hard and without a saddle, cursing the machinery he hated but was sometimes forced to use, his huge shout echoing back from distant hills.

A big man, his father. Fintan Donovan; or sometimes

O'Flaherty, or Shaunessy? He came from a tribe of people who switched names whenever it suited them. He had come sauntering up to Sad Acre on an April morning, a whistling, hands-in-pockets Irish tinker. A beautiful man, tall and broad in the shoulder, a shockhead of black curls and blue eyes, white even teeth and a smile to melt granite. That had been his mother's description. Niall recalled the bouts of drinking, the violent temper and the even more distressing self-abasement that followed; the tears of regret that seemed out of place in so huge and proud a man. As a child, as an adolescent, he had blamed and hated, and loved both of them in turn. Worst of all, he had felt embarrassed by them.

Now, thinking about them for the first time in years, he could see clearly that the faults had lain not with them but elsewhere.

Circumstances had been their undoing, and had led to their eventual downfall. Some tragedies are meant to happen.

His mother had owned the farm. In her own right. Willed to her by her parents, free of debt and of mortgage, or so she had led Fintan Donovan to believe. She was also a stationary woman. The house and the land held her fast. Twice each year she had gone down to Taunton, to visit the bank, to buy shoes and boots for her husband, for her son, but rarely for herself. Niall had gone with her. Seated beside her on what she called the dogcart, pulled by the pony which was nominally his, he became more aware with every year that passed that they made a rare outlandish sight as they cantered along Taunton's main streets. There were still some horse-drawn vehicles to be seen back in the nineteen fifties, but it was his mother's style of dress, her arresting looks which drew the eye. Tall and slender, fair-haired and grey-eyed, she wore the ankle-length dark skirts and high-necked blouses, the swinging capes and wide-brimmed bonnets that had been fashionable in her grandmother's day. Remembering the faint smells of lavender and camphor which hung about those clothes, Niall thought they had probably belonged to, and had once been worn by, his mother's grandmother. A word came to his mind, one that is seldom if ever heard in these throwaway, end-of-the-century days. His mother was a *frugal* woman. Nothing was ever wasted. Scraps of food, of soap, of paper, were recycled and utilised in crazy, time-consuming ways. Clothes were patched, darned, cut down or extended according to need. He seldom recalled owning anything that was truly brand-new.

His first school uniform, bought on his eleventh birthday for his September entrance to the Prince George's school in Taunton, had smelled so strange, felt so stiff across his body, that he feared the wearing of it more than school itself.

Looking back, Niall wondered what it had all been for, so much penny-pinching, such deliberate deprivations; those small meannesses that had robbed their lives of joy, and worn them down.

They had not, by anybody's standards, been poor. Not even marginally hard up. Yet his mother had forced them to live as if they were on the brink of financial disaster, bankruptcy, eviction. Everything used and worn until it was threadbare, and the resultant rags consigned to the milking parlour as udder-cloths, and the discarded cloths ending up on the dung heap, then carried out in autumn and spread to enrich the hungry fields. Nothing wasted, except life itself. In the single instance where his mother had been willing, even anxious to spend money, lay the only purpose which his father considered to be unnecessary.

'School?' he had roared. 'What does my boy want with boarding school? He's already learned all that he needs to in that little place in the village. He can read and write, can't he? And that's a damn sight more than his Dadda can manage! He can milk and clean the sheds. He can drive that bloody tractor like a man grown. He's a fine strong boy, good with his hands. What can a fancy schooling do for him, woman?'

'I want him to have a better start in life.'

'Better than what? Everything he could ever need is right here. He'll inherit from you. One day all of this will be his.'

'No,' she had said. 'There's something you should know. Niall can never inherit. The house and lands were left to me for my lifetime only. When I die the property will revert to my cousin Richard.'

Niall, listening unobserved from a corner of the settle in the dimness of the inglenook, had not really understood.

His mother's face had been sad, her voice solemn, as if she was telling of a death in the family. He felt the familiar lurch in his stomach; he waited for his father's anger at the bad news; his realisation of the long deception.

But Fintan, hands on hips, head thrown back, had roared out his great laugh. 'Then woman dear, there's nothing else for it, is there? You can't afford to die. You'll be obliged to outlive us all. Begod, Alice, for the boy's sake, you had better live forever!'

She had folded her hands in her lap and studied her fingers. 'It means nothing to you, does it? The house. The land.'

'No,' he said, equally solemn. ''Tis a burthen and a nuisance to me, so it is! And it's glad I am that my darlin' boy will never be weighted down with it the way that you are.'

His father was always his most Irish, his most tinkerman, when serious matters were under discussion. Even then, Niall had sensed that the thickened brogue, the feckless ways were exaggerated deliberately to distress his mother.

All his sympathies, his loyalties, were with Fintan. Blood called to blood; there was nothing of Alice in Niall's looks and nature. There were times when he stood deliberately far back from Fin, looked hard at the man, studied every aspect of him, good and bad, and thought with satisfaction: *this is me – this is what I am*.

It was in the boarding school that Niall first learned how to manipulate people and circumstances to serve his own purpose. He was tall for his age, strong and healthy. What he lacked in academic ability was more than compensated for by native cunning. And he had charm.

With Sad Acre Farm so conveniently isolated, he was able to keep private the secrets of his origins, his spartan home life. In the summer holidays he was invited to the homes of schoolfriends; the sons of businessmen and bankers, who lived in the large Victorian villas in Staplegrove and on the Wellington Road. In those houses he experienced for the first time a degree of luxury he had only read about and seen photographed in magazines. At the age of fourteen or fifteen he had long since lost the Somerset burr, overlaid by the Irish lilt of his father's speech. He had learned neatness, good manners, containment, and a diplomatic silence. There were times when he sat at some middle-class table, drinking watered-down wine from Stuart crystal, his hands moving confidently among the cutlery of heavy silver, and he would feel an unholy glee, a wicked joy flood through him. He would look from one pale, dough-featured face to another; listen to their talk of shares and dealings and think in his father's voice, *'Begod! If youse shysters but know'd me for the son of an Irish tinkerman, yous'd have my arse off this chair in double-quick time, and me tipped out of your back door. But not before you'd searched my pockets.'*

Niall had treasured such moments. There were to be other times in his life when he would hear Fin's voice, when the secret of his origins would rip with a terrible excitement through his veins.

He had stood in a city church with Imogen, he in grey tails and topper, she in justified virginal white; the wedding guests, to use Fin's old expression, 'dressed to death and killed with fashion'. Even while he made the vows he was not sure he could keep, while he looked deep into her eyes and saw his own face reflected, still he hugged the knowledge close.

'I am not what you think I am.' He could feel the laughter bubble in his throat. *'Begod! If you knew . . . If you only knew.'*

Imogen

When he's here he drives me crazy. The trail of mess he leaves behind him, room to room; sheets of newsprint, discarded socks, cassettes and videos spilled from their cases, a plate that holds a half-eaten sandwich. The telephone ignored and ringing from beneath a heap of cushions.

First time he has gone away. On his own. First time since we married. I go away regularly. Conferences, seminars, long weekends in interesting places.

He stays put. Yet in my heart I always expected that he would be the one to leave. But his wandering is done within prescribed parameters. With his work, his women, his favourite pubs and racecourses, he travels a tight and regular circuit. Rather like gypsies, moving from place to place; but always the same route, the same routines. Mobile but predictable.

He phones me in late evening, calling up when I am propped comfortably on pillows in the middle of the wide bed, a mug of hot chocolate on the bedside table, a batch of office files pinning my legs beneath the quilt.

There is a curious intimacy about these midnight conversations that would not occur if he was present. For so large a man he has a quiet, almost whispered way of speaking. We had never talked at length on the telephone; now without the distraction of his physical presence, I found myself listening to Niall's voice in a different way. Across the wires I could gauge his mood. I could judge his state of mind, his anxieties, from the faintest nuance, the slightest variance of tone. After the first two or three of these late night-early morning reports of his progress, I began almost to believe that I had discovered the secret path into his mind.

'So how is it going?'

'Pretty good. Very well in fact.' Well, I had known he would say that. He said the same thing whatever the circumstances.

'How's the weather down there?'

'It began to snow this morning. Picture-postcard stuff, powdery and dry, but drifting.'

'Seriously drifting?'

'Nothing I haven't seen before. It isn't going to be a problem. You packed me up with enough food to withstand a siege, and I've found a large woodpile behind the barn. The previous tenant had obviously made good use of his chain saw.'

'What about your cows?'

'The delivery date will have to be put back. Nothing ever gets down these lanes in this kind of weather.' He paused. 'I've made the repairs to the barn my first priority. There was a stack of old straw bales packed at the far end. So when the Dexters finally get here they'll be warm and dry.'

'And you?' I asked him. 'Are you warm and dry?'

He chuckled. I could not remember ever having heard Niall chuckle. 'Oh, nice one, Immie! I'm warm as toast; as for dry, the nearest pub is ten miles away, and the snow lies all about me, deep and crisp and even.'

'It's never stopped you before, as I recollect.' I kept my tone carefully light and free of censure.

I could feel his smile across the wires. 'Let's say, I'm only lightly oiled then. Just juiced-up enough to keep loneliness at bay.' His voice was also light but I could sense an undertone.

'Loneliness?' I asked him.

'Oh, you know – being here on my own – time to think about stuff I thought I had left behind me years ago.'

He had spoken about snow in the lanes as if he already knew

the lie of the country. I said, 'You've been there before – Sad Acre – haven't you, Niall?'

He answered with the nervous eagerness that told me he was lying. 'Of course not!'

I decided to back off. It was years since he had spoken to me about his feelings, and I realised that I quite liked it. I wondered briefly if he had company there with him; but only briefly. I recalled the shed behind the barn, the board with a hole cut in it which lay across the pit which served as a lavatory. Not at all the style of any of Niall's ladies. For they were never country girls accustomed to crude sanitation. It took some feat of the imagination to see his elbow without a bar on which to prop it; to believe him to be so needy that he was reduced to midnight phone conversations with his own wife.

He said, 'Sleep tight,' and I said, 'Yes,' although I knew I wouldn't. Too much to think about; to remember.

I leaned out to replace the handset and the movement sent the stack of office files slithering to the carpet. All those in-depth interviews, meticulously reported; the black and white of printed words that told nothing of the clients' agony, their desperation. I let the files lie where they had fallen, pushed aside all the pillows but one, and switched off the lamp. Immediately the darkness was absolute, thick and black as molasses. I thrust back the duvet in a rush of fear, leapt for the cord which controlled the curtains and snapped them open to reveal the night sky. Back in the warmth of the bed I lay with my face turned towards the window. As my eyes adjusted to the changed light I could see the first flurries of the powdery snow.

There are nights when no matter how desperate I am for sleep, I remain more alertly awake than I often am at midday. My brain begins to spin backwards like a video set to REWIND. This was to be one of those times, and the video was entitled *The Sad Life of Nina Franklin*.

I had promised my mother on that August night of family revelations that I would tell Francesca the inside story of her grandparents' lives. As the fine snow changed to thick and clingy flakes, I began to rehearse the version of events which I hoped would cause the least sorrow to my tender-hearted daughter.

I had so far managed to put off the telling, offering Nina a variety of excuses, pleading pressure of work, the imminent move to the Taunton office; the lack of a suitable opportunity for the imparting of such dramatic information.

The truth was of course that I could see no good reason for raking over these ashes of the past. Francesca, along with several million other early-morning viewers, had seen those in-depth television interviews. What more could she need to put her in the picture?

'So how old were you, Mrs Franklin, when your baby was taken?'

'Twenty – twenty-one. Old enough to be responsible, I might tell you! And we were, you know! There were no day nurseries, no social security handouts for young mothers of my generation. The only help available in those days had to come from within the family.'

'So what happened exactly on that night?'

'If it's exactitude you're after, I can only say that I went out to the woodpile to fetch logs for the fire, and in that few minutes my brother-in-law Alan Franklin came into the house and stole my baby from her pram. But we had no suspicion at the time that the kidnapper was Alan. Everybody knew that his wife Dinah was about to give birth. So why would he bother to steal his brother's child?'

'And why did he, Mrs Franklin?'

Nina had faltered at this point, all her sharpness blunted by old emotion.

'You must understand that I have spent almost fifty years of my life wondering about what happened that night, but not guessing the reason. Not knowing if my child was alive or dead. To begin with, I was the prime suspect. The police always take that view, you know. Crazy though it sounds, they believe that a child is most likely to be murdered by the mother who bore it. I was ostracised by most of my family and by all the villagers in Ashkeepers. We moved to the city, Jack and I. We tried to make a new life.'

'What made you return to Ashkeepers after so many years?'

'After I was widowed I found life very lonely. My grand-daughter Francesca lives in Nether Ash. I decided to move to a property nearby. It was while house-hunting with my daughter that I came across the old Toll House, in a terrible state of disrepair, but with a FOR SALE notice in its garden. As soon as I saw it I knew that I would buy it.'

'And this was the house where the kidnapping happened?'

'Yes – it was.'

'I don't quite see how you could bear to . . . ?'

'Well, you wouldn't, would you?' Nina interrupted. 'What you must realise is that since the age of twenty I had spent my life in hiding. My husband was a probation officer. He worked in the city prison. Prison officers are like policemen. Nobody wants to know them. They have no friends except among their own kind. Which, at the time, suited me very well. I could not have borne to be asked further questions, to face the hatred and suspicion I had known in Ashkeepers; to be suspected at worst of murder, and at best of being a neglectful mother. I wanted to be left alone. And so I was.'

'Didn't that deliberate isolation make life difficult for your husband and your second daughter?'

Nina looked genuinely amazed. 'Why should it? Jack and Imogen were guiltless; they also had each other. I was the one who had let my baby be taken away. There was no way around that. I WAS THE ONE. And I was on my own with that guilt. It was never discussed, that kidnapping of our first baby.

'Jack behaved for the rest of his life as though it never occurred. As though there was nothing to forgive because it hadn't happened.'

The hardbitten young interviewer looked shaken, then nonplussed. If the interview had been rehearsed, then Nina had long since departed from the script; she returned to her earlier question.

'Why did Alan Franklin steal your child?'

'Because his own child had died and he blamed himself. He saw a chance to redeem himself in his wife's eyes, and he took it.'

'So – so – you moved back into the Toll House all those years later – and then what?'

'Strange things began to happen, slight in themselves, but put together they first made me curious and then frightened. Somebody wanted me out of the village. The climax came with an anonymous letter, sent to my daughter and accusing me of murder. At about the same time, I discovered that Alan, my brother-in-law, was dead, and his widow Dinah still lived in the gamekeeper's cottage in the woods.' Nina paused at this point, uncertain now how much more she should reveal. She had not fully answered the interviewer's question about Alan Franklin's motive for his crime, for to do so would involve the revelation of all those old and bitter family feelings. 'I visited the churchyard,' she continued. 'I found Alan's grave, and that of Lucy, his daughter. They had both died in the same year. I decided to pay my sister-in-law a visit. My daughter Imogen accompanied me. Dinah had made a sort of shrine to Lucy's memory. A room filled with photographs and mementoes, flowers everywhere.' And now there was a break in Nina's strong voice, and I thought that she might not be able to continue. But she clasped her hands tight together, and went on. 'When I saw Lucy's photo I was in no doubt. You see – the young woman claimed by Alan and Dinah as being theirs, had looked exactly like my own daughter Imogen – who looks very much like me. The resemblance was strongly marked. If Dinah had been in her right mind, she would never have allowed us into that room. But she was not in her right mind, hadn't been for many years. She spoke as if Alan were still alive, and likely to walk in at any moment. She assumed that I had come to see her because I knew the truth; she told us about her own baby who had died soon after birth, and who was buried under the buddleia bush at the end of her garden. She told how Alan had come home one evening with a newborn infant zipped inside his windcheater. She had known the baby was mine and Jack's, but in her bitterness and anger she had justified the keeping of her. How relieved those two must have been when Jack and I moved away to the city, and no more questions asked.'

Nina had leaned forward then, her face only inches from the horrified features of her interviewer. 'Let me tell you something, young woman! Never run away from trouble! I spent almost half a century in hiding. If I had stayed in Ashkeepers, faced it out, and why shouldn't I have? God knows I had done nothing so very wrong. If I had remained – why then, as Lucy grew up I would have seen that remarkable physical likeness and acted upon it. I've discovered since, that others in the village saw and marked it, but the Franklins were influential people, nobody dared to accuse my brother-in-law, and in any case, there would have been no proof.' Nina sighed. 'All those years I hid myself away, determined to avoid pain. But you know, being hurt is a part of being alive.'

The tears were wet on my face, and I turned into the pillow as if I might find comfort there. Inevitably there were great gaps in Nina's televised telling of her story; it was the detail she had left out, partly from lack of time, but also by inclination, that she expected me to fill in for Francesca.

Trouble was – still is – that my version of events would differ greatly from that of my mother. As told by me, my daughter would learn about *my* childhood. She would know how much it hurts me to see how easily she achieves a closeness to Nina, which no matter how hard I try, I will never have.

The hands of the clock glow green in the semi-darkness. Three in the morning, and I know now that I will not sleep. I feel close to my father at this moment. I had never believed in an afterlife until he died.

I made a silent promise to Francesca and Niall never to repeat the mistakes made by my mother. To consider their feelings at all times, and in all circumstances.

But how am I ever to know if I have successfully kept that promise?

Niall

The snow settled in around him, concealing the dung heaps, the rusty machinery, the sag of the thatched roof. His first hours, first day, had been busy: unloading the pickup, clearing a space in the barn for the vehicle, carrying wood, splitting logs for kindling; pumping water from the well into the several plastic buckets he had remembered to bring with him. On that first night in the house his whole body ached with exhaustion and the biting cold. He built a huge fire on the inglenook hearthstone and heated soup on the primus stove Imogen had insisted on providing. A kitchen cupboard held a selection of oil lamps, and he had brought paraffin and new wicks; but when dusk crept across the windows he decided, for that night at least, to depend on firelight and the powerful beam of his builder's torch. He unrolled his sleeping bag, shook out the blankets and duvet and spread them in the space between blazing fire and settle. He hacked wedges of bread from a crusty loaf, and dunked them in the scalding soup. He ate a whole plateful of apple pie and washed it down with strong black coffee. Settled among the blankets, replete and warm, Niall lit a cigarette and thought about the crate of Becks beer he had left conveniently standing in the hallway. He half rose and then lay down again, his weariness outstripping his need. His eyelids drooped on the thought that perhaps he ought to phone Imogen.

When he woke it was to find snow drifted halfway up the windows, and a terrifying sense of disorientation in which he was a child again, waking in this house to the sounds of his mother making breakfast in the kitchen, and Fin's great voice cursing the temperamental Allis Chalmers as if it understood his every word.

He began to think about the Dexters: two newly calved heifers and their calves. The idea had come to him when filming an advertisement for health foods. While searching for a suitable location, the crew had come across a small agricultural show; Niall had wandered through the flower displays, the home-grown produce tent, the racks of riding gear and rows of brand-new tractors. He was passing the railed enclosures which held pedigree cattle when a printed notice caught his eye.

RARE BREEDS
DEXTERS. SMALLEST, AND RARE AMONG DAIRY CATTLE

IN 1896 A MR DEXTER, AN IRISH CATTLE BREEDER, MATED A KERRY BULL WITH A DEEP-BODIED KERRY COW WHICH HAD VERY SHORT LEGS AND A LARGE UDDER. THE RESULTING OFFSPRING WERE THE FIRST OF THE NEW BREED TO BE KNOWN AS DEXTERS.

THE KERRYS WERE THE ORIGINAL NATIVE IRISH CATTLE, AND HAD BEEN BRED IN IRELAND FOR 3,000 YEARS.

THIS NEW BREED OF DEXTERS INCORPORATED ALL THE BEST QUALITIES OF THIS HARDY MOUNTAIN STRAIN WITH THE ADDED ADVANTAGES OF COMPACTNESS OF BODY, AND AN EXCELLENT CONVERSION RATE OF AVAILABLE FODDER.

DEXTERS ARE EITHER ALL BLACK IN COLOUR, OR A DEEP SHADE OF RED. THEY ARE HARDY AND TOLERANT OF POOR GRAZING CONDITIONS, GIVING GOOD MEAT AND MILK.

Niall's father had come from County Kerry.

He moved closer to the rails, reached out a hand to stroke the velvety black flank, and wondered if his father had known about Dexters.

Almost certainly not.

Fin had loathed the milking herd of South Devons, even more than he detested the farm machinery. Any contact he might have had with the cows of his native land would have been limited to the theft at midnight of a pint or two of milk, wrung from some convenient udder.

He gazed for a long time at the neat black heifer and her tiny suckling calf. Niall remembered that he himself had not loathed his mother's dairy herd; and driving the tractor had been his greatest joy.

He conceded, reluctantly now, that not all of his genetic make-up could have been pure Irish tinker. Something of those old farmers who had built this house and tilled the land over generations must have come down to him through his mother.

He talked to the owners and stockmen who were brushing and polishing, preparing these prima donnas of the dairy world for the showing which would with luck win rosettes and add value to their herd. He noted an address and phone number on the inside flap of a cigarette packet, and filed it away with the hip flask and the petrol receipts in the glove compartment of the pickup.

That was last September.

Since then he had thought about the Dexters every time he hid the hip flask; every time he purchased petrol. When he posed for the rugged, outdoor shots required by the film crew he became increasingly aware of the deception he promoted. Too much booze, too many cigarettes had already begun to affect his health, although, fortunately, not his looks. For the first two hours after waking he felt nauseated and jumpy. Lately it had taken more than a couple of whiskies just to get him moving. When in the bathroom in the early morning he ran all the taps and flushed the toilet to conceal from Imogen the tearing sounds of his smoker's cough. Liver probably shot all to hell, he thought, kidneys likewise. As for his lungs! It was not laziness which required him to pay younger fitter men to do the heavy work entailed in house renovation, but the fear that if pushed to the limit physically, he might possibly drop in his tracks.

Niall knew himself to be weak-willed. Resolutions would be made only to be broken. The answer was to remove himself from temptation, to find a complete change of lifestyle.

When Imogen suggested – no, not suggested but informed him of – the move down to Taunton, he thought, to begin with, only about the racecourse, the pubs, the opportunities for following all his favourite pursuits, indulging his fancies.

And then he thought *Taunton*, and the name of the town hit him like a blow between the eyes. His ability to forget, to push unhappy memories into some dark compartment of the mind, surprised even Niall. Having been reconstituted by marriage, made over by Imogen into some wimpish figure closer to her heart's desire, had confused him so that even for him several years of his true identity had gone missing. Sometimes he wondered who and what the hell he really was. But the trouble with make-overs is that they do not always take. Recently, Niall's veneer of middle-class polish had begun to wear thin; his control would slip, and the Irish tinkerman in him occasionally showed through. That old joyous tingle would rip through his veins and he would hear his own demented gypsy mutter. '*If you knew what I came from – Begod, if you only knew . . .*'

Increasing light from the snowed-up rectangle of window revealed the pale ash of last night's fire, the dusty patina of the uneven floor; the house as it had always been, uncurtained, uncarpeted, spartan. He shivered, suddenly chilled by the penetrating cold of the room. He rose, fully dressed as he had laid himself down on the previous night. Such slovenly habits were possible when a man lived alone. He rubbed his hand across a bristly chin and decided that shaving could also be dispensed with.

He built a pyramid of dry kindling and lit it. He hooked

the ready-filled kettle to the chain that hung suspended from the chimney breast. While the water heated, he stumbled to the kitchen and poured a measure of Camp coffee into a large mug.

It had taken some finding, that supply of Camp.

He had bought a whole caseful, amazing the corner-shop grocer with his plebeian taste. Imogen had also raised her eyebrows at the cheap liquid essence of coffee-and-chicory contained in the thick glass bottle; and the strange, old-fashioned racist label which showed a turbaned Indian servant proffering a cup of Camp coffee on a silver tray to his European master.

'Easier to make,' Niall had told her, 'quicker. Don't bother to pack your electric gadget. You won't have a use for it on Sad Acre.'

He sat before the crackling fire, gulping down the strong brew. Fin had always drunk Camp first thing in the morning.

The hand that held the mug began to tremble. He reached for the hip flask and then remembered it was empty.

Out in the hall, wedged between the Becks, was a slim golden bottle of Glenlivet. He brewed a second mug of coffee, leaving space for a generous measure of the whisky. He returned to the seat before the fire and waited for the spirit to kick in, knowing that until it did he was incapable of further movement. His great effort had been made yesterday, achieving the drive down here without a single nip.

He planned to cut down, to eventually stop drinking altogether.

But not today.

Today he would need all the help that was available to him.

He should have been able to fall asleep pegged-out on a clothes line. The fire burned brightly on that fourth night in Sad Acre, he was warm and fed, his nerve ends soothed by a generous nightcap. He lay on a mattress of foam rubber he had found in a downstairs cupboard, and watched the gusting wind hurl snowflakes at the window.

Two hours after lying down he was still watching and listening. The idea of phoning Imogen again took him by surprise. He reached for the mobile then thought: but I don't do this sort of thing – it could become a dangerous habit – she might come to expect it – and what if I'm entertaining company some lucky midnight and she decides to phone me?

But even as the thoughts drifted through his mind, his index finger was punching out her number.

She answered cautiously as if expecting bad news or a heavy breather. 'Oh,' she murmured, 'it's you again.'

'I'll ring off if it's an inconvenient moment.'

'Don't be stupid,' she snapped, 'it's just that you never ring twice – come to think of it, you never ring once.'

'How would you know, I've never been away from home this long before?'

'No,' she said, 'but I have. When I was at that conference in Geneva I rang you every night, and never once managed to catch you in—'

'Stop!' he shouted. 'Stop it, Immie! You're beginning to sound like those whining apologies for women you spend half your life propping up.' His tone became quiet again, conciliatory. 'No. I didn't mean that last bit. It's just—' The words stuck and would not come, and then he spoke in a great rush. 'It's just so bloody *silent* here. I needed to hear your voice, even if you choose to nag me.'

He could feel his toes curl at her amused tone. 'Oh my! You'll be telling me next how much you miss me.'

'Like I miss a too-tight shoe when I remove it?'

'Why Niall!' she said, 'your repartee certainly improves after midnight.'

'Oh,' he said, 'after midnight I get better and better at a lot of things.'

'So you say. But come on now! How would I know that you're not just boasting?' Her tone was no longer light.

His whisky-induced euphoria began to drain away. The conversation was heading in directions he could not afford to follow. He said briskly, 'I fixed the front door. It no longer sticks.'

'Well done that man!'

'You may well sneer, but there's so much to do here, it's hard to know where to start.'

'Make a list. Begin with the most urgent jobs.'

Her advice was automatic, he had known what she would say and so ignored it. He said, 'Are you in bed?'

'Yes.'

'So am I. It's still snowing here; drifts are over the hedgetops.'

'Which bedroom did you settle on? You had six to choose from.'

He hesitated. 'I haven't even been upstairs yet. I'm sleeping in the living room, beside the fire.'

'You mean you haven't washed or bathed since you left home?'

'There's no bathroom, upstairs or down. Don't you remember? Anyway, if I smell like a skunk there's no one here to notice.'

She was silent for so long he thought she had broken the connection. 'That settles it then.' Her voice came back, strong and determined; her official tone that he guessed was usually reserved for wayward clients. 'I can't possibly live without a bathroom. You will have to install a shower and a flush lavatory *at the very least.*'

He struggled to remain patient. 'Imogen. There is no electricity, no plumbing here. You know that.'

'Buy a generator. Install a proper sewerage system.'

'But that will cost at least – well, thousands! And I don't need to remind you that our lease is for only five years.'

'Generators are portable, aren't they? When we leave, if we leave, we simply take it with us. As for the cost of the plumbing, I think we can stand that, since the yearly rent is so low.'

The unexpectedness of her suggestion, which was of course a capitulation and also an order, simply robbed him of breath and speech.

'Are you there?' she said sharply. 'You haven't dozed off, have you, Niall?'

'No,' he said weakly, 'anything but. I'm just knocked out at your change of heart. I hadn't dared even to suggest such luxuries to you.'

'Don't get too excited,' she said drily, 'it's my own comfort I'm thinking of. I can't imagine going out to that shed and sitting on a splintery plank, especially on dark winter nights.'

'Whatever,' he said. 'A bit of modernisation here will make all the difference.'

'Oh, will it?' she asked, and he knew her mood had changed, again. Whatever he said now, she was clearly going to shoot him down in flames. 'Will civilised sanitation and a few electric sockets stop your drinking and smoking, your chasing and gambling?'

'For Christ's sake, Imogen! Can't you see I'm trying? Why can't you have a bit of faith in me for once?'

'You really want to know?' Her voice had that poisonous edge, that smart-arsed clever note that would surely have incited a less placid man to violence, if not murder.

'You really do want to know this time, don't you? Then I'll tell you. I have no faith in you Niall, because you are a congenital liar. Because before you left, I watched you hide your crates of booze, your stinking cigarettes, in the bottom of the pickup. I know all about your hip flask and the floozies you pick up in bars—'

He switched her off in mid sentence. He raised the phone, made to throw it at the wall. Then he remembered it was his only contact with the white world.

Snow continued to fall throughout the long night. He woke at intervals, rebuilt the fire and fell back into uneasy sleep. He began to remember things he had spent half a lifetime trying to forget. His father's body skewed across the first treads of the staircase. His mother dead in her rocking chair, cause of death according to the policeman not yet apparent. They had brought him from his school in Taunton, the fatherly sergeant trying to prepare him for the double shock of sudden bereavement; for the curious manner of his parents' deaths.

He had never spoken about that time to anyone.

He had preferred to screw and sleep, drink himself into oblivion; find solace in the small illicit pleasures he had raised like a barrier between himself and the normal world.

'Which bedroom did you settle on?' she had asked. 'You had six to choose from.'

His throat had tightened. In his head the words he could not utter were a great shout. 'I can't even face walking up the bloody stairs yet, can I!'

But he would walk up them. He would have to.

But not until he was so drunk that every nerve was numbed, every painful bit of him anaesthetised; his heart dead even though still beating.

Nina

Primrose, who is my best friend and in many ways a very silly woman, has these occasional flashes of insight into my mental state and dire needs which leave me speechless; and it has to be admitted profoundly uneasy.

She and my daughter Imogen, I might say, get on remarkably well together. An alliance which I do not care to examine too closely, since it could be construed as a subtle criticism of me, both as a parent and as a confidante.

Imogen never tells me anything unless she really has to. And then only briefly. Days, sometimes weeks after the event or disaster, it is Primmie who will quite innocently drop the bombshell into a conversation. Primmie who has every fine detail of my daughter's life at the tips of those manicured, rose-tinted fingernails.

Assuming that I naturally know all about it, she will say, 'Isn't it wonderful news about Imogen's promotion. Head of Department. You must be so proud of her, Nina!'

I smile, nod modestly, and say nothing. I bite my lip.

I think, head of which bloody department? And where? For promotion in my daughter's line of work almost always involves what is currently described as relocation and, in my language, uprooting.

And why does Primrose Martindale know all about it, when I don't?

Primmie will then gaze at me with that tender unfocused

look which I suspect is down to short-sightedness, and her vanity in refusing to wear spectacles.

'You didn't know about it, did you dear?'

'I knew it was a possibility,' I lie. Well I would have known about it if the thought of my daughter's unlikely advancement had ever crossed my mind. Almost anything is possible in this life. But to be honest I had always seen Imogen as a settled kind of person. Married for twenty-eight years to the same man. Still living in the house Jack and I helped them buy while they were an engaged couple. Twenty years in the same job. My daughter had become a social worker in the days when it was still a respectable profession.

We fell silent across the teacups.

I rivet my gaze on the ornately-framed photograph of Ashley Martindale, which stands on Primmie's antique lady's escritoire. (Although Jack's desk fills one wall of my little sitting room, I tend to write my letters while seated at the kitchen table.)

I begin to think about Ashley, who is soon to marry Angelique, and who is the link which binds Primmie and me irrevocably together. Ashley, our much-loved and mutual grandson.

Primmie says gently, 'I'll make us a fresh pot of tea, shall I, Nina?' The question is rhetorical. I have never yet known her to wait for an answer.

I sit in her beige-on-beige room, which gives me the sensation of being trapped inside a giant mushroom. She returns with the recharged tea tray which holds a teapot, clean cups and saucers and a piled-high plate of chocolate biscuits. Primrose is the only woman I know who still uses traycloths. Remember traycloths?

Oblongs of heavy linen or fine lawn, appliquéd with satin flowers, or intricately embroidered with crinolined ladies who lead cute little satin-stitch doggies across every mitred corner.

Today's traycloth is pale pink. It matches exactly the delicate bone china. When she comes to my house we sit in the kitchen and drink our tea or coffee out of thick brown pottery mugs.

Not a dainty cup or spoon, not even a tray – never mind its cloth, anywhere in view.

But then, when I entertain Primmie there is never a hip flask to be seen. Her flask is made of silver, expensively antique, chased and stoppered. She often points out its great age. It sits now among the eggshell china. Without reference to my wishes she removes the stopper and spikes our teacups with a generous slug of Gilbey's gin. As I have already mentioned, she has these occasional flashes of insight into my mental state and my dire needs.

I have never worried about Imogen. Never needed to.

She was a biddable child, a well-behaved teenager, which was quite an achievement in the nineteen-sixties era of rock-and-roll and the Beatles. True, we were never close, and that may have been my fault. My own mother ran away with an encyclopaedia salesman when I was quite small. I don't know how relationships are supposed to work between mothers and daughters. Never had the chance to find out. Primrose says that I do not appreciate Imogen. But I do. I truly do! What I would prefer is a little more essential information about her feelings, her intentions. In her father's lifetime all her confidences were given to Jack, who faithfully passed them on to me. It seems now that the chosen go-between is Primmie, an embarrassing choice since my friend is critical of me in areas where Jack was not.

Two days later and I find myself in the gratifying position of being one-up in this game of inside information. I have a visit from Imogen's husband.

Niall, not unnaturally, assumes that I am fully informed about his situation and his plans, when in fact nothing could be further from the truth. He talks for five minutes about a farmhouse and an expected delivery of cows.

Eventually he notices my bewildered look.

'She hasn't told you, has she?'

'No,' I say.

He tells me everything: the rundown farmhouse, the long

lease, his plans for a herd of rare breed Dexter cattle. He does not mention Imogen's new job, and neither do I.

He says, 'You'll be welcome to come and stay just as soon as I've done a few urgent repairs, a lick of paint here and there. Come as often and stay as long as you want to. We shall have five empty bedrooms.'

Last night I had a phone call from Niall. He talked at first about the isolated farmhouse, his arrival there, the snow, eight-foot drifts in the Devon lanes and no thaw forecast. To begin with he sounded cheerful, considering his circumstances. But that was just the whisky talking.

Oh yes, I know all about Niall's little weaknesses, if that is what they are. He knows that I know. We joke about his hip flask. I offered one Christmas to buy him a silver model in the style of Primmie's, but he said wouldn't that look just a mite ostentatious when pulled from the back pocket of a jobbing builder's jeans?

He constantly puts himself down. He is so much more than a jobbing builder. When he married Imogen he was already a successful young actor. He had appeared in television plays. Small roles, it's true, but he could have advanced to greater things.

Something went wrong very early in Niall's life, and coward that I am, and true to form, I pretend not to notice.

We talked trivialities for a long time. Long enough for his mild euphoria to ebb away. I thought about him, alone in that rambling house. I am never altogether certain that he and Imogen are happy together, and I really don't want to know. But Niall had been good to me; he had stayed at my side, supported me through those awful television interviews, and overheated media attention.

I said, 'There's something else, isn't there? It's not just the snow and the loneliness, is it?'

When he finally spoke I could hear an undertone of fear in his voice. 'I think I may have made a mistake in coming here, Nina. A bad one.'

I said, 'If Imogen has agreed to live there it must be all right.' I attempted a light laugh. 'You know our girl. Famous for never putting a foot wrong. Miss Efficiency of the nineteen nineties.'

'She doesn't know what she's taking on.'

'True,' I said. 'She's never been nearer to a cow than a quick glimpse through her car window. Do her good to get her hair mussed and her hands dirty. Perhaps I'll buy her a milking stool for her birthday.'

He said, 'It's a bit more than gaining Imogen's approval. I'll never do that anyway. Gave up trying years ago.' He paused. 'Look,' he said, 'I need to see you, talk to you. Perhaps when the snow has cleared you could come down here. It's a bit rough and ready at the moment—'

'I'd love to come. Just ring me when the lanes are open.'

I relished my triumph. For once I was ahead of Imogen and Primrose in the game of who knows first and most about family secrets. For Niall clearly had a secret, and I did not believe it concerned those little flings he has from time to time with generous and consenting ladies; or the minor gambling debts which I have occasionally settled for him. Oh yes, I know all about his philandering too. I tried at first to feel indignant on Imogen's behalf, until she began to return from her seminars and conferences with the expression on her face of a cat who has lived exclusively on cream for the whole of the weekend.

Modern times, I tell myself, and none of my business. But if my suspicions were correct it was hypocritical behaviour all the same, from someone who has made a career and devoted most of her life to telling other women how to stay happily married.

It is up to the wife to know her husband's needs and satisfy them. I have never forgiven my own mother her desertion of my father.

I did not wait for the snow to clear. Advancing years have made me reckless. I travelled two days later by National Coach, availing myself of the senior citizens' reduced fare. Primrose, who would rather tramp barefoot than be seen on any form of public transport, took it upon herself to feel embarrassed for me. I let her waffle on about the indignity of having to reveal one's age to perfect strangers in order to ride cut-price with forty other people. What I did not reveal, because it is none of her damned business, is that the money thus saved would allow me to travel by taxi without a guilty conscience, and in solitary state and comfort, from the Taunton bus terminal to Sad Acre Farm.

These small economies, although not strictly necessary, give me enormous pleasure.

I told Primrose the well-known story about Charlie Chaplin, who, when already a millionaire, was said to have used pencils down to the last half-inch, and to have lined his shoes with newspaper when they needed repairing. Well, I am no millionaire, as Primrose pointed out. Oh, but I can be extravagant when the need arises. It is the knowledge that I have secured a bargain which gives me the most satisfaction.

I doubted that Niall had found a bargain in the leasing of Sad Acre. I arrived late in the afternoon to find him only halfway sober. He had offered to meet me in Taunton but I insisted on finding my own way to him. He was not altogether reliable when it came to such arrangements, and I had no wish to freeze to death in a Somerset bus station.

The taxi driver, who had sworn he knew the Blackdown Hills like the back of his hand, took so long to find Sad Acre Farm that for decency's sake he finally switched off the ticking meter.

He left me standing in knee-deep snow in what was presumably a farmyard, beside a house which appeared to be in total darkness. I rapped on the front door, and when this produced no answer, I kicked it as hard as my rubber-soled boots allowed.

When Niall finally appeared it was in the ghastly greenish

light of a hand-held halogen lamp, and on a cloud of whisky fumes. While he heated soup on a primus stove and built up the log fire into a great blaze we established that the mistake must have been mine. It seemed I had arrived, not only on the wrong day, but in the wrong week. Possibly the wrong year? I was too cold and weary to argue with him. I slept for twelve hours, fully dressed on the floor, on a slab of foam rubber beside the fire, with my son-in-law snoring heavily somewhere in the background. As I plummeted into sleep my final thought was, oh dearest Primrose, if you could only see me now!

I woke to a crackling fire and a smell of bacon frying. I struggled free of my blankets, sat up and leaned my back against the settle. A mug of scalding tea was pushed into my hand, and tea had never been so welcome. Niall's anxious face hovered over me. 'How are you feeling, Nina?'

I flexed my usually arthritic joints and could find no pain. 'I feel wonderful,' I said. 'If I'd known that sleeping on the floor was so beneficial—'

'You're quite sure? God! I must have been crazy asking you to come down here. I didn't think you'd travel in this weather, especially at your—'

'If you dare to say "at your age" I shall leave at once.'

He smiled and pointed at the snowed-up window. 'You might have a problem there. It could well be April before you and I see the lights of Taunton town again – a slight exaggeration – but you know what I mean.'

He went into the kitchen and returned with two dinner plates loaded with bacon, eggs and fried bread. We ate seated on the floor on piled-up blankets and by firelight.

I said, 'I was worried about you. When you phoned you said you thought you had made a bad mistake in coming here?'

He paused, a forkful of bacon halfway to his mouth. 'I was feeling a bit down that night.' His gaze did not quite meet mine. 'I thought I might have taken on a bit more than I'm equipped to handle.'

'And now?'

He chewed and swallowed and then he sat up very straight.

I was meant to be reassured by the determined squaring of his shoulders, his strong voice. But all he reminded me of was a lying child who wished desperately to be believed.

'I've got it sorted now. In my mind. I know what I have to do here.'

'Well, that's good,' I murmured. 'How does Imogen feel about things?'

He shrugged. 'Who ever knows what Immie thinks or feels? She's agreed to live here. She'll be arriving on Friday with the furniture removers.'

I mopped up the egg yolk with the last square of fried bread, and tried not to think about the cholesterol content. 'That gives us five clear days to bash this place into some sort of order. Where do you suggest that we begin?'

His smile was one of genuine amusement. 'Let me lead you to my kitchen, Nina; where all your questions will be answered.'

I will not go into the separate horrors of that kitchen, no not even to please Primmie who would relish the details of every beetle and spider, every cobweb and mouse-dropping, every sagging cupboard door and especially the rusty iron range.

Niall waited for cries of dismay. When all I said was, 'Ah yes – I can see why you thought I should start here,' his relief was obvious.

'It doesn't bother me,' he said, in the offhanded way that men adopt to justify themselves, 'but Imogen rather took against this kitchen.'

'I can see how she might have wanted a few improvements.'

He sighed upon the word 'improvements'. 'That's it, Nina! I knew you would see it my way. A spot of disinfectant, a lick of paint. After all, we haven't bought the place. We've taken it on a five-year lease. Any changes we make will be at our own expense, and who knows—?'

'Five years is a long time,' I pointed out. 'Anything could

happen. You might discover that you like the farming way of life.'

I had wanted to ask him the question from the moment I arrived here, but had lacked the courage. Now seemed as suitable a time as any to discover what my son-in-law was really up to.

'Niall,' I said, 'you obviously went to some considerable trouble to steer Imogen in this direction.' I picked up the greasy frying pan from where he had left it on the table-top. 'But you are no more used to living rough than she is.' I banged the pan down into the soapstone sink. 'I know you've talked about breeding rare Dexter cattle and keeping a flock of free-range poultry. But I get the feeling that you are here for a very different reason.' I picked up a fork and began to etch patterns in the congealed fat. 'Imogen went through a very bad time last summer, and I must accept full responsibility for that. If I had been more honest with her, more open, she could have been spared the shock of finding out about Lucy, and the discovery of Dinah's body.'

I abandoned the frying pan and sat down again at the kitchen table. I said, 'Imogen won't talk to me about any of it. It's like she's pretending that none of it ever happened. Her father behaved in the same way when Lucy was stolen from us. I'm getting the feeling now that Imogen hates me. Oh, she still smiles and is polite. We were never close, and that again was my fault. But now there's this veiled hostility and a tremendous distancing, and to be perfectly honest with you, Niall, I am finding it quite unbearable.'

He had that scared expression which most men get when a woman becomes emotional or is about to. With an effort I made my voice firm again. 'Has she said anything to you?'

'No. She hasn't spoken to me, on that or any other subject.' He looked directly at me, and for once he was not prevaricating. 'She doesn't talk to me either. I don't know how she feels or what she thinks about anything at all. Except of course my evil habits. On that subject she is most explicit.' He reached out a hand and briefly squeezed my fingers. 'She'll be here in a few days. Perhaps then we can both sort out a few things with her.' He spoke as if surprised at his own recent understanding of Imogen, his insight into her dilemmas. 'It can't be easy for her, can it? New job, the move from city life to country living. And as you said, there's all that bad experience of last year.'

I stood. I said, 'We need hot water, scrubbing brushes, disinfectant and mousetraps, and whatever it takes to remove the rust from that kitchen range.'

He smiled his lazy smile and reached for his cigarettes.

'Now!' I shouted. 'Not tomorrow or next week! On your feet, Niall. Let's get this pigsty cleared up.'

Imogen

When the removal men had finished loading and the van pulled away from the house, I closed the front door and proceeded to do the very thing I had vowed not to.

Some rooms are easy to vacate. A quick glance around the bedroom I had shared with Niall, the pale blue walls and dark blue carpet, and I slammed that door shut.

I lingered longest in Fran's room. Patchwork quilt and yellow curtains, her posters of Paul Young and Leo Sayer taking up most of the wall space. Her porcelain-faced doll, inherited from Nina, sprawled on the pillow. We had given her the largest bedroom, space for twin beds we had said, when she has a baby sister or brother.

It had never happened. Now the room would be my grandson John's, and I hoped he would not be too long alone there. From the window I could just see the swing in a corner of the garden, the treehouse Niall had built for Fran's eighth birthday. I was doing pretty well so far, or so I thought, for a dedicated sentimentalist. Moving house comes high on the list of life's more testing traumas. I believed I had dealt with it all; believed that the family home I had tried to create was not lost forever.

Of course they would change things, Fran and Mitch, in the way that each successive generation stamps its own identity and image on the world. I had invited them to choose any items they would like to keep, but I might have known my dark furniture and deep-pile carpets would not be to their taste. My mother had made me the same offer when she moved from Infirmary Road to the Toll House. But all I really wanted from her was that she should continue to live in the city house, keeping my childhood memories intact, preserving an identity of which I had never been totally assured. I had known even as I said it that I was being unreasonable, unfair; handing her yet another stick with which to beat me; expecting her to preserve memories which meant more to me than they did to her. Since I found out about Lucy, my elder, kidnapped, long-dead sister, I have dreaded entering the Toll House. It was the place to which she was brought soon after her birth, and the place from which she was stolen only days later. I have heard the story told so many times, by Nina and the media presenters, that I can actually see that little blue pram with its shiny chrome mudguards, standing by the window, and the uncle I was never to know in life snatching up the baby and zipping her inside his windcheater, carrying her away into the dark night.

Although she spent only a few days there, time she would never have remembered, I shall always think of that house as being Lucy's home.

I don't know how my mother could bring herself to go back there, to sit in the evenings in that room of bitter memories, and recall the police interrogations, the accusation that she had murdered her own baby. There is a toughness in Nina which I envy but do not possess. Seeing us together people comment on our likeness to each other. But the similarity is one of hair and skin, height and build, facial structure. Unlike seaside rock, our essential lettering is not stamped all the way through.

I can enter a room, a building, and if a tragedy has happened there I am able to sense it. I am never surprised when I experience this dread on going into an old house.

I felt it the first time I set foot in the Toll House.

I experienced it again as I crossed the threshold of Sad Acre Farm. I said nothing about it to Niall. There would have been no point.

The snow in the city had long since disappeared. Out in the country the hills were still snowcapped; the tops of hedges were slowly re-emerging from the deep drifts; the narrow lanes which led up to Sad Acre Farm were slushy but passable. I drove slowly, uncertain of what I should do if I met the empty furniture van making its return journey, and no convenient gateway I could pull into. My anxiety increased as I drove deeper into the network of icy lanes. I began to think about the house I had vacated and to long for the safe city roads and pavements which in this severe weather were sanded and gritted by council workmen. Out here a motorist would be dependent on nature, skilled driving, and a rapid thaw.

My thoughts turned to Niall. Those late night phone calls had disturbed me. After years of mutual indifference there had been a rare intimacy about those conversations. There had been a reaching out on his part to which I had responded shyly, like some young girl who is getting to know a boy and is not quite sure of how she should react. But I was not a young girl, and his present amiability might well be a ploy to gain my approval. Niall needed approval as grass needs rain.

The light was almost gone when I pulled into the farmyard. I should not have worried about a head-on collision with the furniture van for there it stood, empty, in a corner in the yard. This time I had come suitably dressed for the arctic conditions. I wore tailored trousers, an angora sweater and a quilted-silk parka, together with high, furlined boots and a smart cap of tan suede. The front door opened to my touch. As I walked through the hall I could see my furniture carelessly piled up in the rooms which lay on either side. A smell of beer and frying bacon came from the kitchen. The laughter was loud and prolonged. A gap in the door, which still did not close completely, allowed me a clear view of the table. Through a blue haze of cigarette smoke I saw Niall and the two removal men seated among a litter of empty beer bottles and overflowing ashtrays. At one end of the large table stood the primus stove, and above it leaned the tall thin figure of my mother, spatula in hand as she flipped sliced tomatoes and mushrooms and thick bacon rashers expertly around an outsized frying pan.

My hand fell away from the door as I took in her outrageous collection of mismatched garments and the ridiculous red woollen hat which covered her hair. I watched as she divided the contents of the frying pan into three equal portions and shovelled them on to waiting plates. A basket which held thick doorsteps of white bread stood in the middle of the table, with an opened pot of jam from which the spoon protruded. The tablecloth consisted of the spread-out pages of a tabloid newspaper. Illumination came from a lovely old cranberry-glass oil lamp.

For some moments I could neither move nor speak.

On my way through the hall I noticed the two suitcases I had packed that morning especially for instant access to warm trousers and sweaters, dressing gown and pyjamas, make-up and toiletries.

I took two steps back from the door, then three. The laughter continued. I saw my mother pour black coffee into three mugs. I had not been seen or heard. I turned, picked up my suitcases and returned to the car. I pushed the gear into reverse and coasted silently back into the lane, then turned my face and the car towards Taunton.

With the fading of the light a crust of ice had formed across the slush and lying snow. Propelled by rage I zipped back through the dangerous lanes without a twinge of fear. Once again I had been upstaged, usurped, unbalanced by Nina. I wondered why so many demoralising words should begin with the letter 'u'. I went into a skid, spun the driving wheel, swore an unprintable oath and by some miracle got the car back on track. My reckless mood as I drove into Taunton took me straight to the car park of the Castle Hotel.

The hotel stands on Castle Green. It is the most expensive, the most prestigious in the Vale of Taunton Deane. In springtime the stone façade is luminous with hanging vines of purple wisteria; white tubs of hyacinths and narcissi, tulips and daffodils flank the approach path from the car park.

Even as I locked the car and walked towards the entrance, I felt the pleasurable guilt that comes with an act of unjustified extravagance. I stood at reception and was acutely conscious of the elegant staircase which rose up behind me, the rich colours of the carpets, the warm air scented by exquisite arrangements of spring flowers, the muted glitter of cut-glass chandeliers.

The receptionist was young and charming and observant. The state of the roads was touched on. I confessed to not having made a reservation. I had driven, I said, many miles that day (which was no lie) and feared to drive further in the icy conditions. He was sympathetic. He could offer me a single room and a supper tray if I would like it?

Two well-worn pigskin suitcases and my Gold Card were sufficient to confirm my credit rating.

The single room was done out in shades of old rose and silvery-grey; the four-poster bed was painted white, the ruffled bedspread and hangings were an old-rose satin-chintz. There were the usual built-in wardrobes and dressing table, an attractive little writing desk, and a wing chair upholstered in grey velvet. The bud vase on the desk held two sprays of yellow freesia. The bathroom offered thick fluffy towels in various sizes, and those pretty little sample-sized bottles of shampoo, shower gel and bath salts. I poured their combined contents into a deep and scalding bath and soaked my bones until the water cooled.

The supper tray held hot asparagus soup, crusty rolls, smoked salmon and salad and a half-sized bottle of white wine. I had not eaten since early morning, but the very sight of the food revolted me. I switched on the evening television news, and inch by inch, spoonful by careful spoonful, while watching an horrific weather forecast, and depressing world news, I deliberately consumed every last drop, every crumb.

The Castle was the most luxurious hotel in Taunton, probably in the whole county of Somerset? I had not even enquired the cost of a single room with supper tray and breakfast.

I drank the half bottle of wine and lay back among the pillows. I thought with satisfaction of Sad Acre Farm and the bacon fried on the primus, the water which must be carried from a well, the lavatory behind the barn. A four-poster bed, wine and smoked salmon, an en-suite bathroom and out-of-season spring flowers seemed a just revenge for the wrongs that had been done me.

The mobile bleeped from my handbag while I was eating breakfast. I glanced swiftly around the dining room but the only other occupant was seated in the furthest corner. I forked kedgeree into my mouth and allowed the bleeping to continue. When I flicked the ON switch, Niall said, 'Where in hell are you? We've been trying to raise you since yesterday evening.'

Raise me? I found his quaint phraseology amusing. His choice of words were usually an indication of the kind of company he was currently keeping. Somewhere, not too far away, there would be some trendy TV type character, who boasted of flying regularly on Concorde, and who spoke with a mid-Atlantic accent.

'Well – here I am,' I said. 'Consider me raised!'

'Where exactly is here?'

'Taunton.'

'Since when?'

'Since yesterday evening.' The impromptu lie tripped off my tongue as if rehearsed. 'Car broke down in the middle of Fore Street. I'm in a hotel.'

'Why didn't you phone me? You must have known I'd be anxious.'

I smiled at the breakfast table, the pale green table-linen and matching china, the bud vase which held white and yellow tulips, the remains of grapefruit, kedgeree, toast and coffee. 'I'm quite safe, Niall. I couldn't raise you either,' I said sweetly. 'Must be this freezing weather, don't you think?'

'Your mother managed to get down here.'

The criticism in his voice was not implied but blatant.

'How very brave of her,' I murmured. 'Since Nina is at your side, you'll hardly be needing my help, will you? I might as well stay on in Taunton for a few days, take a look at my new office, find my way around.'

I broke the connection abruptly, not trusting myself to remain calm. I poured a second cup of coffee and reloaded my plate with kedgeree. I had lost control of events as I had feared I might. Far from escaping Nina and all the emotional baggage that came with her, I had, it seemed, made it possible, even easy, for her to move in with us; with me.

I began to eat, determined to enjoy every morsel. I lingered long over that breakfast and when it was finished my mind was made up. I would book into the Castle Hotel for a further three nights, and then review my situation. But today I would need to do essential shopping.

A glaze of ice made walking on the cobbled surface risky. I trod warily as I came through the archway that leads from the Castle Hotel on to Taunton's main streets. It was market day, the town was busy. Farmers wearing corduroy and tweed, nailed boots and waxed jackets and carrying thick blackthorn staves, shouldered their way among the shoppers. I tried to imagine Niall adopting the same style, and failed. The yellowish-grey skies threatened more snow. I needed changes of underwear, extra socks and pyjamas. When I packed those suitcases, I had not expected to be dependent on their contents for what might turn out to be weeks.

I found Marks and Spencers, where I bought thermal camisoles and pants, and three sensible nightgowns of a thickness and style that would have seen the Brontë sisters through several Yorkshire winters. After all, with a husband like Niall and a home like Sad Acre – who needed Janet Reger?

Along with details of my new appointment I had been sent a street map of the town. Someone had pencilled a cross to mark the location of the office out of which I should be operating. I went back to my hotel room and hid my Marks and Sparks carrier bags and their contents inside a wardrobe. Life in a hotel has a wonderfully liberating effect upon me.

Already the bed had been made, there were fresh towels in the bathroom, the little shampoo and bath-essence bottles had been renewed. It was a style of living to which I would quite like to become accustomed. I fairly skipped down the elegant staircase, past the impressive arrangements of flowers and out into the gloomy morning. It had started to snow again, but I at least had pavements under my feet, and the exciting prospect of a new job, new challenges and, albeit temporarily, an en suite bathroom and a white-painted four-poster bed in which to sleep.

I phoned the office to check that my arrival there this morning would not be inconvenient. I stressed that my visit was only to familiarise myself with the location and to meet the people who were to be my assistants.

Small courtesies of this kind are never wasted.

I know because I recently attended a course on the proper management of staff.

The snow sifted down like icing sugar. I took note of the street names. North Street led into Bridge Street and between the two curved the graceful wrought-iron arches of the bridge which spans the river Tone. A mist lay across the water and over the ornamental gardens and walks that edge the river bank. There was something about that view which drained away euphoria and false hopes. I imagined the same scene in late March or April, daffodils and tulips, hyacinth and crocus; blossom on the cherry trees, the sun sparkling on the brown, fast-flowing water. It was too cold to linger and yet I found it impossible to move.

I was, I realised, always thinking in this way, always looking forward a few months, a year ahead, dreaming of how life could be in some imaginary future, and never really facing up to present problems.

The here-and-now reality of it all was wintry Taunton, slippery pavements, my only home a shabby isolated farmhouse, currently inhabited by my faithless husband and my interfering mother; and a job which involved me in other women's heartaches.

A stab of pure panic had me gripping the ice-rimed wrought iron of the bridge. I leaned forward and stared down into the water. What in hell was I doing here, wasting money in a five-star hotel when I should have booked into a bed-and-breakfast? I was, I reminded myself, a frugal woman who bought her underwear in a high street chain store; a fool who worked hard to finance her husband's feckless lifestyle, and who, even when chance presented an escape route, had chosen to stay in an unsatisfactory marriage.

A voice in my ear said, 'Shudden bother jumping in, my dear, not if I was you. Not today. That water's bloody freezing.'

The bag lady's home was stuffed into plastic carriers, and wheeled in an old pram. She wore a man's thick overcoat, and a battered felt hat at a jaunty angle. A cigarette hung from her lower lip.

In my line of work training prompts an attitude of caring. I asked, automatically, 'Have you anywhere to sleep tonight? There's a Salvation Army—'

She held up a mittened hand and stopped me dead. 'Don't you worry about me, my lovely. Far as I can see, 'tis you what got the troubles.'

She trundled away across the bridge, and as the pram wheels hit lumps of frozen snow left over from the last fall, I could hear the merry clink of bottles. I walked on into Bridge Street. I had never lived alone. I moved straight from my parents' home to the house Niall and I had bought together. The very thought of a single existence terrified me.

I found the offices I sought on the first floor of an attractive listed building set among lawns and old trees. The refurbishment had been done to a high standard. Even on this day of snow and bitter cold I felt my spirits lift as I climbed the wide staircase, and went into warm and spacious high-ceilinged rooms done out in soft pastel shades, with groupings of comfortable upholstered chairs set around low tables. The contrast with my former shabby place of work was so marked that I sat down abruptly on a blue chair and gazed at the single painting on the far wall.

Here was the imaginative setting that was needed by troubled clients, but so rarely found. Whoever had been responsible for all this deserved to be congratulated.

The sounds of traffic were muted beyond the tall windows. A telephone rang and was promptly answered; music played softly from a hidden source. I relaxed into the chair and pretended that I was a client. I began to rehearse what I would say and do when my turn came to be interviewed. Would I tell it all, pour my heart out, the words stumbling off my tongue, or would I be silent, gazing at my hands, not knowing where to begin because wherever I began the ending would always be the same?

An inner door opened and then closed. I looked up to find a very large man gazing down at me.

He said, 'Good morning. Do you have an appointment?'

I stood, and although I am tall for a woman I found that I was the shorter by several inches.

'Imogen Donovan,' I said. 'I phoned earlier.'

'Why yes.' Pale eyes glittered coldly from beneath his overhanging eyebrows; the handshake was just a fraction too firm.

'Paul Mavsoni. I shall be your assistant.'

'Oh!' I could hear the dismay in my voice. 'I understood that Mrs Stevens would be working with me.'

'Mrs Stevens had to leave very suddenly. A family crisis, I believe. I was brought in at short notice. I am obviously not what you anticipated.'

'Nothing of the sort.' The polite lie came too late. The damage had been done. At a loss for words and to cover my embarrassment, I smiled and walked towards the window.

He said, 'We weren't expecting you until next week.'

'I came down earlier than intended. I wanted to take a look at Taunton, get a feel of the place.'

'You found a house then?'

'Out in the country, towards the Blackdowns.' I turned back to face him. 'The house is not quite fit for occupation. My husband is working on it. I'm staying in an hotel for a few days.'

I had liked the sound of Anna Stevens. We had spoken often on the telephone in recent weeks. I would have answered her questions easily and without resentment. The same enquiries coming from Paul Mavsoni seemed intrusive and edged with criticism. I had always found men difficult to work with. This shambling, bearded bear of a man already intimidated me. I looked down at my booted feet, the quilted parka and thick trousers. I was dressed like a woman from the backwoods. This impromptu visit had been a mistake. I should have worn my black suit and carried my briefcase for this first appearance. Image is everything. I hardly took in a word he said as I trailed him from one comfortable interview room to another.

He showed me the room that was to be my office and the one adjoining which he had taken over from the defecting Mrs Stevens. There was, he said, a part-time secretary who came in every afternoon, and a tiny kitchen and bathroom which meant that we were pleasantly self-sufficient. He had worked there for only a few days but I knew then, that even before my coat was hung on a peg in the entrance lobby, before I sat down for the first time at my neat bleached-oak desk, that his larger-than-life presence would have infiltrated into every routine, every office system, taking over the territory that I had believed would be my own. I followed him back into the reception room. For all his height and bulk, and the awkward, almost apologetic gait that he affected, this man actually moved lightly on his feet. There was nothing clumsy, nothing disconnected about anything he did or said. On this first meeting I already knew myself to be seriously disadvantaged. For very different reasons, but nevertheless, the bag lady on the Tone bridge would have made a more significant impression on him than I did.

Quickly, before I had time to question the wisdom of the invitation, I said, 'Will you have dinner with me this evening? There are several points I would like to talk over with you.'

The heavy black beard and moustache split apart to reveal white and even teeth. The smile certainly transformed him, but I suspected he was well aware of that fact.

'Why yes,' he said, 'I'd like that, Mrs Donovan.'

71

I said, 'Since I'm a stranger in this town I'll leave the choice of restaurant to you. Book a table for eight o'clock this evening and ring me later on this afternoon with the details.'

The note of authority in my voice made me feel marginally better, until I saw the amused and ever so slight raising of his eyebrows. I pencilled my mobile number on a scrap of paper.

'Have you any preference?' he asked. 'Indian – Chinese—?'

'Neither. I prefer my food to be plain and unadulterated.' I smiled as I spoke, but his expression was serious again.

'I'll be sure and remember that,' he said.

I knew before I left the office that to have invited a male, subordinate colleague to dinner, especially on an initial meeting, had been a grave error, liable to lead to all kinds of misinterpretation. Apart from which I had nothing remotely suitable to wear. I looked back across the snowy lawns and frost-rimed trees at the old stone building that would be a significant part of my future life. I located the window of Paul Mavsoni's office, and there was his dark, slightly ominous bulk watching me watching him. I began to walk fast back towards the Tone bridge. I slipped on a patch of concealed ice and was saved from falling by a passing schoolgirl. What I needed was a strong hot coffee and a place in which I could sit quietly and gather my scattered wits.

The coffee shop was a part of a small boutique. I was the solitary customer that morning, for coffee or clothes. The owner was a woman of my own age who, when I explained, understood at once the dilemma of a traveller who has an unexpected dinner engagement in a strange town, when her suitcases contain only sweaters and trousers, spare underwear and socks. The lady's name was Gloria. She joined me at the wobbly little gilt table. She said, 'I do a hire service if that would suit you better?'

'Hire would be fine,' I said. 'I almost always wear black or grey, so whatever I bought today would be a duplicate of something already in my wardrobe.'

She studied me at some length. 'Colour,' she said, 'is what

you need. With that black hair and pale skin you'd look a real dish in scarlet or emerald.'

The emerald dress was definitely not for me. Too little of it above the waistline, and not sufficient of it below.

The scarlet dress was long, close-fitting, slinky. It came with a short, high-collared matching jacket, and shiny black sandals. I had never in all my life worn anything like it.

I stood before the boutique mirror and thought about all the dark clothes in my wardrobe, the greys and blacks, the navy blues. A touch of white or cream in a sweater or blouse was the only variation I had ever permitted.

Gloria, with her upswept red curling hair and purple velvet trouser suit, was more perceptive than I gave her credit. She watched me through the long mirror.

'Colour frightens you to death, dear. Am I right, or am I right?'

'I tend to avoid it, yes.' I began to justify. 'You see, it saves so much trouble. All that matching and mixing. I really don't have the time. I know exactly where I am with dark.'

'Stuck in a rut, dear, that's exactly where you are. With your looks and figure you could wear anything you fancy.' She adjusted the stand-away collar of the scarlet jacket. 'Special date tonight, is it? Well it must be. You'd never have even tried that dress on if it wasn't. If it's making an impression on him that you're after – then that red'll do it for you. You won't need to flutter an eyelash. He'll be knocked sideways when he sees you.'

I thought about Paul Mavsoni in his corduroys and baggy jumper. I had left the choice of restaurant up to him. If his sartorial style was any measure of his taste in venues, we might end up in a greasy spoon café, or a fish-and-chip emporium. I smoothed the scarlet silk across my hips and turned sideways to the mirror. I raised my right shoulder slightly, and what I hoped was provocatively, and peered across the high stiffness of the jacket collar.

I imagined Paul Mavsoni's surprise at my transformation. It could be a crafty means of regaining lost initiative; of making a misleading statement about who and what I am.

I said, 'You don't think the red makes me look a bit tarty?'

'Tarty! I'll have you know that's a Versace exclusive you're wearing. Don't ask me how I came by it. There are certain famous, very wealthy ladies who privately sell on their left-off clothing to discreet buyers like myself.' She tapped the side of her nose with a green-painted fingernail. 'You'd fall down in a dead faint, dear, if I was to tell you who last wore that dress!'

I could feel my heartbeat quicken. Dizziness struck and my vision blurred. Too many cups of Gloria's strong coffee and no lunch. I held on to the back of a chair. Gloria was flipping her way through plastic packets. 'You'll need the right scanties, of course.' She dangled two scrappy bits of red lace before me.

I remembered the Marks and Spencers thermals I had bought that morning. 'I'll need black tights too,' I told her.

The long black silk coat was included free of any hire charge. It was the only garment of the lurid collection which I would not be embarrassed to wear.

The gold-coloured garment bag had the single word *Gloria* printed on it in flowing purple script. As I rushed through the hotel foyer I turned the bag inwards so that its plain side faced out towards anyone who chanced to see it. I wondered if this was how men felt after a first-time shopping expedition to a sex shop. Did their embarrassing purchases come contained in brown paper bags and plain wrappers? Did they skulk and scuttle nervously through public thoroughfares? Did they pray not to fall and break a leg and end up in a casualty department, having their curious acquisitions giggled over by some young nurse or junior doctor?

I fumbled my key into the lock and almost fell into the room, kicking the door smartly shut with the heel of my left boot. I tossed the carrier bag on to the bed and the silken gown slithered out on to the chintzy bedspread. In the shaded lamplight of Gloria's boutique its colour had been muted; in the white glare from reflected snow it was a definite and worrying scarlet. I dangled the scraps of lacy underwear from my fingertips and marvelled that I had been persuaded to pay so much for so very little.

The mobile bleeped and it was him, Paul Mavsoni. I found myself listening to his voice rather than his words: sexy, I thought, intimate, low-pitched and slow, bordering on suggestive. He was making a business dinner sound like an assignation. When he paused, waiting for my reply, I realised I had not taken in a single word.

I said, in my most clipped tones, 'Would you repeat that please. I seem to be on a bad line.'

'A quiet little restaurant,' he said, 'a few miles out of town, never crowded on a Monday evening. I'll pick you up at seven from your hotel. By the way, which hotel will that be?'

'The Castle,' I said.

The silence at his end was prolonged. 'Right,' he said, and again, 'right.'

'See you at seven then,' I muttered, but he was already gone.

There are men who can wear dinner jackets, and men who can't. On the rare occasions when Niall has needed to dress for dinner he has looked ill at ease, miserable even, in formal clothes.

Paul Mavsoni had taken trouble with his appearance. It crossed my mind that knowing he would be picking me up from the Castle Hotel might have given him some hint of what could be required of him that evening. Out of the scruffy sweater and trousers of the morning he was revealed as a leaner, rather rangy figure. His beard and moustache had been severely trimmed; his black curling hair neatly parted. He handed me into the elderly Range Rover as if it were a Silver Shadow, which believe me is no mean feat.

I tend to judge strangers by the way their cars smell. Niall's pickup stinks of cigarette smoke and every surface of its interior is the colour of an oversmoked kipper. When obliged to travel in it, I have squirted every brand of fresh-air spray, but nothing ever masks the odour. On the dashboard and floor there is always a tide of empty crisp bags, McDonalds' take-out cartons, petrol receipts and cassettes called 'The World's Hundred Best Love Songs' and 'Romantic Evenings with Des O'Connor'.

The Range Rover, although vintage, was immaculate within and without. In fact its very age, like a much-loved antique, seemed to lend it a certain cachet. I leaned back into the seat of worn green leather and breathed in the pleasant scents of polish, and lemon verbena which came from a sachet pinned above the windscreen. A portable CD player lay on the dashboard. Paul Mavsoni asked if I would like some music and very soon the sound of panpipes played by a Mexican musician helped to ease the uneasy silence which fell as we drove out of Taunton.

Away from the lights of the town I was vaguely aware of his sidelong glances. I pulled Gloria's long coat close about me so that not an inch showed of the scarlet silk. I tried to suppress an involuntary shiver, and he immediately turned up the heating by several notches. 'Sorry,' he said, 'I should have done that earlier. I had forgotten you would be wearing a thin dress.'

His thoughtfulness was unexpected. Consideration was something I usually gave rather than received.

'Better now?' he asked, and in that instant I wanted to lay my head on Mr Mavsoni's dashboard and sob like a desolate child.

I pressed my hands tight together and sat up straighter in my seat. Something shameful was happening inside me, and I could not control it. The smallest sign of kindness from a stranger and there I was, reduced to tearful gratitude, when all he had intended was old-fashioned politeness.

The restaurant, as he had promised, was small and quiet. Once inside, I headed straight for the door labelled POWDER ROOM. I stood before a full-length mirror and removed the silk coat. Even in the peachy discreet lighting the shock of the red dress again caught my breath. Gloria had insisted that I wear my hair down on this occasion, but I had compromised by substituting a loosely pinned chignon for my French pleat. I fiddled with the untidy tendrils which curled in my neck.

I looked like a middle-aged whore, and felt like a weepy teenager.

I walked back into the restaurant. I gave all my attention to the waiter who was pulling out a chair, unfolding a table napkin and placing it across my knees. A single blue candle burned in a silver holder on the table. Two sprays of white freesias nodded in a cut-glass bud vase. A white, baby-grand piano stood at the edge of a tiny, circular dance floor. The elderly pianist was playing a smoochy selection from a popular musical.

I was looking anywhere but at Mr Mavsoni. My stomach was a tight knot. I wished myself back in my hotel room. I almost wished I was on Sad Acre Farm. When I finally met his gaze I saw surprise and shock, and something else that I could not define. He began to speak, then thought better of it.

The silence became intolerable. I said, 'People seem to be very fond of freesias in this town. I see them everywhere I go.'

'Mrs Donovan,' he said quietly, 'if I hadn't driven you here, and walked with you into this restaurant – I would never have recognised you in that gown.'

I attempted a lightness I did not feel. 'Oh my! Did I really look so different when we met this morning?'

'If you'll allow me to say so, you looked very charming. But now – well, I feel I should have taken you somewhere more – more impressive. This place doesn't do you justice. I wish—'

The arrival of the wine waiter saved him. We ordered mineral water. I began to question him about office routines. I had planned an in-depth, intelligent interrogation but my mind roved elsewhere. I don't even remember now what food we ordered. I only recall that he ate his neatly and with concentration while I pushed mine distractedly about the plate. It was not behaviour appropriate to my new position. I tried to remember the advice I was given on the recent course, especially that which applied to the line which should be taken when dealing with lower-grade male staff.

Firm but polite. Friendly but not familiar. These were not

the specific instructions given, but wrapped up in psycho-babble the message was the same.

So what was I doing here?

Would I, I asked myself, have invited the departed Mrs Stevens to have dinner with me?

No, of course I wouldn't.

But then, there would have been no need to contrive a private meeting with another woman. I would have known instinctively what her thoughts were, where she was coming from. She would have sensed the kind of woman I am. Any wrinkles would have been smoothed out in office hours. The silence between Paul Mavsoni and me, even allowing for concentrated chewing and swallowing, had once again gone on for a worryingly long time.

I peered into my plate of mushed risotto as if it might inspire a subject for conversation. Like – are you married? Are you in a relationship? Are you gay, and if you are, am I broad-minded?

He laid his knife and fork across his plate. He said, 'I'm sorry if you are offended. I meant to pay you a compliment, not annoy you.'

'I'm not offended, not annoyed. You don't have to flatter me, you know.' I pushed my plate away. 'The truth is,' and now I could not believe the words which were issuing from my lips, 'the truth is that I receive so few compliments these days that when one comes along I fail to recognise it.'

I touched the stand-away collar of the scarlet jacket. 'You might as well know that I never normally look like this. I was persuaded into this outfit by a lady called Gloria who owns a local boutique. I was feeling a little low at the time, and not inclined to argue with her. Fortunately I didn't buy the dress and shoes, but only hired them. I had never worn red before. I wanted to see how it felt. Put into words, I suppose it all sounds very juvenile.'

He smiled. 'Mrs Donovan,' he said, 'you look absolutely stunning.'

The admiration in his eyes was genuine. I could feel the blush spread across my face, and he considerately looked away.

He shot his cuffs and touched the lapel of his dinner jacket. 'Seems like Gloria has a lot to answer for. We both owe our fine feathers to her hire department.'

'You mean – you too?'

'I have never owned a dinner jacket, but I thought, after meeting you this morning, and you staying at the Castle . . . Oh, I might as well be truthful about it. I wanted to impress you.'

'And you did. You have. I am totally bowled over!'

We began to laugh in the relieved and grateful way that marks the easing of severe nervous tension. When the cheese and biscuits came, he ordered cognacs. I should have refused the brandy but I didn't. The pianist was playing softly. Amazingly I felt warm and confident, and almost beautiful. I could not stop smiling.

When he asked me to dance I moved into his arms as if we now belonged together. I said, 'My name is Imogen.'

'I know,' he murmured. 'I'm Paul.'

I said, 'This is very unprofessional behaviour.'

'Yes,' he said, 'but we needn't tell anybody on Monday morning. We shall greet each other in the office as if we are total strangers.'

It was the second cognac which did the real damage. I remembered halfway through it why I avoided alcohol, but by that time it was too late.

We had arrived at the stage of tentative intimacy which allows an exchange of personal information. We established that he was a widower, and that I was married. He had a son. I had a daughter and a grandson. I told him about Fran and Mitch, and John. He told me about his twenty-two-year-old son Jake, who was backpacking his way around the world. We talked about anything and everything.

But a fragment of caution still prevented me from talking about feelings. That is until we were pulled into the Castle car park, and I was thanking him for a lovely evening.

Of course I shall always blame that damned pianist and those two cognacs for my unprecedented lack of self control. There is not a woman of my age and generation who does not know the words of that particular song which tells of an evening of enchantment, a meeting with a stranger, and the instant conviction that love is waiting on the far side of the room. And of course it was. And I knew. Even then.

For once in my life everything was right. The time, the place, the man. I had worn the style of dress that a middle-aged grandmother really should not wear. And been told that I looked stunning in it. I had danced for the first time in years, and with a man who was not my son-in-law or husband.

The Range Rover's heater blew warm lemon-scented air; the lights of the car-park glowed misty silver in the falling snow. The man beside me did not reek of booze and cigarette smoke. More importantly, all his attention that evening had been for me, for my comfort, my enjoyment.

When his hand found my hand, when he said. 'You're not happy, are you, Imogen?'

Yes, you've guessed it.

I fell sobbing on the shoulder of his dinner jacket.

He turned towards me and put his arms around me. He held me until the spasm passed. He smelled of discreet aftershave and spearmint gum, and faintly but not unpleasantly of garlic. I said, shakily, 'Gloria won't be pleased. I've smeared make-up all over the front of your hired jacket.'

'Don't worry about it. At the prices she charges, the odd dry cleaning bill won't break her.'

I wiped my face on a tissue from the box he kept in the glove compartment. 'I'm coming apart,' I said. 'Having a breakdown. I'm probably pre-menopausal.' The list of my ills had me snivelling. 'If I ever invite you to dinner again – don't come.'

'It's your marriage, isn't it?'

I sat up straighter in my seat. 'How did you know that?' He adopted an American accent. 'It's my ja-ab, ma'am,' he drawled. 'I'm a marriage counsellor, remember?'

The very best laughter is the hysterical kind that comes immediately after tears. I rocked back and forth, howled and screeched and made a total exhibition of myself. I thought I had never heard anything so funny.

'That's it,' he cheered, 'go to it, girl! Best therapy in all the world, laughter!' Again he took my hand and held it.

Calm once more, I said, 'You're right of course.' His touch seemed to flow right through my body, relaxing every muscle and nerve end.

I had never experienced anything like it. I, who never confided in anybody, was ready, eager even, to tell this stranger all my secrets.

A car pulled into the car park. As its lights swept across us Paul looked at his watch. 'We can't really talk here. There's a little bar still open just across the road. They'll serve us coffee if I ask them nicely.'

The bar was warm and dimly lit and almost empty; the air was smoky but I hardly noticed. We found a corner seat among the quilted red plush. He sat facing me across the glass-topped table. We sipped our coffee and all I saw was the kindness in his eyes, the compelling way he leaned towards me.

'Well then?' he asked, 'if you're so unhappy, why are you still with him?'

I feigned shock. 'I hope you don't ask that particular question of our clients, at least not so bluntly and at the beginning of a consultation. We are supposed to mend relationships, not wreck them.'

'Ah, come on,' he said, 'this is you and me talking. You've been to all the lectures, read all the books. You know as well as I do that when you reach a certain point in a failed relationship, the only solution is a clean break.'

'Easier said than done.'

'What's keeping you together? You say your daughter is married. You are obviously able to support yourself.'

'He needs me.'

'Bullshit!'

The cognac-induced euphoria was wearing off. This man who had promised to befriend me was not saying what I wished to hear.

The tears brimmed again but did not fall.

At once he was around the table and beside me. 'Sorry,' he said, 'sorry. Me and my big mouth.'

'No. You are absolutely right. But I just can't seem to—' How often had I faced a stricken woman who could similarly not express her feelings. I remembered the long and painful pauses, the agonised groping for explanations. Now it was happening to me.

Blessedly, this time he seemed to understand. He returned to his facing seat. 'Tell me about Niall,' he said. 'How long have you been married? How did you first meet?'

The questions were standard, routine; the line was one he would have taken to ease any distressed client into telling her story. I knew this, and yet I wanted to convince myself that his compassionate gaze, his tender tone was special only to me.

I said, 'We married young. Too young. I'm almost fifty years old. I have a twenty-eight-year-old daughter. When we met I was a student. He was trying to get into RADA. He'd had a few small parts in repertory theatre productions. We kept running across one another at other people's parties. We sort of drifted together. God knows why, we had absolutely nothing in common. Save lust. Thirty years ago hardly any couples cohabited. I didn't need to explain this to him. I simply took him home and introduced him to my mother. From that day forward Niall knew that it was marriage or nothing.

'The first few years were pretty good. My mother took care of the baby while I finished my degree course. My parents helped us to buy an old, rundown house and Niall began to renovate it. He made a very good job of it, so good in fact that neighbours employed him to do similar renovations. It built up into a profitable business. I became a social worker. We could afford to go on foreign holidays. And then,' I paused, 'something happened. From one day to another he was changed and I never knew why. He began to drink, heavily. He became unreliable in every way. He started gambling. When I tried to talk to him about it he accused me of trying to brainwash him with the slick and facile solutions I offered to my clients. "Keep it for office hours," he told me.

'In the end I more or less gave up on him. I had my small daughter, my job, a few good friends. When he and I talked it was about the phone bill, the TV licence, the state of the brakes on his pickup truck.'

'But still you stayed with him?'

I shrugged. 'Who can say why anyone stays in a bad situation. Habit? Fear of loneliness, of the unknown? Women like me, the ones who are not particularly interested in starting a new relationship, they stay put out of sheer inertia. They make their jobs, their children, a sufficient reason to get up in the morning, to face another day.

'But then of course, the child, the job, become over-important. I've never admitted this before, but without my work I would have nothing.'

'But you have a daughter, a grandchild.'

'Appropriated by my mother. Both of them. And no – don't tell me I should also be doing something about that. People love you, or they don't. Her grandmother comes first with Fran.'

He said, 'But you must to some degree have allowed this to happen. Didn't you see—?'

I sighed, looked away and then back at him. 'It's more complicated than that. It would take forever to explain it.'

'Tell me,' he said, 'this move to Taunton, the promotion, are you happy about it?'

'No!' I burst out, 'I'm terrified. Already I am making mistakes. Inviting you to have dinner with me was way out of order. But you know that. Personal relationships within the office are not approved of.'

'We've been into this and decided that it isn't relevant to anything.'

'Maybe not to you,' I said, 'but if asked about it, how would I explain?'

He smiled. 'You could say we were having an in-depth, all-round preliminary exploration of where we stand on certain interdepartmental problems.' He smiled. 'Dinner, a couple of dances, and a late-evening coffee can hardly be seen as a wild affair, can it?'

I tried to avoid his mesmeric gaze and could not. He leaned closer. 'I think part of your problem is that you have trouble trusting people. You don't trust me. I can see it in your eyes. Well, I don't blame you. Why should you? We've only just met; but then that same criterion applies to the unhappy people who walk through our office doors.' He leaned across the table. 'Sometimes,' he said, 'you have to take a step into the dark, and hope that if you stumble, some sympathetic friend will be there to catch you before you fall.'

I shrugged, assuming an indifference to his words I did not feel. 'I never step out into the dark.'

'Oh, but you do! You were well into foreign territory when you hired that red dress. Even if you don't acknowledge it, you were changing your image, playing a game, taking a chance as to where it might lead. Maybe you've done other things lately that are not "in character"?'

'The Castle Hotel,' I said slowly, 'an expensive room with a four-poster bed and an en-suite bathroom, and supper trays with wine and smoked salmon, when I should be economising in a bed and breakfast. I feel guilty as hell, but there's a part of me that's saying, "So what! I earn my money, why shouldn't I just this once indulge myself?"'

'You said your husband was working on the house?'

'And so he is. I hope he is. One never knows with Niall.'

I had already told Paul Mavsoni more than I intended, more than he had any right to know. Yet every time he probed a little deeper I heard myself answering.

'It's called Sad Acre Farm. Niall's choice of habitation. He seems to see himself in the role of farmer, of the "gentleman" variety of course.' I glanced up and then away. 'I drove out there on Monday intending to move in, to help him get the place into some sort of order. I hadn't known my mother would already be there. She and Niall get on extremely well together. I drove away before they saw me. My mother makes me feel redundant in any situation.'

'Hence the Castle Hotel and the red dress.'

'Yes,' I said. 'Bloody childish of me, isn't it.'

'No,' he murmured, 'it isn't childish. Sometimes you need to make that sort of statement, for your own private satisfaction.'

Once again I was caught unawares by his warmth, the quiet intimacy of his understanding. Nothing about this evening had gone according to plan, yet all I felt was unbelievable relief that I had found a friend.

He walked me back to the hotel. The moonlight cast shadows on the coils of leafless wisteria which clung to the high walls. The snow bestowed its special silence. We stood close together, not quite touching. If he had tried to kiss me I would have let him.

Not true! I would have responded. Enthusiastically. Things might have escalated, got out of hand? But he did not kiss me. 'If you want to talk again?' he said.

Oh I do. I do. I do. But I didn't say it. 'Goodnight,' I said, 'and thank you.'

I didn't sleep that night. I pulled back the curtains and in the light of the moon the red dress and its jacket seemed to watch me from where I had thrown them across the grey velvet chair. After years of involvement in other people's dramas, of being the counsellor, the confidante, the bearer of off-loaded burdens, I had, at a stroke, become the confider, the counselled; I had shifted my troubles on to Paul Mavsoni's shoulders, and he had encouraged, almost ordered me to do so.

I thumped my pillows, lay on my back and then my side, closed my eyes and opened them again. But my brain was alert, my thoughts as connected and clear as if I had slept deeply for several hours. I saw the whole of my life, all the putdowns, the disappointments, the rare little islands of pure joy. If I had ever thought about the future I assumed it would be a rerun of the past.

I thought about Paul's words. The way he had looked when he said them.

'Why are you still with him?' he had asked again.

Good question. Why was I?

The doubts began to nudge me, like a gentle shove between the shoulder blades.

I could leave Niall. I need never return through those twisting lanes, to that pale-pink ruined farmhouse with its sagging roof and sloping floors. I could find myself a room in Taunton, a bedsitter, in one of those prim, well-kept Victorian villas which stood close to Vivary Park. But even as the plan took wings it lost height and fell back into the real world.

I switched on the bedside lamp, grabbed pen and paper and began to do what I always did when troubled. I made my list of jobs outstanding.

1. *Return* the dress, shoes and coat to Gloria.
2. *Check* the balance in my cheque account. (THE HOTEL BILL!)
3. *Phone* Francesca, Primrose; Sad Acre Farm.
4. *Give serious thought* to the potentially dangerous situation I have allowed to develop between myself and Paul Mavsoni.
5. *Decide* if and what I shall tell Niall about the events of recent days.

Niall

Because of Nina's presence in the house Niall had been forced both mentally and actually to open doors he would rather have left closed. He had planned to ease himself gently back into Sad Acre. One room at a time had been the plan. In the first days, when he had been alone there, wherever he looked he saw horrors in his mind's eye. The image of his father's body wedged across the lower stair-treads. The rocking chair in the kitchen still seeming to move from the momentum of whatever agony his mother had suffered that day in her final moments. The unmilked cows in the crew yard bellowing from the anguish of their swollen udders. The buzz of the gathering flies.

Since coming back to Sad Acre he had dived head first each night into the crate of Becks, had tossed down the whisky as if it were lemonade. He went through all the emotional stages of intoxication. The euphoria, the deep peace which never lasts, the grieving for lost chances, and the ultimate self-loathing. Ah no, it was not what he had intended on that morning when he set out with the loaded pickup, almost sober and high on hope.

Phoning Imogen had been a mistake. Lying to her about his achievements in house and field had imposed an added pressure. He needed the distractions of placing a bet on a promising horse, of long and pointless conversations with the barman in the Queen's Arms, and with Kumar who owned the corner off-licence; a night spent with Maggie, who really understood him. When he had opened the front door and found Nina standing in the porch, he could not at first imagine who she was, or what she wanted. He had resented her presence, the need to provide food, to build up the fire, to find extra blankets for her.

And then, as the evening wore on, his feelings changed. The house, with her in it, became just a house like any other. The ghosts receded into the shadows. The terror he had experienced since his arrival lost much of its power. The spirits of his dead, if not altogether flown, were now perched and watching from a respectable distance. He slept deeply that night without the benefit of Becks or whisky.

Remorse, and the need to justify himself in Nina's eyes, was sufficient incentive to get him moving the next morning. He found the box of cleaning materials which Imogen had packed. Nina set him to washing down the kitchen walls and scrubbing the floor. By lunchtime he was exhausted, but a surface of pale cream paintwork had by that time been revealed on walls and fitments; and flagstones of a soft and mottled blue-grey emerged from beneath the trodden-in grime of years.

Meanwhile Nina set to work on the iron range. Using a wire brush she removed the worst of the rust. A search through the box yielded other brushes and a tube of something black and viscous called Zebo. The tube itself was striped black and white like a zebra's coat. Nina held it up, studied the instruction leaflet. She said, in a wondering voice, 'Oh clever Imogen! Wherever did she find this?' She squeezed a long trail of the thick goo onto the surface of the range, and began to spread it evenly across the rusted iron.

Niall said, 'Looks as though you've done that job before.'

'Oh, I have,' she said. 'My husband's family were farmers. I spent much of my childhood in their kitchen. The first task Grandma Franklin ever gave me was the blackleading of their massive range with Zebo.'

He said, 'So you know a bit about farming?'

'A bit. My husband Jack had three older brothers. They

barely tolerated me about the place. But I was always there, listening and watching.'

Niall said, 'So one of those brothers must have been Alan, the man who stole Lucy?'

'Yes,' she said. 'They were a peculiar bunch, the Franklins. Jack favoured his mother. I always thought those two were the only approachable members of that family.'

Niall said, 'They say the highest rates of suicide are found among farmers.' He spoke provocatively, almost daring her to question the statement.

'Is that a fact?' she said drily. 'I wonder what happened to the original owners of this place? It must have been beautiful once. This would have been a fine house before the rot set in.' She took up a soft cloth and began to buff gently the almost dry blackleaded surface of the range. He was acutely aware of her sidelong glances, the indirect challenge in her tone. 'Five acres of pasture did you say?' she asked him.

'That's right. Five acres.'

'And the adjoining woodland, and the large pond, are they included?'

He said, 'Eight acres of woods, and that's also a part of the leasehold – for what it's worth, which is next to nothing.'

'You mentioned keeping pigs and poultry?'

'Well, yes, I'd like to try some of the old breeds,' he said. 'A few Gloucester Old Spot breeding sows, some free-range laying hens. A goat or two.'

She laid down her polishing cloth and turned to face him. 'Put like that, one would think you were quite knowledgeable. But you didn't fool Imogen, did you? Truth is, you don't know a damn thing about farming, do you Niall?'

He forced a grin. 'I've featured in a few cornflake commercials.'

'I'm serious,' she told him. 'You've already invested money in this project. More importantly, you've invested your own credibility.' She shook her head and laughed. 'Sorry,' she said, 'I begin to sound like Imogen, don't I? But you know what I mean. If you think I'm crazy, then tell me to shut up.'

He knew exactly what she meant. He always knew what Nina meant, always felt comfortable with her.

He said, 'I understand you better when you're crazy. Imogen had warned me before I met you. "My mother," she said, "is as batty as they come. My Dad's okay, just talk to him and you'll survive." But you see, I grew up with madness. I was never surprised or frightened at the oddness of strangers. People with quirky minds, people who do their own thing regardless of what is termed "acceptable behaviour", they are the ones I get along with.'

She shot him a keen glance. 'But we're in the minority, you and I. Eccentricity is all very well, but only when linked to practicability.' She emphasised each word by tapping the blacklead brush sharply against the iron range. 'And it is not practical or wise to disregard eight acres of valuable woodland!'

He did not answer. He filled the kettle and lit the primus stove. 'Lunch break,' he said. He fetched the loaf of bread, the pot of jam, the butter and cheese from a cupboard. 'Toast and instruction,' he said. 'How's that for reasonable behaviour? So tell me what I ought to do.'

The toast was made at the living-room fire with the last of the bread Nina had prudently brought with her. Tomorrow, when the range had been buffed to a gleaming blackness they would light that fire and roast potatoes in the oven. Her mouth full of cheese, butter dripping from her chin, she surveyed him across the table. 'That mature woodland,' she said, 'could be your most valuable asset. You will need several free-range pens, each raised on pillars to provide a scratching area for the hens in winter weather. You will also need shelter for the pigs. There's a fine stand of oak trees in that wood. Oak trees produce acorns. Pigs love to graze acorns. As for the pond, I would say a couple of dozen ducks, Khaki Campbells for preference, would be very happy there.'

He gazed at her, open-mouthed. 'Gawd!' he whispered, 'you're a bloody miracle, Nina.' He closed his eyes, 'I can just see it. Ducks swimming on the pond. Pigs rooting underneath the trees. Hens clucking – and to think I'd written off those woods as useless.'

'Stop it,' she ordered. 'There's a lot of work to be done before we – you reach that point in the plan.'

'I know – I know. But just to have a plan. We shall have to get this down on paper. Work out costs, and numbers per acre.' He began to laugh. 'Just wait till Imogen hears all this. What price now her postgraduate course in Counselling and Psychotherapy. Bet she doesn't know the difference between a Rhode Island Red and a White Wyandotte.'

'Imogen doesn't need to know those things,' Nina pointed out. 'And you'd better remember that it will be her salary which keeps you ticking over until the farm begins to make a profit.'

But he wasn't listening. He gazed up at the hooks which were suspended from the black beams of the ceiling. 'We'll have hams hanging up there. We'll make our own bread.' He turned to the gleaming range, opened the oven door and closed it. 'Bakes marvellous bread, that oven! Always did, and will again.'

His euphoria was such that he did not realise the significance of what he had just said. Nina gave him a sharp glance and looked quickly away. He would tell her the whole story, but only in his own time. And she was very good at waiting.

Imogen

I did not stay in Taunton, did not rent a bedsitter. But you must have guessed I wouldn't.

I considered phoning Niall, announcing my imminent arrival, and then I thought, why should I? That cruddy farm was as much my place as it was his, and I certainly had more right to be there than my mother, who by this time would be running the whole show, single-handed.

Oh, I know what you are thinking, and yes, I was being just a mite unreasonable. Even so, I was not about to pussyfoot around him, to behave as if I was a well-mannered guest in my own home. As I paid my hotel bill and drove out into North Street I anticipated the satisfying pleasure of catching them both on the wrong foot. Niall, preferably, in a drunken stupor, and Nina nursing her chilblains in that freezing house without carpets or plumbing; and my valuable furniture still stacked up in the centre of every room.

Thinking about Niall was always a non-starter. Paul Mavsoni however had all the fascination of forbidden fruit. While returning my hired evening wear to Gloria's boutique I had bought a blouse of heavy emerald satin. I found myself smiling as I drove, imagining next Monday morning, my arrival in the office, slipping off my suit jacket to reveal the flattering green blouse. I might even wear my hair in the loose chignon, and put on the expensive new bra which Gloria promised would give me uplift and separation; and the sheer black tights which caused even Niall to sometimes glance briefly at my legs. Something weird and frightening was happening to me. I could scarcely believe my own thoughts. After years of deliberate understatement it now seemed that I longed to be the kind of woman who turned heads, who caused speculation when she entered a room; who left a disturbed atmosphere in her wake. My smile broadened. I would never achieve any of this, but it could be fun just making the attempt.

A rapid thaw had set in overnight, the sun shone on a wet road. I drove cautiously, remembering the recent skid. Along with the engine's purr I hummed the haunting tune Paul Mavsoni and I had danced to.

My bump of direction is almost non-existent and yet without studying signposts I threaded my way confidently through the maze of lanes and arrived at the entrance to Sad Acre Farm; I turned in and was obliged to brake hard. The gate, all its five bars repaired and in position, had been painted and rehung. I halted just a whisper away from the gleaming white.

I switched off the engine and sat very still. The manure heaps still ringed the farmyard, the rusted machinery was still there. But from all the eight chimneys grey smoke plumed upwards into the blue sky. Curtains now hung in some of the windows. The pickup was loaded high with empty packing cases and assorted rubbish.

It was not what I had envisioned.

I sat for a while and stared at the bars of the resurrected gate. The inmates of Sad Acre had been busy. Just for a moment I suspected Niall of hiring help from the nearest village, but reason told me that even if this had been possible, my mother would never have allowed it.

I began to review my position in all this. Subtly and unexpectedly I was once again the one who had been wrongfooted. And not only by Nina, but even more alarmingly by Niall. This was no time for me to indulge in stupidity or hurt pride, I told myself. I had been all primed to march into the house, look around, sum up the areas in greatest need of attention, and stun them both with my plan of action. I beat on the steering wheel with both fists. I felt a surge of anger more fierce than I had ever known. How was it that my seventy-year-old mother and my laid-back feckless husband, in spite of blizzards, freeze-ups and a total absence of convenience gadgets, had so obviously made a significant start on this business of house reclamation?

Or perhaps a functional gate, and fires lit in every room, not to mention the hanging of curtains, was not after all such a great achievement? But I knew that it was, and the knowledge was bitter.

Until I remembered Paul Mavsoni, the way he had held me when we danced. The promise in his eyes.

There is a dangerous aspect to revenge which, until now, had prevented me from even contemplating it. But the anger had been building slowly in me for a long time. It only required a certain set of circumstances, a spark among the dry tinder of unstable emotions, and there I was, ablaze and aflame.

Paul Mavsoni had found me attractive, had almost kissed me. I hung on to this thought as Niall and Nina emerged from the front porch and walked towards my car.

I thought I knew all there was to know about family resentments. The way ill-feeling backs up and clogs the channels of communication. I hear about it every day from clients, and I may have mentioned that my mother and I each talk across each other's shoulder, rarely face to face. The snide remarks she makes privately about my character and life are whispered to me months later, by well-meaning friends who think I really ought to know what she is saying.

I believed I had nothing new to learn when it came to the sneakiness of loved ones, but I learned a trick or two that morning which will stay forever in my memory.

To begin with I was greeted with smiles and outstretched hands by Nina, who never touches any adult if she can help it.

She is rather like the Queen in that respect, although HM will force herself to press her subjects' humble flesh but only when she is suitably gloved.

Niall's lips brushed my cheek in an unprecedented display of husbandly affection. Both enquired tenderly about my health, the state of the (allegedly) broken-down car; the awfulness of being stranded, alone in Taunton. They led me into the house as if I were an invalid lately discharged from a hospital bed. As if I were fragile. Precious. And here is where the trick is manifested in all its brilliance. If you wish to make a dear one feel guilty; deeply, ashamedly, sickeningly at fault, just be especially nice to that person, even when you know, and they know, *they do not deserve it.*

As they led me from sitting room to bedroom, each one warmed by a log fire, carpeted and curtained, the shining furniture attractively arranged, and smelling of pot-pourri and Johnson's Furniture Cream, I attempted to justify my absence from the scene. I made excuses. I was penitent. I almost grovelled, damn it! But they were having none of it. When it came to twisting the knife, they were the experts. 'No, no,' they said. 'We understood. Truly we did. There was nothing you could have done. Without the car you couldn't possibly have reached us. *But we were worried about you.* We tried to phone you, several times, and then remembered you had said you were also having trouble with your mobile. We know you are deeply involved in sorting out your new job. You were absolutely right to stay in Taunton. Now do stop blaming yourself, dear.' What they didn't say was – but the public telephones were still working, weren't they? You could have reached us one way or another. *Nina made it in a taxi.* They didn't need to say another word. I was saying them all underneath my breath.

I admired their handiwork; fulsomely, gushingly, over-the-top stuff! And to be fair, they must have worked the clock round to achieve so much within a week. I said as much and Nina laughed.

'This husband of yours has a good turn of speed when

pointed in the right direction. One room at a time, I told him. He's very good at following orders.'

I looked at Niall and was amazed to see the fatuous grin spreading on his face. I longed to slap him, instead I smiled, I snapped my fingers. 'Gosh darn it!' I drawled. 'I wish I'd known sooner, mother. Now I can see where I've been going wrong. I've obviously never given him the right instructions.'

We sat at the well-scrubbed kitchen table. I remarked on the beauty of the old blue flagstones, was suitably astonished at the gleaming range. The stains were gone from the sink, the flies from the windowsill. A note of genuine respect leaked into my voice. 'You must both be exhausted,' I said, 'but now it's my turn. Just tell me what needs to be done, and I'll make a start.'

Nina said, 'We've really only completed three rooms. The kitchen, the sitting room, and my little bedroom.' She uttered the last three words without batting an eyelash. Perhaps she had rehearsed her part, perhaps she thought I hadn't already marked the significance of the twin-bedded guest room which overlooked the orchard; both beds made up, but only one in use; my little tapestry chair positioned by the window, Nina's housecoat draped across it.

I said, 'So you're planning to stay for a bit, are you?'

'Only as long as Niall finds me useful. There's the master bedroom still to be sorted out. Niall is sleeping on the sitting-room floor at present. We thought it better to wait until you arrived. I'm sure you'd rather supervise the arrangement of your bedroom furniture personally.'

I blinked at her mention of a 'master bedroom'. It was unlike Nina to suffer delusions of grandeur. All right, so it was quite a large house, but even so! Perhaps she was rehearsing her description of Sad Acre for the eventual telling to Primrose Martindale?

'And of course,' she continued, 'I shall need to go home for a few days. I've left Roscoe with Primrose, and he and Gorbachev don't really get along too well. I shall bring Roscoe back with me. He'll think he's in dog-heaven. All those trees!'

She treated me to that assured smile. 'As soon as we've sorted out your bedroom, dear, Niall can run me into the bus station in Taunton. My National Coach ticket is still valid.'

'I'll drive you in myself,' I told her. One look at Niall's face and I knew better than to try to dissuade her from returning to Sad Acre. I followed her up the echoing stairs and into the spacious bedroom she had already decided was to be mine and Niall's.

'Now, you will almost certainly need new curtains,' she was saying, 'and as for the carpet—'

I stood at the long window, which gave a clear view of the paddock. The cattle shelter which Niall assured me he had repaired was still in its tumbledown condition. There had been no mention of the Dexter cattle. Dense woodland adjoined the neatly hedged field. Lying snow still streaked the blue and misty hills.

I thought about Taunton, about Paul Mavsoni's lean and rangy body; the faint smell of garlic on his breath which should have been off-putting and wasn't.

With Nina in residence here, my occasional absences from home would hardly be noticed. It struck me for the first time that what Niall really wanted was not a wife but a mother.

I would not until now have believed myself capable of deep deceit, of such shameful manipulation of circumstances. When talking to clients I had often heard the excuse, 'It was all very innocent really. I took good care to make sure that my little affair never hurt anybody.'

It could be reasoned that by excluding myself temporarily from Sad Acre I was about to do my husband and mother a great favour.

I turned back to Nina. I said, 'You and Niall work very well together. I'm really most grateful to you.' For once I did not have to force the sincerity in my voice.

She smiled. 'All I want is for you to be happy here, Immie.'

'Oh, I will,' I said. 'I already have a very good feel about the future.'

Niall

The change in Imogen was so marked that even he had become aware, and slightly suspicious of it. He waited for the catch, the snag, because he had learned that with women, any favourable alteration in behaviour often carried with it a penalty, a payoff. He had braced himself against her reaction to her mother's presence in Sad Acre. Not that tension between the two of them would have troubled him greatly; what actually stopped him dead in the water was Immie's good humour, her praise of their efforts.

He and Imogen and Nina had made a great team that first weekend. Between them, the room Nina chose to call the master bedroom had been transformed from a dusty storeplace for old bedsteads and moth-eaten blankets to a charming and promising retreat which might in time (and supposing Imogen's new mood lasted) put fresh life into their marriage.

On her way to the first day in her new office Imogen drove Nina to the Taunton bus station. Niall was not at his best at seven thirty in the morning. Bleary-eyed, unshaven, in dressing gown and slippers, he had nevertheless come smartly to attention at the sight of the green satin blouse, the dangling jade earrings, the new looser hairstyle. He had wolf-whistled her across the yellow tablecloth (which since Imogen's return had replaced the more interesting back issues of the *Daily Mirror*) and she had smiled and touched the wayward hair that escaped the chignon.

'You look lovely, dear,' Nina had said.

'It's not quite *you* though, is it?' He had sounded churlish, sour, resentful. He wanted to add, 'So what are you up to?' but with Nina present didn't quite dare to.

'I've been rethinking my business image,' said Imogen, 'while I was down in Taunton.'

He felt reassured. Now that was exactly Imogen.

'I'm dealing with distressed, abused women,' she went on. 'Women in crisis, at risk, often suicidal. I took a good look at myself in a full-length mirror. What I saw was severe, repressive, schoolmarmish, and unsympathetic. While wandering around Taunton I found this little boutique place. The owner was very helpful. I explained that I wanted to loosen up, look more – more approachable. I bought some earrings, a few blouses.'

'Just so long,' he said, 'as you are only approached by your female clients.' He had meant only to tease her and was surprised at the tide of crimson which spread across her averted face.

'Male clients,' she snapped back, 'are as rare as snow in August in my job.'

'That's because men grin and bear it,' he said mildly. 'You won't find many blokes crying their eyes out on a stranger's shoulder.' Again, he had intended only to inject a little humour, but this time the colour drained abruptly from her face. 'What do you mean? What are you accusing me of?'

Puzzled, he looked to Nina for help.

Nina said, 'I think perhaps we should make an early start this morning, dear. The traffic could be heavy on a Monday.' She looked meaningfully at Niall. 'If you would bring my suitcase down and put it in the boot?'

With Nina gone, and Imogen absent for twelve hours of every weekday, he began to appreciate the full measure of his isolation. He had never noticed any lack of company in childhood. There had seemed to be a constant stream of visitors trudging through the farmyard and in at the ever-open kitchen door. Relatives and neighbours, the dealers in pigs, calves and chickens; gypsies looking for work, the vicar from the next parish.

The recent blizzard had ensured his privacy; dark mornings and evenings had precluded the random visits of curious neighbours. But the day would come when he would have to face them. He had already worked out that those men who farmed in the area in his parents' time would now be in their late seventies or eighties. His mother had never been known as Mrs Donovan, always as Miss Frances, old Treddinick's daughter. But the country people in these parts tended to be long-lived. Farms were handed on to sons and grandsons. It needed only one elderly gossip, with a long memory and a loose tongue . . .

An easement in the bitter weather was allowing movement again in the lanes and fields, and smoke from the Sad Acre chimneys was a signal for miles around that the farm was again in occupation. He stood at the newly painted gate and watched his wife's car out of sight. Something had happened to her lately, and he would need to think about that, work out quite what it might mean for him, this new loosened-up Imogen, with her jazzy blouse and the wispy hair curling sexily on to her collar, the dangly jade miniature pagodas hooked into her earlobes.

As he turned back to the house, as he gazed at the sagging ancient thatch, the crazed pink walls, *he saw his mother*. His first reaction was the same resentful adolescent anger he had felt as a boy. I wasn't even thinking about her, and here she is, come back to haunt me and twice as threatening as when she was alive.

He knuckled his eyes, closed and then opened them but she was still there. He thought, this cannot be happening to me. Not in broad daylight, with the sun shining out of a clear sky. She was standing in the porch, smiling at him. That special, possessive, *hungry* look in her eyes that unhappy, love-deprived mothers reserve for their only sons. She was wearing the faded pink dress and sunbonnet. Her fair hair hung in wisps about her neck. He felt the old fear twist his stomach. Let me go, he groaned aloud. Let me go. I can't help you. I am the child. You are the parent. I can't put the world right for you. I know you want me to murder him for you. But I can't. He's my Dadda, and I love him.

Niall stumbled back into the house. He stood beside the shining black of the kitchen range, warmed himself at the fire and rubbed his hands across his stiffened face. He knew what had caused the 'visitation'. Hardly a drink had he taken since Nina's arrival and Imogen's return. It didn't do to cut down so drastically and abruptly. The same sort of thing happened to deprived alcoholics, he had heard them tell about it. Pink elephants, rats on the ceiling, and all that! Had he reached that stage? Blindly, he sought the Glenlivet only to find it had been tidied away into a cupboard. He was not an alcoholic; just desperate for a drink. He didn't bother looking for a glass, but drank straight from the bottle, which he then tossed carelessly into the swing-bin. One thing about an empty whisky bottle that could always be relied upon. It was strictly no deposit – no return.

The cork memo-board, brought with them from their old house, now hung in a prominent position on the kitchen wall. In the space of the weekend it had sprouted a great crop of memos, lists, timetables, and significant dates, all in Imogen's firm, straight-up-and-down script, and held in place with coloured pins. The longest list was headed NIALL – THINGS TO DO AND BUY. He pulled it loose from its securing pin. It began with GENERATOR and ended with PASTA.

Nina

The National Coach had deep and comfortable seats, a hot-drinks machine and the kind of cramped toilet facilities found on transatlantic jumbo jets. I was the only passenger that morning. I sat back in my front seat and let the warm air thaw my toes and fingers. With a cup of coffee in my hand, and a panoramic view of the Somerset landscape available through the wide windscreen, I wondered for the thousandth time why young people insisted on driving pesky and expensive cars that were always breaking down and cost a mint of money.

Superimposed on the flat fields and swollen rhynes of the Somerset Levels was an image of Imogen's tense and anxious face. I had sensed a brittle, dangerous excitement in her that morning. I should have been gratified by her easy acceptance of my presence over the weekend, her insistence that I should return as soon as possible to help with the organisation of the house. She had talked about the overgrown garden, the neglected orchard. So much to be done, she had said, and she down in Taunton for five days of each week. And then came the flattery, that was so unlike her. Niall, she insisted, would move mountains for me, while for her sake he could hardly be persuaded to leave his armchair. She became confidential. 'He never talks about his early life, but I believe his mother died while he was still a boy. I think,' said my daughter in her counsellor's voice, 'he sees you as a mother substitute. In a way, he needs you more than he needs me.'

'I'm very fond of him,' I told her. 'I suppose I regard him as the son I never had.'

I would not, until now, have dared to make such an admission, especially to Imogen.

'Well that's wonderful,' she said, 'so everyone is happy!'

Her enthusiasm stunned me. I tried to work out just what it was that I had done right, so that if necessary I could repeat the miracle at some future date. Perhaps it was the hours of work I had put in on that rusty kitchen range? Or the semi-sobriety of Niall over recent days? Or, and this was more likely, had something extraordinary happened while she was allegedly stranded in Taunton, unable to make contact with us in a world which bristled with the technology of instant communication?

I gazed at the ribbon of road, watched the overtaking, anti-social cars, inhabited mostly by a solitary person; drivers who needed a mobile phone wedged between ear and shoulder to assure themselves that there were other people still living on the planet. From time to time we picked up passengers along the way, students or people of my own generation. A nod and smile from each new arrival on the bus established just sufficient contact to be friendly but not intrusive.

I arrived in Ashkeepers soon after midday.

Primrose, who had turned out to meet me and was unsuitably dressed for the arctic weather in stiletto heels and sheer nylons, shivered in a corner of the bus shelter; but the warmth of her welcome was gratifying. After hot soup and toast, and a couple of brandy-spiked coffees, we settled down among her beige-on-beige upholstery, with the photograph of Lucy, Tim and Ashley facing us from the coffee table.

'I want to know everything,' she said.

Roscoe, whose welcome had been positively ecstatic, now lay across my feet as if to ensure that I could not stir another inch without him. I looked at Primmie's eager face, felt the dog's restrictive weight across my feet, and knew that I did not belong with Imogen and Niall, never had and maybe never would. I had intended to put a gloss on recent days, to tell it as if it had all been a great adventure. I had my pride after all, but as the warmth of the soup, or maybe it was the splash of Old Napoleon, spread through my veins, my vision misted over. I heard myself say, 'Oh, Primrose, I am really worried about them.'

'Well, yes,' she said hesitantly. 'Niall is a dear, of course, but he can be a little unreliable.'

'Not Niall! I'm talking about Imogen. She's behaving very oddly.'

Amazement made Primrose incautious. 'That's exactly what Imogen always says about you.'

I could have taken umbrage. On reflection I probably should have. But my need to unburden my worries was urgent. I took a long drink of coffee and ate two of Primmie's superior brand of biscuit. 'You never worry about Imogen,' she prompted. 'You've never needed to. She's in every way the ideal daughter.'

I snorted inelegantly. 'But have I been the ideal mother?' I set my cup down and leaned back into the oyster-satin scatter cushions. I began to tell Primmie about the isolated farmhouse, Imogen's week-long absence which had not been satisfactorily explained; her change of attitude towards me; her pressing invitation that I should return to the Blackdowns as soon as possible, and stay as long as I wished to; her purchase of a rather gaudy satin blouse and swinging green earrings, which in a subtle but worrying way had made Imogen a woman to be noticed.

Primrose began to laugh. 'Listen to yourself, Nina. Every word you've spoken is optimistic. Every change you've mentioned is for the better.'

When I continued to look doubtful she said, 'It could be that they are having a bit of a mid-life crisis; a difficulty with commitment. Perhaps they need counselling?'

'Don't you dare use that drivelling claptrap, to me of all people,' I shouted. 'When did you or I ever have the luxury of a "mid-life crisis"? When were we ever considered to be in the need of counselling? We had plain, old-fashioned worries and troubles. And what did we do? We got on with it. That's what!'

I gulped down the last of the now cold coffee. 'And may I remind you that Imogen is herself a counsellor, in case you had forgotten.'

'Well in that case,' said Primrose, 'it may well be a matter of "physician heal thyself".'

She was probably right.

We both looked to the photograph of Lucy, Tim and Ashley: my dead daughter, Primmie's dead son, and our mutual grandson.

I said, 'So tell me about the marriage plans. Is it to be the village church, or St Margaret's, Westminster?'

'Neither. They've decided against getting married. Ashley and Angelique intend to live together.'

I walked the few hundred yards which lay between Primmie's home and mine. She lives in a pretentious grouping of mock-Tudor horrors known collectively as Homesteaders' Valley, a small enclave where the three linked and private roads are named Ranchers Close, Farmers Crescent, and Pioneer Way. My own little house was built around 1745. It has three crooked chimneys, a white picket fence enclosing a small front garden, and the bedroom is haunted by two harmless ghosts. One is a baby who wails piteously from time to time, and the other is an elderly woman who is said to resemble me, and who is frequently seen gazing from my bedroom window. In the few years of my occupation of the house, I have grown used to these companions and would miss them if they disappeared.

I did not even consider Imogen's suggestion that I should call in the bishop of the diocese with a request for their exorcism.

Before opening the garden gate I stood for a moment or two and assured myself that all was safe and as I had left it: the diamond-paned windows, the heavy slab of oak that was the front door, the high wooden fence at the rear, and its sheltering row of poplars which concealed the permanent travellers' settlement which lay in Witches' Hollow.

Since the painful events of last year, it seemed to me now

that this little Toll House was my only secure place in an unsafe world. I had moved from the city to this village of Ashkeepers, determined to discover what had become of my kidnapped baby. With Imogen's help the mystery had been solved. But as so often happens in such cases, the resolution had thrown up other questions. A dull ache throbbed behind my eyes. I needed to sleep in my own bed for a few nights, to phone Ashley and Angelique; and to pack sufficient clothes for what promised to be an extended stay on Sad Acre Farm.

I also needed to reserve two seats on next Monday's National Coach. One for myself and one for Roscoe.

That peculiar instinct which most mothers have regarding their offspring was informing me now that Imogen, ideal daughter and model wife, was about, for the first time in her life, to do something very stupid, if not downright dangerous.

Imogen

What I expected to be awkward turned out to be easy.

He called to me from the slip of kitchen. 'What would you prefer – tea or coffee?'

We opened for business at nine thirty. I arrived early in the office, but he was earlier. I walked in to discreet lighting, the smell of coffee perking and the strong and inescapable scent of Taunton's freesias, two vases in reception, one on my desk.

'Coffee,' I called back, 'black, no sugar.' I hung my coat on a peg, exchanged my boots for high-heeled courts, checked my hair and make-up in a wall mirror. As he came through the door, a coffee mug in each hand, I slowly slipped off the jacket of my black suit. The Wonderbra kept its promise. I caught him staring and turned my head away before I smiled. All I lacked was the accompanying stripper's music.

I sat down at the desk across which I would soon be facing my first client. Paul Mavsoni seated himself in the client's chair. As if we had worked together for years he said, 'Not too many appointments this morning. May I suggest we allocate the new ones to you, and the two follow-on cases are mine.'

When I did not answer he said, 'Something wrong?'

'This arrangement of the furniture. Desk in the middle of the room, client and counsellor facing one another across a slab of wood. I don't like it, Paul.'

'Was it different in your former office?'

'No. But I was not in charge there.'

He picked up my coffee mug and placed it with his own on a side table. 'Right,' he said. 'Just tell me how you want things.'

I said, 'Desk pushed back against the far wall. My chair and the client's placed near to the desk but at an angle, so that we are facing one another.'

'Yes,' he said slowly. 'I see what you mean. Makes for a less formal approach, friendlier, more receptive.' He smiled. 'But I would have said you were all of that, never mind the desk.'

I thought, but you don't know me. Misled by the tarty red dress, the Wonderbra, the silly way I kept on smiling at him, he must think I was easy to get close to. Or perhaps just easy.

It crossed my mind that I was turning into the very type of woman favoured by my husband; and it didn't worry me at all. I held the telephone and the vase of freesias while he lifted the solid desk and stood it where I indicated. I moved the upholstered chairs into various positions; when I found what seemed to me the most favourable placing he said, 'Let's try it out. Let's see if propinquity makes a difference.' He handed me my coffee; when we sat our knees touched. I eased my chair back to leave a foot of space between us. He leaned forward and looked into my face. He said, 'We'd better do this properly, don't you think? I'll be counsellor, you be client. If it doesn't work, I can always put the desk back in its old position.'

I immediately felt foolish. I said, 'I don't know how to be a client,' which wasn't true. I had learned a lot just lately, but he didn't need to know that.

'Did you never role-play when you were training?'

'Well – yes. But that was – that was not for real.'

'And if you talk to me now it would be?' He edged his way forward in the chair. I stared down at his corduroy-covered knees. I remembered the way he had held me when I fell sobbing on the shoulder of his dinner jacket; how his touch seemed to flow right through my body, relaxing every muscle and nerve end.

As if he had climbed into my mind he said, 'Perhaps it takes a red dress and a dinner jacket?'

'Perhaps.'

'You went home at the weekend.'

'How did you know that?'

'I enquired at the Castle. They said you had checked out.'

Something moved inside my chest, my stomach muscles tightened. He had cared enough, was interested enough to go looking for me. My reactions to him were all physical, my body responded urgently while my mind was still trying to catch up.

'So how did it go? Was your mother still there?'

We both heard the slam of the outer door, footsteps on the stairs.

I moved back to the desk, he to the little secretary's office. Before the inner door opened to admit my first client, Paul Mavsoni touched my shoulder. 'Lunchtime?' he asked.

'After work would be better,' I told him.

As I greeted my nervous unhappy lady, and led her to our new improved seating arrangement, I was already rehearsing the convincing lie I would need to tell my husband to explain my late arrival home that evening.

One in four women is physically assaulted by her partner. Violent behaviour by men is used to exert control over the women with whom they live. Most of these men have normal friendly relationships with people who are not their partners. This deliberate use of power can take forms other than physical abuse. Sleep deprivation, criticism of her looks, her mental abilities, keeping her short of money, a prisoner within her home; threatening to maim, disfigure or kill her. There is no typical abuser, or abuse.

My client was tall and very thin, at a guess in her mid fifties, dressed conservatively in shades of grey that matched her hair. She sat down with the scarf still wound around her lower face and neck.

When making the telephone appointment, Paul had told me she refused to give her name. This reluctance to be identified was not unusual.

Before I could introduce myself or welcome her she said, 'He'll kill me if he finds out I came here.'

I led her to the blue chair and she sat like a frightened and obedient child.

'Don't worry,' I said, 'he won't find out.'

She spoke in a rapid mumbled whisper, the cause of which became obvious when the scarf slipped down and I saw her split and swollen lips, the severe bruising of her throat.

'I've often thought about coming here, but couldn't find the courage until now. You see,' she said, 'I knew I had to seek help from somebody when I started to keep a knife in my pocket. I don't suppose I would ever use it on him, but just to be thinking about it—'

The words came out in a great rush, her face red with shame. Under the heavy tweed coat she wore a woollen cardigan which had button-down pockets. I watched her fumble with a button, and withdraw a small but efficient-looking kitchen knife which had a thin sharp blade and yellow handle.

She touched the blade with one finger and then looked wonderingly at me. She said, 'The subject of his sermon yesterday morning was "Love within the Family". Last night he gave me the worst beating yet.' She attempted a nervous smile but found the effort too painful. 'I thought about going to see his bishop, but you never know, do you? Men tend to stick together. Even if he believed me, what could he do about it?'

I said, 'The important thing is that you have come to us. That you are no longer alone with the problem. *You do not have to put up with this, you know.*'

She played with the knife compulsively, as a little girl might play with a favourite doll from which she fears to be parted.

'I would never use it, you know,' she repeated.

I was not so sure. She was very near the edge. Maybe I could have persuaded her to hand the knife over, but what was the use? I had no doubt that her kitchen held a dozen other similar weapons. With great reluctance and fearful of discovery she had come to talk. The time for analysis and advice would come later. Much later. There was a lot to tell. A childless marriage, which she said was his fault. She had proved her ability to have a baby, and with merciless insight she acknowledged that it was this very fact which had caused the breakdown of the relationship, the subsequent beatings. The child had been conceived long before she met her husband; as she put it, 'a love child, born out of wedlock'.

I imagined my daughter Fran shuddering at the use by any woman of such an antiquated and defeatist term. It was when the adoption of the child was being arranged that my client first met the young clergyman who was to become her tormentor; her violent husband.

'He was different then. So supportive and understanding. Within six months of meeting we were married.' She paused. Her lower lip had begun to bleed and she touched a tissue to it. 'We both wanted children. After two years of trying I went to my doctor. Tests were done and I was told there was no reason why I should not conceive. When I told my husband he went crazy. He said how dared I involve strangers in our private matters. He refused to take a fertility test. It was then that the trouble really started. He said it was my fault that I couldn't get pregnant. That it was God's punishment for the sin I had committed before we married.'

'How old were you when you married him?'

'Twenty-five.'

'So the abuse has continued over many years?'

'Fourteen, maybe fifteen years. I can hardly remember any more.'

I did a quick addition. I studied her thin lined face, her grey hair. No woman of forty should look as old as she did.

She began to press the point of the knife into the tips of her fingers. 'He's always sorry afterwards. Sometimes he cries like a child and swears it will never happen again. I asked him once why he did it, and he said I had annoying habits. He's very critical, you see. His shirts have to be ironed in a certain way. He's a vegetarian. He once banged my head against the wall because I had used a spoonful of beef extract in the soup. And then of course there are the endless accusations that I am unfaithful to him. Given your past history, he says, how can I ever trust you?' She sighed and moved uneasily in her chair. 'I can't altogether blame him,' she went on. 'I'm not very organised, and there was the other man's baby – and when I couldn't give him a child of his own – I know when he hits me it's got nothing to do with a creased shirt collar or beef stock in the soup.'

I said, 'I am sure you're right. But you have nothing to be ashamed of. You must never blame yourself. *No man has the right to assault his partner.*'

'But I can't help thinking it must be something about me that sets him off. His parishioners think the world of him. He does so much good in the village. Everybody likes him, trusts him.'

'Have you a friend, someone you could confide in?'

The sound that came from her throat was bitter. 'Who would believe me?' she asked. 'He usually hits me in places where the marks won't show. Last night, he lost control. He's getting worse. I sometimes wonder if he's mentally ill.'

'No,' I said, 'he has a problem, certainly, but believe me he knows exactly what he's doing. I think you are in danger. Great danger. We can help you—'

'He'd kill me,' she repeated, 'if he knew I had told you all this. I'll have to think about it.'

I said, 'There are many options open to you—'

She began to sway; again she pressed a tissue to her mouth. 'I – I think I might faint,' she said. 'A drink of water?'

I hurried into the little kitchen. I filled a tumbler with water, and took time to switch on the kettle to make her a hot drink.

When I returned to my client all I found was the swinging door which led from the office, and a bloodstained tissue on the blue chair.

We closed the office at four thirty. Paul left almost at once saying he had things to do. I stayed on, for several reasons.

We arranged to drive separately to a restaurant he knew out in the country. Meanwhile I needed to phone Niall with my excuse that I had paperwork which could only be done here in Taunton. 'Don't bother to wait up,' I told him, and smiled as I used the cruel phrase he had so often used to me.

Where there is trust, deception is easy.

I should have felt guilty, but I didn't. If I had known I was to dine out I would have brought a change of clothes. As it was, my faith in the Wonderbra and green blouse would have to do. I tried to work on the files Paul had said were urgent. But I thought instead about his no-colour opalescent eyes.

I stood before the wall mirror and applied fresh make-up. I loosened my hair from the chignon, piled it on top of my head and secured it with the tortoiseshell combs I had bought in Spain and never used, and which had lain forgotten for a year in a pocket of my briefcase.

He was sitting at a corner table, in the bar, in a pool of lamplight. I recognised him by the set of his shoulders and the back view of his head. My heart thumped so hard that I could scarcely breathe, I felt a deep sweet ache in the pit of my stomach. I seemed to have moved from the first to the final stages of burning passion without the intervening flashes of cold reason which might have saved me.

If I had been busy changing my appearance so had he. As I slid into the facing seat I couldn't help staring at him. The long black curling hair had been clipped short. The beard and moustache which had concealed much of his face was gone. There was still a faint blue shadow on his pale skin, where the razor had not quite done its business, but revealed was the strong and bony jaw, the cleft chin, the slanting Slavic cheekbones. He looked vulnerable and ten years younger, and when he smiled at me the first clear sight of his long-lipped mouth turned my bones to water.

He stood and looked towards the bar.

'White wine,' I said, 'a small one.' I watched him walk away and thought about the lie I had told Niall. I was not used to lying, had never needed to until now. If we talked exclusively about work, Paul and I, would it somehow cancel out the deceit? The trouble was, once begun, one lie would lead to another.

He returned with the drinks. I preferred mineral water, but white wine sounded more sophisticated.

I had made sure that Paul did not hear the call I made to Niall. I could have told my husband that I was meeting a colleague for an after-work drink, but he had behaved so oddly at breakfast that I doubted I would have been believed. Already I was being careful. Telephone lies were easier.

The wine was sharp and stinging on my tongue, and although I took small slow sips my head almost at once felt light and swimmy.

I said, more by way of distraction than true concern, 'My first client this morning – I shouldn't have left her alone for a single second. State she was in anything could happen. Supposing I read in the local paper that a vicar has been stabbed? I know I handled it badly.'

'If she means to do it,' he said, 'she will.'

'We've no name, no address.'

'She'll be back.'

I said, 'You seem very certain.'

'I've heard a lot of murder threats. I worked in King's Cross for five years.'

But for the brief statement that he was a widower and had a son, this was the first personal information he had volunteered.

'You don't remember me, do you?' he went on. 'Spain, nineteen ninety-two. You spoke at a conference. I sat at the back of the room. I was very impressed by your arguments, and by you.'

I said, 'There were so many people there. If we had been introduced I'm sure I would have remembered.'

'We weren't,' he muttered. He was drinking cider, the rough brew straight from the wood. He grabbed his glass and looked into the amber-coloured liquid. 'I heard on the grapevine that you were taking over the Taunton office. I applied to be transferred here, and was told that no vacancy existed. And then Mrs Stevens resigned and here I am. I shouldn't be telling you any of this, should I?'

I knew what he was saying, and the knowledge sent me spinning. It was all too fast, too soon, but perhaps for me it was the only way that love could happen. If this was love? How should I know? My skin prickled as if I had fallen into a bed of nettles. I was dizzy with desire. My throat and mouth were so dry I could not speak. I imagined myself in his bed, doing things I would never do with Niall.

He leaned across the table and ran his index finger down my face, from my eyelid to the corner of my mouth. 'I'm not wrong, am I?' he whispered. 'Tell me I'm not wrong.'

I shook my head, like a rabbit transfixed by headlights on a lonely road on a dark night.

'No,' I croaked, 'you're not wrong.' Still feeling like a mesmerised rabbit I leaned towards him across the table. I had never kissed a man who was moustached and bearded; now, I thought regretfully, that he was clean shaven, I would never know what it felt like. He tasted of rough cider and still smelt faintly of garlic. Maybe he knew something I did not. Perhaps garlic and cider were aphrodisiacs. The kiss grew more passionate. The groan which vibrated in his throat reverberated in mine. We pulled apart to see the back of the retreating waiter who had presumably come to tell us that our table in the restaurant was ready.

In the first week of May the skies cleared, the rain clouds slipped northwards and warm air from Devon blew across the Blackdowns. I watched the leaves unfurl on the beech trees, and grass grow lush and green in Niall's meadow field. I began to identify birds, thrush and robin, blackbird and what might have been a swallow. Wild orchids appeared in the steep banks of the lanes.

My mother returned to Sad Acre Farm, and life took on a cosy pattern: home-cooked meals instead of Marks and Sparks frozen dinners, washing and ironing done regularly, rather than our crumpled clothes being hidden away in cupboards. The rooms of the house, newly papered and painted, carpeted and curtained, were becoming charming and homelike. At any other time I would have resented Nina's skills, her ability to get along with Niall, her knack of cajoling and persuading him that the long hours worked in the house and field would, as she put it, one day bring their own reward. It was their singlemindedness, the way the two of them were focused and at one about the reclamation of Sad Acre, that allowed me to keep my secret. When I arrived home in the blue dusk, the time of day which the people who lived in these hills called 'dimpsey', it was to find them in the kitchen, Niall proud of his swollen blistered hands, my mother of her aching back, sitting among the supper dishes, radiant and contented, and congratulating one another on the small successes of their day.

A delicious meal was always waiting for me; a clean cloth, and wild flowers in a copper jug in the centre of the table. I was greeted with smiles, and treated with the sympathy which they considered due to one who had driven to and returned from Taunton, with a long and tedious day of paperwork and the burden of other people's troubles sandwiched in between.

I allowed them to spoil me.

If I felt an occasional twinge of guilt at their obvious concern, I reminded myself that my paycheck was financing our day-to-day living expenses, and would continue to do so for some time yet.

When Paul and I were in the office, that haven of blue chairs, white walls, vases of daffodils in March and April, muted sounds of traffic passing through Taunton, I would watch him as he worked at the computer, as he welcomed clients, as he made tea and coffee, and washed up mugs, and I would find it difficult to believe that what happened between us out of office hours actually took place. We made love in positions I would once have thought anatomically impossible for people in their late forties, whose spines were no longer as flexible, whose stamina was failing. I lived from one soft spring evening to the next, from weekend to weekend. I never once looked any further forward. I told whatever lies were necessary. Because I was happy I was a nicer person. There were times when the magical secret threatened to spontaneously combust. After a Saturday allegedly spent shopping in Taunton I would carry the proofs of purchase into the farm kitchen: a small bottle of Old Napoleon for Nina, a large bottle of Glenlivet for Niall, a pound of their favourite Ardennes pâté, a jar of olives and a box of cream cakes, all from the Somerset County Stores. And as they exclaimed their pleasure at my thoughtfulness, I was tempted to be offhand. 'Oh, it's nothing,' I longed to say, 'you deserve a little treat or two. Of course a few cream cakes can't begin to compare with the fun I'm having. Did you ever do it in the back of a Range Rover, Niall? Or across a government standard-issue desk?' I would gaze into their trusting faces while a voice in my head was shouting, 'If you only knew! My God, if you only knew!'

After midsummer we moved into a different league. I had been careful to let Paul set the pace, I made no demands and, consumed as I was with curiosity and lust, I never questioned him about his past life.

I had studied his file, of course I had. Born in London. University for three years. A short spell in the probation service, and then an unaccounted gap of nine years. He had come into our counselling service eight years ago. He had worked in several major cities, including London. He was listed as a widower with one son. His age was given as fifty-two. His Taunton address was that of a tall Victorian house close to the office. His name was beside the bellpush which, when pressed, would ring in the topmost flat.

I knew because I confirmed these details very early one morning, before full daylight, parking my car in a side street and creeping around the Victorian villa like a private investigator.

May and June had been cool and wet. Good grass-growing weather said my mother, who had taken to trotting out these farming legends as if she had herself been reared by a herdsman rather than a village doctor.

July came in hot and dry, and the hay yield, so my two self-styled agricultural experts informed me, was as heavy and as sweet as they had predicted. I said I was happy for them, but heaviness and sweetness had quite other connotations in my own life, although of course I could not say so.

There were a lot of things I did not say in those long hot months, questions I should have asked Paul Mavsoni, small mysteries I turned away from. But as I have already stated, where there is trust, deception is easy.

Business was slow through July and August. It was the holiday season, people spent time in their gardens and on beaches. Family problems eased, arguments and tensions were harder to sustain in temperatures of ninety degrees Fahrenheit. For this was high summer in England and the living, as the old song said, was easy.

For the first time in my life I also spent a lot of time on beaches. Taunton, I discovered, was just a short drive away from several private little coves. I tanned easily and quickly.

I explained my Mediterranean appearance to Niall and my mother as being the result of lunchtimes spent on the rear lawn of my office building.

On two occasions I saw my battered client, once in Goodlands Gardens, and once in the Friday market. She wore an ankle-length faded print dress, and her hair was scraped hard back and secured with a rubber band at the nape of her neck. At the sight of me she averted her gaze and walked rapidly away in the opposite direction. Her damaged face and throat had healed but she moved stiffly, and I wondered what new injuries were concealed beneath that long skirt.

I didn't want to think about her, and yet I was drawn frequently back to Goodlands Gardens, and the market. I scoured the weekly newspaper for headlines about domestic dramas, and found nothing that could even remotely have involved her.

In the first week of September, the extra staff I had requested, and for whom I had waited all summer, finally arrived. Now, counting Jan the part-time secretary, we were a workforce of four people. Mary was a fifty-six-year-old widow, motherly, soft-spoken, with blue eyes, wavy silver hair and a pink, unlined complexion. She fitted in right away, and I was able, thankfully, to reorganise my workload. Mary was good with the most deeply distressed of our clients. She would have handled our abused vicar's wife far better than I did. There was just one drawback to her presence in the office. Unlike Jan, who worked on flexitime and was absent for long chunks of each day, Mary was constantly with us.

There would be no more long and meaningful glances, no burning kisses dropped on to the nape of my neck; no lunchtime frolicking across his desk or mine.

To allay any possible suspicions, Paul now lunched alone off sandwiches and coffee in his office, and spoke to me only when absolutely necessary. Also alone, I took to grabbing a salad or a bowl of soup in a pretty little green-and-white café in the narrow, ancient thoroughfare known as Bath Place.

Between Bath Place and the Taunton public library, there is a small, partially enclosed garden, shaded by trees and with facing wrought-iron benches set on a central square of paving. I fell into the regular habit of sitting on one of those benches. The September sun had mellowed to a pleasant warmth; the lunchtime shoppers and the tourists wandered in and out of the attractive boutiques and specialist food shops of Bath Place. I thought about Paul, about his voice, his eyes, his body, and how the circumspectness of our daytime behaviour had increased the abandonment of our evening loving. I wondered how much longer this concealment of our feelings for each other could possibly go on. It was the first time I had dwelt seriously on the future, and I didn't like the route my mind was taking.

Sitting on that bench, I admitted to being caught up in a dangerous madness; yet when later that day Paul suggested we should spend the weekend together, I began immediately to plan the series of lies I would need to tell Niall and Nina to explain my absence from Sad Acre Farm.

Guilt was making me increasingly cautious.

I feared discovery of my affair with Paul by my superiors at head office far more than any showdown with Niall and Nina. On the early morning drives into Taunton and on the evening returns I began to realise how very little I actually knew about him.

I had known next to nothing about Niall when we married, but I was young then and it hadn't seemed to matter.

It was only recently that Niall had accused me of an indifference towards his early life that, at the time, I hadn't even noticed. In truth I wasn't all that curious about it even now. If Niall had wished to tell me more about his childhood, his family, he had already missed his chances over several years. With Paul, my need to know everything about his life was becoming urgent. I longed to hear about his dead wife, the backpacking son who sent him postcards from exotic places. I began to invent a childhood for Paul, loving parents, a secure home. I could never envisage brothers or sisters. Like Niall, like me, he had that hint of remoteness in his nature, a hard-learned self-sufficiency that identifies the solitary child.

No matter which way I steered the conversation, Paul, for whatever reason, continued to block me whenever my questions became probing. I had never visited his flat. I did not even know his son's first name. Our meetings were arranged around our work schedules, and in isolated venues. We dared not risk being seen together in Taunton. Too many late nights in the office would also, on my part, not have been wise. I needed time alone to work out what was happening to me, yet there I was telling him now that a snatched hour here or there was not enough; that we ought to spend more time together.

The offer from Paul's sympathetic friend of a holiday bungalow in Dawlish Warren, vacant from Friday until Monday, was too good to pass up.

I invented a seminar in London, about whose exact whereabouts I was carefully vague. When I went into unnecessary detail about the subjects to be covered, my husband and mother hardly took in a single word I said. Pigs and the housing of them, their breeding potential, had lately formed the subject of every conversation between Nina and Niall. For weeks past they had lived and breathed pigs. I could have announced my imminent elopement with Prince Charles and my mother's response would have been, 'Well, that's nice, dear!'

I packed a weekend case on the Friday morning and told them I would be back late on Monday.

They waved me off absent-mindedly, their faces turned already to the pig pens and the pregnant sow.

The bungalow overlooked the ocean; it was warm and comfortable, and stood at a considerable distance from its nearest neighbours. It was shabby, and furnished in the style of the 1920s, wicker chairs and sofas, chrome and glass tables, orange and blue rugs and cushions, and a set of Clarice Cliff pottery jugs and bowls that Paul treated carelessly, even when I told him they were Art Deco and worth a fortune. The kitchen was almost as antiquated as that of Sad Acre Farm. A bulbous, yellow-painted fridge stood in a corner beside a small gas cooker which had the name NEW WORLD embossed on its grey-and-white mottled enamel. There was a wooden meat safe with a wire-mesh door to discourage flies, and a metal dolly-tub for washing clothes, complete with washboard and wooden tongs.

I said, 'Your friend doesn't seem to need much in the way of modern gadgets.'

'He isn't here very often.'

I waited for more information on the anonymous friend, but Paul had already turned away and was striking kitchen matches in order to light the ancient gas stove. I was tempted to ask, 'Do you come here often?' but I didn't need to. It was obvious that he knew every inch of the bungalow, had long been familiar with all its contents.

We had never spent a whole night together. To fall asleep in his arms and wake up to find him beside me in the morning should have been magical and tender and reassuring. The falling asleep bit after prolonged love-making was all I had hoped it would be, but I woke the next morning to find myself alone. When I looked from the window I saw him pacing on the shore, his head and shoulders bent as if he faced a howling gale even though there was only a light breeze blowing.

I had bought a glamorous leisure-suit of dark red velvet from Gloria, especially for this weekend adventure, but it seemed inappropriate now and I left it folded in my suitcase. Instead, I put on jeans and a fresh shirt and sweater. I waited for his return before starting to make breakfast. I did not trust the gas cooker and felt a curious diffidence about opening drawers and cupboards in Paul's absence. When he finally returned I sat on a kitchen chair and watched him make toast and coffee and poached eggs. We ate in silence and when the meal was finished I washed and stacked the dishes.

Something was not quite right; perhaps it was the strangeness of our being together in a domestic situation. A man who had lived alone for many years might well find the constant presence of another person irksome. I hung the tea towel on a hook, I fidgeted with cutlery, opened and closed drawers and cupboards.

I said, 'What is it, Paul? Have I upset you in some way?'

He looked up abruptly. He had the bemused expression of someone who had been too long in a dark place. 'No,' he said. 'Not you.' He smiled. 'Sorry. I'm not very good company in the early morning. Never was. One of the few benefits of living alone – you can be as morose and miserable as you like until after breakfast, without upsetting anyone.'

I went into the bedroom. I retrieved the duvet and pillows from far corners of the room where they and several other items seemed to have drifted during the long night. I remade the bed. There could not, I reasoned, be very much wrong with a relationship passionate enough to wreck a bedroom. I could not remember a single night with Niall in which the sheets had been more than slightly wrinkled.

I went back to the kitchen. He was sitting as I had left him, staring at the hideous mottled gas stove. I crept up behind him, twined my arms around his chest and shoulders and laid the side of my face against his. I could feel the sharp ridge of his high slanting cheekbone, smell the freshness of his aftershave. I edged my face around until I found his long-lipped mouth.

Two hours later I admitted that getting dressed that morning and remaking the bed had been a waste of energy and time.

In the afternoon we drove out to the estuary at Starcross. The weather was changing. The mild and golden October of recent days now had a nip of winter in the air. We parked the Range Rover close to the mud-and-sand flats, and watched them come alive with the wild birds flying in from distant places. It was warm in the car. We were both content and relaxed from our recent gymnastics. Now, I thought, there was time to talk, time to ask him the kind of questions which were threatening to build up an impenetrable wall between us, all the questions which could no longer be answered with a few dismissive words.

I had rehearsed my lines. 'Paul,' I would begin, 'I have told you just about all there is to know about myself, my family and my life. Now it's your turn. I want to know—'

As I began to speak a magpie flew down and perched on the Range Rover's bonnet. Out beyond the estuary, above the blue-grey line which marked the meeting place of land and water, the sun was going down spectacularly in a lake of streaky crimson. The bird, its black and white plumage silhouetted against the rosy light, remained motionless and watching us.

According to my mother to see a single magpie was unlucky, and although in theory I considered such tales to be total rubbish, I began to look anxiously at distant trees and hedges, willing the magpie's mate to appear and join him, which would, supposedly, nullify the threatened ill luck.

I sneaked a sideways glance at Paul, who had become unnaturally still and watchful; he was staring back at the magpie, a look of pure terror on his face. All at once there was a fluttering of wings and a second magpie came to sit on the Rover's bonnet. 'Ah,' he muttered, 'the *cucaratchi* has a mate.' The relief in his voice was ludicrous. In Mexico they call the magpie *la cucaracha*. Not quite what Paul had said, but close enough. My hearing is acute. I know exactly what I heard. I wanted to question him about it but he seemed to sense my intention and managed to forestall me. So often lately he had known or guessed my most private thoughts. He relaxed into his seat, reached for my hand and began to stroke my fingers. I felt calm again, all my tension eased.

He said, 'You find me secretive, don't you?'

'Well – yes, as a matter of fact, I do! We've talked for hours about my life, my problems, but I know virtually nothing about you. About your life.'

He shrugged. 'Nothing much to tell. I never knew my parents. As a child I was passed like a parcel from one set of relatives to another. I married in my early twenties. We were childless for ten years and then, when Keiron was born, my wife was found to be suffering from an incurable cancer. She died two years later.'

As he spoke he removed his fingers from my hand. 'It's a depressing little tale. Keiron was the only good thing that ever happened to me. But he has his own life now.' He paused. 'Perhaps you can begin to understand why I find it easier to listen to other people's troubles, rather than dwelling on my own.'

I was stunned, overwhelmed by what he had told me. I felt like a child who had handled what he thought was a firework, only to discover that it was a bomb.

What could I say? Sorry seemed inadequate. I reached out a hand and then withdrew it.

He said, his gaze still fixed on the magpies, 'And in case you were wondering about it, I've lived alone since Ann died. You are the first woman—'

'I'm glad!' I said. I spoke impulsively, but immediately felt that I had blundered, had assumed too much, about him and his feelings.

The afterglow had faded from the western skies. A lemon light was shading into violet where land and water merged.

We sat in an uneasy silence. I said, 'Perhaps we should be going back?'

He said, 'Not just yet.' He nodded towards the two birds, still as motionless as polished mascots on the Rover's bonnet. 'Better not disturb them.'

I made my voice incredulous. 'You're seriously superstitious, aren't you?'

'I'm – careful.'

'Oh, don't worry,' I laughed. 'If you're nervous of upsetting them I'll shift them for you.'

I had opened the door, had one foot on the ground, when he leaned over, grabbed my arm violently and pulled me back inside. I thought at first that he was joking, that it was some sort of new game, until I looked at him full face and saw mixed fear and anger.

I settled back into my seat and quietly closed the car door. 'Look,' I said gently. 'My mother goes in for this sort of mumbo-jumbo. I was throwing spilled salt over my left shoulder and wishing on the new moon before I could walk. It's harmless enough as long as you don't let it rule your life.' I smiled but he did not smile back, so I shouted at him. I said, 'I would never not drive my car because I was afraid to upset a couple of magpies.' I could hear the anger in my voice. It might well have been Niall I was yelling at. We were, I now realised, having our first serious disagreement. He realised it too. He put an arm around my shoulders, turned my face towards his and kissed me. He began to tell me about shelducks, black-backed gulls and widgeon. He told me about the sounds of crooning made by eider-ducks as they dive for food. He described the intimate life of puffins which, he said, build their nests underground in disused rabbit burrows. As a ploy for cooling temper it really worked. The sound of his voice was mesmeric. I was startled when of their own accord the magpies flew suddenly upwards in a single flash of black and white. We watched them skim across the eel grass and disappear into the darkening sky.

One for sorrow, Nina would have said. Two for joy.

I whispered, 'I'm sorry Paul. I had no right to complain

because you are superstitious. Truth is – I half believe in all that silly stuff myself; and I don't want to. That's why I lost my temper.'

He said, 'You know I love you. I've never felt like this about any other woman. I want us to live as if the past had never happened. What's that corny saying? Today is the first day of the rest of my life? Let's begin again – together, put all the pain and disappointment behind us.'

He had never said he loved me until now. His arm rested heavy on my shoulders. The scent of lemon verbena wafting from the sachet above the driving mirror seemed stronger than usual. Since becoming beardless he had started to use an expensive aftershave. It was only now that I recognised the fragrance; it was one I had bought for Niall on his fiftieth birthday. I remembered the day last summer, the celebration in my daughter's garden, the chocolate cake she had baked, the melting ice cream, the circle of garden loungers and two-year-old John, the object of everyone's attention, splashing in his plastic pool, a blue cotton sun-hat perched on his white-blond hair. I tried to blot out the memory. Fran, blonde and suntanned in her pink dress. Niall laughing, a smudge of chocolate icing on his chin. Mitch, serious and focusing his camcorder on the antics of his young son. I could no longer visualise myself in that happy group, although I had been present.

As we drove out of Starcross I looked out across the twilit mud flats, and for one terrifying moment I saw myself, hovering and alone, in that dark place between land and sea.

Nina

Imogen had given me a free hand.

'Have a free hand, mother,' she said. She had been talking about the house, the reclamation of dusty rooms and arranging of furniture, the laying of carpets and the hanging of curtains. She was also talking about something else.

I was unpacking china and saucepans from the cartons she had once neatly labelled KITCHEN. I watched her as she spread folders from her briefcase across the big pine table.

Something was different about her; a change so profound that the marking of those cartons might have happened in another life, on a distant planet. I could see by her blank gaze that she had no recollection of ever packing the blue-ringed bowls and dishes, the copper-bottomed pans. Imogen had moved not only into a different house, but another dimension, a place in which Niall and I had no reality for her.

If I had not known her so well I would have thought my cool, unemotional daughter to be dangerously in love. But this was hardly likely. She was a grandmother, a very serious person and devoted to her job. Two-thirds of her time was spent with women who lacked the strength of mind and purpose to sort out their own domestic troubles. Such people are counselled lately for every slightest problem. Where, in this nannified female environment of dysfunctional families and hysterical women in which she spent her days, would my daughter have found a man who could put that look of dreaming on her face?

Niall had noticed.

How could he not? Although we never talked about it, he had long been aware of Imogen's attitude towards me, the fierce way she had protected what she saw as her private territory. The fact that she was now not only willing but anxious to turn over to me all responsibility for the day to day running of her home, and the organisation of her house and garden, indicated a change so amazing that I knew in my bones he and I should both be suspicious of it.

I have this theory (so far not quite proven), that a determined seventy-year-old, if strongly motivated, might be able temporarily to halt the march of time and start moving backwards down the decades, and so confuse, if not delay, the ageing process.

I was seventy last year. This year I decided to be sixty-nine again. You may well laugh, but while admitting to seventy I could not have found the nerve to drive a tractor, milk a cow, herd pigs through an unfenced beech wood. I did all those things and more in the first ten months of this reversible year, because a voice in my head told me that I could. Age is a state of mind. I felt older at forty than I do now. Oh yes, I have had my aches and blisters, my stiff joints. But so has Niall.

From January to July we reeked of liniment; our blistered hands and feet were a patchwork of plasters. In the last two months we have become limber; our joints no longer creak and ache, our feet and hands are blessedly callused. We no longer rush about the place like headless chickens, achieving little, but have learned to walk slowly and purposefully like seasoned farmers. We take turns at shopping in Taunton on a Friday. Niall goes in the pickup. I travel in and return with Imogen. It means a long day in the town but I take it gently. Taunton has a certain charm for me, a terrifying feeling of familiarity which I try hard to attribute to tales I have read about it.

I once attempted to talk to Imogen about this but, as is usual these days, her attention was elsewhere. She is concerned only with the present.

So I tried my theory out on Niall. We were sitting outside in the late evening sunshine packing eggs into crates, checking them for cracks and cleanness. 'Do you think,' I asked, 'that it is possible to know a place, I mean *really know* it, even though you have never previously visited it in your whole life?' This sort of conversational opening can be risky; I already had a feeling that I would tell him more than was wise. The danger is that he is a good listener. He treats the most bizarre of my questions with respect.

'All depends,' he said, 'on your state of health at the time.'

I could see what he meant. 'Yes,' I said. 'Well, supposing you had slept well and were not hungover, or suffering from indigestion. Suppose you were just ambling along, on a pleasant summer morning in these unfamiliar streets. You discover that a river runs bang through the middle of Taunton. You stand for a while on the river bridge. Heavy traffic drives across that bridge. You breathe in exhaust fumes. An aeroplane drones overhead. Formal gardens line the riverbank on one side. There are flower beds edged with blue and white lobelia. There is a centrepiece of scarlet salvias. You can see a café, white chairs and tables, striped blue and white umbrellas. You can smell the coffee. You decide to go down there, sit under one of those umbrellas, order a cappuccino, kick off your sandals underneath the table, rest your aching back and feet.'

I looked doubtfully at him. He was not even smiling.

'There are steps,' I went on, 'leading down to this riverside café. But as you walk down them the sky clouds over. The plane disappears, and so do the cars and lorries. You can hear the clip-clop of horses' hooves. Coming towards you are two men who wear knee-breeches and tricorn hats, they are carrying what looks like a sedan chair. They halt beside the café entrance, except that the café has changed into a heavily timbered building with a sign above the door which reads CHOP HOUSE. PROP. SILAS CHAFFEY. There are rough wooden benches beside that door. There is a dank smell coming off the river. You sit down because your shaky legs will carry you no further. There are several men seated on those benches but they pay you no attention. You speak to them, you laugh and ask if this is a film set you have blundered into, even though you know it can't be. They continue drinking and talking as if you had not spoken, as if you were invisible. Two of these men are not strangers. You know them. And it is that instant recognition which terrifies you. You close your eyes against their faces, but their images are imprinted on your inner vision. You sit very still and listen to your rapid heartbeat. The thin dark man is Silva Lee. The red-haired giant is Georgie Barnacle. Silva is a Romany gypsy. Georgie is a Toll House Master. He has a gypsy wife named Coralina. You know these things to be true because you have always known them. Silva Lee is a dangerous man; he is staring at you and that stare burns right through your closed eyelids. When you open your eyes and look upwards you see once more the blue and white stripes of the café umbrella. A cup of cappuccino is on the table. Traffic roars across the Tone bridge. A tiny silver aircraft leaves a vapour trail across the cloudless blue. Children are feeding ducks at the water's edge.

'You ease your sandals from your burning feet, but your body is cold; you begin to shiver. You gulp down the scalding coffee. You tell yourself you were not dreaming, neither are you crazy. You saw what you saw. But who would ever believe you?'

Niall regarded me without surprise. 'I believe you, Nina.'

'Don't humour me, Niall.'

'I thought you knew me better than that.'

And of course I did. 'Sorry,' I said. 'Trouble is, I have difficulty believing it myself.'

'No you don't,' he said quietly. 'Not really. I think you are sure it really happened.' He wiped the shell of a small brown egg and placed it carefully into the open crate. He said, 'Sometimes the corner of a veil lifts. It happens when we are deeply worried about something or someone. I see my mother sometimes.'

As he spoke he looked away towards the beech woods, and I wondered again just how familiar Niall was with Sad Acre Farm.

I had never felt able to ask him the direct question; my craven instinct to leave well alone was still intact. But I recognised now that we were talking for the first time on another, deeper level. This was a Niall I had never dreamed existed: thoughtful, acutely sensitive, and willing to believe the unbelievable.

I said, 'I'm concerned about Immie.'

'So am I.' The egg crate was full and he closed the lid carefully and secured the hasp. 'Something going on down to Taunton, don't you think?'

It was not in his nature to make such an admission. For a moment there I heard the burr of Somerset in his usually accentless speech. I said, 'Something going on somewhere, but what?'

He nodded. 'It's got to be her job or connected with it. I've smelled alcohol on her when she comes home late.' His face was flushed. 'She doesn't drink. She doesn't sleep around – at least, she didn't.'

'A man?' My incredulity amused him, but his smile was wry.

'She doesn't want me,' he said. 'So think about it, Nina! New clothes, perfume, late nights; none of which is on my account.'

'There was a time,' I confessed, 'when I wondered about her trips abroad. She would come back with a certain look about her.'

He said, 'She tried to make me jealous.'

'And were you?'

'No. I knew she had no time to be unfaithful, and anyway she wasn't the type. All her energies went into that damned job. I actually wished that she would loosen up a bit. Have a drink or two, smoke a cigarette, flirt a little. Perfection is very hard to live with. Now,' he said ruefully, 'when she's lying her head off, doing the sort of risky things I've always done, I'm as jealous as hell.'

I would not have thought him capable of jealousy. But what did I know?

I said, tentatively, 'Perhaps she feels that it's her turn to have a little fun? She will soon be fifty – maybe she thinks that she deserves it?'

'You're absolutely right. I don't have a leg to stand on, do I. But Immie's such an innocent. She knows damn-all about real life. All her experience of domestic trouble is second-hand. She advises beat-up women to leave their husbands. If those women had any sense they would know what to do about such bastards without being told.' He sighed. 'I don't want her to get hurt, Nina. The world is full of smooth-talking con artists.' He caught my speculative look. 'All right,' he laughed, 'but I never *hurt* anybody. I never make promises I can't keep.'

He began to stack the egg crates, ready for direct deliveries on the following morning. We were in the habit, he and I, of drinking bedtime cocoa. Niall called it hot chocolate, which made it sound less elderly and cosy. He drained his mug and put it in the washing-up bowl. He said, 'I'll check on the new sow before I turn in.'

He may have intended to visit the pregnant sow, but from the uphill path which led to the farrowing pens he would also have a clear view of the road down which Imogen must travel.

There were nights when she was late home. Just lately there had been nights when she did not return at all. Her explanation, vague and grudgingly given, was that she had become involved with extra-curricular work in a women's refuge, and the occasional crisis required her presence.

I did not believe one word of this. How he felt I had no way of knowing, but I could make an informed guess. Ten minutes later I heard Niall's step on the cobbled yard and then the sound of a car door slamming. I grabbed my cocoa and made for the back stairs. Whatever went on between the two of them, I did not wish to know about it.

There was a rocking chair in the house, an item to which Niall had shown a strange aversion. When I asked if I might have it in my bedroom he had carried it upstairs at once. I sat in it now beside the green dormer window, and watched a brown moth flutter dangerously close to the hot pink glass funnel of the oil lamp. When Imogen had given me a free hand, my first act had been to move myself up the short flight of stairs which led to the attic. Over the years, various owners and tenants had carried out questionable improvements to the farmhouse. Niall had already ripped out the imitation brass cowl above the sitting-room fireplace. Someone must once have bid for a job lot of nylon carpet patterned in orange and purple swirls, for it spread like a deadly fungus over many of the rooms. Gradually, he was revealing the lovely old pine boards that had lain beneath the carpet, sanding and waxing them until they glowed. It was only in the two large attic rooms that acceptable improvements had already been made; here the walls had been relined with new pine tongue and groove, a false ceiling fitted, useful cupboards built in, and window seats inserted in the embrasures of the dormer windows. Surprisingly, no rubbish had accumulated up here, only a few cobwebs and dust which were easily removed. On a rainy April afternoon Niall and I had moved my bed, a table and two chairs, a small upholstered armchair, and other odds and ends, up to the top of the house.

If Imogen had required an explanation of my anti-social seclusion I would have cited the wonderful views, the feeling of safety I experienced when sleeping directly underneath the thatch. But she hardly seemed to notice my absence from the first-floor guest room. Over the summer months I had acquired a few creamy sheepskins for the floor, a shelf of favourite books, the cranberry-glass oil lamp; blue and white curtains for the dormer windows and matching cushions for the windowseats, from which I can see the winding lanes which lead to Taunton.

From the rear windows of the attic I can see the two fields and the acres of woodland which currently comprise the holding. In the further field we have had, since springtime, a dozen ewes with their lambs at foot. Niall plans to have the ewes share their grassland with free-range turkeys for the Christmas market. Our pigs and poultry are housed in raised wooden pens within the beech woods. The nearer, larger field is occupied by Niall's pride and joy, two Dexter heifers and their calves.

He is beginning to show a hitherto unsuspected head for business. Like many of his generation he now tends to think and speak in slogans, an encouraging turnaround since his former style was to think in terms of racetracks, whisky and fast women.

Niall is rarely, these days, hungover at the breakfast table. His tan is the genuine article, the result of haymaking in June, and the building of his own hen houses and pig pens, under the day-long sunshine of the recent summer.

His slogans are varied. The first and most successful was DIRECT SELLING. To begin with, this ploy was used in order to sell eggs. He visited a few of the new housing estates which are springing up around neighbouring villages. His first customers passed the word along. Now he delivers to three hundred homes and, as he says, the potential is endless. DIRECT SELLING from the tailgate of the pickup is turning out to be COST EFFECTIVE. He is thinking now of packaging his home-bred pork and lamb to sell on the egg-round. The acres of woodland, neglected for half a century, are long overdue a thorough thinning-out. By November he intends to have a supply of bagged-up logs to add to the egg-round. Even Roscoe is under training to work for his Winalot and beef bones. Since he sees himself lately as a sheep and cattle herder this is no hardship for him.

Only the Dexters are so far ornamental and non-profit making. But their day will come.

From my lookout post in the attic window there are times when I see more than I wish to. Observation can be two-edged. When Imogen returned home from her weekend away, her so-called seminar in London, she was travelling fast, too fast to notice the car which followed her through the lanes at a discreet distance. Whoever he was, he stopped short of the final slope which leads down to Sad Acre. It was almost dark, but I could make out the size and shape of what might have been a Range Rover. Such vehicles are common enough in rural districts, but why was he parked up there, without lights and for two hours? I was tempted to tell Niall; or, more to the point, to warn my daughter that she had been followed. But to do so would have been to reveal myself as a spy, a secret watcher, one who meddled in the affairs of others. I could have taken that chance; could have stirred the already simmering pot with a long spoon. But if I had, would it have made any difference? Some tragedies are meant to happen.

Since moving myself into Sad Acre Farm I have learned a thing or two. Interesting stuff, but nothing that leads to peace of mind. The tenancy of a small farm or holding, it seems, is viewed by the rural community as a pearl of great price. When there is also a spacious if shabby house on offer, and the whole package is situated in what is known as a 'conservation area of outstanding beauty', how, our neighbours were asking, did Niall Donovan, one-time builder, plumber, gardener, and bit-part actor, manage to secure a five-year tenure and, it was rumoured, at a knockdown price?

Not that a word of this was ever spoken directly to Niall. He continued to be absent whenever neighbours called. It was left to me to apologise for our Dexter heifers when they strayed into Widdicombes' herd of Friesians; or for our sex-mad cockerel who went a-courting regularly up to Bob's farm.

It was at such times that I began to be aware of the local curiosity about us. Situated as we were at the end of a rutted, narrow lane, in a house which was screened by trees on three sides, I had mistakenly imagined that we were invisible to most. Since our entire stock was made up of determined escapees, there were frequent opportunities for aggrieved neighbours to appear on the doorstep or by the farm gate. Conversations always, eventually, took the same turn. The complaints about our cows, sheep, pigs, hens or newly acquired goat would be lodged in a firm, no-nonsense manner. I would apologise, cringe, beg or grovel, according to the gravity of the offence. We exchanged a few predictable comments on the weather. No rural conversation is complete without them. There would be a pregnant pause, and then the inquisitor would get down to the real purpose of his visit. Not quite looking at me he would ask, 'That 'ud be your son, of course, the young master?'

'Son-in-law.'

'Ah well. Same difference. Not that we'm nosy or anything like that, but as I said to Mother, his face looks familiar . . . ?'

'Ah!' I would cry, 'well, I know why that is – he's appeared quite often on TV.'

'Oh! You don't say so! Well I never! The television, eh! What sort of programme?'

'Farming matters,' I would say firmly, 'and subjects connected with farming.' My glacial look forbade any further questioning, I hoped. But a long and baffled stare from the questioner was followed by the acute observation that Niall was 'one of they "gentleman" farmers, was he?'

There were many such enquiries. As spring gave way to summer and increased activity was noted on Sad Acre, I was frequently waylaid while gathering eggs and feeding pigs. Our nearest neighbour, Bob, whose land abutted on our beech wood, was the most persistent of them all. It was he who first raised the question of Niall's tenancy. His ruddy face peered over the hawthorn hedge one sweet June morning. In his arms he held our black, virile, and incurably polygamous cockerel. With one practised movement he tossed Nero over the hedge, to land fluttering and outraged at my feet. 'Dratted bird,' he complained. 'Always up to my place he is, bothering my hens. Fox'll get him, you mark my words. Heap of feathers he'll be one of these fine nights.'

'We are putting in electric fencing,' I said sharply. The offended Nero, who was still ruffling his feathers, began to stalk off and I made to follow.

Bob said in a quiet voice, 'There was Donovans farming on Sad Acre in my granfer's time. Same family would it be, do you think?'

I paused halfway between hedge and pig pen. When I turned back to face him he was grinning broadly. I recognised the sneaky nature of the challenge but refused to rise to it. 'I know nothing about the history of the farm,' I said. 'You may have noticed that since we moved here, we've all three of us been too busy to draw breath.' I included Imogen in our number in order to add weight, and not because she deserved it. 'And now,' I said, 'if you will excuse me, I have pigs to feed.'

I walked away in a dignified manner, but his voice still floated slyly across the hedge. 'I remember old Donovan, meself. Irish, he was. Hell of a temper on him. Of course he was young when he first showed up here. Where he come from nobody could tell. Had a young 'un with him according to Granfer. Queer little cove – great slanty eyes and dark frizzy hair. Never spoke a word to nobody, that boy! He was here for a summer and then he disappeared. My old granfer said the gyppos took him off, said he'd seen it happen. But granfer's sight was failing by that time, and anyway, he was a lying old sod, he'd make up any daft yarn when he was the worse for cider.'

'Teetotaller yourself then are you, Bob?' I asked sweetly.

It took almost a minute for that particular penny to drop. When it did, he shot me an evil but more respectful glance, turned on his green-wellied heel and marched away.

But not for long.

He was back the next morning, waiting beside the hedge. This time with a lamb tucked under his arm.

'Bugger keeps getting in among my ewes,' he muttered.

This time I was not apologetic. 'I can't imagine how,' I snapped. 'The fencing is new and so is the wire, and that lamb is too fat to get through any but the largest hole.'

'Knows all about farming, do you missus?'

'I should do. I was brought up on a farm, and my husband was a farmer's son.' This was not altogether a true statement, but I didn't care. The bafflement on his face was worth a shoal of lies.

But Bob was not so easily deflected. He handed me the lamb across a spray of pale pink dog roses. He said, 'Funny the way the tenancy of Sad Acre never come on to the open market?'

I took the lamb. 'Oh, but it did,' I began to say, and then realised that I owed this man no explanations of what was, after all, Niall and Imogen's business.

'Can't stop,' I said brightly. 'Things to do. I'm sure you must be busy too.'

Determined to have the last word he muttered, 'Folks is talking, missus, that's all! Just thought you ought to know.'

I had promised Fran that she and Mitch and John should visit Sad Acre just as soon as the house was in a civilised condition. I explained that by civilised I did not mean the final curtains hung, or the last cushion plumped and in its place. Civilised in this case meant the installation of what town-bred people considered the amenities essential to survival. A flushable lavatory, the provision of hot baths, and electric sockets into which could be plugged a washing machine, a microwave and vacuum cleaner.

The generator had been our first and most important purchase, but the power it provided was not boundless. We tried to include Imogen in the vital choices of working electrical equipment which must now be made, but her only contribution was to agree sweetly to all our suggestions, saying that she was quite sure Niall and I 'knew best'.

The bathroom was installed in what had been the smallest bedroom. The plumber from Taunton had viewed the sloping floor and low ceiling as a challenge. The job took a little longer and cost more than first estimated. But we were left with a larger than usual bathroom and the triple blessings of a shower, a deep bath, and a flush loo. Painting and papering, we decided, could be done on winter days, when nothing much was happening outside. Other decisions were equally simple. Our most urgent needs were in the kitchen. A washing machine was installed, and a microwave to provide the quick and easy meals which were all we had time for in that first hectic summer. The vacuum cleaner was dragged out of storage, but there was little enough time and energy left over for it to be pushed often across the few carpets we had laid.

By the end of October we were in a decent enough state of order to contemplate visitors, providing of course that they were blood relatives and willing to overlook the odd inconvenience or discomfort. I could not for instance imagine entertaining Primrose, whose eyebrows would have touched her expensive blonde hairline if confronted with the beetles, spiders, mice, and a suspected couple of squirrels which were currently moving indoors to live among us as the autumn nights grew colder.

You may think from my recent preoccupation with my son-in-law and daughter that they are the most important people in my life.

Not so!

Admittedly my circle of relatives and friends is not extensive. I have never believed in spreading myself too thinly. It was not until my granddaughter phoned and said, 'What about a long weekend visit, Grandma?' that I realised how much of this year had been devoted to these two middle-aged delinquents with whom I seem to have thrown in my lot.

'Wonderful!' I told Fran. 'Come as soon as you can though. This quiet mild weather won't last much longer.'

'Next weekend?'

'Yes,' I said, 'oh yes please!'

'I'll phone again on Thursday,' she said, 'to let you know when we shall be arriving.'

I checked the linen cupboard; spare duvets and pillows needed to be aired. I made out a shopping list for food and wine, all of which could be bought at the County Stores in Taunton. Two hours later when I was passing the mirror in the hall I was shocked at the sight of the wild-looking woman reflected there. My hair had not been cut since Christmas. The skin of my hands was rough and callused. The strange assortment of garments which I threw on every morning would have shamed a scarecrow.

I remembered the times when Imogen had bullied me into regularly buying clothes and shoes; into visiting a hairdresser at six-weekly intervals. It was a clear indication of my daughter's preoccupation with her secret life in Taunton that my appearance had been allowed to deteriorate to a level which shamed even me.

Not wishing to leave anything to chance, I phoned ahead and made a hair appointment. The list for the County Stores was in my handbag. Niall would collect the unusually large grocery order when he drove into Taunton on Friday.

I felt organised, capable. I needed handcream from Boots, warm tights and a pale pink lipstick.

I sat tidily in Imogen's car, knees together, hands folded. I began, in my head, to plan menus for the weekend. The November morning was still and overcast. Our neighbour Bob was already in his field, ploughing golden stubble into dark red rows of turned earth. The trees were still tawny-yellow, hardly a leaf fallen.

I had announced at supper last evening that Fran, Mitch and John would be coming to spend the weekend with us. Niall had expressed great pleasure at the news; Imogen had continued to eat chops and drink coffee as if I had not spoken.

Come to think about it, she had not said a single word since my announcement. As if she had read my thoughts, she said now through clenched teeth, 'I would have liked to be consulted before you made arrangements to invite visitors down for the weekend.'

I turned my head and upper body as far to the right as the pesky seat belt would permit. Imogen's face was pale with anger. She was driving much faster than was safe in these high-banked, twisty lanes.

I said, reasonably, 'They are not just any old visitors, dear. Fran is your daughter. John is your grandson. It must be nine, ten, months since you saw them. I thought you would be overjoyed.'

'I am. I am,' she insisted. 'It's just that you are so high-handed, mother. Does it never occur to you that I might have a life of my own? That my sole function in life is not to work seven days a week, in order to fund you and Niall on that joke of a farm you are both so keen on?'

I decided, magnanimously, to ignore her final sentence.

I said, 'And what plans have you made that are more important than seeing your only child and grandchild?'

'You wouldn't understand.'

'Too bloody right I wouldn't!' I could feel my temper rising and I tried to control it. In a quieter tone I continued, 'You may remember how a few months ago you gave me what you termed "a free hand". You should have made it clear at the time that this freedom had its limits. That it precluded me from issuing holiday invitations to our nearest and dearest. It seems to me,' I was so angry now that if she had not been driving at speed I would have slapped her, 'it seems to me that all I am really "free" to do is the cooking, cleaning, washing, ironing and general skivvying in your house. And then, if I have any time left over, then I am also "free" to feed the hens, collect the eggs, milk that crazy goat, and deal with the neighbours' ever-increasing gossip about you and Niall.'

I probably shouldn't have included that last bit, but she does provoke me. She took a bend too fast, swerved, almost landed us in the ditch, straightened up and drove on; but slowly.

I wondered which bit of my tirade had brought on such a violent reaction. I decided that in the circumstances, silence might be golden. We travelled without speaking until we reached the outskirts of Taunton. As we came into Staplegrove she said in a small voice, 'What sort of gossip about Niall and me?'

'Oh. A lot of hints and innuendo.' I could have said more, but didn't. Let her wonder!

'What hints? What innuendo? Don't be so infuriating, mother! Why must you always be so awkward?' She was looking straight ahead.

We were into the rush of early morning traffic. I smiled. The kind of triumphant grimace that she would sense even if she could not see it. I said, 'Whatever is the matter with you lately? One would think, that is, if you were not such a worthy and truthful person, that maybe you had a guilty conscience.'

Oh I know, I know. You are absolutely right.

It was nasty of me. Below the belt. Not the sort of remark a fond mother makes to her only daughter.

But, as I said, she provokes me.

'If you really want to know,' I relented, 'our neighbours are curious about Niall. There's talk of some old farmer also called Donovan, who farmed Sad Acre years ago. They also want to know how Niall managed to secure the tenancy of the house and land, when every farmer's son for miles around has been trying for years to get his hands on that ramshackle house and rickety sheds.'

Her breath exhaled in a long sigh. 'Oh,' she said, 'is that all.'

'There was also a tale that this old farmer called Donovan was a wild Irishman. I was thinking – could this possibly have been Niall's father?'

'Haven't you asked him?'

'No,' I said. 'Of course I haven't! If Niall wants to tell me, he'll do so in his own time.'

'Oh fine,' snapped my daughter. 'Lucky old Niall. All the courtesies observed in his case.' Her bitter glance swivelled sideways. 'What a pity it is that you don't mind your own damn business where I am concerned.' She ground the gears, swore and beat the steering wheel with the flat of her hand.

In a dangerously quiet voice she said, 'You had better remember in future, mother, just whose house you are living in.'

I was so astonished that for a moment or two I could only gape. I decided that she had lost her mind. That constant contact with dysfunctional women had suddenly become contagious.

I have always wanted to shout, 'Stop this car!' but the opportunity has never arisen. It usually happens in TV dramas when the heroine is about to be raped or have her throat slit. You know and she knows that the car will not stop. It isn't in the scriptwriter's plot.

But Imogen and I had no script, no plot. I was careful to shout the magic words only when we were on a clear bit of road. Imogen stopped dead, then leaned across and clicked my door open. Without exchanging another word I got out, walked stiffly away, and did not look back. As rows went it had been a brahmah. I might even have enjoyed it, if I hadn't felt so guilty.

The hairdresser scrunched up a lock of my hair between thumb and forefinger and informed me that it needed a special shampoo, a heated oil-conditioner and a radical restyling. It was my morning for being intimidated by younger women.

Shorn and conditioned, I located Debenhams, where I bought tan coloured slacks and a sweater, both of which carried the expensive label usually favoured by my daughter. At the very last moment I also chose a matching quilted jacket. I left the store all decked out in my new fine feathers, with the shabby outfit in which I had arrived pushed into a Debenhams carrier bag.

My favourite young assistant in the County Stores needed to look twice before he recognised me. Reassured and confident again I decided to forgive Imogen. It would, I thought, be a nice gesture on my part to present the olive branch in person. I would take her out to lunch. Somewhere special.

I recrossed the Tone bridge, carefully not looking at the flight of steps which led down to the café and the river bank. I walked along North Street and into Bridge Street. I decided against phoning her; if I appeared before Imogen all dressed up and tidy-looking, the chances of an immediate reconciliation would be that much stronger.

I walked slowly in the mild and quiet morning. I thought about the hard words she had said. That I had said. It had all been so unnecessary, so childish. I walked faster, anxious to sort the matter out, and then put it behind us. I had never actually visited Imogen's office. Preoccupied as I was, I took a wrong turning, missed the front entrance, and found myself entering from the rear car park. There was a strip of lawn to one side, some forsythia bushes, a bank of dusty laurels. Here it was, I thought, that Immie had acquired her summer suntan. Or so she said.

The dark green Range Rover was so well camouflaged by the laurel bushes that I almost missed it. I moved closer to its mud-spattered rear and felt a coldness ripple in the nape of my neck, an unpleasant crawling sensation.

I recalled the night when Niall had waited for Imogen's return, and all those other times when from my attic window I had seen a Range Rover and its dark-haired driver watching Sad Acre from the high ground beyond the lane.

I approached the vehicle without stealth; my shoes made no sound on the damp grass. They were standing very close together. I recognised the back view of Imogen's new scarlet woollen coat; the silver filigree combs which secured her dark hair.

Perhaps it was shock which sharpened my powers of observation, which enabled me to register so many small details in one single disbelieving stare.

He was taller than Immie by at least six inches. His bent head was thatched with thick short black curls; his ears were pointed. He wore a suit of drab-olive corduroy and a white rollneck sweater. On the hand which pressed Immie close to him, he wore a heavy diamond-studded gold ring. To me, frozen as I was in my involuntary role of Peeping Tom, the theatrical kiss seemed likely to go on indefinitely. Just when I thought they might both collapse from lack of oxygen, he raised his head, stared across my daughter's shoulder, and registered my presence.

As he looked towards me my sense of horror grew stronger. I knew the flat planes of that face, the high distinctive cheekbones, those no-colour eyes which had the glitter and coldness of chipped ice.

Reason told me that this could not be Silva Lee.

Silva was a character in an old book I was reading; a gypsy who might or might not have existed in the eighteenth century.

Any moment now this man would warn Imogen of my presence, and what could I say?

'How about a spot of lunch, dear?' hardly seemed adequate in the circumstances.

There are certain compensations that come with advancing age; an instinctive, life-preserving caution protects the elderly psyche. Severe shock tends to be assimilated gradually. The scene I had just witnessed would once have provoked in me an immediate and startled reaction. Heaven knows what I might have said and done when in my fifties!

Now I simply backed away, turned, and walked out into the street without undue haste. My heart rate had accelerated but only slightly. Don't even begin to think about what you saw, I told myself. At least, not until you have found a café, and are safely seated with an extra-strong coffee in your hand.

I came into the centre of town, and there at the entrance to Bath Place was the pretty green-and-white café which Imogen frequented. I looked in at the window and saw that every seat was taken. I found a sandwich bar in High Street, bought an egg-and-cress on brown bread, and a giant-sized takeaway coffee.

I wandered back into Bath Place, clutching my Debenhams carrier, handbag and lunch. Halfway along the narrow thoroughfare I came into a little garden from which access could be gained to the public library. Both benches were unoccupied, which was fortunate since I doubted if my trembling legs would have carried me much further.

I ate and drank, my mind still deliberately blank. But once I had tossed wrapper and plastic cup into the nearby bin I could no longer control the amazing images and thoughts which filled my head.

What exactly had I seen?

My prim, respectable, long-married daughter had been locked in a passionate clinch with a stranger. The fact that his features were as familiar to me as my own served only to compound the mystery. As for adultery, unfaithfulness, well why not? If the media was to be believed, fornication was the favourite pastime of nine-tenths of the population. When I was young it was chorus-girls and actresses, the idle rich and the aristocracy, who could be relied upon to provide the more lip-licking scandals. It was expected of them.

Nice girls were married in white in the 1940s, having 'saved' themselves for their future husbands. Those who read the racy bits in the *News of the World* on a Sunday afternoon denied ever having bought it on the following Monday.

Bath Place was thronged with strolling shoppers on that soft November day. I could hear American and Australian voices mingling with those of the local people. The little boutiques and speciality shops were very attractive. The fishmonger's window, filled with a colourful platter of exquisitely arranged seafood, looked like a still life painted by someone famous.

In other shop windows were displays of handcrafted silver jewellery, hand-painted silk scarves, pottery and watercolours. The WI shop sold fresh vegetables, homemade jams and pickles, hand-knitted soft toys. The American lady now halted by the fishmonger's window began to read aloud from her guidebook.

'Bath Place. Formerly known as Hunts Court. The dwelling place in the eighteenth century of Taunton's sedan-chair men.'

'Hey, Billie-Jo!' she called to the girl who was viewing the handcrafted silver bracelets, 'can you believe this? It says here that sedan-chair men lived in this cute little alley back in the seventeen hundreds.'

'What's a sedan chair, Mom?' The young voice was bored, indifferent.

'Why, I'm not too sure, dear. I think it was some kinda—'

They moved away and I was tempted to follow, to explain about sedans. But a sense of inertia kept me on the bench; there was surprising warmth in the November sunshine, crisp brown leaves rustled at my feet. I was aware of the bulk of Taunton's public library to my right hand. If I turned my head a fraction to the left I could see the denim-clad rears of the departing tourists.

I settled myself comfortably among my bags and parcels. In view of the shock I had experienced that morning, I was amazingly relaxed, almost apathetic. I remember thinking that I should be worried about Immie, and the scene I had witnessed behind the laurel bushes. But sitting there, in the golden light of that late autumn, a distance seemed to stretch between myself and the pressures of the world. I thought about Fran and John, and the coming weekend. I was happy. Contented.

Now, I must make it quite clear that I did not fall asleep at this point. I did not even doze. Therefore, what happened next could not possibly have been a dream. In fact, there was nothing dreamlike about the sudden disappearance of the sun behind a black cloud, or the chill which spread throughout my body. I attempted to move, my intention being to go back to the green and white café, now that the lunchtime rush was over. But my legs and feet had become ramrod stiff. My inertia deepened into stupor. I knew a moment of pure panic while I wondered if I was suffering a stroke, but since I did not know what the symptoms of stroke were, I decided not to worry about it. I closed my eyes and then opened them, but nothing could halt what happened next. The public library was beginning to fade in the sinister way that scenes grow dim in horror movies. In an effort to hold on to my own reality, I sat up straight, buttoned my new jacket, fiddled with my handbag, blew my nose on a pink tissue, touched my recently cut and coiffed hair. Within seconds the library had totally vanished. *But I was still me. Nina Franklin. Born 24 May, 1928* in the village of Ashkeepers. I was still the elderly woman who had quarrelled bitterly that morning with her only child. I was the one who had left a long grocery order at the County Stores, in preparation for her granddaughter's weekend visit. I held fast to the memory of the egg-and-cress sandwich I had just consumed, the strong hot coffee. I ran my tongue across my front teeth and discovered a bit of that same cress lodged between them. I pulled it loose and found the sight of it infinitely precious and reassuring.

The bench on which I sat remained surprisingly intact in view of the fact that all about me was dissolving and changing. The bright little shopfronts had by now been replaced by the shabby half-doors and leaded-pane windows of the cottages of the 1700s, and I realised that this was no longer Bath Place in which I sat, but Hunts Court. The smell from the open drain was overpowering. I fished in my handbag for a wad of tissues and clapped them across my mouth and nose. I thought about Henry VIII, who had carried a clove-spiked orange in similar circumstances; or was it Cardinal Wolsey?

The oaths and shouts of excited men were coming from the spot where the public library had stood. The impulse to turn my head became too strong to resist.

I looked down into a sawdust-lined hollow and saw that I was positioned directly above a pit where a cockfight was in progress. The scene churned my stomach, yet I could not turn away from it. The rowdy men were of all ages and classes. There were young boys and grandfathers; rough labourers stood shoulder to shoulder with fine gentlemen who wore silk waistcoats and cravats.

The betting was heavy. Money passed swiftly from hand to hand.

The main protagonist, star of the show, was a large black gamebird which closely resembled our own lovelorn Nero. As I watched he fought one contender after another, his unfair advantages being a pair of sharp silver spurs fastened to his heels, and a powerful beak which left his opponents featherless and bleeding, and frequently dead.

When the sport was over and the crowd dispersed, the two owners whose birds had survived the carnage remained in the pit, tenderly cradling their victorious stock and bathing the bloodied heads with a milk and water mixture.

Meanwhile, the life of Hunts Court continued; the bedraggled-looking women were quite unmoved by the horrific happenings in the cockpit and continued to gossip on doorsteps, while their underfed children played some complicated game which resembled hopscotch.

I sat for what seemed to be an age. From time to time a small child would come close to my bench, but none spoke to me or even glanced in my direction. The women were equally oblivious of my presence.

In my strange, disconnected state of mind, it was some time before I realised that although I saw and heard these people clearly, I was quite invisible to them. It was at this point that I began seriously to doubt the evidence of my senses and the balance of my mind.

I rose with difficulty, and went down into the cockpit. The men who tended their gamebirds were the same sedan-chair carriers I had seen only weeks ago beside the River Tone. I knew their names.

The fat one was called Treedy, the other was Preddy.

In addition to the trade of chairmen, I also knew them for murderers and thieves; although I could not have told you, then or now, quite how I came by such dangerous knowledge.

They were speaking in whispers. I walked across the blood-stained sawdust and stood close enough to catch the rank odour of their rarely-washed bodies. The men showed no sign of knowing I was there, but the gamecocks stared straight at me from dulled and bloodied eyes. As I came closer they trembled and shrank back into their masters' arms.

'Bide still there!' roared Preddy as he slapped a milk-soaked rag across the creature's head. The fine black bird had sustained more damage than I expected, despite the advantage of his silver spurs; he was looking at me now with what I will swear was instant recognition. The white fowl held by Treedy was equally nervous and aware of my presence.

I was visible only to the animal world, and they, thanks be to heaven, were unable to inform on me.

Treedy and Preddy continued to minister to their wounded champions. I settled myself on an adjacent stool, intrigued by the possibilities offered by invisibility. I paid little attention to their conversation until I heard the words 'Toll House', and the names of Georgie Barnacle and his wife Coralina, and that of her cousin Silva Lee. My mind ceased to wander. I no longer doubted my sanity; this was no dream-state, no hallucination.

I had known for some time that I had only to take one voluntary step in a certain direction to discover that other dimension of time that exists alongside our own. It had taken the unusual and worrying events of the day to lower my resistance and allow the door to open. If there is such an experience as precognition, then why should there not be retro-cognition?

A knowledge of the past could, in my case, be more valuable than information about the future.

I began to think about the events last year in the village of Ashkeepers. For want of a better word, there had been certain 'apparitions' in my house.

While I searched for information about my child, kidnapped half a century ago, there had been signs and pointers which I had chosen to dismiss as superstitious nonsense. There was the non-existent baby whose despairing cries had wrung my heart, and the aged, white-haired woman who appeared regularly at my bedroom window, although such a person could not possibly have stood there. All I had needed to do then was ask them what it was they had to tell me, and all the ensuing heartache and searching, the suicide of my sister-in-law Dinah, could have been avoided.

I saw now that I had been given an introduction into what could be ever deeper experiences. The relevance of the past to present-day mysteries was still unrealised by most people. This tapping into an unsuspected source of knowledge was not a unique skill.

Anyone could do it.

It needed only a certain state of mind—

I felt a hand on my shoulder. A girl's voice was asking, 'Are you feeling ill, dear? You've been sitting here for hours, and it's beginning to get dark. We saw you from the library window.'

I looked up into the concerned young face of the librarian. I said in my best old lady's style, 'Oh dearie me! I must have dozed off. How very silly of me. I was supposed to be meeting my daughter here. I must have missed her.' The lies tripped so merrily from my tongue that I was tempted to overdo the act, and have her believing that I was, in fact, completely gaga.

I stood up with as much agility as my stiff limbs would allow. 'Not to worry,' I told her, 'just point me in the direction of the taxi-rank and I'll be extravagant for once, and take a ride home.'

The taxi-rank was only yards away in Corporation Street. As luck would have it, my driver was the very one who had almost failed to find Sad Acre last winter on my first trip up there. He remembered me.

This time he knew the way.

It was unfortunate that Imogen and I should meet in the farmyard. As we walked to the front door she said, 'If you're trying to prove a point by taking a taxi – let me tell you now – you didn't have to! I would have been happy to give you a lift home.'

Imogen

I was relieved to see her.

She stepped out of the taxi in the manner of a dowager duchess, tipping the taxi driver; all sleek silver hair and wearing an outfit I might have chosen for myself.

No wonder I had failed to recognise Paul's description of her in the car park.

'Don't look around,' he had whispered, 'but we are being spied on by some elegant old dame who appears to have wandered in here by mistake.'

I had become increasingly uneasy when by six o'clock that evening she failed to come home, and Niall had heard no word from her. I was standing at the farm gate when the taxi came rattling down the lane. I opened the gate and the car door. As we stood face to face in the porch light I guessed from her stricken looks that she knew what I had never wanted her to know.

The elegant old dame had been my mother.

I had rehearsed my apology for the morning unpleasantness; I intended to take all the blame upon myself. I should never have said what I did, never have provoked her. As for dumping her in Staplegrove and leaving her to walk into town, especially at her age, that was unforgivable and I meant to say so.

She left her parcels in the hall, and made straight for the light and warmth of the kitchen. Niall was outside, in the sheds, doing something totally boring with pigs or chickens, for which I was thankful. I needed desperately to talk to her. But privately.

I made a large pot of tea, and spread butter on fingers of cinnamon toast, which is her favourite teatime snack. She drank the tea, but the toast grew cold. There was a remoteness about her which terrified me. So far she had spoken not one word, which was quite unlike her normal behaviour. When I began to apologise for the morning's trouble she stopped me with a wave of her hand and a shake of her head.

I refilled her teacup, and was shamed by the realisation of how seldom I performed the smallest service for her.

I began again.

I said, 'I should never have said those dreadful things to you. I am so, so sorry. I should not have—'

Once again she held up her hand. 'I don't want to hear this,' she said. 'It's unimportant. It doesn't matter.'

'But it does! I'm such a bitch! You have to listen to me. Help me.' I could hardly force the next words past my front teeth, but I had to tell somebody.

'There's a reason for my bad behaviour. I'm having these mood swings – I, well the truth is – I'm pregnant.'

She noticed me then; raised her head and looked straight at me.

'Don't be stupid, Imogen,' she said. 'You are almost fifty years old, your child-bearing years are far behind you.'

The words were so typically Nina, their content so exactly what I longed to hear, that I started to weep and could not stop.

She comforted me then. She said that we would forget the events of the morning, it was the menopause that caused the moodiness. She knew all about it; had led my poor father what she termed 'a dog's life' when she herself was my age.

I almost believed her.

Whatever she had seen in the car park that morning, she now forbore to mention in the face of my distress. I was more grateful to her than I had ever thought I could be. But her face was white. She was clearly exhausted and it was all my fault.

'Bed,' I said. 'You go up and I'll come and tuck you in.'

She smiled and went, and I felt my love for her, so rarely admitted, well up and threaten to bring back the tears.

I filled a hot-water bottle and made her a mug of hot chocolate. The evidence of her caring was all around me: the warm and colourful kitchen, the comfortable rooms, the stocked fridge and freezer; the notice board and its memos of all she thought we should be doing; the comfort and reassurance, so readily given when I asked for it. Except that I had asked for it so rarely, if ever, and was never grateful when it came.

When Fran and Mitch arrived on the following day, my daughter's first words to me were, 'Whatever have you done to Grandma? She looks worn out.'

The accusation was so well deserved I could not argue with her.

'I've been thoughtless,' I admitted, 'but don't worry, I'll make sure she puts her feet up from now on.'

'Gran's not a "feet-up" sort of person, but really, Mum! You and Dad should know better than to let her do so much. You do realise, don't you, that she's seventy years old?'

It was not a good beginning to a weekend visit which I would rather, in any case, have postponed. When dealing with my daughter I need time to gather my defences, decide on which attitude I shall adopt in any specific circumstance; especially the circumstance of my being pregnant. Whatever I do or say I can never expect to win Francesca's unqualified approval. In my present mood and state of health I could foresee only misunderstandings and hurt feelings. One way or another I had managed to alienate my whole family. I needed to redeem myself, to be seen as a caring, loving mother, grandmother and daughter. I made a start by doing what I should have done many months ago. I reclaimed my kitchen from Nina, put on an apron, rolled up my sleeves and began to prepare dinner.

The weekend was pleasant; the weather still mild and quiet. I insisted on doing all the cooking, Niall and Mitch took care of the washing-up, which left my mother free to be with Francesca and John while I did my penance at sink and stove.

From the kitchen window I could see them in the farmyard and the near fields. From the upstairs windows I observed them in the beech woods. I watched as my mother introduced the pigs and hens, the small black Dexter cattle, the white goat. The delight of Fran and Nina in one another's company was something I had never fully admitted. Now, I saw the way they laughed together, walked arm in arm, leaned confidentially into one another, and I could not bear it. I wanted to be a part of that charmed circle. I longed for John to run to me as he ran to Nina, shouting a greeting, holding his arms up trustingly for her embrace. Loving her. With me he was always hesitant, his smile shy, his kiss a swift touch on my cheek, before he ran away.

I loved him deeply, painfully and secretly. He had grown so much since I last saw him. I thought of all the stages of his development that I had missed. It was possible now to hold a conversation with him, but it was not to me he addressed his questions. He was already three years old and he scarcely knew me. Where had I been, what had I been doing, thinking of, in those years? He was at that chubby stage when little boys are at their most charming. His dark blue eyes were fringed by thick black lashes. His shock of fine, white-blond hair, its colour inherited from Jack, my father, always surprised and delighted me. He had Fran's looks, not mine, not Nina's. He was boisterous, noisy, had the occasional tantrum. He was also sweet-natured and endearingly polite.

It was possible that in the coming year he would have a brother or a sister. In the three mornings of their stay, Fran had made an early dash for the bathroom, and although she had not said a word, at least to me, the sounds of morning sickness are unmistakable to any mother.

Fran cornered me on the last evening of the visit. I thought she might mention her condition but instead she said abruptly, 'What's wrong with Gran?'

'Nothing,' I said. 'What should be wrong with her, apart from tiredness, which as I told you, I am sorting out.'

'Sorting out!' Her tone was scathing. 'What do you ever "sort out" for any of your family? All your time and energy is spent on total strangers. We might as well not exist for all the time you ever spend with us.'

She leaned closer. 'I think Gran should go back to Ashkeepers. All the gossip has died down now. She needs rest and quiet, and she will never get that here with you and Dad. She will be happier in her own little house, with Mitch and me living down the road, and Primrose just around the corner. She's absolutely stressed out. Surely even you have noticed?'

'No,' I snapped, 'I haven't noticed, because there is nothing to notice. She came back late from Taunton on Friday. There was no explanation of where she had been or what she had been doing. It was only then that she began to look different. What you would probably term "spaced out".'

'No I wouldn't! I never use stupid expressions like "spaced out".'

Fran's usually sweet face was creased with anger. I wanted to touch her hand but did not dare to. It's your hormones, my love, I wanted to say. Pregnancy does that to you.

'It is not possible to get pregnant while having hot flushes.'

'Fertility is almost nil after a woman's fortieth birthday.'

'A woman who has failed to conceive a second child before the age of thirty is unlikely to achieve motherhood in middle age.'

I dredged up the myths, the old wives' tales, the superstitions. I studied the books and the young women's magazines.

I was in my fiftieth year.

I was menopausal.

Not pregnant.

Signs of the menopause.

'Periods will become irregular before ceasing altogether.

Some weight gain can be expected at this time. Mood swings are frequent. Hot flushes, rashes, dryness of the skin—'

Oh yes! Oh please! I had all of that and more, didn't I?

There was nothing to worry about.

I gave up my struggle with the zip of the black office skirt, and put on a loose dress and long floaty scarf, the ends of which hung concealingly over my ever so slightly protruding stomach.

Niall

There had been too many women in his life.

He wondered why this should be, since he had never cherished any of them, had never sought them out. Yet still they continued to attach themselves to him.

There were few people whom he really cared about. John, his grandson. Francesca, his daughter. Nina, his mother-in-law.

There was also Imogen, about whom he had grown increasingly ambivalent in recent years.

For Niall it was impossible to give love where that love was not immediately reciprocated.

He found the tale of Robert Browning's long and thwarted courtship of Elizabeth Barrett difficult to believe in. Not that Niall was a man who would ever be familiar with the names of poets, or their love lives. But it had been a wet Sunday afternoon, and he had watched the TV film through an alcoholic haze. Even so, his attention had been held by the young and virile Browning, and his persistence in forcing his attentions on a sick, drug-addicted, middle-aged frump, not to mention her smelly old dog.

There had to have been a strong incentive for such a man to propose marriage to such a woman. Perhaps it had to do with the fact that young Robert was a penniless poet, while the Barretts were an influential and well-heeled family. And Elizabeth herself had a substantial private income. 'Romance of the century'? Only fools would believe that. Niall began to collect a stock of such instances which proved the cunning and deceitfulness of these allegedly devoted lovers. One and all, they were gambling men and women, willing to risk everything for a chance to hit the big-money jackpot in the lottery of marriage. Remember Edward VIII and Wallis Simpson? Whereas the young Niall Donovan, having been as handsome and virile as any poet Browning, had married Imogen Franklin for love alone.

Or so he chose to believe.

The trouble had been that Imogen Franklin, girl of his dreams, had not really loved Niall Donovan in return, and certainly not with the excitement and tenderness he had expected and needed.

Thirty years on, and all he felt now for that idealistic boy was a certain wry amusement.

Niall never remembered a day, an hour, when his own parents had been happy, smiling, in accord. His father had married his mother for her land and money.

Sad Acre Farm had been appropriately named in those days. Theirs had been not so much a marriage as a fight to the finish; which had culminated in the death of each.

Niall had believed, in his innocence, that for him it could all be different. He had studied the dark-haired, white-skinned Imogen with her smooth brow and calm gaze, and could not imagine her ever shrewish and scolding.

He had been only too right in his initial estimation of her.

Imogen was over-conscious of her own superior brand of dignity ever to lose her temper, raise her voice, throw things at him. What he had not allowed for was her lack of passion in other areas of their life together. Their lovemaking had long since been restricted to once a fortnight, and always with the light out. If he found himself from time to time in beds other than his own, who could blame him?

He suspected that the poet Browning had also wandered from home occasionally, and was it any wonder?

Now, after thirty years of marriage to a totally predictable wife, one who could be relied upon to keep the same style of dress and hairdo, to never so much as bat an eyelash at another man, to manage all practical and financial matters; something was going disastrously wrong.

It wasn't fair. There was no reason for her recent outrageous behaviour. Just as he was cleaning up his own act: off the booze, smoking less, forswearing (or almost) the pleasures of the random willing lady, there was the hitherto faithful, boring but still beautiful Imogen, shortening her skirt length, quite literally letting her hair down and, he suspected, doing those risky things he himself had done, and enjoying the experience.

It was indecent. At her age. Well into maturity and a grandmother! It could not even be put down to mid-life crisis. He himself had been through that particular minefield in his early forties; and anyway, surely that delightful aberration was allowed only to men.

More disturbing still, for reasons he could not begin to imagine, Nina had also started to act strangely.

On the day before Francesca's visit she had spent a long day in Taunton. There had also been major trouble on that day between Imogen and her mother. Neither woman had told him what it was about, but he had caught the atmosphere, sensed the tension, overheard a few of their high words. It must, he thought, have been the first outright slanging match ever to have occurred between them. In other circumstances he might have considered it a good thing. Sometimes it paid to clear the air, have a good old barney.

But all he could see was the new, made-over Imogen, who spoke these days, when she spoke at all, in a dreamy disconnected fashion, as if she no longer lived in the same world as himself and Nina.

And there was Nina herself, who throughout Fran's visit had needed to struggle for normality. He alone had not been deceived by her laughter; her attempts to behave towards Immie as if nothing had gone wrong between them.

He needed them both, wife and mother-in-law. Not as they were now, but as they had always been; Nina supportive, Imogen conservative and calm. If they were set on changing course, either or both of them, this was not a good time.

His consumption of whisky had lessened in proportion to the number of livestock which depended upon him.

It had not been an intentional cutting-down. He had hardly noticed it happening until the need to restock the Glenlivet became virtually unnecessary.

First had come the Dexters, two recently calved heifers with their unweaned calves. Their pedigree names were long and fancy, and not intended for daily usage. The mothers, so he was informed by their former owners, were regularly known as Gypsy and Ellie. Ellie was the smaller of the two. The calves had yet to be named. Niall had favoured flower names for the two little females, and Nina had agreed.

Gypsy's daughter was named Poppy.

Ellie's calf was Bluebell.

To himself and Nina the little herd was known collectively as 'The Girls'. In those first spring months they took more of his time and energy than any project he had ever undertaken. The farming skills he had learned in childhood and as a young boy came back slowly. The feisty behaviour of these rare breed cattle was not quite what he recalled of his mother's herd of lumbering South Devons.

Nina had thought, cosily, that the heifers would be company for one another; that their calves would play together. She had seen them as two single-parent families living happily ever after, but within hours of their arrival it became very clear that bovine new neighbours behave exactly like their human equivalents.

Each calf was kept close beside its mother's flank while Gypsy and Ellie, heads lowered, glared suspiciously at one another. Territories were quickly marked out. Gypsy, being older and larger, took possession of the sweetest patches of new grass, the deepest noonday shade beneath the tallest hedges. All of this she achieved with the superior air of one who knows she is the boss-cow.

Niall had also not taken into account the skittishness of healthy young females. When their time of the month came around both heifers showed a turn of speed which would have shamed greyhounds.

Gypsy, when in search of a mate, could jump a five-barred gate from a standing position.

Ellie, with a handsome bull in mind, would behave like a water buffalo, leaping brooks and ponds in her abortive search for romance.

Periodically the victims of their raging hormones, the heifers were never to find the satisfaction intended by nature.

The Artificial Insemination Centre was only twenty minutes drive away. Niall thought it the easy option, but since he could not yet afford to buy a pedigree bull, it appeared to be the next best thing.

He studied the paperwork sent to him by the AI office, selected the name of a Dexter bull from the impressive list, and on an August morning of high wind and grey skies when Gypsy was showing all the usual danger signs of thwarted passion, Niall made the phone call.

The AI man arrived at the field within half an hour. He put on a plastic apron and long plastic gloves, and with Niall holding Gypsy's leather halter to steady her head, the large syringe was applied to her rear end. It could not have been the climax she had dreamed of. But nine months hence, who cared?

Ellie, in spite of her subordinate position in the hierarchy, was the more determined of the two heifers when it came to satisfying her carnal instincts. According to her previous owner, she had found for herself a lusting bull while still well under the bovine age of consent.

This premature mating had resulted in the birth of the undersized Bluebell, who even now was only the size of a small lurcher dog. Underaged sex had also stunted Ellie's growth. The child bride needed time to recover and grow a little before being subjected again to the trauma of motherhood.

He succeeded in keeping her unsullied until mid-October, in spite of her determined attempts at fornication, and efforts to escape; by which time her repressions and frustrations were reaching danger levels. Niall doubted that her experience at the hands of the AI operator would give her any joy either, but she would at least be in calf, and settled for the next nine months.

Ellie, being small even for a Dexter, should in theory have been easy to handle. Niall had not thought it necessary to fit her with a bridle. Confident that he would be able to hold her as easily as Gypsy, he stood at her head while the AI man approached, syringe at the ready. But Ellie was not to be so easily cheated of her conjugal rights. Eyes rolling wildly, head lowered, she bucked and jumped like a Wild West steer, with Niall still clutching her neck in a desperate embrace. After several abortive lunges with his syringe the AI operator was willing to give up, until Niall remembered an old trick of his father's when dealing with a stroppy cow.

The tenderest, most vulnerable part of a cow's anatomy is her nose.

Grab her there, pinch hard, and endorphins are released into her brain which will render her sleepy and docile. Niall shouted an alert to the AI man then, taking tight hold of Ellie's head, he thrust his fingers hard up her nostrils, tweaked and twisted until he felt her slacken and lean into him.

Down at the business end of the operation the syringe found its target. The job was done, and Ellie hopefully in calf.

The weather changed suddenly in mid-November. The first frosts had the beech leaves spiralling down; smoke rose in straight plumes from the chimneys of the house. A fire was lit in the grate of the black range, and Nina began seriously to experiment with baking in the ironclad ovens. Watching her brought back to Niall memories of his mother at the same task. Temperature, he recalled, was tested by placing a sheet of greaseproofed paper on the oven shelf. If the paper turned a shade of light brown the signal was for casseroles, slow roasts and milk puddings. When the greaseproof crisped up rapidly to the colour of burnt ochre, that was the time to cook pastry and other high-temperature dishes.

There was a uniqueness about the food cooked in this

outdated fashion, something that was not to be found in the most expensive restaurant; an amazing flavour, texture. Even porridge, left to simmer gently overnight in the cooling oven, was an epicurean dish in its own right.

This would be their first full winter on Sad Acre. Remembering last January's snows he resolved that this time he would be provident, prepared. This time around there would be livestock to cater for. He began to count up the jobs to be done. The roof of the cattle shelter had still to be repaired. He would need to lay in stocks of fodder; hay and straw.

He made notes for himself and pinned them on the cork board in the kitchen. 'Enquire about hire of chain saw. (Trees to be felled in woods.) Cost out price for sale of logs per bag. Silage next year? Frost precautions. Purchase of second-hand tractor now urgent. Service the pickup. Hedging – ditching? Contract out, or have a go myself?' He would wake at two in the morning, leave the warm bed, go down to the kitchen and chalk up an addition to the list.

In between all the serious planning, the anxieties and the satisfaction he felt when a project he had doubted turned out better than he could have hoped for, he would hear his father's voice with its lilt of County Kerry, and the hoarseness caused by whisky and the smoking of Wild Woodbines. 'Pigs can see the wind, boy! Just you watch them when a westerly is blowing. They'll follow the wind with their sharp little eyes. They can see the rain coming long before it falls on us.'

According to Fintan the cow's sweet-smelling breath dated from the birth of Jesus, when the foreign cows had breathed on him to keep him warm.

Never kill a black slug, boy! 'Twill bring you the very worst of luck.

His father had a host of myths and warnings about trees and flowers.

Never burn elder. If you do, the Devil will come and live in your house.

Willow must always be chopped, not sawn.

Hawthorn is the luckiest of all woods, save for the blossom, which must never be allowed indoors.

If you pick the season's first daffodils, it must be a large bunch. If you pluck just a few, you can be sure your poultry flock will fail.

To see a single magpie is unluckiest of all!

Nina

When Fran and Mitch suggested that I hitch a ride with them back to Ashkeepers, I at first refused.

Mitch insisted it would be no trouble. He pointed out that the Toll House was just over a mile from their village of Nether Ash. We could pick up a box of groceries and be home before the fall of dark.

I hesitated for several reasons.

I was just getting the knack of managing the iron monster, which, when the wind was in the right direction and the fire drawing well, cooked the perfect roasts, the cakes and pastries one sees illustrated in glossy cookbooks.

And then there was Niall's list of urgent jobs to be done before winter set in; I felt a stab of guilt at the thought of abandoning him to Imogen's doubtful care. Every time I glanced up at the cork board the list was longer. Mine is the final generation of women to believe that their menfolk should be looked after, coddled. Just as well, I hear you mutter. It was mothers like me that turned out helpless sons who just about managed to fasten their own flies; who sat at the table and expected their meals to arrive on time, and who never ever washed up, or made a bed.

My husband Jack had grown up in such a family. Mother and grandmother, both of whom believed that a woman's place is in the kitchen, trained him in the art of helplessness when it came to domestic matters.

But I too would not have had it any other way. It gave me huge satisfaction to have him dependent on me.

Niall pointed out that the chest freezer was packed to its limits, so he would not starve. I saw for myself that but for a pre-dinner drink and a very small nightcap he was off the alcohol altogether. The longer I thought about it, the more attractive the idea of home became. I had a sense of tensions building between Imogen and Niall, and there was that preposterous attention-seeking outburst in which she declared that she was pregnant. So many problems. Not to mention the lounge-lizard type I had seen her kissing in the car park. My daughter and her husband needed time alone together.

I needed to talk to Francesca and Primrose.

And then there was Mr Barnacle, estate agent; known to his friends as Monty because of his likeness to the deceased general, but to me as George. He had been the previous owner of the Toll House. There was some mystery in his life, from which I had speedily distanced myself. I had more than sufficient troubles of my own, and anyway the man annoyed me for several reasons. But I needed urgently to see him on a matter of business, of the sort that cannot be done on the telephone but requires confrontation.

Primrose, forewarned of my return, had aired and dusted, switched on the heating and stocked the fridge. Her gardener had given my lawn its final before-winter cut, and tidied up the borders.

I stood on the flagged path and appreciated the charm of the place.

Perhaps if I had stayed put in Ashkeepers, if I had outfaced the village gossip after Dinah's suicide, and not run away to Somerset and the distraction offered by Niall and his troubles? What then? Perhaps I could have reconciled myself to living out the rest of my life in this little house?

But I had run away. For the second time in my life I had turned my back and fled. The FOR SALE sign leaned drunkenly across the picket fence. If there had been any offers, any interest shown in the property, George Barnacle had failed to tell me about it.

His behaviour regarding the Toll House had been strange from my very first contact with him. Having failed at first to admit that he was himself the owner of the property, he had then proceeded to hamper the sale to a point where I began to believe it would never be accomplished. Added to which, he had left me to dispose of the contents of a garden shed packed from floor to roof with mouldering books.

The strange thing was that the single volume I had rescued from the stacks of mildewed rubbish would change my ways of thinking and my whole life. It was bound in green leather, the lettering on its spine picked out in peeling gilt. I had glanced idly at the title and almost dropped it from surprise.

I opened the stiff and speckled cover and found I was in fact holding *The History of the Village of Ashkeepers* by one Montague George Barnacle, who had died in 1930. I began to read it on a January afternoon with snow drifting halfway up the windows, Roscoe snoring at my feet and a full wine glass of Harvey's Bristol Cream standing at my elbow.

It was written in the long-winded style of turn of the century authors, but Montague G. Barnacle had grabbed his readers' attention on the opening page. I had skimmed the first paragraph and been hooked.

'Ashkeepers – known formerly as Moors End – the custom of local inhabitants of collecting and keeping the ashes of witches burned at the stake on the village green—'

I soon realised that it was not so much a history of the village as a record of the Barnacle family, beginning with the first known bearer of that curious name, and commencing in the year 1750.

'In the following pages,' wrote Montague G., 'I shall tell the stories of those times as they were told to me when I was a young man, by my grandfather Barnacle, who was a mighty raconteur and accomplished in the expressive oral tradition of his time. I have no reason to doubt the absolute truth of these tales, and have verified many of them by diligent research of my own. Montague G. Barnacle. The Toll House. Ashkeepers. May 1928.'

The first George Barnacle was born in the Shepton Mallet House of Correction in the 1740s. He was taken from his mother when only hours old, and delivered to the poorhouse by the village parson.

The identity of his mother was never to be established beyond all doubt, and Georgie's first experience of female kindness was the mercy shown him by Pennina, the young wife of the Toll House keeper, to whom he was apprenticed at the age of six or seven.

Georgie's hard life in the Toll House, *this same house in which I now sat, warm and well fed, sherry glass in hand*, made poignant and fascinating reading.

My especial, personal interest was the high-born and beautiful Pennina who had made an unlikely marriage to the dour and elderly Toll House keeper, Ezra Lambton.

Pennina is a seldom-heard name which, according to my father, had been handed down through his family for several generations.

All my life I have been known as Nina, but my birth certificate hints at a more interesting story.

Now if you were me, and in possession of such a book, and such revelations, wouldn't that provide sufficient incentive to keep you reading to the final page?

Well, I hadn't read to the final page. The dramas of my own life had erupted last summer, and I had been forced to abandon the tale of George Barnacle, now grown to manhood, and his gypsy wife Coralina, as they stood in the Taunton Assize Court.

Once again I experienced the dispossessed feeling of a house owner who is waiting for a purchaser. The FOR SALE sign seemed to mock my intentions of working in the garden or doing any serious cleaning in the house. After all, since I intended to sell the place, as Primmie said, why bother! She had her own alternative plans for the spending of my days, which apparently involved busy mornings together, shopping and lunching in the city, and boozy afternoons in her mushroom-coloured armchairs, our heads laid on oyster-satin cushions, our feet propped on beige velvet pouffes; a tray of brandy-spiked tea or coffee and plate of chocolate biscuits within easy reach.

To be truthful, I was secretly grateful for her insistence that I was in need of a hedonistic couple of months in which to recover from the rigours of the farming way of life, and the strain of witnessing at close quarters the ups and downs of my daughter's marriage.

Under Primmie's indulgent regime I regained lost weight, my backache vanished, and my chapped hands healed. I had not realised how weary and troubled I had actually been while living on Sad Acre.

Primmie's kindness now tempted me to confidences and revelations I had sworn not to indulge in.

I quite naturally began with all the good news. I described Niall's and my reclamation of the house, the installation of the generator, the proper loo and bathroom. I explained his transformation of the scrubby woodland and rough fields into a profit-making habitation for livestock.

But Primrose, who is nobody's fool, said, 'Now tell me what really happened down there that made you appear ten years older. Not,' she hastened to add, 'that you don't look your old self now, dear. But for the first few weeks after your return – well, to be honest, you seemed as if you had been seeing ghosts. And not the friendly sort that hang out regularly in the Toll House.' She giggled. 'Even I have learned to live with the woman who looks out of your bedroom window. I give her a wave whenever I'm passing. Just as if – well you know – just as if she was a real person. I feel a bit silly sometimes. I tend to look left and right first in case anyone is watching. After all dear, she isn't really there, is she?'

I had not meant to get into a discussion of the supernatural with Primrose, who was clearly not disposed to serious study of the subject. She is my dearest and most trusted friend, and we have mutual shares in our grandson Ashley, but committed clairvoyant she is not.

On the other hand, although she has never heard the crying of the baby whose tiny ghost lives in the region of my built-in wardrobe, Primrose 'sees' repeatedly the shade of the woman I believe to be Pennina Lambton, which proves that my friend occasionally has more sensitivity than I give her credit for.

'Primmie,' I said reluctantly, hesitating even then to reveal the depth of my personal convictions, 'that woman you see – in a certain sense *she is real*. She lived in the Toll House in the seventeen fifties. She was a high-born lady who became a highway robber, and married the Toll House keeper as a cover for her crimes.'

Primmie's eyes grew wide. Her pale pink lips formed a silent Oh! She said, 'How do you know all this, Nina?'

'There's a book, a history of the village. The estate agent Barnacle left it in the garden shed. His own family, it seems, were also involved in what happened here centuries ago.'

'And this woman's name? The one who was a highway robber?'

'Pennina Lambton.'

'And your full name is Pennina Lambton Franklin.' She wagged her head of impossibly golden curls in that knowing way that makes me long to hit her. 'I wasn't prying, dear. But I happened to notice it on the form you filled in when you applied for that old persons' half-price bus pass you insist on using.'

I could almost hear the clicking of her brain cells as she put two and two together. 'She will have been an ancestor of yours – this lady? This high-born Pennina?'

I nodded.

Primrose settled herself deeper into her armchair. She said, in tones that were meant to be comforting, 'Well, never mind, dear. Even though she was criminally inclined, she was aristocracy after all.' She leaned forward anxiously. 'I take it she was truly upper-crust?'

'Oh without a doubt,' I reassured her. 'Daddy, I believe, was a baronet. Lord Lieutenant of the county and all that, don't you know! Lived in a castle, according to the Barnacle who wrote the village history.'

'There you are then! You have nothing to be ashamed of. Rather the contrary, I should think.' She grew thoughtful. 'The blue blood will, of course, have come down to Ashley through you and your family. I shall have to look into it for him. He might wish to have the family crest embossed on his notepaper.'

I stared at her, stunned into silence by her rampant snobbery. She was sitting upright in her chair. There was a gleam in her eyes that I had learned to mistrust. Primmie on a mission was virtually unstoppable. 'This Book,' she said, speaking in capital letters as if it were the Bible, 'I feel it is my duty to read it.'

My face must have revealed my misgivings for she added swiftly, 'For Ashley's sake, you understand. Not because I wish to pry into your private matters.'

Oh, but she did! She couldn't wait to begin prying. She closed her eyes and I knew she was mentally surveying my little sitting room; the bookshelves, the desktop, seeking the source of all that fascinating information.

'I've got it,' she cried triumphantly. 'It's that mouldy-smelling old book you keep on your coffee table!' She paused. 'I've often wondered about that book, Nina. You frequently seemed cast down, depressed when I caught you reading it.' She smiled the smug and irritating smile of a lottery winner who has scooped a record payout, having invested a pound in a single line. 'Your worries are over, dear. I shall share your burden. You need no longer be alone with so much precious information.' She breathed in deeply, and the double row of matched pearls rose and fell on her magnificent bosom. There were tears of pure joy in her blue eyes.

'The Lady Pennina,' she murmured, trying it for size. She picked up the portrait photograph of Ashley and held it at arm's length. 'Every inch the aristocrat. The shape of his head! That aquiline nose! I always knew he was very special!'

'Hang on,' I interrupted, 'I haven't yet worked out just how I am related to her. There is no record so far in Barnacle's book that she ever bore a child.'

'Don't be silly, Nina! One only has to look at you to see that you are her descendant. Why, the very first time I saw you I remember thinking – that is no ordinary lady. There are times of course when you look – well – less than bandbox. But that's just another sign of your good breeding. Even the poor Queen has her off days, and goes about with her head tied up in one of those frightfully common coloured headscarves.'

'Oh, thank you Primrose,' I smiled. 'Perhaps you can pass on that comment on my good breeding when you next see my daughter.'

She walked me home that evening; she made straight for my sitting room and the coffee table. I found her gazing down at the mildew stains on the old green leather binding with a look of reverence on her plump face.

'We could start tomorrow. Since you still look tired, I could read the book aloud to you. I was in amateur theatricals years ago, I can do all kinds of voices, accents.'

I nodded, too weary to argue. 'I'll come around tomorrow afternoon,' I said, 'and we'll see how it goes.'

Surprisingly, it was to go very well.

As a reader, Primrose proved to be well up to BBC Radio Four standard. She could easily have coped with *Book at Bedtime* and the *Late Night Story*. It was actually pleasurable to lie back in one of her luxurious armchairs and hear the drama spoken, while the December gales howled around the house, and the early dusk came down across Ashkeepers village.

I had read two-thirds of the book when overtaken by events which put all thoughts of Georgie Barnacle and Pennina

Lambton from my mind. I insisted that Primmie should start her reading at the point where I had stopped. If she wished to begin at the beginning, she was welcome to do so in her own time. Before she began to read I filled her in briefly regarding the events which had brought young Georgie Barnacle to his present situation. How he had been suspected by the militia of complicity in the abduction of Lord Roehampton's baby son, and the murder of the nursemaid. How Georgie's doubts about his impending marriage to the gypsy girl Coralina Lee had been resolved by his need to escape from the Toll House and from Ashkeepers. About his agony of mind when he discovered the truth about Pennina Lambton.

'She was,' I told Primrose, 'a thoroughly bad lot.'

'Oh, I don't know, dear. Back in the eighteenth century, who knows what pressures she was under? And we don't know that she was really guilty of anything, do we?' Primmie patted her curls, sipped her Lapsang Souchong and smiled. 'I am sure that when the time came for your Pennina to face her accusers, she behaved like a lady – a true blue aristocrat to the very end.' She opened the book and began to read at the page I had indicated.

'The Taunton Assizes were held in April.

'The people of the town regarded this yearly assembling of judiciary and prisons as being a rare brand of entertainment which would in the fullness of time be bound to culminate in several public hangings and, if they were lucky, that most thrilling show of all, the burning of a wicked woman at the stake. Shop fronts and signboards were repainted. Hotels and lodging houses were refurnished to house the visiting judges, counsellors and attorneys.

'George and Coralina, having bathed in the river and arrayed themselves in their new fine clothing, set out on the flint road which led down to Taunton. As they came into the town many eyes turned to gaze upon them, for they made a handsome couple. George, with his great physique and shock of red curling hair, made the perfect foil for Coralina's slender darkness. As they walked under Castle Gate and paused on Castle Green,

Coralina said, "Leave me here, George. Let me sit on the grass and wait for you. I will surely die of fright if I must go into that great house of cold stone."

' "I cannot leave you here. We must stay together. I need to show milord that I am wed and settled in my life." He took her hand and led her up the steps of the Assizes; they came into a vast press of jostling people; he could sense the tremors that ran through her body. They came into the public galleries where the crowd of spectators was already great. By the use of his shoulders and elbows George made a way for both of them towards the front, where the view of the courtroom was uninterrupted. Coralina, eyes downcast, did not dare to look about her, but George, confident of Roehampton's goodwill, gazed boldly around him, familiarising himself with the already seated judiciary and the court officials.

'Silence was called for, and the rabble in the public gallery came gradually to order. The first prisoner was brought in, a boy of fourteen years, a skinny ragged urchin who wept without cease, and was accused of stealing the Mayor's silver cup.

' "Are you guilty of this crime?" George recognised the voice of Pennina's uncle.

' "No, your honour," sobbed the youth.

' "If it please your lordship, he was found with the said cup underneath his jacket," said a turnkey.

'Roehampton passed sentence without hesitation. "Seven years transportation to the Americas. No appeal."

'The next prisoner to appear was a man of eighteen years, who stood accused of the rape of an eight-year-old girl. An account of the crime was given by the mother of the girl, and confirmed by the child. The rapist admitted to his sin, and was sentenced to be hanged; again without hope of appeal, and within the week.

'There followed in quick succession two further sentences of hanging. One for the theft of a horse, and the other for highway robbery.

'The next case to be heard was that of a young woman who, when accused of poisoning her husband, protested her innocence while tearing at her hair and clothing, and weeping loudly. The only evidence against her rested with her brother-in-law, who clearly disliked her. She was ordered to be burned at the stake, the sentence to be carried out within the month on the green of her home village.

'But in her case at least it seemed that the judiciary were prepared to show some mercy. Her plea to be allowed to appeal against sentence was granted.

'The morning's business had so far been conducted at a fast clip. Now there was a lull; a hushed excitement rippled through the spectators in the public gallery. By the remarks of those who stood nearest to him, George concluded that this last case of the day was to be one of vast importance.

'A door slammed, there was a rattling of chains; a murmur which became a roar erupted through the building as two prisoners, a man and a woman, bodies bent, hands bound, legs shackled, were brought in to stand before Sir Jeffery Roehampton.

'Pennina, her once handsome figure draped in many ragged shawls, made an especially sorry sight.

'George felt the blood drain from his head and face. Coralina moved closer to him and held on tightly to his hand. "'Tis the Lady Pennina," she whispered, "and her lover."

'"Yes," said George, "and the judge is Pennina's uncle, and no friend of hers."

'The charges against the couple were many, and announced by the clerk in ringing tones.

'"Here stand accused on this fifth day of April the Honourable Hugo Fitzgibbon, Gentleman, of Exeter in Devon, and his partner in evil, the former Lady Pennina Roehampton, known latterly as Mrs Lambton, wife of the tollkeeper Ezra Lambton of the village of Ashkeepers. The crimes of this pair are all the more reprehensible in view of their gentle birth and high position in society. The least of those crimes being robbery of stagecoach passengers travelling on the King's Highway, and of trespass and sundry other thefts and deceptions. But we are not concerned this day with minor matters." The clerk drew breath, raised his head and stared directly into the faces of the two accused.

'"Pennina Lambton – Hugo Fitzgibbon. You stand before this court to answer charges of the unlawful taking away and likely murder of a male infant, name of Neville Roehampton. The said child being torn from the arms of his nursemaid and removed from his home by Hugo Fitzgibbon, aided and abetted by Pennina Lambton. The same Hugo Fitzgibbon having also, in order to ensure her silence, wickedly stabbed to death Emily Green, the infant's nursemaid, since Fitzgibbon's face was known to her, he being a family member and frequent visitor to the castle."

'George looked down on the pale drawn faces of Pennina and Hugo. His body felt numb, as if turned to stone, but his mind raced feverishly, foreseeing the possibilities of danger to Coralina and her family should Pennina seek to save herself by implicating the Lees and Lovells in her crime. But surely she would never do that. He bent his head to Coralina's urgent whisper. "This will be a bad day for us, husband, if that woman should confess to the judge where she left the boy last autumn. Mayhap she will say that 'twas my people what took him in the first place?"

'George said, "She would not be so wicked! Whatever else she might have done, she is still a highborn lady and truthful."

'They stood together in a little wooden box which concealed their leg-fetters, but afforded a clear view of their upper bodies, hands and faces. Hugo had lost his high-and-mighty airs, his ruddy complexion. Pennina was wan and sickly looking. Both had the air of animals caught in the jaws of an iron trap; it was almost possible, George thought, to smell their fear. He remembered Pennina's former kindness to him and felt a stab of pity for her.

'The importance of the case was heightened by the blood relationship between accused and judge. There were other differences. Pennina and Hugo, unlike their needy fellow felons, were not called upon to state their own version of events, but relied upon a number of hired attorneys and counsellors to give evidence on their behalf. Protestations were made by lawyers of mistaken identity; and malice aforethought shown towards the accused by certain members of the Roehampton family. The judge grew ever more restive while listening to those long-winded statements until at last, his patience exhausted, he called a halt to the proceedings.

'"Bring Mrs Lambton to stand before me," he roared. "She shall speak for herself. As for that lampoon beside her, I have no wish to hear him."

'Pennina, escorted by a turnkey, came slowly forward towards her uncle. He spoke at first in a conversational, almost pleasant manner, leaning towards her across the bench, smiling at her.

'"You may recall madam, a certain morning last year when I came to see you at the Ashkeepers' Toll House. I warned you then about your irregular way of life, and the dangers attendant upon it. You would have done well to heed my words." He paused. "I am giving you this chance to explain your part in the crimes of which you stand accused. But I warn you now, be truthful in what you tell me, madam. If you lie I will show you no mercy."

'Pennina looked out across the packed courtroom and then upwards to the public gallery. Her gaze locked into that of Georgie Barnacle, and then took in the presence of Coralina at his side.

'She lifted her right hand and pointed. She said in loud and ringing tones, "You need look no further, my lord, for the guilty parties in this awful business. They stand together up there – the red-haired man and his gypsy trollop."

'There was a silence, and then a stamping of feet and a pandemonium of shouting. By the time order was restored in the courtroom, George and Coralina had already been hustled below and stood arraigned before the judge.

'"So," said Roehampton to Pennina, in the same pleasant tone of voice, "perhaps you will be good enough to tell us,

Mrs Lambton, just how this young man, your former servant, comes to be guilty of the crimes of which you and Fitzgibbon stand accused."

'Pennina spoke up in a sincere voice. "He was up at the castle on the night my half-brother was stolen, and so was his woman, the dancer Coralina. Between them they killed the nursemaid Emily Green and stole the child. On the following morning, George Barnacle, alarmed by the visit of the militia, confessed all to me and showed me the child hidden in my barn. At some time in the night the Lees came to the Toll House and took possession of the babe. I was alone at the time, a defenceless woman. There was nothing I could do to stop them. I asked the purpose of the abduction and was told that my father would soon be asked to pay a ransom for his son's safe return. That is the truth, my lord, although it pains me greatly to say it."

'Judge Roehampton feigned astonishment. "A truly dramatic tale, lady! But I do not understand why, since you have known all this time of your half-brother's whereabouts, you chose to keep silent on the matter?"

' "But these gypsies are dangerous people, sir! I dared not speak up lest I risk the child's safety."

'Roehampton smiled. "You have a persuasive tongue, niece. But then you always had. How thoughtful of you to continue to consider the child's safety when your own neck is so close to the noose."

'The mockery in her uncle's voice enraged Pennina. She pointed a shaking finger towards the place where George and Coralina stood. "Look at them!" she shouted. "See how the guilt is writ plain on both their faces. Ask *them* where my half-brother is, and how he fares!"

'The judge turned towards George. He asked in a level tone, "Do you have knowledge of the whereabouts of Neville Roehampton?"

'George, overawed by the grandness at close quarters of the curled wigs and the fine apparel of the court officials, and aghast at the treachery of Pennina, could not find his voice.

'It was left to Coralina to speak up. She said in her husky

tones, "The babe is safe. It is true he is with my people, in the charge of my aunt Estralita, who loves him as if he were her own. But he was never in danger from us."

'"And how came the child into your aunt's care?"

'"He was brought to us in the forest by Lady Pennina. She told us she feared for the little lordship's life, that he was in mortal danger, that there were those at the castle who would have him dead."

'"And did she say from whom the child was in this danger, and why?"

'"Why, from your own self, my lord, since the late birth of a son to your older brother meant that you yourself could not now inherit the castle should your brother die."

'"Ah!" The word was spoken on a long sigh. "So now we have it all, the whole wicked tarradiddle."

'Pennina cried out, "Do not listen to her, uncle! Can you not see? Under the modest calico and petticoats stands a loose and evil woman; you are exchanging words with a gypsy trollop. They are all a pack of mongrels known for their fluency in lying! And George Barnacle, my once faithful servant, has chosen to live with them and adopt their ways."

'"And you, dear niece, are noted for your adherence to the truth, are you? You have lied before. It is your habit to accuse others of theft and murder." Roehampton slapped the flat of his hand upon the bench-top. "Enough," he roared, "of this charade! Bring Ezra Lambton before us."

'Ezra came shuffling his way into the well of the courtroom. He looked old and broken and totally bereft, but he spoke in a strong voice and with conviction.

'He told of the ever increasing lawlessness of Pennina and her cousins. He spoke of the night of celebration at the castle, when Hugo Fitzgibbon brought an infant back to the Toll House, concealed underneath his bloodstained cape; and the disappearance of that same child in the hours that followed, and the token search of the house by the militia. He revealed how a young nursing mother and her babe had been brought to the Toll House for the express purpose of misleading the militiamen, and to provide a temporary wet nurse for the stolen infant Neville Roehampton.

'In a voice which trembled, Ezra confessed to driving a cart into the forest later on that same day; a cart on which rode Pennina his wife, with the Roehampton child and many sacks of vittels.

'He had heard his wife tell Silence Lee that the babe's life was in danger, and that she would return and reclaim him when the peril was past. Meanwhile, the Lees and Lovells should remain in the deep forest until such time as she judged it was safe for them to leave.

'The judge gazed compassionately on Ezra Lambton. He said, "So what think you now to your wife's accusation against George Barnacle? What say you man, in the matter of these crimes?"

'Ezra raised his head and spoke up, again in a strong voice. "The woman Pennina lies, your lordship. The woman has lied since that accursed day when I first met her. She is at her most dangerous when she is sweetest. As for Barnacle and his wife, they are innocent of all crimes."

'No charges were brought against Ezra Lambton. Coralina and Georgie Barnacle were likewise free to go upon their way, although all three were instructed to wait upon the judge in his private room in the rear of the Assize Court, where he would later have matters to discuss with them which would be to their advantage.

'Hugo Fitzgibbon was sentenced to be hanged by the neck until dead, for the murder of Emily Green and the theft from its parents of an infant child.

'Pennina Lambton, for her complicity in these crimes, was ordered to be burned alive, at the stake, on the green of Ashkeepers village, at a time and date to be decided by her uncle, Sir Jeffery Roehampton.'

Primrose had not faltered in her reading, but her face was pale as she closed the book and laid it on the coffee table.

I rose, picked up the tray and went out to her opulent kitchen. I rejected her assortment of exotic teabags, and put a handful of ordinary Typhoo into the teapot.

I took my time over making the tea, finding clean cups and saucers and adding a small bottle of Old Napoleon to the tray. I judged that she needed a few minutes alone in which to review her previous opinion of Pennina, yet still retain that lady as a suitable forebear for Ashley.

She accepted the mahogany-coloured tea with a grateful glance, and drained the cup. As I gave her a refill, I said, 'Not quite what you expected, was it?'

She swallowed, bravely. 'Well no, dear. I thought it would be more sort of – well you know – more like Georgette Heyer.'

Never having read a book by Georgette H., I was in no position to offer judgement.

I said, 'I imagine it's going to get worse before it gets better.'

Primmie looked anxious. 'Do you think the author described the actual execution?'

'We could always skip a few pages ahead and find out.'

'Oh no, dear! That would be most improper, not at all the done thing.'

I smiled at her range of adjustable moral values, which allowed a titled lady to conspire at child abduction and murder, and yet balked at sneaking a readers' preview of what happened a couple of centuries ago.

'You don't have to read it aloud,' I said, 'if you think it might be too upsetting.'

But she shook her head and assumed the expression of a Christian martyr. She would read every last horrifying word. For the sake of Ashley who, if I was any judge, wouldn't give a toss about his aristocratic forebears, one way or the other.

December came in cold and dry. Primrose and I shopped for Christmas presents. Resolved as I always was to post early, I bought sheets of stamps in the village post office, for cards I would forget to send until the final posting date had long passed.

I walked slowly through the village streets.

A few people nodded briefly in my direction, but none spoke. They were remembering, as I was, the notoriety I had brought upon their quiet community when I set out to discover the truth about Lucy.

Lucy. Coming back to Ashkeepers had awakened regrets I was finding it difficult to live with. There were all the things I had never done with her. Never pushed her out in the shiny blue pram. Never saw her take her first unsteady steps, heard her speak her first words.

I tried to imagine her daily walk to the village school from the cottage in the forest, where she had lived with those two thieves whom she believed to be her parents. Had Dinah walked with her through the changing seasons, or had Lucy roamed alone down those green paths? I have said it before and I will say it again. The most evil, the most deadly crimes are those committed within the family. Trust is abused, suspicions are smothered; secrets are kept and wickedness excused.

And so it must have been with Lucy.

If Jack's grandmother, his father and brothers had ever looked askance at the girl who did not physically resemble any one of them, but who was, so I have been told, my own living image, those doubts were never voiced.

And Jack and I, heartbroken, each turned inwards by our personal agony of mind, had resolved to cut all ties with Ashkeepers, and both our families.

Now, it is my bitter and frequently recurring regret that if I had come back and taken just one look at the little girl who lived in the woodland cottage, I would have known the truth. Dinah and Alan. They hadn't found her biddable, this child they had named Lucy. Beautiful but wild. Sweet-natured but strong-willed. Had they ever doubted, ever regretted their abduction of her? Probably not.

That they had loved her, been devoted to her, there can be no question. For this much I am grateful.

My wanderings had brought me to the lych gate. I passed through into the churchyard, and took the path that led down towards the Franklin family graves.

Alan had outlived Lucy by only a few months. They had been buried together. The last time I had walked here the headstone looked weathered and stained by lichen. Long before I reached it I could see how the marble now gleamed brilliantly white in the overcast morning. I came close and saw that a third name had been added below those of Lucy and Alan. Picked out in fresh gold leaf, the new inscription read simply: 'Dinah. Beloved wife and mother.' At the base of the stone was etched the final comment on their lives. 'Together in life, and in death they were not parted.'

Shock paralysed my legs and brain.

I could not move away, neither could I work out what had happened. Someone had organised the cleaning of the headstone, ordered the new inscription.

My thoughts jerked disconnectedly around my head. It had never occurred to me to wonder where Dinah had been buried. If it had ever crossed my mind I might have recalled Granny Franklin once saying that suicides were not permitted burial in consecrated ground, but were put into unmarked graves beyond the churchyard walls.

Times had obviously changed.

The voice in my ear, obsequious and loathsome as ever, was saying, 'Stonemason made a good job, don't you reckon, Nina? Your Imogen'll be pleased as punch when she sees it.'

The pain in my chest was raw and bitter, but the face I turned towards Jimmy Luxton was bland and smiling. If the sexton intended to upset me, and of course he did, then I would disappoint him. 'Yes,' I said, 'It looks very fine. As you say, my daughter will be delighted.' I took a few steps away from him and then turned back. Still smiling, I asked, 'Can you tell me where Tim Martindale is buried?'

Jimmy nodded knowingly. 'Was wondering how long it 'ud be before you twigged on to that. Funny – them two, Tim and Lucy, husband and wife, killed together in the same car crash yet buried separate from one another.'

He pointed to a small neat slab of granite only yards away. The inscription, in black lettering, said simply, 'Timothy Martindale. Beloved son of Primrose, husband of Lucy and father of Ashley.'

Primrose, whose taste in jewellery and clothes inclined towards the ornate and overstated, had in this case opted for quiet dignity. Maybe it was fanciful of me, but I felt a surge of anger that Tim, who had been Lucy's husband, had been separated from her and laid alone in this narrow grave; while Lucy who had never belonged to Alan and Dinah rested with them in eternity.

I began to walk home, but instead of arriving at my own door I found myself pressing Primmie's bell, the one which would set off the chimes of 'Una Paloma Blanca'. Unless we have an arrangement to drive early to the city, she is by habit a late riser. She opened up reluctantly, peering uneasily around a small gap, dressed in robe and slippers, her hair in a net, her eyes still puffy from sleep.

She stepped back and I entered. 'Sorry,' I said, 'I didn't mean to—'

'Don't worry,' she smiled. 'It's high time I was up, and anyway, now that you're here you can make the coffee.' She disappeared, and I made for her overheated kitchen. Surreptitiously I opened a small window and then plugged in the percolator. I selected two flowered china mugs from her vast array of expensive tableware. I found bread and slipped four slices into the toaster. I set butter and marmalade on the table, plates and cutlery. And all the time I was thinking about Tim and Lucy. Primmie must at one time have been deeply involved with Alan and Dinah Franklin, how could she not have been? Yet she never really talked about them.

She returned, still in robe and slippers but with her hair combed and her face washed. Primrose, without her make-up and jewellery, the hem of her baby-pink dressing gown resting on the tops of blue velvet slippers shaped like mice, was so much less intimidating than usual that we had scarcely sipped our coffee when I burst out, 'Why did you allow the Franklins to bury Lucy in their family plot in the churchyard and not with Tim, her husband?'

Even as I spoke I realised it was not the kind of question one expects from a friend, along with the first coffee of the day.

She set her mug down on the table and began to crumble her toast. 'Ah,' she said, 'you've seen it, then?'

My voice was louder than necessary. 'You might have warned me! It was Imogen's doing, wasn't it? Having the stone cleaned, and Dinah's name added to it.'

Primrose reached for her gold-rimmed glasses, which she only wears when viewing TV or when among old friends. The spectacles changed her. She gained time by adjusting them on her shiny nose, and with that action I saw her as an elderly woman, a little confused by the changing world, and trying not to show it. Attempting to adjust to the younger members of her family, and not always succeeding. Someone who worried secretly, while pretending to be blasé. A woman exactly like myself.

'None of my business,' I muttered. 'Your affair entirely. Sorry.'

'As a matter of fact,' she said gently. 'I've been meaning to talk to you on that very subject.' She sipped her coffee and chose her next words with obvious care.

'A bit difficult to get around to – not an easy subject to approach – you being so terribly disturbed still about Lucy – and all that; and if you don't mind me saying so, too ready to blame Imogen, who is only doing her best in a tricky situation.'

I pulled myself upright in the chair and planted my elbows on the table. 'I do mind you saying so. I mind very much.

Matters concerning Lucy and the Franklins are for me to decide. Immie had no business putting Dinah's name on that headstone. She didn't even consult me. As for that cosy little addition "Together in life, and in death they were not parted", how dared she even think about the Franklins in such cosy, clichéd terms.'

'She didn't.' Primrose still spoke gently but now there was an edge of scorn to her words. 'The cleaning of the stone, the new inscriptions, were done at my expense and at my suggestion. Imogen did the necessary paperwork. You were not consulted, partly from consideration for your feelings, but mainly because I anticipated this precise reaction from you.'

She pushed her coffee mug away. She said, 'I don't wish to lose your friendship, Nina, but certain things have to be said.' She swallowed nervously, and I began to see that this was not going to be easy for her either.

'Losing your first child in such terrible circumstances was a tragedy, and no one denies that. Discovering the truth of what really happened was in a way even more horrific, since by that time Lucy was dead. What you don't seem to realise is that you are not the only one who suffered in all this. I needed only to see you and Imogen together to know that you have never given her the caring she deserves. You were always looking back across your shoulder, yearning for your lost child, when all that time you could have had Immie's love. And there is,' said Primrose, 'there is my own situation. Have you ever spared more than a passing thought for how I feel?'

No, not really, Primmie, was the honest answer.

Primrose, her house, her clothes, her lifestyle, had always struck me as being light years away from Dinah and Alan and that house in the woods. The very notion of the three of them sitting down together and talking was ludicrous, and yet at some point that is what they must have done.

'After the accident,' she said, 'there was an inquest. Lucy had been driving. No other vehicle involved. The verdict was accidental death. The baby, Ashley, had been taken to Dinah and Alan once the hospital had confirmed that he was unhurt.

The maternal grandmother, it seems, is always deemed the closest and most important relative in these situations. But the social workers had got it all very wrong. It was Dinah Franklin who behaved so strangely. She wouldn't allow the child across her doorstep.

'"Take him to Primrose Martindale," she said, "we don't deserve to have him." And so he came, tiny and trusting and bewildered, with all his paraphernalia of pram and buggy, high chair and cot, and enough toys and gadgets to fill the whole house. Primrose looked meaningly at me. "I dealt with my grief about Tim in the only way I knew how. I had lost one child, but I had been given another. The Franklins had deliberately refused the only consolation available to them, but their loss had been my gain. In a muddled sort of way I felt grateful to them for their rejection of Ashley. When they asked if Lucy could be buried in the Franklin family plot, I could see how desperately important it was to them. You've heard the expression "crazed with grief"? Well, that is how they were. Alan made it very clear that Tim was not included in their plan, but at the time it didn't seem to matter. These were our children and they were both dead, and to be honest about it, I blamed Lucy for Tim's death. In a bitter vengeful way I felt justified in handing her body back to the Franklins for burial. It was only lately, when Ashley asked why his parents had not been interred together, that I began to have doubts about what I'd done.'

Through a haze of tears I looked at Primmie in the Mickey Mouse slippers and granny glasses, and I felt humbled and ashamed, and a lot of other emotions I was not accustomed to admitting.

'You did absolutely right,' I told her, 'and I am an arrogant bitch who should have her mouth stapled.'

'Don't be too hard on yourself, dear. Remember, I lived through those times. I dealt with the problems as they happened, while you have had it all dropped on your head several decades later.'

'Yes,' I said, 'but you stayed put. You reared Ashley and made a damned good job of it. You saw to it, when the time came, that Dinah's name was added to the Franklin headstone. You face up to life – and I don't.'

Her tone was mild but the look she gave me could have penetrated reinforced concrete.

'It's not too late, Nina. If you would only stop dwelling on the past and consider those who are living – and selling your house is no solution – where would you move to? At our age we need stability and quiet.'

I refilled the coffee mugs with a stronger brew. Stability and quiet. It sounded boring, yet I knew that she was right. I relaxed in my chair, let my shoulders slump and my head hang. But Primrose was not quite finished with me.

'There is also,' she said, 'the matter of Ashley. He was rejected as a baby by his grandmother Dinah. It seems a shame that now, having learned the truth about his mother's parentage, he is again being rejected – and this time by you. Why is that, Nina?'

I shrugged. 'Well, I may have neglected him a bit. But I don't know him, Primrose. It's not so easy to get close to an adult grandchild. He's in his twenties, for goodness' sake! I can't buy him a cuddly toy and a bar of chocolate and invite him to the pantomime at Christmas. I don't know what to do, where to begin. I thought he was going to marry Angelique. I was hoping that we could get together at the wedding. And now they're not going to get married but live together. I don't even know if I approve.'

Primrose laughed. 'Get real, Nina,' she told me. I don't know how she comes by these weird un-English expressions. I suspect she watches *Top of the Pops* and *Neighbours*. All the same, I knew exactly what she meant.

'First rule of being a successful, well-loved grandmother,' she continued. 'Mind your own damn business, and keep your mouth firmly shut. And while we're on the subject, you might do well to apply the same principle to Imogen and Niall. That marriage is far less likely to come to grief if you stay in Ashkeepers and leave them to get on with it.'

'Are you suggesting that I am an interfering mother?' I was

on my feet now and thumping the table with my clenched fist. (A silly gesture which I was to regret later on when my hand swelled.) 'You have never been more wrong in your entire life.' The injustice of her accusation and the pain in my hand brought tears to my eyes. 'If you only knew what is going on down in Taunton at this very minute, you would revise your opinion of my saintly Imogen.'

'If you mean her affair with Paul Mavsoni, I know all about that.'

'You know all about it?' I exploded. 'How dare you know things about my daughter that I don't!'

The farcical nature of that last remark made us both smile. Hesitantly it is true, but the situation was defused, which was all that mattered.

I sat down. 'I spied on them,' I said dully. 'I hadn't meant to, I just came upon them accidentally. Immie doesn't know that I know.'

'She tried to tell you, but you won't allow it, will you Nina? You're adept at changing the subject, switching a conversation when it looks like turning into a true confession.'

I was forced to look admiringly at her. 'When it comes to character assassination,' I said, 'I really have to congratulate you. You've left me without a shred of dignity – do you know that? What's more, I wouldn't have thought you had it in you. I can't remember when I was last told so many home truths in so short a time.'

'So what do you propose to do now?'

'I don't know.'

'Spend a few months in Ashkeepers,' she advised. 'Leave Immie and Niall some time alone to sort out their problems. Now that Fran is expecting her second baby she'll be glad to have you close by.'

Punch drunk from the drubbing I had already taken, the news of Fran's pregnancy, coming from Primrose, failed to rouse me to the pitch of anger I might once have reached.

I know when I am beaten.

'Right,' I said. 'You're absolutely right of course.'

She smiled. 'I'll do Christmas if you like. We could invite Ashley and Angelique, and Fran and Mitch.'

I said, 'Yes. That would be very nice,' and felt depression settle on me. I remembered last year's celebrations: the string of dancing Santas looped across the mock Tudor stucco of Primmie's front elevation, the festoons of coloured lights which were timed to flash on and off to give maximum migraine levels to people who never usually had headaches. The turkey, the flaming pudding, the brandy butter, the mince pies. Bing Crosby singing 'White Christmas' while English rain poured down the windows. Boxes of dates and Turkish delight. Crackers which held plastic whistles.

And then I remembered John, who was three years old, and whom I had hardly seen in the past year. He would adore those dancing Santas, the flashing lights. He would cheer the flaming pudding, blow the whistles.

'Yes,' I repeated, and this time with more enthusiasm. 'I'll get the drinks in. Ashley and Angelique could stay over at my house – that's if they wish to?'

'I'm sure they will wish to. But it will be up to you dear, to make the first move.'

Imogen

'Imogen,' he said, 'you sprinkled salt on this potato, didn't you?' It was not so much an enquiry as an accusation.

'Yes Paul,' I said, holding on to my temper with difficulty. '*Mea culpa.* I always rub salt into the skins of potatoes before I bake them.'

He winced, as if I had applied salt to some raw part of himself. 'You shouldn't have done that,' he said. 'You must never help someone to salt. It's a sure sign that quite soon you will be helping that person to sorrow.'

My head felt swimmy, my bra was too tight as was the waist band of my skirt, and yet I was constantly and ravenously hungry. I watched disbelievingly as he pushed the offending vegetable to the far side of his plate. I leaned across the table, speared his potato with my fork and made a production of eating it myself, salted skin and all.

'Satisfied now?' I asked him.

He nodded, not the least bit offended, and with that intent expression on his face which made me long to hit him.

Oh, I would help him to both salt and sorrow, just as soon as I was sure what ailed me!

I felt the nausea rise in the back of my throat. I should not have eaten that second baked potato. Surely this queasiness must be more than mere morning sickness?

But what was I thinking about? 'Mere' was not a word that could be used about any symptom of middle-aged pregnancy.

Procreation was for the young, and they were welcome to it. At some stage in the evolutionary process some evil chance had decreed that women should have an in-built facility for maximum suffering, which proves to me that God must be of the masculine gender. My Christmas present to myself was to be a pregnancy-testing kit which, with Christmas Eve just two days away, I would not have the courage to use.

The only good news to come my way was that Nina would be spending Christmas with Primrose Martindale. Fran, Mitch and John were to come to Sad Acre on Boxing Day. As for my own plans, I had done no shopping, made no preparations, and neither did I propose to do so.

If the preggy-test was positive I intended to tie concrete blocks to my ankles and jump in the River Tone.

What I really needed was a friend, a woman of my own age, in whom I could confide; someone who was not judgemental. But there was no one. Which was superbly ironic when you think about it, given the nature of my job.

Paul never once remarked on my mood swings and my thickening waistline, and that in itself was suspect, since most of my anger was directed his way. I watched him eat his ham and salad. I felt impelled to nag him. Surely he could sense some change in me?

I said, 'You should have eaten the baked potato. You'll be hungry long before teatime.'

He had this way just lately of not quite looking at me. His gaze would graze the side of my face and then slide down across my shoulder. He was doing it now.

'Don't worry,' he said kindly. 'There are some cream doughnuts in the fridge. I won't starve.'

We were sitting in the little office kitchen, which was as close to a domestic situation as we were likely to get. The last time I had dropped broad hints that a visit to his flat would be more private and less costly than regularly eating out, he had returned to the office on the following morning bringing a tiny microwave oven and a table-top fridge. The thought crossed my mind that it needed only a bed and a TV, and he and I could live here illegally, rent-free and, as the saying goes, 'on the job' in every sense.

Until, that is, some official turned up from head office and questioned our cosy arrangement; or Mary blew the whistle on us. As it was, a drawer which had held spare folders now contained assorted cutlery, a tin opener, a whisk and a ladle. A shelf of the stationery cupboard had been cleared in order to accommodate microwave dishes, plates and glasses, and two white candleholders complete with fancy red candles.

Red was the colour of sin.

All this madness had started with the hiring of a red dress; which thought led directly to Gloria, woman-of-the-world. Paul's recent mention of cream doughnuts was almost my undoing. My stomach churned. 'I'm going to the post office,' I lied. 'I may be some time.'

Walking briskly in the cold grey afternoon cleared my head; the nauseous sensation retreated and I was able to think. I needed to see a counsellor, but I couldn't. Forget professional confidentiality. Notes would be taken. I was still on probation in my job as head of department. There were those who would love to step into my shoes; who would love to see me demoted on the grounds of mental instability. Paul, for instance. I reminded myself daily that he was my subordinate, except that it didn't feel as though he was. Never had. I should have spoken out long ago, put him in his place, wherever that was.

I walked down the sloping path which led to Gloria's boutique. The long bow window displayed a single garment; a gold-shaded lamp cast an inviting glow which spilled out on to the pavement. I pushed open the door and stepped inside, into tropical heat and the scents of sandalwood and coffee.

Gloria appeared through a doorway, glamorous as ever. She wore a floaty thing in her favourite shades of lavender and purple. The red curls bounced merrily as she purred a greeting.

'Well, well! I've been waiting for you. It's taken a bit longer than I expected, but I knew you'd be back.'

I moved into the café area of the small shop, took off my coat and sat on an insubstantial gilt chair while Gloria manned the machine that produced the best cappuccino I had ever tasted.

Carrying two steaming cups she came to sit with me.

'Peaky,' she said, studying me above the cup's rim. 'Having husband trouble, are you?'

'No. He's behaving better than he has done for years.'

She quirked a thin black eyebrow. 'Then dare I suggest problems with a lover?'

This could not possibly be a serious question. I was not good romantic material in Gloria's critical estimation. The aura of thermal underwear and thick flannel nightgowns is hard to dispel from the memory of a woman whom I had once paid extortionately for the few inches of scarlet lace which she termed 'scanties'.

I hesitated. I could tell her nothing, or everything. She was the only person in the world whom I could trust.

The thought was so awful that I began to weep.

Gloria said nothing. She thrust a box of pink, rose-scented tissues across the table, and continued to drink her cappuccino.

'That bad, is it?' she asked when I finally achieved control. If I had sobbed and hiccoughed in the presence of any other woman I would have felt impelled to apologise and then to leave. But Gloria took hysterical customers in her stride. I remained in my chair, she continued to gaze enquiringly at me.

I said, 'It's a long story.' I heard myself making the typical opening admission of a desperate client.

From a fold of the floaty garment she produced a packet of Dunhills and a gold cigarette lighter. She lit a cigarette and pushed the packet in my direction. I pushed it back.

'Pity,' she said. 'There's nothing like a fag when you've got troubles. I've got a drop of Gilbey's if you'd sooner.'

'No,' I said, momentarily distracted by this novel approach to counselling. 'Better not. Wouldn't do to go back to my office smelling of strong drink.'

'You work in that marriage guidance place, don't you?' She drew hard on the cigarette. 'Bloody awful job that must be. Don't know how you stick it.'

I watched the blue smoke trickle slowly from her nostrils, and was reminded of Niall.

'How did you—?'

'Not much I don't know, darling! There was a paragraph in the *Gazette* when your office first opened. Photos of you and your assistant. Dishy-looking fellah. Sinister type, though quiet-spoken. He came in here once. Hired a dinner jacket. Brought it back all smeared with lipstick and face powder. Same weekend you hired that red dress, come to think about it.'

I put my hands up to my burning face.

She began to laugh and the smoke caught in her throat and almost choked her. 'So it *was* you!' she spluttered. 'I wondered at the time – you know – putting two and two together. But then I thought no, she's not the sort to kick her heels up. She'll probably have worn her thermal vest with that red frock, and anyway he's not her type.'

'Well, I didn't, and he was. And the dress was a huge success.'

'Too successful if you ask me. Blokes like him should carry a government health warning. I thought the minute I clapped eyes on him – watch yourself girl, this one is danger on two legs!' She stubbed out her cigarette in a purple ashtray and lit another.

I said, trying to regain a little dignity, 'I am his supervisor. He is a subordinate member of my team.'

She shook her head. 'Oh you poor lamb. I'll bet he never even had to ask permission. He'll have had you on the back seat of that Land Rover – and you wouldn't have been doing any supervising!'

'Range Rover,' I corrected her, and then wondered how she could have known. But before I could ask her, she had stubbed out her second cigarette and was searching her handbag for a fresh packet.

'So start at the beginning,' she said. 'I'll just light another fag and then I shall be all ears.'

I moved uneasily on the wobbly chair. I was not sure that I could trust her. She seemed already to know a worrying amount about my life. I rose and began to gather up my bag and gloves.

She said, 'I'm not a gossip. Anything you tell me will be strictly between the two of us.' I sat down again, wishing to believe her. Suddenly curious I asked, 'Why do you want to help me? You know what my job is. I might be expected to seek help from my colleagues.'

'So you might. But you can't, can you? The minute I saw you walk in here today I thought, poor cow. This woman is in deep doo-doo – big time, and not a soul in this world she can turn to, saving me, of course!'

Her sentiments were my own on seeing a troubled client, if not in those precise terms; I had seldom, no never, heard the female predicament expressed so succinctly. If I hadn't been so close to tears I would have giggled. I felt a rush of affection for her, a warmth I am sure my own clients have never felt for me. I began to talk. I told Gloria things I have never before put into words. When I reached the point in the saga which included Paul Mavsoni, her head began to nod.

'You were ripe for it, sweetie! I could tell, when I saw you trying on that red gown. If it hadn't been him, it would have been the first presentable chap who paid attention to you.'

'Oh no,' I said, 'it wasn't like that. I fell in love with him, you see. I have never felt remotely romantic about any other man. I couldn't bear him to be out of my sight. Just one look from him could turn my bones to water. When he touched me – even accidentally – I –' I paused, too embarrassed to continue.

Gloria laughed. 'Don't be shy. We both know what you wanted from him. You were lonely, bored, vulnerable. I saw how it was with you, and I pushed you into doing something about it.' She studied her lilac-painted fingernails. 'That's why I feel responsible now for what has happened. But I never dreamed that persuading you to buy a pair of red lace panties would get you into this state.' She pointed her cigarette at me as she searched for words. 'How could I have known you would be so bloody serious about it all? A bit of fun is what I thought.'

Her voice shook with impatience. 'I expected you to come back and thank me for correcting your lack of dress sense, not to accuse me of ruining your life. It was only a sexy frock for heaven's sake. I couldn't have guessed it'd end up by turning you suicidal, or that he of all people would be the cause.'

'I'm not!' I wanted to advise her that a responsible counsellor never mentions the 'S' word to a client. But Gloria obviously made up her own rules as the situation developed. 'I am *not* suicidal,' I repeated, 'and I don't believe you have ruined my life.'

'Pretty damned near it,' she said, 'I can read your body language.' She slapped her hands palms downward on the table.

'Look,' she said, 'let's stop messing about and get down to essentials. You fell in love with him, you said?'

I nodded.

Gloria shook her red curls at me. 'No. Oh dear me, no! All this "in love" crap is an illusion. Personally, I blame Mills and Boon and Barbara Cartland.' She leaned forward. 'Watch my lips, sweetie. There is *liking* and there is *lust*, and the sooner you admit that, the better you will feel. The ideal solution would be for a woman to have two husbands. One for friendship – and one for bonking.'

I stared at her, transfixed. I remembered the years of training sessions, the seminars, the text books. All my earnest attempts to analyse failed relationships, to advise on the saving of foundering marriages. Words like trust and empathy.

'I wouldn't mind betting,' she said slyly, 'that you quite like your husband really, but you fancy that gypsy-looking fellah something rotten. Am I right, or am I right?'

I would not have used those precise words but I was bound to agree that she was bang on target, and I said so.

She smiled her satisfaction. 'So,' she said. 'Now we've sorted that out, let's talk about your other problem.'

'What other problem?'

'Ah, come on now. You didn't walk down here just to tell me you are lovesick.'

I reached for her packet of Dunhills, put a cigarette in my

mouth and lit it. One inhalation later I was diving for the door which was coyly labelled 'Little Girls' Room'. The awful sounds of my dry retching filled the premises. A wad of pink tissues pressed to my face, I returned to Gloria on trembling legs, and sat.

She studied me for several moments. She said, 'So what was that all about?'

Now that the opportunity had come I found it impossible to tell her. I looked at the coffee machine, the racks of elegant evening wear, the displays of costume jewellery.

Gloria said, in sympathetic tones, 'Are you ill? Come to think about it – you look ill. You're not bulimic, are you? Or do I mean anorexic? I never really know which is which.'

'I'm pregnant,' I blurted, 'at least, I think I might be.'

Her explosion of laughter could be heard beyond the Tone bridge. 'You can't be,' she cackled, 'you're too old.'

'I'm not that ancient! Women older than I am get pregnant all the time.' At that moment I actually hoped that I was pregnant, just to prove her wrong.

'Oh, come off it! Those women are having fertility treatment. It'll have cost them several thousand pounds to conceive, when a few years earlier they could have achieved the same result for the price of a Chinese meal and a bottle of plonk.' She sighed. 'Oh what am I going to do with you? It's always the same with you serious intense types. Don't you understand? For him it's just a bit of fun. For you it's the romance of the century. It won't do, you know, sweetie.'

I said, 'Fact is – I've rather gone off him, if you know what I mean?'

'I can understand that. Nothing like thinking you've got a bun in the oven to kill passion stone dead. I noticed earlier that you were beginning to refer to him in the past tense.'

I regarded her admiringly. With training, Gloria would have made a first-rate counsellor, she never missed a single nuance. And yet, that very training might have killed her spontaneity, her uncanny intuition.

'It's not just my – my health problem,' I told her. 'He has

some rather worrying obsessions. He's superstitious to the point of being manic.' I told her about his salt phobia, the business with the magpies, and all the other rituals which governed Paul's life, and threatened to engulf mine. 'Even worse,' I said, 'he's never taken me up to his flat, even though he lives alone.'

'Perhaps he doesn't live alone. Perhaps he's got a mad wife stashed away in a locked room.' She wasn't joking now. 'For all you know he could be a drug-pusher, a fence, a murderer released early for good behaviour.'

'Don't be stupid,' I snapped back. 'Our organisation would never have employed him if he was even remotely suspect. He will have been thoroughly vetted. Anyway, I've read his CV and his character assessment from head office.'

'Head office,' she mimicked in a prissy voice. 'They'll only know what he's chosen to tell them. How thoroughly do they check up on new employees? As for CVs, they're as much use as a wad of toilet paper, less in fact! Don't you read the newspapers, watch the television?' All kinds of nutters get into your line of business lately.'

I prepared to argue with her, then I remembered the unexplained nine-year gap in Paul's employment record. Nine years was a long time. I rejected the doubts which came flocking to my mind, and Gloria, sensing that she might have pushed me further than was wise, adroitly brought me back to the subject of my interesting condition. She clapped her hands smartly together, and all her metal bangles jangled. 'Right,' she said, 'I'm going to close up early, business is slow anyway, and take you down to Boots' family planning counter. There we shall select a suitable product, which will settle once and for all if you are really up the duff or just menopausal.'

I didn't argue with her. Her presence could be quite fortuitous. If I manoeuvred her wisely, it would be Gloria who made all the embarrassing enquiries, who selected the test kit and bought it on my behalf; allowing me to hover in the background, unrecognised and never to be remembered by any member of the Boots' staff.

It didn't work out like that; these things never do, do they?

Just to be in Gloria's company is to become conspicuous by association. The leopardskin fun fur, the swathes of purple chiffon wound about her head, the high-heeled black leather boots in which she tripped along Fore Street, meant that we were noticed by every male from the ages of eight to eighty.

Inside the store she moved unerringly to the metal rack which was labelled FAMILY PLANNING. I stood a pace behind her and gazed bemusedly at the display of home pregnancy test kits.

Boots' own (blue box) was the cheapest at £8.55. First Response (red and white box) came next at £8.75. Then there was Clear Blue (blue, white and pink box), £8.95. The most expensive was Predictor (white and pink box) £11.45.

I hovered for so long that Gloria became impatient.

As if we were shopping for groceries in Tesco, she announced in bright and ringing tones, 'Oh look! Clear Blue has a free offer on it, they're giving away a flowered mug and a herbal teabag with every twin-pack test kit.'

I grabbed the blue, pink and white box, the mug and teabag, thrust them at Gloria with a twenty-pound note and hissed, 'Pay for them, will you, I'll see you outside.'

It is now Christmas Eve and the blue, pink and white box is still wrapped in tissues and hidden at the bottom of my handbag. Paul and I exchanged gifts last night while sitting in the restaurant where he had taken me on that first evening, when I had worn the red gown.

He gave me an outsize box of chocolates.

I gave him the most hideous, the most kitsch present I could find; a lucky hare's foot, silver mounted and designed so that it serves also as a key ring. He received it with a painful gratitude which shames me. It appears that it was the single magic talisman he had always wanted, but had never managed to find.

The very thought of those milk chocolates set my stomach heaving. He had not bothered to gift-wrap the box but handed it over in an outsized carrier bag, which was immediately spotted by Niall as I entered the kitchen.

'For my mother,' I told him, 'a little extra present for all her hard work throughout the summer.'

Niall said, all unsuspectingly, 'That's really nice of you Immie. Nina loves milk chocolates.'

There are times when I hate myself even more than usual.

Niall

A popular brand of milk chocolates in a beribboned box, with a sentimental cover picture which depicted two fluffy white kittens gambolling through a clump of bluebells. Niall knew that Nina hated milk chocolates. Terrys Gold in the plain dark red box was her preferred choice. Imogen, better than anybody, also knew this, and could not possibly have forgotten.

Yet she had just looked him straight in the eye and told him a blatant lie. And he, unbelievably, had gone along with it.

As he had gone along with all her aberrations in the remarkable year that was now ending. He no longer expected her behaviour to be rational. She came and went without explanation. Lacking Nina's presence on Sad Acre they were forced to acknowledge one another's existence; there was nothing and no one to cushion the shocks and sharp edges of their failed relationship, which should have been decently buried many years ago.

It seemed unjust that at a time when he had wrestled his own life into some sort of order, Imogen should have chosen to fall spectacularly to pieces.

Whatever, or whomever, had caused her disintegration it was obvious that she could no longer cope with the consequences. If it was a man, and of course it must be; Niall could not imagine any other reason for a woman to exhibit so total a collapse; then perhaps it was Niall who should be talking to her.

But what could he say?

As a skilled and habitual philanderer, he was better equipped than most men to turn informer on his own sex. But he and Imogen had never acquired the habit of exchanging confidences. Until now he had been only mildly curious as to the identity of her secret lover. It had to be someone who worked in her office; where else did she spend time? He pictured some lanky, whey-faced do-gooder, all metal-rimmed specs and damp handshake, highly trained, as Immie was, to interfere in other people's lives. Just thinking about the two of them roused a spurt of anger in him. 'Patronising bastards!' he muttered. 'What do they know about anything?' He passed a few satisfying moments imagining himself striding into one of their group counselling sessions, and informing the captive clients of exactly what was going on between their mentors.

If he really wanted to he could easily discover who the man was, but why should he bother? If Imogen's distraught and sickly looks were any measure of her state of mind, something spectacular was about to happen, or had already taken place.

He told himself he didn't give a toss, knowing in his heart that he cared far too much for comfort.

The high-backed inglenook settle was still the warmest seat in the draughty house. He built up the log fire and allowed himself a glass of Guinness and a small cigar. Damn it all, it was Christmas Eve and little cheer of any other sort was going to come his way. A recent TV film had shown the plight of a Mr Rochester, who had a mad wife locked away in his attic. Niall had experienced a rush of fellow-feeling for the man. He fantasised about incarcerating Immie in the attic bedroom in which she had taken to sleeping since Nina's departure. He could almost hear the gratifying scrunch as the key turned in the old lock, and the beat of his wife's fists on the solid panels of the door. He began to work out ways of delivering her food and escorting her to the bathroom, without risk of escape. Their neighbours were virtually unaware of her existence. If old Bob or Silas had ever glimpsed her comings and goings, they would have mistaken her for some officious pest from the Inland Revenue. Lord knows, Immie looked and acted the part of a government inspector to perfection. Or at least she had, until recent months. The executive image, so carefully cultivated, was slipping more each week. *Dishevelled* was a word that came into his mind; the other word that occurred to him was *suicidal*.

His own life had been a mess for so many years that, self-centred as he was, still he recognised the signs of despair in others. He had sat in hundreds of bars and both told and been told hundreds of sad tales of desertion, broken hearts and dreams. The solution then had been to order up another drink, and to keep on ordering until the landlord invited him to vacate the premises, or his money had run out.

But this was not some boozy no-hoper, it was Imogen whose function in life was to set the world to rights for other less fortunate people.

All his resentment towards her, his fantasising about locking her away in the attic room she had fled to, in order to escape his unlikely attentions; it all came down in the end to one single word.

Guilt. It was a pressure he had rarely felt, or admitted to feeling. But now she was on his mind at times of the day when he had formerly been tranquil, contented. Her wild eyes seemed to follow him around when he was shepherding the Dexters, checking on the breeding sows, collecting the warm eggs in the frayed wicker basket once used by his mother. He could no longer remember whose decision it had been a year ago to move on to Sad Acre. He searched for something or somebody he could blame, but always came up with the same result. The only face that fitted the frame was his own. He thought about the wasted years, their separate lives lived out beneath the same roof. The years ahead which promised a slow decline into a lonely old age.

The gusting wind rattled the loose frames of the window, and blew a flurry of raindrops against the glass.

He remembered another rain-sodden Christmas Eve in this house, the river in full spate, the lower fields under water, the rutted lanes a quagmire; and the Irish travellers' wagons caught axle-deep in mud and unable to move.

He must have been young, nine or ten years old. Considered capable anyway by his father of bringing the herd of South Devons single-handed out of the waterlogged meadows and on to the safety of higher ground. He needed only to lean his head against the settle's back and close his eyes to see again the pale and swaying rumps of the frightened cows, to feel the mud sucking at his boots, pulling him in so that he could scarcely move forward. He had just managed to drive the herd through the gateway which led into the first of the safe fields when his own situation had become perilous. He called out but knew that nobody would help him. Above the sounds of wind and rushing water he could hear his mother screaming at his father, both of them concerned only with their own hatred of each other, never giving him a thought.

He was into the bogland up to his thighs, sinking deeper every time he moved, when a voice beyond the hedge shouted, 'Bide still, boy! I got a rope here. I'll chuck one end over to thee. Tie it round your middle. Tie it tight, mind!'

It was a poor bit of rope, thin and frayed. Three times it snaked towards him, and three times he failed to catch it. Afraid to move another single millimetre he risked a swift glance upwards to where his saviour stood on a patch of stony ground. He registered a skinny youth, black tangled hair, patched clothing, strange eyes. 'This time!' the boy yelled. 'You better catch it this time, you *dinilo*!' Something about him reminded Niall of his own father. Perhaps it was a certain look, or the thick brogue of County Kerry in the speech. 'Do you want to drown then, you silly bugger? One more try now. If you miss it this time, honest to God I'll be off and leave you sinking, so I will!'

The impatience in the voice was not assumed. The wild-looking boy would do exactly what he threatened. Niall focused every nerve end, all his fading willpower, upon the rope which once again flew out towards him.

This time his frozen fingers locked on to the hempen strands; he fumbled the rope around his middle and tied as many clumsy knots as he was able. The youth, his legs spread wide, began to pull, but the weak effort caused Niall to sink even deeper. He closed his eyes, faint with terror and the loss of hope. He heard the boy shouting again, and then felt the rope grow taut around his middle. He opened his eyes to see a small grey donkey, the other end of the rope tied round its body, being backed up the slight slope of dry ground, with the boy hanging on its ears and swearing at it.

Niall came free with a great sucking sound that he would hear again in nightmares. He lay on the rough ground, shivering and mud-encrusted. He felt the rope being untied from his waist, sensed the unexpected sympathy of the youth who stood above him.

The head of matted curls was inclined towards the farm-house. 'That's a bad master you've got there, boy! The miserable old sod should be out here saving his own cows from the waters.'

'He's not my master,' Niall had gasped, 'he's my father.'

The youth became very still. He stared down into Niall's face. 'Begod,' he whispered, 'so 'tis true what they say then. You have the look of him about you. Poor little divil that you are, better I had left you to drown than to save you for him.'

Niall had said nothing to his parents about the tinker youth, the rescue, and their strange conversation. His life had been saved and he had not even said thank you! He searched among his small store of treasures, found a pearl-handled penknife and a green silken kerchief of the sort worn by the gypsy men. When the early dusk of December came down upon the wet fields he made his way out towards the huddle of vans which crowded underneath the beech trees.

They sat on upturned buckets around a fire of glowing brushwood. Niall stood absolutely still. Through the bare twigs of the blackthorn hedge he saw how the firelight leapt and fell across the green and red paintwork of the wagons, and lit the features of the long dark faces of the three women and two men. He found the scene unbearably poignant. The way in which these wild-looking people sat companionably together, laughing and smoking their little clay pipes, touched a deep need in his boy's heart. In Niall's experience of his own family, such rare moments of leisure were reserved for argument and recrimination. He had learned to fear the very proximity of his parents to one another, and could only relax when one of them was in the house and the other in field or shed.

He realised now with a sense of shock that it was actually possible for certain grown-ups to like each other.

A lurcher dog caught Niall's scent and began to growl. The older man stood up and walked towards the blackthorn.

''Tis the young 'un from the farm,' he called back across his shoulder. Turning to Niall he asked, 'What brings you to us then?'

'I was looking for your son, sir.'

'And what would the likes of you be wanting with our Padraig?' The man's voice hardened. 'And he's not *my* son.'

Niall held out the penknife and the neckerchief. 'He saved me from the flood. But for him I would have drowned. I want him to have these.' He paused. 'Tell him – tell him Niall Donovan said thank you.'

'Donovan, eh? Then you'll be Fin's boy?'

Niall nodded.

The man took the gifts. 'I'll be sure and tell Padraig what you said, and I'll see to it he gets these. He's away just now. He's off down the country. But we'll be seeing him again come Easter Sunday. Tell your father how Tip Monahan was asking after him.'

Niall lingered beside the hedge, nervous of the tinkers, yet part of him craving to be one of that tight little company around the fire, smoking a clay pipe, laughing with them.

In the morning he watched the coloured wagons wind their way towards the Blackdown Hills. Those few moments of contact with them had changed something fundamental in him. A sadness seized him as they passed from view. He knew then that this small group of wanderers must have been his father's close kin. The men might have been his uncles; the boy Padraig his cousin?

Niall wondered, with a new maturity of insight, how his father, being Irish and having once lived a free life, could bear to be constrained to live now beneath a house roof and with an English wife and son.

He had wanted to run to Fin, grab his hand and follow wherever the tinkers led. But fear of his mother, of her possessiveness, her strangeness, held him fast. It was a terror which was to govern all his subsequent dealings with women. Only with Nina had he ever felt easy; he wondered how much he succeeded in fooling her, and concluded that it didn't matter.

In all his extra-marital adventures he had always been the one to walk away. The most recent, and if he was being honest, the most stupid, had been with a forty-something housewife who regularly bought his free-range eggs from the back of the pickup.

They had gone through the usual suggestive, slightly smutty routine in which the lady customer hefts a couple of brown eggs in her hand and makes great play with the expression 'free-range'; bats her eyelashes at him and invites him in for a coffee.

Boredom had set in as early as his third session in her lilac-walled, pink-carpeted bedroom. Tangled in her purple nylon sheets it crossed his horrified mind that maybe he was getting past it. Well, the lady herself was no spring chicken. The train of thought which led from his delivery of fresh eggs to the expression 'spring chicken' appealed to his sense of the ridiculous. The silent laughter swept him upwards on a rare tide of honesty. He began to think about terrible things like ageing, and impotence, and loneliness.

For the first time in his life, Niall had experienced a debilitating feeling which he recognised as being shame.

In years to come he would believe that it had been those slippery nylon sheets which had set off something revolutionary in him. He had driven slowly back to Sad Acre, and although he had struggled to deny it, he began to see himself as pitiable, the sort of bloke who, if he wasn't careful, might end up by being labelled as a dirty old man. He parked on a windy hillside and looked down on the tidy fields of Sad Acre, the grazing Dexters, the neat sheds which housed pigs and hens. He thought he might pack in the egg-round. Or he could employ a lad from the village to do it for him. He had always refused to acknowledge that this day would have to come, and now that it had he feared it more than death itself. Or did he? He began tentatively to sort out his feelings and found that having faced up to his own inadequacies, all he felt now was a vast relief. He deliberately allowed his stomach to sag, so that a roll of spare flesh hung over the waistband of his trousers. He had been aware for a couple of years that he needed distance spectacles. An optician's appointment would be his next move; as would the pouring of his dark-brown hair tint down the bathroom sink.

He waited for Imogen to notice the altered, reconstituted Niall, but if she looked at him at all it was with the same amused contempt she had always shown him.

Nina

I called them on Christmas Eve and was informed by my daughter's bored voice, 'Sorry we are not able to take your call – blah – blah. Please speak after the tone.'

I do not talk to machines.

I made this perfectly clear to Imogen when that abominable gadget was installed. I slammed down the handset. Either they were at home and disinclined to speak; or, and this seemed more likely, they were down in Taunton, separately, and on a bender. So who was minding the livestock? Who would be getting up at first light to do the jobs that I had done?

Having tried to speak to them and failed, I should have put them from my mind and got on with enjoying my own Christmas. Except that I couldn't, and I said as much to Primrose.

She tut-tutted. 'Don't fret about it, dear. You can't be in two places at once.'

Thank you Primmie, for this week's most obvious statement.

'I hate it,' I said, 'when I phone and nobody answers.'

'They'll be sure to ring you,' she said blithely, 'first thing in the morning.'

I was not so sure.

When I telephoned Imogen a week ago she cut me short with some lame excuse about being desperately tired and needing to go straight away to bed.

What does she ever do to make her even mildly weary?

She sits for hours and hours each day. In the car. In her office. In an armchair when she deigns to spend a rare evening in her own home.

As I told her, if she is in this pathetic state of health in middle age, how will she feel when she reaches (if she ever reaches) my age?

I explained to her the plight of her generation.

No stamina. Push-button housework. A nannified existence from cradle to grave. A philosophy that says 'to want is to have'. If a 1990s' criminal so much as stubs his toe, or suffers mild depression, a battalion of social workers will rush to comfort him and give counsel. He will be persuaded that every ache and pain, all his inadequacies, are down to the fact that his parents didn't love him, or that he wasn't breast-fed.

As for the nineties woman! Oh I could hold forth for hours on that subject. And then I remember Fran and her generation, who manage their lives with more wisdom and style than their parents have ever shown.

Primrose says that I am in danger of becoming an irascible old woman. Perhaps I should take notice of what she says. Her judgement is often disturbingly acute.

On the other hand, a bit of irascibility can add a certain spice to life.

I am rattling on in this irritating way about my daughter and her husband to conceal from myself that I am paralysed with fear at the thought of meeting Ashley Martindale.

I believe this stupid behaviour is called displacement activity? Whatever it is called, it isn't working.

I slept last night in Primmie's guest room so that we might breakfast together and make an early start on preparations for Christmas lunch.

Another little scheme that isn't working.

By mid-morning I have already burned my hand while removing a tray of mince pies from the oven, and cut my finger while chopping parsley and slicing carrots.

So I shall be obliged at lunchtime to hold out to Ashley a

hand of welcome that is bandaged and plastered and smelling of antiseptic, instead of the warm pressure of grandmotherly fingers I had planned.

I have tried to fix a definitive picture of him in my mind. I go back to first impressions, formed long before I knew there was any connection between us. While waiting in his office a few years ago, to put my house on the market, I studied Ashley – up-and-coming young estate agent, seated at his desk of pale grey wood, in his blue shirt and darker blue tie. There had been a knife-edged crease in his navy-blue trousers; his shirt sleeves were rolled back a discreet few inches to reveal a gold watch on his left wrist, and fine reddish hairs glinting on his forearms. A lock of the same fiery shade of red had fallen disarmingly across his forehead. He pushed it back at intervals, and I had uncharitably suspected him of practising the gesture before his bathroom mirror.

Half-dozing in the warmth of that May afternoon I began to invent a life for him; several lives. I saw him still living at home with a devoted mother; or as having a nagging wife and four unruly children. Relenting a little, I wiped clean the image of the family man and awarded him a smart little mews cottage and a glamorous live-in partner.

I couldn't have been more wrong about him, could I? Poor fellow! Orphaned in infancy, brought up by his grandmother Primrose, he lives alone in a small flat in the city centre. There had, so Primmie said, been one or two girlfriends, but nothing serious until he met and fell in love with Angelique.

Their meeting and subsequent closeness had come about two years ago when Ashley had rescued the love of his life from a squat occupied by a weird religious cult who called themselves the Children of God. Angel had turned out to be the daughter of Lord-somebody-or-other. But as Niall had commented, she was not at all the snooty mare one might have expected her to be.

So you see, in spite of his unpromising beginnings, my handsome estate-agent grandson has created for himself a life more interesting than any I could dream up.

The lunch preparations were complete. The setting of the

table was done by Primmie, who has a most refined touch in such matters. I used Roscoe's need of a run as an excuse to escape from the overheated kitchen. I pulled on my warm boots and heavy coat, clipped my dog's lead to his collar and set off at a brisk pace for the village.

It was a cold and breezy morning; the dark grey clouds were so low they almost touched the church spire. The early churchgoers had long since departed for their own hot and steamy kitchens, where presumably they also basted turkeys and peeled brussels sprouts and carrots. I stood for a moment at the lych gate, turned away and then on impulse turned back, pushed it open and walked through.

I moved without purpose down the familiar path. I noted abstractedly the names of the long-dead carved on lichen-spattered headstones, the frost-blackened flowers in stone vases. Around a bend in the path I came suddenly upon Ashley, tall and dark-overcoated, standing beside the grave of Tim, his father. There was every reason why he should have been there, on this of all days, but the surprise I felt must have shown on my face. My legs kept moving while my mind blanked.

As I drew near he spoke. 'I never knew them,' he said defensively. 'At least, not to remember.'

'No,' I said. 'I never knew them either.'

'Sorry,' he said. 'I sort of forget your part in all that happened.' He nodded towards the grave where Lucy lay.

'She was your daughter.' He spoke as if he had only just then realised that fact. 'She was your child and she never knew *you*. I am her child and I never knew *her*.'

'Perhaps,' I said, 'the time has come for us to get to know each other?'

He gave me a long and nervous look. He said, doubtfully, 'We argued pretty heatedly, you and I, about your house sale.'

'That was to do with property. People always argue about money and property.'

'I know,' he smiled, 'I'm in the business. If I'd realised then that you were my grandmother—'

'It wouldn't have made any difference. Ask Primrose. She'll

tell you that I'm argumentative by nature. A stroppy old woman.'

'Actually,' he said, 'she speaks very fondly of you.'

'That's because she's a much nicer person than I am. You may find,' I warned him, 'on closer acquaintance, that you don't much like me after all.'

'I don't have that many relatives,' he said, 'that I can afford to be choosy.'

'Well, that's honest of you. And you're quite right. I am also a bit on the short side when it comes to kith and kin.'

He took my arm and we walked back towards the lych gate. It felt oddly comforting, that closeness. I thought about the sleepless nights in which I had rehearsed a dozen different venues and dialogues for this meeting, none of which resembled the exchange which had just taken place.

I thought about Jack who had wanted a son, and who would have loved this tall, redheaded grandson.

Happiness comes sometimes from the most unexpected sources. Ashley gave my arm a firm squeeze. In a voice that was rough with an emotion I had not expected from him, he said, 'We've got a lot of catching up to do, you and I. I want us to spend time together, get to know each other. I've just realised,' he said, 'that I have a whole new family still to meet.'

'Why yes,' I said, 'there's your Aunt Imogen and Niall her husband, and their daughter Fran and husband Mitch and little John. You met them once at a bonfire party, but at that time I didn't know – you didn't know—' My voice failed, choked by the tears lodged in my throat.

'It's all right,' said Ashley, 'and it's going to get better. Much better.' He paused. 'There are things I need to know, stuff that only you can tell me.' He sounded like a man who needed to lay to rest a whole family of ghosts. 'If it won't upset you too much, I have questions about Alan and Dinah, and your husband – Jack – my real grandfather?'

'It won't upset me,' I reassured him, and as I spoke I knew that at last this was in fact the truth.

As we approached Ashley's car I could see the pale oval of

Angelique's lovely face turn anxiously towards us. She wound down the window.

'Happy Christmas, Nina!' she cried, and I felt my heart lift. I found myself anticipating, even longing, to be back inside Primmie's house, that exaggerated version of a Santa's grotto, enjoying the sort of Christmas I had never known, even as a child.

It was not until we tuned to the television news channel on Boxing Day morning that we learned of the serious flooding in the vicinity of Sad Acre.

Fran and Mitch, who were due to drive down there that day, wisely abandoned all hope of going.

We tried at intervals to reach Imogen and Niall. In the end we left messages and greetings on the answering gadget, which even I was forced to admit sometimes had its uses.

I had packed Barnacle's book in my luggage so that Primrose and I could continue with our reading of it over the extended holiday of Christmas.

As it turned out the book was to remain in the suitcase, while present dangers took precedence over long-past dramas.

Imogen

'The worst floods for one hundred and fifty years. Low-lying farmland is especially under threat . . .'

So said our local radio station on Boxing Day morning, while also forecasting more heavy rain.

'Rubbish,' shouted Niall, 'it was much worse in nineteen sixty-three, or was it sixty-four? We were cut off for three weeks. No milk collection. We made as much butter and cheese as we were able, but gallons went to waste down the drain.'

He spoke bitterly about those days and I calculated that he would have been ten years old, maybe less. There had also been fear in his voice and I began to wonder about his childhood.

I joined him at the kitchen window from which we watched the rising waters begin to creep across his fields. He moved to the dark end of the kitchen where waterproofs hung and gumboots stood.

He said, 'You'll have to help me, Immie. I can't do this on my own. The pigs and hens are safe enough. The woodlands stand on high ground. The whole of Somerset and Devon would have to be four foot under before the floodwater reached up that far. But the Dexters and their calves will have to be brought up into the barn within the next hour.'

I said quietly, 'The floodwater frightens you, doesn't it?'

He did not answer but handed me a yellow oilskin and a pair of gumboots which belonged to my mother. I tried again to drag some response from him. I said in a deliberately provoking tone, 'You were born here, weren't you? In this place. In this very house. You are constantly dropping hints – why don't you just tell me?'

He answered in an aggrieved voice. 'How smart of you to work out that much all by yourself. I was beginning to think you would never catch on.'

I stamped my feet hard down into the boots, and pulled on the creaking oilskin. Exasperation brought me to the verge of screaming at him. I snapped shut the fasteners on the oilskin. 'Niall!' I shouted. 'Why does everything have to be a guessing game? There are times when living with you is like taking part in some lunatic TV quiz show. Quite simple, innocent, everyday matters are wrapped up in mystery; and even when you actually manage to tell me something, I'm never sure if it's the whole truth. You have never talked about your family, or where you come from.' I paused. 'There is something seriously amiss with you Niall, and I am really worried about it.'

His reaction was unexpected. His head jerked back as if I had punched him on the jaw. I had never confronted him quite so directly with his lies and subterfuges. He had a sick defeated look and I decided to capitalise on it. 'Come on now – stop ducking and diving. If you were born here and grew up here, why make such a secret of it? Why couldn't you have told me when we came to look the place over?' I paused. 'Unless of course you have a cupboard full of skeletons and would rather keep them hidden? Somebody get murdered here, is that the answer?'

He was shrugging himself into a waterproof jacket. His sudden pallor surprised me. I grabbed his arm and pulled him round so that his gaze met mine. But once again I had misjudged him. I had believed he was staggering on the ropes, almost down if not yet out. But already he was recovering his normal cool. The ghost of a grin was twisting his mouth. 'Well now! Will you just listen to yourself. For a woman who comes from a long line of witches, highway robbers and kidnappers, you're mighty free with your accusations about other people's families.'

'If you are talking about my Uncle Alan and his wife Dinah, what you say does not apply. That kidnapping was a one-off crime.'

'Agreed,' he said. 'But don't you know that it's your *mother's* kin who were the bad lot? Why, poor Nina was even named for Pennina the witch who was condemned to be burned alive on Ashkeepers Green.'

I remembered the copy of Barnacle's book lying on the bedside table in the attic room. He obviously knew more about its contents than I did. 'You've been reading my mother's book,' I accused him.

'She wouldn't mind,' he said, and I knew it was true, and the fact enraged me.

I made my tone deliberately insulting. My smile was patronising. 'But Niall, you never read anything more taxing than the horse-racing news. How ever did you cope with a grown-up book?'

He should have been withered, but he wasn't.

The grin on his face had widened, and become wolfish, triumphant. 'Oh, I managed, Imogen. I couldn't pass up a chance to check up on your aristocratic forebears, now could I? And what a revelation that was! What a family I have married into! Makes my own Irish tinker-bogman's bloodline look quite respectable.' The lure of one-upmanship was making him reckless, loosening his tongue. I registered the Irish tinker-bogman part of his admission and squirrelled it away for future use. What really alarmed me was the fact that Niall, having read the whole of Barnacle's book, now knew more than I did about the Lambert family and their history. There should be a moratorium on old sins, old crimes. I said as much to him as we walked out into the slanting rain. 'It's all a long time ago Niall. Let's forget it.'

'Oh really?' He laughed. 'But you started this, Immie. As you so rightly pointed out, I'm not your literary man. A dead-slow reader me, thick as two short planks. Believe it or not, I'm on my second read-through of old Barnacle's tale. I've just reached the bit where your ancestor Pennina is about to be hauled off to her place of execution.' He glanced sideways at me. 'Ah, you haven't read that far have you? Lots of catching up for you to do – in every department. And no. We shall not be forgetting about it, no matter how long ago it happened.'

We were moving downhill towards the brown swell of the river. There was as yet no sign of the Dexters and their calves. 'You'll be amazed,' he said, 'when you read about the tricks those eighteenth-century females played on their menfolk. Barnacle tells it all, exactly as it happened.' He grabbed my shoulder roughly, swinging me round to face him, and I almost lost my footing on the marshy ground. 'But you'd know all about that: clandestine meetings, secret lovers?'

He reached out a hand to steady me but I recovered my balance unaided, angry at the unfairness of his accusation. 'What about yourself?' I screeched. 'You could write a sex manual based solely on your own experiences.'

'Ah,' he yelled above the rush of wind and rain, 'but I've never pretended to be other than I am.'

'Oh yes you have. You forgot to tell me that your family were Irish tinkers – a bogman's bloodline, I think you called it?'

So great was our fury with one another we had by now forgotten the Dexters; the marshy ground on which we walked. With every step I was sinking deeper into mud.

'I have an Irish name,' he taunted, 'did you never wonder where that came from?'

'Not really. It's not the sort of detail that interests me. But since you've raised the subject – where did it come from?'

Once again he grabbed my shoulders and this time he shook me, although gently, and I knew a line had been crossed and I had taken that one step too far that can never be retraced.

He was not shouting at me now but speaking in a low voice, and in spite of the gale I could hear every last word.

'"It's not the sort of detail that interests me,"' he mimicked. 'You're a cold bitch, Imogen. Clever, but a cold bitch. You don't give a monkey's toss about anything or anybody. Always too absorbed in yourself and your own little world to give a second's worth of thought to the people who are nearest to you.' The taunting note was no longer in his voice. He meant every word. 'That job you rate so highly – have you never asked yourself why you chose it, why you do it? I'll tell you why! Women like you, empty vessels, obsessed by their looks, their style, their own precious image, they have no real lives of their own. They are forced to warm their hands at other people's fires. They get off on listening to other women's troubles. I'll tell you what your problem is: you live life at second hand because that's the only way you can cope. Those women who come to your office, they probably think you are some sort of guru, the wise woman who can put their lives to rights. And you love it, don't you? Except that lately something peculiar has happened to you. You appear to be falling apart, and I'm wondering why. One thing I'm sure of. If you've got yourself into a mess you'll have no one to turn to. You've never bothered much with Fran, and even your mother has gone back to Ashkeepers to escape your bad temper. And you have no friends.'

He paused. 'Have you ever realised that? You have no friends.'

Even as I struggled to deny it I knew that what he said was true. The only other people in my life apart from family were Gloria and Paul Mavsoni, neither of whom could remotely be considered in terms of friendship.

Tangles of wet hair stuck to my face. I was cold to the bone and there was a deep ache spreading through the pit of my stomach. I looked at Niall's unforgiving face and began to perceive, if only dimly, what it was that I had done; that I was still doing. But before I could speak a plaintive bellow came from a blackthorn thicket and the two Dexter heifers and their calves came slowly into view.

Even I could see that the cattle were distressed. Niall had warned me about the heifers, which had never been trained to the halter and were therefore difficult to lead and unused to being driven. Their relief at our arrival was quite touching. They followed us out of the lower fields like trained dogs, with only minutes to spare. The flood barriers were proving inadequate against the volume of water, the river banks were breached in several places, and cows, I learned, in spite of their large heads, have very tiny brains. Niall assured me that left to themselves the little herd would have stayed close to the false haven of the blackthorn thicket until swept away and drowned by the rising flood.

We trudged back to the barn in silence. Once inside, Niall laid down fresh straw bedding and filled the hay racks. He gave each beast a handful of cattle-nuts, rather as a mother might reward a child for good behaviour. In no time at all the Dexters were munching contentedly, their thick black coats were drying and the exhausted calves slept.

I sat on a straw bale and caught my breath. I was seriously out of condition, unlike Niall who was fitter than I had ever known him.

He said, 'You okay?'

'I will be in a minute.'

'You look very pale.'

'I'm not used to herding cattle in a tempest.'

'Thanks for helping.'

'It was nothing. They came home like tame poodles.'

'They don't usually. When the vet comes out here I have to chase them round the field for ages. I'll need to train them to the halter if I want to show them. You helped to save their lives, especially the calves.' I sensed his embarrassment at the admission. He gestured towards the Dexters' short legs. 'Another twenty minutes and they would all have been goners.' He was suddenly talking to me in the matey way he spoke to Nina. When he discussed the cattle his eyes shone, his tone was all enthusiasm. He was Niall – yet he was not Niall. Not as I had known him. Against my will I found myself warming to this lean, weather-beaten version of the man who was, after all that had happened, still my husband.

'I did nothing,' I told him. 'You would have managed very well without me.'

'No,' he said, 'I might not have gone down into those fields at all on my own. You must have noticed that I almost left those poor beasts to perish anyway.'

'Well no,' I said. 'I trusted you to know what you were doing.'

He covered his face with his hands, and since he was not given to making dramatic gestures I felt alarmed. 'What is it, Niall?' I asked him.

The words came in a great rush. 'I was just a kid. The flood came up suddenly in the lower fields, and my mother sent me down to the river meadows to bring in her herd of South Devons. I had just got them through a gateway on to dry ground when I lost my footing and slipped into a patch of bogland. I was in up to my waist and sinking. There was no point in shouting for help. I had left my mother and father quarrelling here in the barn. It was the kind of bitter row that would drag on for hours. I had seen it all before.'

'So what saved you?'

'A gypsy and his donkey.'

He paused and I could see how hard he found it to continue.

He said, 'I'd heard stories about people getting sucked down into the marshes. I tried to keep very still but even so, in no time at all I was in up to my armpits. I began to imagine the mud filling up my mouth, then my eyes and ears. I tell you, Immie, I nearly died of terror. Years later, even in summer sunshine, I find it hard to walk down there, to pass that spot.' His mouth twisted at the recollection. 'There was a band of tinkers camped up in the top lane. They had a youth along with them, odd-looking cove; he spoke County Kerry Irish, like my own father. He threw me a rope and tied the other end around his donkey's neck. I shot out of that bog like a cork from a bottle, but the fear stayed with me.'

'I can see how it would. So what did your parents say when you told them?'

'I didn't. I drove the herd home and into the shed. By that time the fight had moved into the kitchen. I knew better than to approach either of them. There was always a risk that I might intercept a blow that was not intended for me.'

'You mean they actually struck one another?'

'Struck, kicked, bit, scratched, tore each other's hair out.'

'They must have hated one another, I mean *really hated*.'

'Yes,' he said slowly, 'but if my mother had been acquiescent, allowed him to hit her without ever retaliating – then I could at least have felt sorry for her, tried to protect her. But when it came to ill-temper she was Fin's equal. She pushed him down the back stairs on one occasion; he was drunk and his arm broke in the fall, but she still kicked him as he lay moaning on the floor. She was a frail-looking woman and she must have known he would retaliate as soon as he was able, but he never once broke her spirit.'

'Did they – were they ever violent towards you?'

'No,' he said, 'but I was careful not to give them cause, and anyway, there was always too much going on between the two of them. As long as I did my chores about the place, they hardly registered my existence.'

'But it sounds as if you admired your mother?'

He smiled meaningly. 'Well, she didn't need your sort of marriage guidance, did she? Or a battered wives' refuge. She settled her own scores in her own way. Fin suffered for years from severe stomach upsets. I don't know whether she meant to poison him or just make him suffer. He died believing that he had stomach ulcers. But there were plants growing in my mother's herb-patch that would have killed an ox.'

'What about the neighbours?'

'Oh, there was talk! This farm is isolated, but people notice things like black eyes and split lips. But times were different then. Folk tended to mind their own business. The sort of visitors we had in those days were hardly likely to interfere. Except for the village parson. I believe it was he who insisted in the end that I be sent away to school in Taunton.'

I sat very still, not wishing to distract him. Tears scalded my eyes. I thought about the small boy sucked down by the marshland with a gypsy and his donkey coming to the rescue. I began to trace an uncertain link between the terrified child and the man Niall had grown into. I glanced up and found that he was looking anxiously in my direction.

He said, 'You're not well, are you?'

'I'm all right. Just cold and wet.'

'I should not have forced you to cross those rough fields. You've looked sick for weeks. You may be coming down with flu or something.' As he spoke he was moving towards the barn door. 'I think we have some tinned soup in the cupboard. I'll heat it for you, while you have a hot bath and get into some dry clothing.'

It was his kindness that disarmed me. As the barn door shut behind him I held my face in my hands and howled. I stood up and the pain in my stomach grew stronger and spread around into my back.

It was not flu or something I was coming down with. I believed I was about to suffer a miscarriage.

Nina

Niall phoned on Boxing Day.

He apologised for not replying to the messages we left on his answering gadget. The floods, he said, had not reached the house or the higher fields, but it had been touch and go there for a few hours. The Dexters were safe, also the hens and pigs. He enquired about our Christmas, and said how disappointing it had been not to see little John and give him his presents. He rambled on in this uncharacteristic way and I could hear the prevarication in his voice. I waited to hear the real reason for his call; when he continued to chatter, I broke in, 'Is Imogen handy? I'd like a word with her, if I may.'

'She's not well at the moment. As a matter of fact, she is sleeping.'

'What is it? Flu or this nasty virus that's going the rounds?'

He sounded embarrassed. 'I think it must be women's trouble. She didn't really say.'

'Oh come on, Niall,' I said, 'be a bit more explicit.'

'She helped me bring the Dexters in from the floodland, and then she sort of collapsed with stomach cramps.'

I said swiftly, 'I'll be with you tomorrow.'

'But it's Christmas. The National Coaches won't be running.'

'Yes they will, Niall.' I let a small silence grow between us. 'You do want me to come, don't you?'

'God – yes! I don't know which way to turn here. With

226

Immie sick and these damned floods – and oh, everything is in such a mess.'

I had never known carefree Niall to be in a state of such desperation.

'Are the roads to Sad Acre passable?'

'Yes,' he said, 'quite clear now. Ring me when you get into Taunton. I'll drive down to collect you.'

'No,' I said firmly, 'there's bound to be a taxi waiting on the rank in Corporation Street, or in the bus station.'

I made a phone call to reserve my seat and Roscoe's and repacked my suitcase.

Primrose expressed deep disappointment at my sudden departure, but understood my reasons. 'At least leave me the book for company,' she begged. 'I had just reached that exciting bit where Pennina is about to be burned at the stake on Ashkeepers Green.'

'Well I'm sorry,' I said, not really meaning it. I was slightly miffed at her ghoulish anticipation of the unpleasant end of my namesake-relative. 'But I still have a lot of long winter nights to get through on Sad Acre Farm, and I shall need some diverting reading.'

'How long do you plan to stay there?'

'As long as I'm needed.'

The light was already fading when I arrived in Taunton. A lone taxi stood in a corner of the bus station, its driver delighted to find a fare which would keep him absent from his home for a few more hours.

'Bloody Christmas,' he muttered, as we drove across the Tone bridge. 'Goes on for far too long these days, if you asks me.'

I agreed with him with such fervour that he became quite chatty. He slowed as we crossed the bridge, so that I might appreciate the height and the muddied state of the waters.

'Mind you,' he said, 'that river used to flood real bad in the olden days, specially in North Town.'

'North Town?' I asked. 'Which area would that be?'

He began to speak with the dedicated passion of a local historian. 'Why, back in the seventeen hundreds the floods stretched from French Weir Lane up to North Town Bridge. It was a damp and dirty place; had a bad reputation, full of stagnant ponds and seething ditches. A relative of mine was said to have been landlord of the Black Horse Inn, which in those days stood close to the Turnpike Gate House, so you can imagine the rough sort of customers who favoured that pub! Highway robbers, I shouldn't wonder, and all kinds of riff-raff!'

I leaned so far forward in my seat that my chin almost rested on his shoulder. 'This Turnpike Gate House?' I asked him. 'Would that have been a toll house?'

'Of course,' he said, surprised that I should have needed to ask.

I said, 'It wouldn't – you don't know – if it's still standing – that toll house?'

'Shouldn't think so! Mind you, there's a few old buildings still in place around that spot. I took a fare along there only last week. She was looking for some office that has to do with marriage guidance.' He almost spat from sheer disgust. 'Load of old cod's if you ask me. Me and my old woman – we settle things between us. Don't need no outside interference.'

I said, without thinking, 'My daughter works there.'

'Oops!' he muttered, 'sorry an' all that!'

'Not at all. I quite agree with you. Load of old cod's.'

'You visiting these parts?' He glanced back at me through the driving mirror.

'My daughter and son-in-law. He farms in a small way.'

He said, almost shyly, 'You interested in old Taunton then?'

'I'm very interested.'

He settled more comfortably in his seat and cut his speed. 'Not many women want to talk about the olden days. My missus 'ud sooner watch *Coronation Street* on the box than talk about French Weir or Bath Place. You got some special connection p'raps?'

'You could call it that. I've a strong suspicion that an ancestor of mine was sentenced at the Taunton Assizes to be hanged for the crimes of kidnap and murder, sometime in the late seventeen fifties.'

'Cor,' he said. 'Well, bugger me! Some folks is real lucky in their dead relations.'

I smiled. 'That's a matter of opinion,' I told him. 'I don't think my daughter will be so charmed to learn about her violent ancestors.'

'She'll be the marriage-mender?'

'Yes,' I sighed, 'that's her. In a nutshell.'

It was fully dark when we turned into the farmyard. I paid him and tipped him more than I'd intended.

'If you'll give me your card,' I said, 'I'd like to talk to you again. About Taunton in the old days and the hanging and burning of witches.'

Niall was waiting for me in the front porch. He picked up my suitcase and moved with it towards the stairs. Roscoe trotted happily to his basket by the fire as if we had never been away.

'Leave the luggage,' I told Niall. 'I want to talk to you before I see Immie.'

He followed Roscoe and me into the kitchen. The big black kettle was singing on the trivet, the teapot warming on the range-top. The dim light shed by the single oil lamp mercifully blurred the room's state of muddle. Niall made the tea and placed the pot and two clean mugs before me on the table; he shook an empty biscuit tin and apologised, then seated himself in the carver chair close to the fire.

'Milk?' I asked.

'Sorry,' he said, 'we don't seem to have any.'

'A farm without milk,' I said, 'is like a pub with no beer.'

For the first time I could remember we were awkward with each other. He smiled uncertainly. We drank the scalding black tea. He did not look at me. Finally he said, 'I don't know what to say to you, Nina. You really shouldn't be here. To drag you back at Christmas too. Immie was furious when I told her you were coming.'

'You didn't drag me back, I volunteered. And Imogen is my daughter after all. I wasn't doing anything important up in Ashkeepers. Just sitting around with Primrose, eating and drinking too much and feeling morbid.'

'Well I'm grateful,' he said. 'I just wanted you to know that.'

'What's going on here, Niall?'

We continued to sip our black and bitter tea and attempted to out-stare each other.

'I don't know,' he said at last. 'I was hoping you could tell me. You've seen how she's been in the past year.'

I said, 'She doesn't talk to me, never has done.'

'I've tried,' he said, 'I've really tried. I did a lot of thinking before we moved down here. I wanted it to be a fresh start.'

'I know,' I said, 'and I admired you for that. I also wanted it to work out, for both of you. What neither of us allowed for was Imogen's feelings. We've always taken her for granted. Assumed that she would always be there, reliable and unchanging. Ask yourself, Niall – why should she? Why the hell should she?'

He said, 'She's having an affair.'

'I know.'

His eyebrows shot up into the middle of his forehead.

I said, 'I saw them. Together. Kissing. They didn't see me.'

I rose and began to walk towards the door. 'I'll just go and say hello.' I looked meaningly at the sink crammed to overflowing with dirty dishes. 'And then you and I will roll our sleeves up.'

The door of the master bedroom stood halfway open. I walked in as quietly as the uneven floorboards would allow. Imogen was sleeping, her long dark hair spread out across the yellow pillowcase, her ringless fingers clutching at the edge of the duvet. Her normally pale skin had whitened to a shocking pallor, and I remembered Niall's words, 'Women's trouble. She sort of collapsed with stomach cramps . . .' I also recalled my own words. 'She doesn't talk to me. Never has done.'

Not true, Nina! Not true!

Immie *had* talked to me, quite recently. Or at least she had tried to.

'I'm pregnant,' she had said.

And what had I replied? I eased myself carefully down into the tapestry armchair which stood close to the bed. She had been begging for my help, looking for some understanding of what she was going through. Recalling her distraught appearance, her strange behaviour, I knew now that her need for a sympathetic ear must have been acute.

And what had I done?

I had turned my back, refused to listen, deliberately mis-understood her. I had said, in effect, if not in words, your problem. Not mine.

She stirred, and as she turned to face me her eyes flicked open and a frown line drew her brows together. I reached out to touch her hand but she withdrew it before I could make contact.

'Go away,' she said. 'Leaving is the only thing you're good at, Mother.'

She closed her eyes and turned her head into the pillow, and I rose from the chair and left her, as she had requested.

Niall had washed a mound of dishes, cutlery and saucepans, and made a token attempt at tidying the kitchen. I found him pouring hot water on to chocolate powder. Two filled hot water bottles lay on the table beside a plate which held doorstep-sized cheese and ham sandwiches. As usual, it had taken only a small shove from me in the right direction to get him moving. Muzzy with tiredness, I wondered irritably why Imogen had never learned the knack. Then I remembered the way just a moment ago, she had closed her eyes in order to block out my face. Perhaps she was right after all; perhaps I should not have come here? But it was too late now to go back to my old bad habits of non-involvement. I had knowledge which could not be denied, and which would not let me rest. Up in the attic bedroom I noted vaguely the signs of recent occupation. The wrinkled bedsheets, a pair of Immie's black tights thrown across a chair, the scent of her perfume on the pillows. The cold was intense up here. I put on thick pyjamas and a heavy woollen robe, and propped up in bed, a hot bottle at my feet, the other on my knees, I ate the sandwiches and drank the hot chocolate, although I would have sworn ten minutes ago that I was not hungry. I was touched by Niall's unexpected thoughtfulness. I tried to imagine the three of us together, behaving like normal people, relaxed and at peace in this ancient pink-washed house. I curled down beneath the quilt and felt the warmth spread through my body. In my mind I roved down the back stairs, up the front stairs, through the low-ceilinged rooms which Niall and I had won back from mouse-droppings and dust to simple charm.

Imogen should have been a part of it; of the reclamation of the thistle-ridden fields, mismanaged woodlands, and tumbledown shed. Of the whole farm; the whole delight that was Sad Acre. But she had, I reminded myself, deliberately excluded herself from the life we lived here. The house was no more than a roof she returned to each evening; the fields and the cattle a pretty view from her window. 'Feel free,' she had told me; and I obeyed her to the letter. And now, months later, here we were, faced with the reckoning. Question was – which one of us three would be willing and able to pick up the bill?

There was a secret life still going on in this house that was not of our time or experience. There were certain haunted rooms, certain cold treads on the staircase, the heart-stopping sensation when turning a corner in the long passageway which connected kitchen and scullery with what Niall always referred to as 'the good rooms'. There was the rocking chair which Niall had been only to happy to banish to the attic; a chair which towards evening would start gently to rock, although no human sat on it.

Imogen

I suppose I had known all the time that I wasn't really pregnant.

And yet I might have been. It was not impossible. It had happened to other forty-something-nearly-fifty women. There were all these mature mothers who appeared with their bundles of joy on breakfast television and told the world how late motherhood had changed and enriched their lives. The partners of these ladies, on the rare occasions when they put in an appearance, had a careworn, shell-shocked look about them, as if pushing a pram when on the brink of drawing one's retirement pension was not altogether to be recommended.

I wondered what Niall would have thought about it Or, come to that, Paul?

The question now was purely academic. Since there was not, and never had been, a baby, the question of paternity did not arise. There would be no need for a cot, a pram, a high chair. No collection of tiny white baby garments. No nursery.

When the stomach cramps began I knew that all I had suffered in recent weeks was what text books describe as 'a menopausal interruption in the normal female cycle'. I had not allowed myself to think further than the pregnancy testing kit, which still lay intact in the bottom of my handbag.

Only now can I see how the phantom baby gave purpose to my life. While remaining ambivalent about the whole thing, in the part of the mind which operates at such times on autopilot

I had visualised a second daughter. A sweet amenable child who would love only me. So great had been my gift for self-delusion that I'd imagined myself into morning sickness and weight gain. I was even crazy enough to attempt to confide in my mother, who had turned out to be shamingly right, as she so often was. Now that the fantasy was over and I could no longer blame pregnancy for my aches and pains and mood swings, now that I was free, I began to realise just how weak and miserable I really felt.

When I collapsed dramatically on the day of the flood, Niall had carried me up the front stairs to what was snobbishly known, thanks to Nina, as the master bedroom. Thinking about it now, this action of his was surprising since he never, if he could avoid it, used that staircase. So once again we are sharing a bed, a room, and nothing has been said about my recent occupation of the attic.

My mother, with heavy-handed tactfulness, returned without comment the tights and dressing gown and other oddments of mine which she had found in what was now her undisputed top-floor territory.

So all is as it was. Normality has been resumed.

Or has it?

The days which follow Christmas are always anti-climactic. Except that in our case, Niall and I had sidestepped all the celebrations this year. I kept to my bed for a full week. Niall lit a fire in the bedroom fireplace, and Nina came to sit beside it on those cold grey afternoons of late December. We exchanged the odd word, but mostly I feigned sleep while she read Barnacle's book.

We had nothing of importance to say to one another, she and I.

When Niall came to bed I feigned sleep again, lying at the far edge of the mattress, fearing I would scream if he so much as touched me.

I think he must have sensed the way I felt, for he behaved as if I were not there, as if I were invisible.

Between the two of them, my silent mother and my switched-off husband, I began to doubt my own existence.

Christmas is a dangerous time for families. Any family.

Expectations are never quite fulfilled. Old hurts tend to surface more readily among all that goodwill. I returned to my office on the stipulated day, saying nothing about my recent indisposition. For that is all it was. I could laugh about it now. Or thought I could.

The telephone never stopped ringing that first morning. The swing door caused a constant draught. It seemed that a good proportion of local marriages had foundered that Christmas. Women who had soldiered on through beatings and male indifference gave up the ghost in the festive season.

Paul and I exchanged hardly a word until the final client left and the outer door was locked. He pushed his hands through his hair and rubbed his face.

'Christ,' he said irritably, 'what is the matter with these women? On days like this I begin to think the entire female population is unhinged.'

I don't object to dirty swearing, but profanity upsets me.

He mistook the expression of disapproval on my face. 'Okay. So that remark was chauvinistic. But there are times when it would help to hear the man's side of the story. Have you noticed how many women come here on their own?'

Of course I had noticed, and the reason was obvious to me. 'Husbands and male partners,' I told him, 'are unwilling to have counselling because they are unable to face their own inadequacies. You know that, Paul. We've talked about it often enough. When a relationship is in trouble your typical man pretends that nothing is wrong, or if it is, it can't be his fault.'

Paul shrugged and turned away.

I said, 'There you go! You're doing it too. Would *you* ask for counselling if you were in trouble?'

It was a light remark, made jokingly, but his reaction surprised me. He began to stride around the office, rearranging chairs, emptying ashtrays, switching off lights. I could sense his pent-up anger. Although nothing had been said I knew that it was over between us. It was not a good situation, for him or for me. We still had to work together, see each other daily. I was coming to realise that I had put myself in a risky position. I still found him attractive, but behind the flash of white smile and sensuous voice there lurked a definite threat.

It occurred to me later that evening, in the pub, watching him as he stood at the bar, that there was something lupine about him. Christmas television had included a wildlife programme about wolves; the way they select their prey and then stalk it. I thought of all the times I had been alone with him, and although he had given me no real reason to fear him I felt uneasy.

He returned to the table and set two coffees down. I looked up at him, hoping the dismay I felt did not show on my face. He sat and began to drop sugar lumps into his cup, and then he stirred it so violently that the coffee spilled over.

'I think,' he said, 'you and I need to sort out a few things.'

'Oh yes?' I asked in a flat tone. I was trying to follow the advice I gave to clients: to be non-confrontational. I got it wrong, my meekness seemed only to inflame him.

'Yes! Like what in hell has been the matter with you in recent weeks? I've obviously done something to upset you. I hoped the break at Christmas might have given you a chance to consider your behaviour. Obviously it has not. I tell you, Imogen, I'm sick of this cold-shoulder routine of yours. Apart from being unreasonable, it is also extremely childish. I've tried to be understanding; after all, it's down to your time of life, isn't it? Menopause and all that.'

He sounded like the very worst type of patronising and insensitive male. The scarcely repressed rage in his voice and body triggered a reaction of near-craziness in me. I wanted to shock, hurt, destroy him.

And so, I told the most alarming lie that I could think of. I said, 'I'll tell you what is wrong with me, Paul. I am three months' pregnant.' You could, as the saying goes, have heard a leaf fall.

A look of utter bafflement crossed his face, and then his features settled into an unreadable mask. There was a long pause and then he said, 'Pregnant, are you? Well, there's a thing now. Let me put you straight on something, darling. Whoever has knocked you up, it isn't me.'

Having told the first lie, I was forced to tell the second. I said, 'I haven't slept with Niall for five years.'

He said, 'You must have been sleeping with some other man then. You see, I've had the operation.' He raised his hand and made a scissoring motion with his two first fingers. 'Snip-snip,' he said, 'so if you're looking around for someone to blame – it isn't me.'

I hated him then. Enough to maim him. Kill him. Bury his body deep in concrete on a half-completed motorway construction.

I remembered my first client in Taunton. Beaten up by her clergyman husband. I recalled the loving way she had stroked the knife concealed in her cardigan pocket. I studied the broad pale planes of his face; the cold no-colour eyes. Now I saw those eyes narrow with suspicion. 'So who is the father? If it isn't Niall, and it can't be me, who else have you been playing around with?'

I almost confessed at that point. I almost said, 'But there is no baby. I just said it to upset you.' And then I thought, why should I? Let him be jealous. I began to push the argument further. I said, 'So how do I know you are telling me the truth about this operation? Look in the files, Paul. Count up the number of men who have used the same glib excuse to their pregnant partners.'

'It's the truth,' he said.

I leaned across the narrow table until my face was almost touching his. 'Prove it! Show me a medical certificate that confirms you have been gelded.'

I was ashamed of what was happening, yet in a curious way exhilarated by the recklessness of it. I saw with satisfaction the dull flush slowly stain his white face, and the pulse that throbbed in his jaw.

And still I sat there, confident that he had done me all of the damage he was capable of doing; complacent to the point of stupidity. That was when he bunched his fist and hit me. Again and again.

We were sitting in a secluded alcove, unheard and unseen. It was still early in the evening. The landlord was deep in conversation with his only other customer at the far end of the bar. My eyes squeezed closed against the awful anguish in my face, I sensed Paul's sudden absence, I heard the outer door slam. It was at least a minute before I fully registered the awkward angle of my neck, the throbbing agony in my cheekbones. The metallic taste of blood that filled my mouth.

I opened my eyes and saw the pool of blood spreading on the glass-topped table. I tried to work out what had happened, but my mind refused to accept what my senses told me. All I could think about at first was the sheer indignity of what had just occurred. Women like me did not suffer physical abuse from husband or partner. Women like me knew all the answers. Women like me?

I was alone on a December night, in a strange pub, in a town which was still unfamiliar to me. I had just suffered several violent blows to the face and head from the fist of my secret lover, who was also my office subordinate, and who had walked away as if nothing had happened. This traumatised wreck was me, Imogen Donovan, who thought she knew all the danger signs of impending brutality; who had read the books, attended the seminars, given years of working life to advising similarly abused women.

Abused? The word, in relation to myself, did not apply. Could not. The room began to swing and dip, my stomach churned. I hung on to the table-edge and willed myself to regain control. My role was that of rescuer, comforter, adviser.

But who rescues the rescuer?

To whom could *I* turn, now that it was *my* turn to be needy?

These thoughts, as I set them down, appear to have been well reasoned. Coherent.

They were not.

Such thinking as I did while huddled in that alcove was frantic and muddled. Even so, certain facts appeared to be unarguable. Firstly, I could not drive home, neither could I take a taxi. Any taxi driver, seeing my face and condition, would drive me straight to Accident and Emergency without prior consultation. I could not phone Niall to come and collect me, for obvious reasons.

I would not be permitted to spend the night in the very cheapest of Taunton's hotels without giving a convincing explanation of my injuries, and accepting first-aid treatment at the very least.

I could not stay much longer in this pub. Paul's hasty exit must have been noted by the landlord and his customer.

A few more minutes and mine host would be over, collecting the empty coffee cups, staring at my face.

The heating in the pub did not extend into the alcove. I was still wearing my dark raincoat, which I now remembered had an attached hood. I pulled the hood up over my head and covered as much of my face as I was able. The lighting in the bar was dim. I picked up my bag, stood, swayed, and then forced my legs to take the short walk to the door.

When the landlord called 'Goodnight' I automatically made to reply and found that I could not speak. Outside, in the street, I leaned against the pub wall and my head cleared a little in the cold night air. I was in no state to drive. I was not sure if I could walk. I remembered what Niall had said when we were rescuing the Dexters. 'You appear to be falling apart and I'm wondering why. One thing I'm sure of. If you've got yourself into a mess you'll have no one to turn to . . . you have no friends. Have you ever realised that? You have no friends.'

There was Gloria! There was, to be truthful, only Gloria. I thought about the distance which lay between this pub, and Gloria's flat above the boutique. I began to walk unsteadily through the frosty evening. What else could I do?

Gloria, very wisely, had one of those intercom gadgets through which a visitor must announce his or her name and business before gaining admittance.

Since I was unable to do more than gurgle and hiss, and hold a persistent finger on the doorbell, some time elapsed before Gloria opened up.

A white mist was rising off the River Tone. The streets of the town had that peculiar quiet which is noticeable between the jollifications of Christmas and the drunken revels of New Year's Eve. Tomorrow night it would be a very different scene.

Gloria, having looked through the spyhole, and satisfied herself that the caller was female and known to her, opened up her door and peered out through the gap permitted by the safety-chain.

'Imogen?'

I nodded.

She switched on an overhead porch light. I threw back the hood of my raincoat. I heard the sharp intake of her breath.

'Ker-rist on a donkey!' she gasped. 'So that bastard did you over, did he?'

She drew me inside. As I climbed the stairs to her living quarters I could hear the sounds of bolts being shot and the chain adjusted. I walked along a carpeted passageway and into a lamplit sitting room. Frank Sinatra was singing 'Come Fly With Me' on the stereo, and I felt safe for the first time that evening.

The warmth of the overheated flat hit me like another fist blow. As the backs of my knees met the sofa cushions I fell sideways and passed out.

Gloria, I now discovered, was unexpectedly houseproud. I opened my eyes to find her spreading towels behind my head and on either side of me. I could hardly blame her for these precautions since the sofa was covered in pale pink linen and as she so rightly said, I was bleeding like a stuck pig.

Having taken care of her soft furnishings she turned her attention back to me. Her expression was a mixture of anger and concern. 'You should go straightaway to Casualty, but you know that, don't you.'

I nodded.

'But you won't go, will you?'

I grunted.

'Right,' she said, 'well, I can see why you wouldn't want to. Too many awkward questions, eh?'

As she spoke she was easing me out of the raincoat. With a large pair of kitchen scissors she cut my best roll-necked cashmere sweater straight up the middle, and peeled it away from my damaged neck as if it were the skin of a banana.

Eyeing the sweater's expensive label she grimaced, and then laughed. 'Perhaps you can make a cardigan of it,' she joked; and then gasped as she took in the full extent of the damage done by Paul Mavsoni. 'Oh, shit,' she said, awestruck. 'I know I've got my Girl Guide's badge for first aid. But something tells me that the Guides' Association weren't thinking of this amount of damage – Imogen, I don't know if I can help you this time.'

I held up my hands in a gesture of supplication.

She sighed. 'This may seem cruel,' she said, 'but I'm going to fetch a mirror and show you just what that swine has done to your face. Perhaps when you see it . . .'

I shook my head and the room spun round me.

'Okay,' she said. 'Okay! I'll clean up the worst of the mess and we'll reconsider.' She brought bowls of warm water, antiseptic, cotton wool balls, and a tumbler with an inch of brandy in it. It was when I attempted to drink that I discovered the loosened teeth and split lips. I also discovered my lost voice.

'My husband,' I croaked, 'and my mother. They'll be worrying about me.'

Gloria paused in her swabbing and wiping. 'You're in shock,' she said. 'Even if I drive you home, what sort of reason will you give them for the state of your face? You look as if you'd gone fourteen rounds with Mike Tyson.'

'You could phone them. You could say I'd had a bump with the car. You could say that you are a colleague and that I'm spending the night at your place. Please,' I pleaded. 'Please.'

Nina

After the floods came severe cold.

On the day before New Year when Imogen returned to work the sun had shone in a blue sky; hoar frost lay thick on the fields and hedges. I felt a lift of the heart that afternoon as I walked up to the beech woods. I fed the hens and collected eggs, and thought how seldom in my life I had known such satisfaction in a simple task.

In the days since my return to Sad Acre I had cleaned the house, caught up with the laundry and shopped for food with Niall in the County Stores in Taunton.

I was pleasantly tired but not exhausted. I had baked cakes and bread that morning, and a suppertime casserole simmered in the oven. My daughter's household was again in order. Before leaving the high woods I paused and looked down into the valley. Once again the river ran peacefully between its banks; the Dexters grazed across a meadow. The whine of the chain saw came from the yard where Niall cut logs and bagged them for next week's deliveries.

Fran and Mitch were due to visit us at the end of January. Ashley and Angelique had promised that quite soon they would spend a weekend with us.

My daughter was not pregnant, and never had been.

It was not unusual for Imogen to be late home. First day back at work, we told each other, she had probably been overwhelmed by weeping clients. Niall and I ate our share of the casserole. We took our coffee and slices of my freshly made chocolate cake into the sitting room and finished the meal while watching the local television news.

Roscoe slept before the crackling log fire. Niall dozed in his armchair. I fought against sleep but must have lost the struggle. The ringing of the telephone woke me.

Niall reached for his mobile and mumbled hello, his voice and face still blurred with sleep. I watched him come fully awake, saw his expression change from mild alarm to horror. I heard him say, 'Give me your address. I'll be there in half an hour.'

The reply from the other end did not please him. 'But why not?' he demanded. 'If things are that bad she should be in hospital. Why isn't she?'

At this point I cried out, 'What is it? What's happened to Immie?' but he motioned me to silence.

'All right,' he told the caller, 'if you're absolutely certain. But I don't know you, do I? I'm not happy about this. Let me speak to my wife, and then give me your address.'

There followed a few confused minutes during which Niall was obviously struggling to make sense of the sounds coming down the wire. Satisfied at last that it was Imogen he spoke to, I heard him say reluctantly, 'Well if you're sure. Yes I know where it is. I'll be over tomorrow morning.'

I waited for him to tell me what had happened. When he did not I said at last, 'What is it? For pity's sake, Niall . . .'

'She's had a bit of an accident,' he said slowly. 'Nothing major, according to her friend. She's a bit shaken up, got a few cuts and bruises. She's staying in Taunton overnight. With a friend.'

'What friend?'

'You may well ask. Some woman with a cockney accent.'

'What sort of accident?'

'Seems the car skidded on an icy stretch not far from her office. Hit a lamppost – so she says.'

'You don't sound convinced?'

'I'm not. There was something a bit off – the woman sounded nervous, shifty, a bit embarrassed.'

'At least,' I said, 'she isn't with the boyfriend.'

'We don't know that, do we?'

This was all too true. Since the move to Taunton there were whole areas of Imogen's life in which we had no part.

'But you actually spoke to her?' I asked him.

'If you could call it speech. She had problems enunciating. It sounded as if she was speaking through a pound of raw liver. But yes. It was definitely Immie.'

I said, without a second's hesitation, 'She's been beaten up.'

I expected Niall to laugh, to tell me not to be foolish. But all he said was, 'By whom?'

'By one of the aggrieved husbands or partners of her women clients. You can't keep poking your nose into other people's private lives without, sooner or later, getting your face slapped.'

It had been more than a slapping. Much more.

She should have been in a hospital bed and I told her so.

Niall brought her home and she could scarcely walk or speak. He had questioned the friend who was called Gloria and owned a boutique, and who was clearly the source of Imogen's recent stylish outfits.

This person had denied all knowledge of what had happened. According to her account, she had simply played Good Samaritan, asked no questions, and believed what she had been told.

Niall asked plenty of questions, and believed nothing. Like where was the car, and were the police involved? And why was Imogen lying? In the end, and reluctantly, Immie gave him the keys and admitted that the Metro was standing unharmed in her office car park.

I remembered yesterday morning up in the beech woods, the blue and endless skies, the white frost, and the peace I had felt, believing that the worst was behind us, and a new year just beginning. Now, from one day to another everything was changed. People were changed.

Niall, easy-going, come-day-go-day Niall was suddenly focused, galvanised as I had never seen him, and displaying a monumental anger. An anger it was going to be difficult to maintain in view of the terrible injuries that had been inflicted on his wife's face. Obtuse though he was, surely even he would see that she needed sympathy rather than blame. Some man had done this to Immie. Deliberately, repeatedly and without mercy, her beautiful face had been made unrecognisable by a large fist.

Not that she was about to admit this. Even when her first pathetic spur of the moment lie had been revealed, she at once came up with another version of her beating. Imogen, the cool and collected one, whose life was organised, to whom nothing eyebrow-raising ever happened, had just taken the kind of punishment regularly doled out to her clients by their *husbands* and *partners*. And I wondered why. What could she possibly have done or said to deserve such treatment?

I had heard of delayed shock, but seldom of delayed anger. While Niall, on his return from Taunton, had raged through the house, kicking furniture and thumping table-tops with his bunched fist, I had remained calm, knowing that something disastrous had happened, and that life for the three of us would never be the same. Not that life had been all that marvellous in the first place. But we had never lied to each other, blatantly; knowing we were not believed but repeating the untruths just the same. It hurt me just to look at her. Listening was even more distressing. Every laboured word was an attempt at concealment.

Version number two of her mishap now involved an unknown assailant. A mystery mugger who had waylaid her in her office car park. When asked why she had lied about a car crash Immie pleaded confusion and disorientation; an excuse it was impossible to refute, since we had no medical assessment of her injuries and their effects. It was at this point that my own suppressed anger surfaced. I had so far gone along with her determination not to see a doctor. I had protected her from Niall's excessive zeal, his insistence that we should at least call in the local GP and report the whole business to the Taunton Constabulary. But as the hours passed I began to question my judgement. It was on the afternoon of the second day after her return home that my patience finally ran out, fear took over, and I dialled the number of the surgery in a nearby village.

She had insisted that only sick people stayed in bed. The doctor was middle-aged, fatherly. I waylaid him in the porch and gave him a swift rundown on events as I knew them. I accompanied him to the sitting-room door, ushered him in, and then fled to the kitchen where Niall waited. Some time elapsed before the doctor joined us. He sat at the kitchen table and drank the tea I put before him.

'It's bad,' he said. 'Even worse than it looks, if you can believe it. Her jaw may be fractured. Her nose is definitely broken. Her eyes are severely contused and the sight of the right one may be affected.'

'And her brain?' I asked.

He sipped his tea and chose his words with care. 'She's taken a bang to the head, but I could find no obvious signs of brain damage. She seems connected in her mind. But as I told her, these injuries should have been dealt with immediately. A delay such as this makes treatment infinitely more difficult.'

Niall said, 'Straight after the accident she went to a friend's flat in Taunton and stayed the night there. She came home in the afternoon of the next day and was adamant that she did not need a doctor. My wife is not easily moved once her mind is made up.'

'As I have just discovered, Mr Donovan.' The doctor smiled. 'But I find most women can be persuaded when it's pointed out that their looks will be permanently ruined without treatment. I want you take her straight away to A and E in Taunton. I'll give you a letter for the senior registrar.' He paused. 'By the way, what actually happened to her? She seems very confused on that subject.'

Niall said, 'Good question! We've had two versions so far. Neither of which we are inclined to believe.'

'She's in a bad way,' said the doctor. 'She's taken a severe beating to the face and head. It's not too surprising if she's muddled about what happened.'

The doctor rose, thanked me for the tea and handed a folded note to Niall. 'Taunton – straight away, Mr Donovan. I've given your wife a sedative to ease her pain on the drive down. I'll be in touch with the registrar this evening.'

I walked with him to his car. He was still not totally convinced that Imogen would consent to hospital treatment.

He wound down his window and said before driving away, 'Your daughter is hiding something; protecting someone. For her own safety you must find out what exactly happened to her.'

Imogen

I wished he had killed me; wished that I was out of it all, at peace on a mortuary slab, beyond questioning, beyond pain, and most of all, beyond guilt.

There was time on that awful drive to the hospital for me to study their faces, their undamaged and familiar features. Niall's thin-lipped with rage, white about the mouth, his eyes blazing, his jaw taut.

Nina's face, crumpled and suddenly old, feeling my pain for me. And the worst of it was – *they didn't deserve this. Any of this!*

You could say I had asked for it.

There were many who would take that view.

I am inclined to think that way myself.

You could also say I had been lucky.

Supposing I had not been sitting in a public bar, with possible witnesses just a step away? I remembered all the isolated places I had been with Paul; even in my office he could have killed me and never been suspected. Oh yes, I had been very lucky. Except that I didn't feel it. Like I said, I wished he had finished the job. Put me out permanently. For even if my nose grows straight again, the swellings in my eyes and jaw subside, the bruises fade, I will be left with the scars that do not show. Loss of confidence, of self-respect. Of pride. I know these things, you see. Who better? I am that wise woman, the marriage guidance expert, the counsellor, the clever bitch who knows all about men and women and their turbulent emotions; the way their minds work, the way love can turn to hatred. Except that I have never known anything at first hand, have I? Oh, I had witnessed clients' battered faces, their bruised and knife-slashed bodies, their unremitting fear of the perpetrator; their destroyed lives. But it's not the same.

Now I stand in what must be a unique position in my line of business. Perhaps a thorough beating should be the required qualification for every marriage-mender? In future I shall be able to say with utter conviction, 'I know how you feel. I know what you're going through. Believe me – I too have been there.'

Nina

We walked into Accident and Emergency, Niall and I supporting her on either side. As we passed through the automatic doors she stumbled and collapsed. Nurses came running, Immie was lifted on to a trolley. Niall handed the GP's note to a tall white-coated boy who looked too young to be a doctor. Immie and the nurses meanwhile, had disappeared from our view behind yellow flowered curtains.

A bank of dark green sofas flanked a white wall. Niall and I sat down as instructed and waited. We waited a long time. He disappeared at intervals to smoke, muttering that he had almost kicked the habit, but what the hell! He brought me bitter coffee in a Styrofoam cup and a pack of stale chocolate biscuits. The biscuits reminded me of Primrose, and I had a deep yearning to be back in Ashkeepers, sitting on her beige sofa drinking her coffee and nibbling her superior Cadbury's assortment. At that moment I would gladly have exchanged the sights and sounds of this terrifying place for Primmie's claustrophobic sitting room and inconsequential chit-chat.

Just for a moment I actually contemplated flight. But it was not an option. I was as deeply involved in this damned mess as were my family. Niall and I were called into a small, cluttered office where the extent of my irresponsible behaviour was soon made clear to me by the senior doctor who was caring for my daughter. His hard words were all fired in my direction. Regardless of the circumstances, never mind that Immie had chosen to remain in Taunton, had refused medical attention, it seemed that I was to blame for the present deterioration in her condition. Niall attempted to intervene, to defend me, which only brought a storm down on his head. Why, he was asked, had the police not been informed? What exactly was going on here? What had really happened? What was Niall's part in all this? And were we, in fact, really the husband and the mother?

I realised, belatedly, that we were being accused of more than neglect. We were suspected of actual involvement . . .

I said, very quietly. 'Why don't you ask my daughter what happened to her? She is the only one who knows the truth.'

'I would,' the doctor said, 'but unfortunately she is unconscious. She is at this moment undergoing a brain scan. So you see, your account of how she sustained her injuries is all we have to go on.'

People who work in casualty departments are right to be suspicious. Not all the injuries they treat are accidental or self-inflicted. Even when the police came to interview us, I could see only too well how our lack of action on Imogen's behalf could be construed as guilty behaviour. The lapse of time between her being injured and our arrival with her in Casualty was too great.

Notes were taken. Names, addresses, occupations. What they really wanted to know we were unable to provide.

Fifty years ago and I had been in a similar position. The accused with no defence. I had been down this road before, when my baby was stolen. Now it was happening again, with my second daughter.

Strange, isn't it? How guilty a policeman can make you feel when you haven't committed any crime?

They told us to go home. To come back later that evening. It seemed unnecessary for both of us to drive back to Sad Acre. Niall had stock to feed, animals which required attention. We decided that I should remain in Taunton, have a meal and meet him back in A and E, when, with luck, we would have better news.

As I walked away from the hospital the early dusk of January was already thickening; the cold quiet air was promising another night of hard frost. I had dressed in the smart tan quilted jacket and matching trousers, having reasoned in a muddled way that among suspicious doctors and policemen it would not do to appear too eccentric or shabby. The outfit, although smart, did nothing to offset the bitter cold. I pushed my hands deep into my jacket pockets, and began to walk away from the spot where Niall had dropped me off. I came up to the Tone bridge. The river was calm, glassy. Only green shrubs in tubs broke the greyness of Goodlands Gardens. There were lights in the café but I was already awash with what passes for coffee in hospital vending machines.

I walked on, keeping my mind deliberately blank, attempting to save myself for what I would need to face later in the evening. I stared unseeingly into shop windows, aware only of my own reflection. Finally, no longer able to face the intense chill, I wandered into one of those trendy bistros, all white wrought iron and trailing houseplants, and outrageous prices.

I sat on a wobbly chair, dizzily grateful for the steamy warmth. This time I chose decaffeinated, and since I intended to stay there for as long as possible I cravenly ordered a Danish pastry with it.

Gradually the blood returned to my fingers and feet. I began to look about me; the bistro stood in a small and fashionable court. Directly opposite was a boutique with one glamorous evening gown displayed in its window.

The name, stencilled in gold across the door and above the window was GLORIA.

I tore the Danish into tiny pieces, ate the currants and licked the cinnamon filling from my fingers. I drank the decaff which tasted and smelled like gravy browning.

The bistro began to show unmistakeable signs that it was closing. The staff started to move with purpose, whipping cloths from tables, rattling crockery and glass, counting the day's takings. I sat for as long as I dared. When I finally left a chorus of relieved 'goodnights' followed me into the court.

I paused beside Gloria's door, but only for a moment. That lady wasn't going anywhere. She would keep for another day.

We were told by a staff nurse that Imogen was conscious and we could see her for a few minutes.

She lay in a corner bed with yellow curtains pulled around it. Against the white of the pillows and bedspread Imogen's injuries looked worse than ever. Her eyes peered out through narrow slits between ledges of black and purple flesh. Her nose was strapped. The deep lacerations across her chin and cheekbones had been stitched; they must have been caused by a heavy sharp-edged ring. Her jaw and neck were severely bruised and puffy. Her lips were split and swollen. Her head had been shaved just above the left ear to reveal a wound we hadn't known existed.

Niall held her hand on the one side, and I on the other.

We murmured the useless mixture of concern and endearments that people resort to when there is nothing of consequence that can be said. There were chairs at the bedside, but before we could sit down we were summoned to the doctor's office.

He was still hostile, still suspicious. He shuffled the papers on his desk, removed his gold-rimmed glasses and began to polish the lenses. He was finding difficulty in speaking to us, as if the words stuck in his throat.

'The scan?' Niall ventured.

'Clear.' The reply was terse, grudging, as if it would have given him satisfaction of a sort to frighten us with bad news. 'Even so, she is quite badly injured. We've done our best to put her face back together; it's her mental state that will be the ongoing problem.'

'Has she told you anything?' I asked.

'Not one word. Not to hospital staff or the police.' He placed his hands on the desktop and spoke directly to me. 'She's your daughter. You waited forty-eight hours before bringing her to us. Surely in all that time she told you something?'

His estimation of the time lapse wasn't strictly accurate, but this did not seem the moment to argue with him.

'She lied,' I said. 'We were given two versions of what had happened to her. Neither of them believable.' I felt the time had come to strike a blow for our side. We at least deserved to be heard. I said, 'I know you think that I – we – have been neglectful of her. I know we should have brought her to you sooner, and for that I am sorry. What you need to know now is that she may well be still at risk. She is a counsellor – broken marriages, battered wives. I believe she is shielding someone. Some violent husband who is blaming my daughter for breaking up his marriage.'

'This,' said the doctor accusingly, 'is something else we should have been told when she was admitted.'

'There's hardly been time, has there?' Niall's face flushed with anger. 'So now that you know, what can you do about it?'

'No visitors, except husband and mother.'

'Are you sure?' Niall asked, 'Can you trust us to sit at her bedside? For some reason known only to you, you think I did this, don't you?'

I put a hand on his arm. 'I think we'd better go. This is getting us nowhere.' I turned to the man in the white coat who, now that I was really studying him, looked weary unto death.

I said, propitiatingly, 'Thank you for speaking to us. We appreciate what you have done for Imogen. Are you sure,' I pleaded, 'that she is not in any immediate medical danger?'

His smile was tired, which increased my guilt.

He said, 'I've pinned her jaw, and set her nose. The rest of her injuries will mend with time and good home care.'

'I take your point, and I'll see she gets it.'

We left, and as we walked through the aching cold towards the car park, something broke inside me, and tears welled up from a deep place. I heard myself sobbing with an intensity and desperation I had not felt since Lucy had been stolen.

I halted beside the pickup and faced Niall.

'What have we done to Immie?' I demanded. 'She's the only truly good person I have ever known. Her whole life is concerned with helping other people. Not because she is well paid, or gains any glory from it. But because *that is the way she is!* It just isn't fair that she should have been a victim. Because whoever did this to her, and for whatever reason, *that is what she is.*'

Niall put an arm round my shoulders.

'It isn't your fault. You couldn't have prevented what has happened. It's that bloody doctor, his attitude and his nasty mind; the things he said, they got to me too. You and I should not have to feel guilty.'

'Yes we should, Niall! We haven't appreciated her, given her credit for what she does. Oh, I've paid lip service now and then, but if I'm being honest, I've thought privately that Immie and her co-helpers were just one big joke. I never realised the risks involved when dealing with violent people. It all sounded so cosy, gossipy; advising women how to hang on to their wandering husbands, how to deal with their stroppy teenagers.'

Niall said, 'I intend to find out who did this. First move tomorrow will be a visit to her office. We need to know who she saw recently, if there were arguments with anyone.'

'Her office! We should have notified her office! It never crossed my mind—'

Niall started the pickup engine and began to move slowly through the car park. 'Funny,' he said, 'it's only just occurred to me too, but none of her staff have enquired about her, have they?'

Imogen

He came to see me.

Breezed in as if nothing terrible had happened, wearing his rumpled corduroys and rollnecked sweater. If I had not had loose teeth and a wired jaw, I would still have been speechless. He looked so harmless, sexy in a cuddly sort of way. *Nice*.

The curtains were no longer drawn round my bed. I saw him strolling down the ward, a staff nurse at his side, a bunch of freesias in his hand. The two of them were smiling and chatting as if they were old acquaintances. And that, of course, was exactly what they were.

Paul was well known in this place. Saviour of distressed women; defender of the oppressed. It had always been Paul who brought injured clients out to A and E; his size and his aspect providing a deterrent to any victim's violent partner who might be lurking in the bushes.

In order to visit me he would not have needed to identify himself. When it came to being trusted, he was rated far above my husband and my mother.

The young nurse took the flowers and returned almost at once with them neatly arranged in a glass vase. In her other hand she carried a mug of coffee which she handed to Paul.

I wondered, light-headed with shock, what would happen if I wrote on my scratch pad, 'This is the man who beat me up'?

I would probably be sectioned.

He sat by my bed, one leg crossed nonchalantly over the other. He sipped his coffee, which had come from the kitchen and not the machine.

The beds on either side were empty, but still he leaned close to my ear and whispered. 'They tell me you refused to name the one who did this to you.' As he spoke his shoulders lifted and a spasm of fear passed across his face, and I knew then his relaxed air was assumed. In my totally helpless condition it gave me some small comfort to know I had this slight power over him; but then I saw his eyes and knew I must be very careful. Since the wiring of my jaw I had decided that for some time to come, even if I was able, I would not speak. Speech, in times of pain and weakness, tends to be impulsive.

With a biro in my hand there was time for forethought and caution. I reached for the scratch pad.

I wrote in careful capitals. 'I DON'T REMEMBER ANYTHING ABOUT IT.'

His shoulders relaxed, his anxious look vanished. His pent-up breath exhaled in a long sigh. He smiled.

'How wise of you, Imogen,' he said. 'But try not to worry. I will personally make sure that whoever did this dreadful thing to you will never do it again.' He was speaking now in his normal tones. Any medical staff who happened to be passing would see only his serious concern for an injured colleague. His glib promise did not reassure me.

I looked at his right hand wrapped around the mug of coffee; at the heavy gold ring studded with diamonds which he wore on his middle finger. There was obvious grazing on his knuckles where they had come into contact with my front teeth. I touched the lacerations on my cheeks and chin, and stared accusingly at him until his gaze dropped. If I should need to prove he was the one . . . ?

'Don't even think about it,' he whispered. 'I hurt my hand in the office. Caught it in those damned swing doors. Several people saw it happen.' He paused. 'I thought the landlord of the the Dragon might have remembered you leaving. I was in there last night. Had an after-work drink with him. He didn't recall us being there at all. Neither together, nor singly.'

I pointed to the scratch pad and its message.

'Okay! Let's keep it that way, shall we,' he said.

It was not a question but an order.

An order that contained an underlying threat.

A nurse was approaching up the long ward. Paul raised his voice to a pitch she could not help but hear. He pointed to the multi-hued freesias, and again he smiled at me. He said, 'They smell of spring, don't they? I remembered they are your favourite flowers. Don't worry, Imogen. You'll soon be out of here and convalescing. Perhaps Niall could take you on holiday? Somewhere in the sun. You both deserve it.'

Paul knew that hell would freeze over before I went on holiday with Niall. He was aware that freesias were not my favourite flowers and he kept telling me not to worry, which in the circumstances was bizarre.

'They say I can go home tomorrow,' I wrote on the scratch pad.

'I'll phone you,' he promised. 'Even if you can't answer, it's important that we maintain contact. I can keep you up to date with what's happening in the office.'

It all sounded so right, so normal. The staff nurse was beginning to hover. I leaned back against my pillows hoping to convey extreme exhaustion.

'I think . . .' she began.

He smiled his sweetest and most endearing smile, and I saw her melt. Oh! How well I remembered that bones-to-water feeling. He put up both hands, expressing his contrition. 'Sorry,' he said, 'I hadn't meant to stay so long, but Imogen is my supervisor and she is also a very special lady. I had to reassure myself . . .'

His duplicity appalled me. It crossed my mind that he had done this sort of thing before. What he had actually needed was reassurance as to my continued silence.

Two men in white coats were making for my bed.

'The orthodontists,' Staff Nurse informed me. 'They're hoping to rescue as many of your teeth as possible.'

I saw another spasm of what this time might have been guilt twist Paul Mavsoni's mouth. Or perhaps he had been suppressing laughter?

Late that night, when Niall and Nina had gone home and I was drinking tepid milk through a straw, I began for the first time since 'the accident' to review my 'case'.

The ward was quiet; one dimmed light still burned above a distant bed. My brain, although heavily sedated, began to attempt a sluggish assessment of what had happened to me. And why. I went back in my mind to that evening in the pub. What he had said. What I had said. But my memory of those fraught few minutes was genuinely hazy.

What I did recall was what at the time and before he hit me had seemed an irrational fear of a nice man, a colleague – who had never shown any signs of violence or even ill temper. He had displayed occasional irritation. But so had I. Had my subconscious somehow managed that evening to pick up on Paul's concealed antagonism, his hatred, so that I almost felt the blows before they landed? And if so, what had sparked him off on that particular night?

My head began to ache, and when I tried to focus my gaze on a passing nurse I felt the ward itself begin to dip and sway. I closed my eyes and fought down nausea. I resolved that once at home, I would refuse all further sedation. This was no time for muddled thinking; I would, from now onwards, need to be sharp, focused and alert.

What had happened to me was not domestic violence; not an uncomplicated case of wife-bashing. All at once, that particular crime seemed simple and straightforward. *I had an enemy.* A dangerous man who might possibly be psychopathic. *And that man had been my lover.* Half a dozen well-chosen words from him could ruin my entire life.

Nina

We brought her home, woozy from sedation, unable to speak, incapable even of nodding or shaking her head to convey yes or no.

Anticipating her refusal to remain in bed, I had this time made proper preparations to nurse her downstairs. A stack of pillows on the outsized sofa, a lightweight blanket if she should want it; a low table within hand's reach which held all the necessary bits and pieces she might need. I had written out a menu of semi-liquid foods from which she could choose; I had provided a bottle of mineral water and a glass. Niall lit the sitting-room fire and filled two log baskets. I switched on the pink-shaded lamps to make the room cosy.

Once installed on the sofa Immie tried to smile. It was then it all became unbearable and I rushed quickly to the kitchen, overcome completely by the sheer horror of what had happened to her.

A week ago her smile, although rare these days, had been well worth waiting for. Now, Niall and I had been told, it would take several months of complicated dental work to restore her mouth to the normality the orthodontists hoped for, but could not guarantee.

I clutched the rim of the kitchen sink and said the word 'bastard' several times over in a loud voice. I tried to imagine what sort of man would pound his fist into a woman's face until the flesh resembled raw meat and the bones smashed.

She slept a lot in those first days, a natural sleep that was not dependent on tablets or the hypodermic.

Heavy bruising now showed up on her hands, which had also taken a pounding as she tried to protect her face during the attack. No bones were broken, but her fingers were stiff and clumsy.

Sometimes she cried out but did not wake, and I knew she was reliving in dreams the night of the attack. My conviction that Imogen knew her attacker grew stronger with every day that passed. Her injuries had the look of deliberate malice, of blows inflicted in good light and well aimed, not the kind of random damage which might have been done by a stranger in the almost total darkness of her office car park.

In that first month we made two trips to Taunton to the orthodontist, and to the surgeon. The swellings had begun to subside, the bruising almost faded; Immie slept less in the daytime, but still she did not speak.

Niall employed a retired farm worker who disliked his retirement. Joe came out to us from the neighbouring village for three hours every morning. The log-delivery business was growing daily in the bitter weather, and Joe was, to quote his own words, a dab hand with the chain saw.

I, on the other hand, made beds, washed dishes, prepared meals, at what was for me a record speed.

Most of my day was spent with my daughter.

I reflected at times that never in all her life had I given so much time to Immie, or tended her with such concentration. Looking back on those weeks I know now that it was the strangest and most intense time of my whole life. On a practical level Imogen needed help with bathing, dressing, coping with her long and heavy hair. On the semi-liquid diet which was all she could cope with, her weight had begun to drop at an alarming rate. I turned overnight into an amateur dietician, working out calorific values and the nourishing qualities of porridge and cream soups, and then persuading her to swallow sufficient to keep the soul within her body.

Her hair needed washing, but considering her wired jaw,

taped nose and stitched face we decided that shampooing was out of the question, and that I was far too nervous to attempt such a task.

After a particularly difficult ten minutes of wrestling on my part, with clips and pins and combs, only to have the whole mass fall back down about her shoulders, she snatched up the scratch pad and wrote in large letters, 'CUT IT!'

I said, 'Are you sure?'

She pointed to the scissors which lay among the assortment of gadgets on the little table. I picked them up, and again I asked, 'Are you absolutely certain?'

I saw her lips twitch. Something sparked between us, and and we became conspirators, about to do the unthinkable. She wrote, 'Niall won't like this!'

I said, entering into the reckless spirit which had seized us both, 'So who is asking Niall's permission anyway?'

I draped a towel round her shoulders, lifted a strand of heavy hair and promptly abandoned the sewing scissors for a large orange-coloured kitchen pair which I fetched from the cutlery drawer. Sawing my way from right to left I cut an experimental swathe, which even I could see was ragged and uneven. Immie put a hand up to her head. 'Shorter,' she wrote. 'Much shorter.'

I had never in my life cut anybody's hair. It required courage. I stood back, appalled at the mess I had already made. As for the shining tresses which lay on the carpet, I decided not to look at them.

I began again, this time wielding a comb above the scissors in what I hoped was an almost professional fashion. I took off at least two more inches. If anything the use of the comb had compounded the disaster. Instead of a sleek shining cap, her head now resembled a floor mop.

I said, weakly, 'Immie, I am sorry, but this is not going to be what you wanted. You would have been better off employing a pudding-basin barber.'

I explained the Beatle-style haircuts, ahead of their time, which were given to schoolboys in Ashkeepers sixty years ago.

Immie was intrigued. 'Tell me more,' she wrote. 'You mean they actually used a pudding-basin?'

I fetched a hand mirror from her bedroom, and handed it to her.

She studied the uneven lengths, the chopped ends.

She wrote 'WHAT WE NEED HERE IS A PUDDING BASIN.'

I hurried to the kitchen and returned with an assortment of plastic bowls. We tried them on her head for size, finally finding one which she approved. I began, fearfully to snip my way around the basin's rim, trimming away the ragged bits with the nail scissors. It seemed to take forever, and when it was done my hands were shaking. Tentatively I lifted the basin away, and then pulled the comb through what remained of the thick short hair. I held up the hand mirror and waited.

The delight in her eyes was more than I had hoped for. She wrote at great speed, 'Wonderful!!! Thank you.'

We looked down at the long lengths of shorn hair, a lifetime's growth, never cut till now. She wrote again, 'When the Jacobs need shearing you'll make a great job of it. I can't wait to see Niall's reaction. I look like a cross between Ringo Starr and Paul McCartney.'

We began to laugh. Immie's shoulders shook and her chest heaved, which was as close as she could get to mirth.

I wanted the moment to last forever: the closeness, the sheer happiness; the connectedness which I had thought could never happen.

A sound from the kitchen warned me of Niall's return. I picked up the basins and left the sitting room, carefully closing the door behind me. Niall was pinning a note on the cork board.

He eyed the plastic bowls with some surprise.

'I've cut Immie's hair,' I warned him. 'You'll find it a bit of a shock, but it's what she wanted. So make sure you say all the right things.'

I prepared a tea tray, making a strong brew to settle my still quivering nerve ends.

Niall must have been diplomatic, even downright flattering,

for when I carried the tray into the sitting room he and Imogen were holding hands. He had gathered up the shorn locks and declared that he would keep them always. They were gazing devotedly at each other.

It was all so Barbara Cartland I was torn between tears and raucous laughter. I set down the tray and left them to their reconciliation. I picked up the kitchen scissors, wiped them and returned them to the cutlery drawer.

As an aid to marriage guidance they had proved a most unlikely tool.

I had noticed, when I handed the minor to Imogen, that she placed her free hand across her nose and mouth so as not to see the damage.

Niall

It's okay for blokes to cry.

He had learned that much from Fin his father, who was capable of running through the full scale of emotions, from screaming temper to heart-rending sobs, all in the space of twenty minutes.

So Niall could have shed tears and not felt embarrassed, except that to do so would have upset Imogen even more than she already was.

She might even have seen tears from him as pitying or patronising. You never knew with Immie.

It was the haircut that did it. The bare and vulnerable look of her; the white nape of her neck suddenly revealed; her ears, which were smaller than he had realised, and sort of pinkly transparent in the fire's red glow. He had needed to turn away, look out of the window until the stinging in his eyes had passed. But at the same time he was also ashamed of how good he sometimes felt about her damaged face; how easy he now felt in her company. Imogen, beautiful, poised and flawless, had terrified him. His initial reaction to the mugging had been one of horror; it was if some exquisite statue or painting had been defaced and ruined. Oh my God, he had breathed when he saw her that morning in Gloria's flat. My God, she looks barely human. How will she survive this mutilation? How will she bear to go on living? He had wanted to cover all the mirrors; even the dark glass of the microwave door might give back her reflection.

He tried to work out what manner of man would do this to a woman, and for what reason. With his mind shocked into a rare state of introspection he also began to see, dimly, what it was that had eaten away at him over the long years of their marriage. How, instead of growing together, Imogen had easily outstripped him in every department.

He had never become accustomed to the fact that with the onset of middle age she had achieved all her goals, realised her potential. As for her looks; why just lately, while approaching the Big Fifty birthday, she had become – well, radiant was the only word that came to mind.

He thought about the way he had invariably pursued what he privately termed 'comfortable' women. He could only feel at ease, confident, with those ladies who were less than perfect, flawed in some endearing way.

He reviewed them; closed his eyes and watched the long procession march across the years. He had loved them all, fiercely and protectively, some for their unruly hairstyles, others for their crooked teeth, or their scruffy shoes and uneven hemlines.

He smiled, remembering the bedrooms, the backdrops to his pitiful conquests. After the cool blues and whites of the room he shared with Immie, it was the fake tigerskin bed throws, the pink nylon sheets, the tarty black satin baby-doll pyjamas that had turned him on. He remembered red plastic shades on bedside lamps, telephones in the shape of Mickey Mouse, the voice of Elvis throbbing from a stereo; plastic daffodils in a green vase. *Kitsch* was how Imogen would have described such things, but some perverse streak in him had made bad taste seem sexy and exciting.

Looking at Immie now, in pain and helpless, he felt a sharp sense of his betrayal of her. All those unnecessary lies, all that ducking and diving. Seeing himself as a bit of a devil, the only one among his boozy mates (they could hardly be called friends) who was not hag-ridden, henpecked, he had clung to his laddish image. Now, so strong was his self-loathing that he only dared to gaze openly at his wife when she was asleep.

He experienced the bleak pain of knowing he had made mistakes that could never be rectified.

He had longed for a son, but there had been no more children after Francesca.

He loved John, his grandson, with an aching love that wanted to keep the child impossibly safe; to give him the whole world.

Niall sat in his armchair and watched Imogen sleeping. Their lives had been such a mess, and for such a long time. This beating she had suffered. Nina's belief was that Imogen knew her attacker. He had heard somewhere that such atrocities were usually committed within the family, or by a lover. He began to remember the way she had changed since coming to Sad Acre. The twinges of jealousy he had felt (and could hardly believe in) when she altered her prim style, wore bright satin blouses, jade-pagoda earrings, and shortened her hemlines.

He had known then that Imogen was an innocent when it came to relationships with men. What first-hand experience had she known of the rough edges of life? Her years had been lived solving other women's problems.

Niall knew now that he should have taken better care of her. He should have made it his business to seek out this 'lover'; if that is what he was, and vet him. But even as the thought came to his mind, he recognised the incongruity of it. He tried to imagine himself marching up to some stranger, tapping him on the shoulder and demanding the sort of character reference which would make him acceptable as Imogen's 'bit of rough on the side'. But even as he chuckled at the impossible image, a cold hand seemed to move inside his chest. He had failed once before when he should have been watchful.

He remembered his parents. The way they died. Or the way the police had said they died.

Niall had always felt he should have been there that weekend. He had known his mother's heart was failing.

He had known, oh God, how well he had known, about Fin's heavy drinking.

The truth had been that he was sick of the pair of them,

weary of the whole business; of the fights that he had witnessed between them all his life. He had chosen to stay down in Taunton, with school friends who lived in normal homes where parents who, even if they did not love one another, treated each other kindly and with respect.

If only he had come home, as his mother had begged him to, that weekend. When the police drove him back to Sad Acre it had been too late. If only he had made it his business to investigate what was going on with Imogen, and this chancer who had been parking his Range Rover under the beech trees in the top lane.

In her present weakened state it was impossible to question her, but there was nothing to prevent Niall from visiting her office. From asking around. There must be somebody in Taunton who knew about this joker. Total anonymity was impossible. Especially for a geezer who imagined he could patch up other people's lives.

After all, it was hardly a bloke's job, was it? A pretty wimpish occupation, really. Which did not make the man less dangerous.

Nina

Niall and I talked around the subject of Immie's silence. We made endless guesses about the actual scene of the attack, the reason for it; the identity of what the Taunton police called the perpetrator.

They were taking it seriously, those policemen. A detective sergeant drove out to Sad Acre to interview Imogen now that she was, as he put it, feeling stronger. On the mend. On the mend?

Well, if that was the case, I told him, I had seen no evidence of it. She continued to write what few words she wished to impart on her scratch pad. She still needed help with bathing and dressing; and going up and down the stairs unaided was impossible for her, due to recurring dizziness resulting, we believed, from the head-blows.

It was, I pointed out, nine weeks since the 'incident' (police jargon is contagious) and my daughter still no more independent than a small child.

Spring crept up on us.

Cocooned as we were inside the house, and the weekly visit to the hospital in Taunton our only contact with the real world, it was becoming increasingly easy to believe that nothing else mattered beyond Imogen's needs, and her eventual recovery. I scarcely noticed April.

It was Niall who forced me to admit that she wasn't getting better. Gradually the metal pinnings that held her jaw in place had been removed. A small, hardly noticeable bump on her nose, which she was told would disappear in time, remained as the sole evidence of the break.

All other swelling and bruising had long since vanished. She had lost a lot of weight. Her face was thin and very pale. But, the doctors reassured us, once she began to eat solid food, and get out into the fresh air, all would be well.

The orthodontist had done, and was still doing, a wonderful job on her damaged teeth. We were told in May that there was no longer any reason why Immie should not be speaking, or eating a normal diet.

But she refused to do either.

There were other things she would not do, like walking further than the few steps it took to go from house to car and back again; like driving her car. Like looking in mirrors, or taking an interest in what she wore. I had succeeded in weaning her off the daytime wearing of pyjamas and dressing gown, but her selection of shabby jeans, track-suit bottoms and baggy sweaters was small improvement.

Looking through her wardrobe one day, hoping to find some more cheerful garments, I came across a beautiful red velvet leisure suit, guaranteed, I thought, to raise her spirits. But her revulsion on seeing the outfit was so extreme that I hid the suit in my attic cupboard.

The days of her heavy dependency on me were over, yet in so many ways she was still needy. She was reluctant to eat solid food. She made no attempt to resume her life. The only improvement in the situation was the reconciliation between her and Niall. It was an odd, one-sided courtship, since only Niall spoke. But perhaps they had found the answer to their problems? Without Immie's vocal and frequent putdowns Niall seemed to gather confidence, to find a way of approaching her that was tender yet assured.

As for myself. Devoted as I had been, and remained, yet the strain was beginning to tell. Reluctant to leave her alone, I too was confined in the house. On lovely May mornings we ate breakfast together in the kitchen, the door and windows open to the sweet air. Niall talked about his day's plan; Joe arrived on his rusty bike, pulling off his bicycle clips, tapping politely on the open door, then coming in to drink a mug of sweet strong tea, and impart the village gossip.

Imogen, her mouth still painful, ate only thin porridge. When the men had gone into the fields she washed the breakfast dishes while I dried them. She would perform any task I gave her, peeling vegetables, preparing salad, loading the washing machine. What she would not do was anything that took her beyond the confines of these four walls.

Niall mowed the long grass in the orchard and set out the garden furniture beneath the trees. When she showed no inclination to sit outside, he bought an expensive hammock with canopy and cushions, but she refused to use it.

We noticed her habit of carrying the mobile phone from room to room. Some days it rang twice, three times; sometimes a week would pass and nothing. After one of those calls Immie would shut herself away in the bedroom she shared with Niall, and miss meals.

I took to listening at closed doors, but as she never spoke to her caller I was none the wiser. And then one evening she went into the kitchen, leaving the mobile in her armchair. Niall snatched up the gadget, swiftly tapped out the 1471 number, and relayed the information to me in an urgent whisper. I wrote it down on Immie's scratch pad, ripped out the evidence and hid it in my handbag. I found, on investigation, that the phone number of my daughter's mystery caller was always the same and had a Taunton code.

When I dialled it the next morning a man's voice announced the name of the counselling service, and asked how he might help me. I rang off without speaking and went into the barn where Niall was working.

'Those calls are coming from her office,' I told him.

'I thought they might be.'

'What I can't understand,' I said, 'is why a call from one

of Immie's colleagues should have such a devastating effect on her. Each time it happens she suffers a setback. What can they possibly be saying to her?'

Her next hospital appointment was for the following Monday. She was accustomed to being dropped off and collected later, when Niall and I had done the weekly big shop.

This time, after leaving her safe in the care of a familiar nurse, Niall and I drove to the office car park, alleged scene of the attack. I noted the dark green Range Rover in its usual slot behind the laurels. I recalled the winter's day I had wandered through there, and come upon Immie and the man called Paul in a Hollywood-style clinch. I remembered the way he had looked at me, and I felt uneasy.

Niall also paused and studied the Rover. He had come prepared with a notepad and pen. He jotted the car's number, peered in at the windows, walked all round it. 'This,' he said, 'belongs to the joker who parks up in the top lane and watches the house.'

The marriage-menders' workplace was nothing like I had imagined. For me, the whole concept had always smacked of petty officials poking their bureaucratic noses into that most private of relationships, the one that exists between cohabiting partners and married couples.

The appropriate setting for such goings-on would, I had thought, be institutional: cream-painted walls, brown-varnished doors, uncurtained windows and a floor made of cheap tiles, with metal chairs and a brass spittoon. I had visualised it so often and in such fine detail; even down to the clanking, bulbous, old-fashioned radiators which were only ever lukewarm, and the curious smell of misery which permeates such places.

We walked around to the main entrance, and the building itself was my first shock. The rear view from the car park had given no hint of the ancient façade and the neat formal gardens which fronted what must once have been a small Elizabethan manor house.

Several organisations were housed within its walls. A notice in the hall informed us that Imogen's lot were situated on the first floor. There was no lift, so troubled women were presumably expected to belong to a youthful age-group. Niall and I climbed a curving staircase which could have featured in a period scene from a Gainsborough film of the 1940s. A glass-walled vestibule led to swing doors, and since the reception desk was unmanned we pushed on into what I can only describe as a very large, high-ceilinged room.

Oh, but what a room!

All blues and whites with touches of pink. Thick carpet, floor-length curtains, comfortable armchairs, fresh flowers.

My expectations had been coloured by recollections of shabby 1950s' baby clinics, doctors' waiting rooms, and Ministry of Food offices where we queued for identity cards and ration books long after the war was officially over.

The world had moved on, had improved beyond belief, leaving me in a time warp and fifty years out of date. And if I could be so mistaken about furnishings and decor, how many other, more serious prejudices was I harbouring? So this was the place to which perfectly nice, ordinary women came when they felt impelled to tell their darkest and most painful secrets to a stranger.

We stood inside the swing doors and waited to be noticed.

Our original intention had been to investigate the car park, and although nothing much had been said we both had our private suspicions regarding the dark green Rover. The visit to Imogen's office had been a spur-of-the-moment impulse, but here we stood, with Mary Grey bearing down upon us, a sheaf of folders in her arms. There was no polite manner of retreat.

I muttered, 'What are we doing here, Niall? What reason do we have for coming?'

'We don't need one. Let me do the talking.'

I had never met Mrs Grey, but we had spoken at least twice weekly in recent months. I had relayed messages and conveyed my daughter's answers to questions of procedure and policy. My impression that this was a very nice lady was confirmed as she came smiling towards us.

We were led to an arrangement of several low chairs set around a coffee table. From what I had learned when acting as go-between for those phone conversations, I assumed that it was here group therapy sessions took place. There were two other, glass-enclosed areas of seating, where clients who required privacy could be interviewed.

We were offered coffee, which Niall declined. His new assertiveness amazed me. He at once took charge of what felt suspiciously like an interrogation. After Mrs Grey's enquiries about Immie's health had been answered, he got down to what I now realised was his real reason for this visit.

'Mr Mavsoni?' he said. 'I would like a word with him.'

A flicker of nervousness showed on the receptionist's face. 'I'm sorry,' she said swiftly, 'he's not available at present.'

'His car is in the car park, and we're quite prepared to wait.'

The uncompromising tone of Niall's voice had her flustered. 'What I meant was – he's with a client. A difficult case which could take some hours yet—'

Niall said, 'Somebody has been phoning my wife from this office; calls which leave her extremely distressed, and God knows, she doesn't need any further upset.'

'I call your house, Mr Donovan, but I always speak to Mrs Franklin here.' She turned to me for confirmation and I nodded.

'No,' said Niall, 'these calls come through to Imogen's mobile. Very few people are aware of that number.'

'Are you sure,' she asked 'that the caller is ringing from here?'

'I've had Telecom monitoring every single word.' He sounded convincing, but if Telecom were on the case, Niall had neglected to inform me.

'If the nuisance continues the police will have to be informed. Perhaps,' said Niall, 'you could relay that message to any interested party.'

We were ushered out through the swing doors. I looked back as we reached the last treads of the staircase, and sensing that we were being watched, I caught a fleeting glimpse of Mrs Mary Grey's blue dress and grey hair.

We walked in silence through the car park and back to the side road where Niall had parked Immie's car. I wondered what he was thinking, what he was planning. I belted myself into the front seat.

He sat for a moment or two, tapping the steering wheel.

I said at last, 'Are you disappointed that you didn't see him?'

'Not really. Just as well in the circumstances. I'm not ready for him yet. I don't know enough about him. I just wanted to get a feel of that place. Build up a picture.'

'And did you?'

'Ye-es. Something odd going on there, Nina. He was listening, you know, in one of those side rooms. The door to our left was not quite shut, and that receptionist kept glancing towards it.'

'Yes,' I said. 'She seemed quite nice on the telephone. Now I'm not sure about her.'

Imogen

I came out of the treatment room and made my way down to the hospital foyer. I went, as I always did, to the long green sofa that stood against a white wall.

They were not there.

The sofa was unoccupied. Nobody stood at the coffee machine.

I waited for a while, not knowing what to do, where to go. I felt the panic rising, like yeast in dough; it swelled, grew huge, until it filled every cell in my body.

Hot tears began to roll down my face.

It had happened as I had known it would. I had been abandoned. They were sick of me, and who could blame them. I don't know how long I stood there; it could have been an hour or seconds. And then Niall's arms were around me, holding me close. I laid my head on his shoulder, clung to him, and he patted my back as if I were an infant.

'It's okay,' he kept saying. 'The shopping took longer than usual. I'm so sorry, darling. But we're here now.'

They led me out to the car, holding my hands. On the drive home I sat with Nina in the back seat. She kept an arm about me, handed me tissues, and gradually I ceased to weep. We drove into the farmyard and I went to the car's boot to help them carry in the shopping. A single carrier bag held a packet of Rice Krispies and a box of assorted fruit yoghurts, and nothing else. I looked at their embarrassed faces and knew they had been lying to me.

Ten minutes later, when I was changing a smart dress for the comfortable old jogging suit in which I felt safe, the mobile bleeped and the awful words that came down the line told me exactly what Niall and Nina had been up to.

'You sicked your bloody husband on to me,' he whispered. 'How dare you! Don't ever do that again – I'm warning you – I'll get you—'

He cut the connection. I stood at the open bedroom window, and watched the grazing Dexters move slowly and methodically across the newly mown meadow. Niall was so proud of his small herd, his haystack; the silage he had made in spring. The egg-round and the logging business were helping to make the farm a viable proposition. Nina was beginning to talk about beekeeping. Selling honey. I envied my mother's deep involvement in all Niall's projects. I had lived so close to them in recent months. Except for the brief trips into Taunton with my husband and mother, these fields and woods, this shabby old house, had become my whole world. Yet still I had no part in anything that happened here.

There was a walk-in cupboard in the bedroom from which, when its doors were open, voices floated clearly upwards from the kitchen.

I was hanging my posh frock in that cupboard when I heard my mother say, 'You're so much closer to her these days. Has she ever mentioned this Mavsoni?'

'Not one scribbled word,' said my husband. There was a rattling of saucepans, the clink of cutlery and china. 'I was talking to one of the nurses. I asked her – sort of offhand – if Imogen had been visited by any of her colleagues when she was in hospital. She told me how that charming Mr Mavsoni had called in regularly, always bringing books and flowers.'

'Not really surprising,' murmured Nina. 'They have worked closely together—'

Niall sounded angry. 'Don't try to bullshit me, Nina. I have a very bad feeling about this bloke. I know what you're up to, and it won't work.'

Again my mother's voice was hesitant. 'Do we tell her we've visited her office?'

'I think we have to. That receptionist could mention that we've been there.'

'But what reason can we give?' Nina sounded worried. 'We had no business being there – not really.'

Niall said, 'Curiosity. We wanted to see for ourselves where the mugging happened. Once on the premises it seemed only polite to go up and have a word with her kindly and concerned workmates.'

Now there was admiration in my mother's voice. 'I didn't know you were so devious,' she laughed.

He said, 'This isn't funny, Nina. Immie could have been murdered.'

'I know,' she said. 'When I see the pitiful state of her, I'm also ready to do murder. The man who did this must be found and punished.'

'Somebody is going to pay,' my husband answered. 'No matter how long it takes, or what it costs, I'll have him.'

The whirring of the blender masked all further conversation.

I sat on the bed, my legs too weak to hold me upright.

Through the open window I could see clearly the outline of the dark green Rover parked under the beech trees in the top lane.

Some of Paul's telephone threats had been that he would ill-wish me if I ever thought of naming him as my assailant.

I believed him. Believed that he possessed the means to destroy me by the power of thought. The power of his evil thought. His repeated taunt was that I was still sick. 'Not getting any better, are you? Can't eat, can't sleep. Can't leave the house. Useless, aren't you, Imogen? Mummy still doing everything for you? Poor old thing. She looks quite worn out. You should be ashamed of yourself. As for dear Niall, your protective hubby. Whoever would have dreamed he would buckle on his armour and rush to your defence? He'd soon change his tune if he knew the truth about you. Snow-white Imogen, the frigid ice-queen? Poor deceived Niall. He never guessed you were a whore underneath those long skirts and sober black. Remember that red frock, and those two scraps of silk lace? Remember the way you tore them off? Just couldn't wait, could you? I've seen some sex-starved women, but darling – you broke all records. And then there was—'

I could break the telephone connection. I could stay within the house. I could refuse to speak on the grounds that impulsive speech might incriminate me.

What I could not do was deny Paul's power over me. A year ago, six months ago, I would have ridiculed the notion of ill-wishing. We had actually talked about it once.

'Overlooking' was what he'd called it. He cited instances of people whose lives had been destroyed, who had grown sickly and then died as a result of a relative or neighbour's malevolent thought-waves.

'After all,' he had said, 'there are certain people who have the benign gift of spiritual healing; and everything in the universe has its other face. Think about it, darling. Overlooking is nothing more than the dark side of healing.'

His eyes were hypnotic, his tone convincing. Even then, and against my better judgement, I had half believed him.

And yet there were times when his control of my mind was less than total. Against my will the dangerous thoughts edged into my head. I could speak if I really wanted to.

I could say out loud, to Niall, to Nina, to Gloria, to the police, 'It was Paul Mavsoni. He did this to me. He is a seriously dangerous person.'

The mobile bleeped, right on cue, as it always did when I had mutinous thoughts. He seemed to be able to tune into my brainwaves. I picked it up, pressed the button. He said, as he always did, 'Don't even think about it. One wrong word and you know what will happen. Be a pity, won't it, if anything nasty should happen to Fran your daughter, your grandchild . . .'

Nina

We were into September, and the only change was in the weather. The fierce and enervating heat of July and August gave way to cold nights, and mild days of golden light. Imogen, shut away in the dimness of the house, kept fast to her sofa like the heroine of some Victorian melodrama. She read books and magazines, listened to music, and waited for the sound of the bleeper on her mobile phone. Roscoe sat at her feet, behaving like Elizabeth Barrett's lapdog. On one of her hospital check-ups Niall and I were called in yet again by the senior doctor.

'We are becoming increasingly concerned,' he said. 'Mrs Donovan's physical injuries have healed. There is no longer any reason why she should not speak, eat a normal diet, or resume her previous lifestyle.'

Niall and I glanced helplessly at one another. What did he expect us to do about it? We had heard all this before. We could hardly force-feed her with roast beef and Yorkshire pudding, or drag her willy-nilly around the fields and woods. As for returning to her office!

'I know – I know,' said the man in the white coat, 'you must be sick of hearing me say this. But you are the ones who are closest to her.' He leaned forward and addressed Niall. 'A pretty personal question I'm afraid, and I apologise for it. But the state of your marriage – is it—?'

'Never better.' Niall spoke with utter conviction. 'In fact, I can say it has never been so good. We had hit a bad patch, several bad patches if I'm being truthful, and in the weeks before the mugging I was on the brink of chucking it all in, and disappearing. But the shock of what happened seemed to change things, changed both of us. You see,' Niall said simply, 'she needs me now. For the first time since we married, Immie's turned to me, trusts me. It's the most wonderful thing that's ever happened to us.'

'Are you sure, Mr Donovan, that with the best of intentions you are not in some subtle way encouraging this pleasant state of dependence in your wife? Especially since it seems to be to your advantage.'

Niall hooted. 'Subtle? Me? Ask my ma-in-law here. She'll tell you I'm about as subtle as a hand grenade. No, doctor, I'm doing all I can to persuade my wife out of this depression. But nothing works. There's something going on with her that we don't know about. Surely you can't think that we enjoy seeing her in this state?'

The doctor turned to me. 'What do you think might be going on, Mrs Franklin?'

I paused before answering, wanting to get it right. I was enraged at the unwarranted attack on Niall and the slur on his motives. Bloody doctors! What did they know?

I said, keeping my voice carefully neutral. 'Before my daughter was attacked she had begun to behave very oddly. Unlike herself, unlike the quiet responsible caring person she had always been.'

'People do change, Mrs Franklin. Women approaching their fifties often take a long and critical look at their lives—'

'It was another bloke my wife was taking a "long look" at,' Niall burst out. 'If it's any of your damned business! Perhaps he's the one you should be treating to these snide insinuations.'

'Do you know who this man is, Mr Donovan?'

I quickly intervened. 'No we don't, and if we did it has no bearing on the situation.' I stood up, giving Niall a long hard look. I opened the door, obliging him to follow, leaving the senior man standing by his desk, astonished at our temerity and lack of proper respect for his white coat.

The beautiful autumn stayed with us.

I thought about nothing else but my daughter's agoraphobia, for that is what it was. Short of burning the house down, I could see no possible way of removing her from it. Since I could not drive, and Niall worked from sunrise till nightfall, I could not even suggest a trip in the car.

Then one morning, with the sun showing up the cracks and peeling paintwork on the kitchen walls, I had an inspired thought. Immie hated the smell of paint, she was allergic to it, it made her nauseous. What if we were to insist, Niall and I, on redecorating the downstairs rooms of the house before winter set in? Paint a single door or window frame in any enclosed space and the smell will spread upwards into the attics. Imogen would be forced to take refuge in the orchard, and that first move back to normality would surely lead on at least to a shopping trip in Taunton?

I found Niall in the barn, packing eggs into boxes for next day's delivery.

'How much redecorating are you thinking of?' he asked.

'Well, the kitchen is urgent. So is the sitting room. The front hall could do with—'

'Can't afford it,' he said, 'and anyway it might not work.'

'You don't have to afford it. Consider it as my Christmas present.'

I could see he was prepared to argue. 'Look,' I said, 'We can't go on like this. I am as much a prisoner as Imogen. I don't know if I can face another winter cooped up here.'

'Don't you think,' he said gently, 'that maybe you do too much for her?'

'Yes,' I said, 'but so do you. Perhaps a little less consideration would be a wise move at this stage. Make the house unbearable for a few weeks. See what happens then.'

'You're determined to do this.' He paused, examined a brown egg, then placed it carefully in the box. 'Well, okay. But on one condition. I shall pay you back as soon as I can afford to. And another thing. It's time you had a day off. You'll need to go into town to choose paint and wallpaper. Joe's grandson can give you a lift in. Meanwhile, you'll have to tell Immie what your plans are.' He sounded doubtful and I rushed to reassure him.

'She'll be thrilled,' I gushed. 'She can choose the colours and the style she wants. It'll take her mind off things, stop her brooding; she might even speak?'

I was talking rubbish and we both knew it. But Niall was too kind to point this out. He patted my arm. 'I'll have a word with Joe,' he said, 'arrange for your lift into Taunton with Jason.' Niall was humouring me. But who could blame him?

I never know what to talk about when in the company of teenage boys. Jason was learning the undertaker business, he aspired to becoming a funeral director. Having had my three-score years and ten, I was myself a little too close to requiring his services to find a discussion of his career prospects a comfortable option.

It was obvious that he loved cars. Fast cars. He had, he told me, passed his driving test just four weeks ago. I clung to the seat belt I normally loathed, and consoled myself with the fact that nobody knew these twisty dipping lanes better than Jason. He had been travelling up and down them since birth. He did not even find it necessary to hoot, as did most other drivers, when turning any of the many blind corners.

The car, he informed me proudly, had cost all of £400. I began to talk about papering and painting, and my need for a reliable decorator, as a distraction from the blur of passing hedgerows, and his habit of keeping one hand on the steering wheel, and the other hand hanging out the window.

Jason knew the very man.

Totally reliable he told me, stamping hard on the accelerator, and hauling on the steering. Gavin had recently refurbished the Chapel of Rest. Very tasteful job he had made it too. And quiet! Why, the people in the Chapel had hardly known that he was there.

I held on to the edge of my seat and refrained from observing that most of them were dead. I was becoming hysterical. I pulled myself together and asked for this paragon's last name and address. I instantly regretted my question when the hand which alone controlled the wheel began to rummage in the glove compartment. Heart in mouth, I assured him I would find the business card he sought. Five minutes later, having rummaged through chocolate wrappers and empty cigarette packets, and having dislodged several curiously named, foil-wrapped items on to the floor, I found the paint-stained square of white card.

Hands shaking, face burning, I stuffed the packages of condoms back into the glove compartment. Jason, not one bit put out, observed, 'Always go prepared – that's what I say!'

I thought about Joe, his grandfather, who touched his cap and always knocked politely on our open kitchen door. Generation gap? But Joe couldn't drive a car. He just about coped with our ancient Ford tractor. He would never have made a funeral director.

I asked Jason to drop me off in the vicinity of High Street. I thanked him for the lift and he grinned engagingly, waved the hand which was rarely on the steering wheel, shouted, 'Any time!' and vanished in a black cloud of exhaust fumes.

I stood for some moments beside a travel agent's window gazing at, but not really seeing, advertisements for holidays in Ibiza and Cyprus. My legs felt unsteady, my pulse rate rapid. I began to walk. As I turned the corner into High Street I saw with relief that the OPEN sign was hanging on the door of the green-and-white café which stands at the entrance to Bath Place. I went in and claimed my favourite table from which I could look down the long narrow thoroughfare and view its ancient buildings.

I ordered toast and a large pot of strong tea. It was still early; I was the café's first customer that morning. Out in Bath Place the shopkeepers were taking down their shutters. The ladies at the WI shop were once more about their usual Friday business of setting out their wares: homemade cakes and jams, pastries and pickles, handknitted sweaters and patchwork quilts. A small queue was already forming beside their shop door.

This view of normal living was reassuring yet painful. I ate and drank very slowly, wanting to prolong the moment. How easy it was, when caught up in a nightmare as we had been since January, to forget that for most other people life was humdrum. Imogen and I had lost a summer. All around us at Sad Acre crops had grown and been brought to harvest. Cows had calved, pigs had farrowed. Even the wild cats which lived in the haystack under the Dutch barn, and which were so deeply suspicious of us they almost never revealed their offspring, had led their kittens out one April morning and paraded them across the farmyard, as if even they sensed safety in the total indifference of these three humans who were their close neighbours.

Niall, because his livelihood, his very survival, depended upon normality had continued to live in the real world. He had even benefited, if that was the right word, from the horror which had left Immie and me suspended in no-man's-land. Imogen's neediness had reawakened Niall's love for her. His anger at her situation and his protectivness had engendered in her a love and respect she had never previously felt.

I alone, from the very best of motives, had done, and was still doing, the wrong things. Like a grief that would not go away, the spasms of guilt swept over me again and again. 'Perhaps you do too much for her,' Niall had said. It was true. What he did not know about, and I could not explain, was my lifelong neglect of my daughter in every way that counted.

Now, because of the way I am, have always been, I was over-compensating. Trying to atone for the omissions of many years in a few months. Strange how clearly I could see this while eating toast and drinking tea in Bath Place.

My resolve, which had until now been half-hearted, stiffened. It might be a cruel act to fill the house with workmen and the smell of paint, but strong action needed to be taken, and quickly.

I walked out into September sunshine, found a phone box, and left Niall's name and number on Gavin's answering gadget. I wandered around the shops, had lunch in the Goodlands Gardens café, then made my way to the taxi rank in Corporation Street. I had carefully avoided the little garden which lay between Bath Place and the public library, recalling the out-of-body experience I once had there.

The driver remembered me. I tapped on his window and he said, 'Hello there! Hop in. Where'll it be then? Same place as last time? Sad Acre Farm?'

I said, 'Eventually. But first of all I would like you to detour around the area that was once called North Town.'

He pulled out into heavy traffic, driving safely with both hands, his gaze fixed on the road ahead. We came into North Street and crossed the Tone bridge.

'You still interested in that old Turnpike House?'

'Yes,' I said, 'very much so.'

We came into Staplegrove Road where the traffic thinned, and turned into French Weir Avenue, where my driver halted. He waved a hand, first left and then right.

'Reckon this must have been the area called North Town two hundred years ago. French Weir on the one hand. Flook House on the other.'

'And the turnpike gate, the Toll House, where were they?'

He scratched his head. 'I've been looking into that. You got me thinking, see. I looked at some old maps. From what I can make out, that turnpike was somewhere close to Flook House, which is nowadays the borough council offices.'

'You've done very well,' I said admiringly.

His smile was modest. 'Local knowledge. You can't beat it.'

He turned the ignition key and glanced sideways. 'Where now? You want to look at Flook House?'

'Not just now,' I said slowly. 'I've had a long day, and my family will be worrying about me.'

'Whenever you want,' he said cheerfully. 'You know where to find me.'

I was disappointed. I felt certain that no sign of Georgie Barnacle's Toll House could possibly have survived in an area which housed borough council offices. Harry (we were now on first-name terms) talked about his family; asked about mine. We were in sight of the Blackdown Hills when he said, 'There's something else you might like to know about old Taunton. My missus; now like I said before, she's not interested in local history. But I mentioned North Town to her and that old turnpike, and up she comes with the queerest tale you ever did hear. Now you know how these old yarns get handed down in families; bits left out, bits tagged on, 'til you can't say what is truth or what's invention.'

He paused, changed gears as we approached a hill. 'But my missus. she swears by what her grandmother told her. Seems like her family kept a pub called the Black Horse back in the late seventeen hundreds. This inn stood close to the turnpike gate, and the story goes that a foul murder was done down there in the nearby fields. A young woman was beaten to death, and her body was found lying in a bed of wild garlic.'

He glanced sideways at me. 'You all right?'

I nodded yes, but he braked, then halted. 'My God,' he said, 'I'm so sorry. I should never have told you such a tale.'

'I'm okay. Really I am. It's just a bit similar to something that happened recently in my own family. Nobody died. But she could have. Oh yes. She could have.'

We travelled in silence until we reached the farm gate. I paid him and he stuffed the notes into his pocket but refused the tip. I said, 'I might need you again quite soon to drive me into town.'

'Any time,' he said, and as he spoke I saw enlightenment hit him like a blow between the eyes.

'That was your daughter. The poor woman who was mugged last New Year in a Taunton car park?'

'Yes,' I said. 'That was Imogen. My daughter.'

Later that night, while Niall and Imogen slept, I read Barnacle's book to the last page. The parallels were all there. All that remained was for me to persuade my daughter that she should also read it.

Imogen

I had known for several days that I was growing weaker.

My head ached, my limbs felt heavy; the will to move, to eat, to breathe, grew less with every phone call from him.

He had said that this was how it would be. That I needed to be punished. That I had failed him. He was sorry that he had no option but to make sure that I continued to sicken. *To sicken even unto death.* Those were his very words.

If he had been my client I would have categorised him as suffering from a serious personality disorder.

The thought came out of nowhere. It hit me with the force of a lightning bolt. I was watching from the bedroom window on that September evening. He was sitting in the Range Rover, up in the top lane, looking down on the farmstead. Wishing me ill. Wishing me dead. Sending me sick thoughts. I wondered why it had taken me so many months to reach such an obvious conclusion about his state of mind.

But he had not been my client, had he? I thought I loved him. And what infatuated, middle-aged woman under the spell of a charismatic lover will pause to analyse him, to tot up his peculiarities, and admit that he is marginally insane?

I began to consider the categories of disorder he might be experiencing. Obsessive-compulsive? Hysterical? Paranoid? Histrionic? Passive-aggressive? Personality disorder is not a mental illness. The sufferer is neither psychotic or neurotic, but has a distorted view of the world around him, making it difficult for him to cope with relationships, and inclined to blame others.

I remembered the way Paul functioned. His charm. His ability to empathise, to flatter; to be all things to all people. And then there was his dark side. His refusal to confide; to share his thoughts, to be open and giving; the superstitious fears that governed his every thought and action. Relief flooded through me as I began to realise that I was actually capable of distancing myself from him; of being objective about him. I recalled the way he had come into my life; the series of events, as told by him, which had led to his appearance in my office. That tale no longer seemed plausible; and if he had lied about one thing why not another?

Perhaps his whole life had been one huge deception?

The man called Paul Mavsoni might well be his own sick-brained invention. If this was indeed the case, why was I allowing him to dominate me? To kill me, slowly?

Disconnected thoughts tumbled in my head, making me dizzy, reckless, daring. When the mobile bleeped I did not answer.

I carried the phone into the bathroom, sat on the edge of the bath and stared at the locked door. I had not looked closely at myself full-face in a mirror since the night of the beating, when Gloria had forced me to view what Paul had done. Now I found courage to examine my changed looks in great detail.

I stood before the bathroom mirror. They had done their best, those surgeons. They had also warned me that this was as good as it would get. What I saw now was a face that resembled a puzzle which was missing a few pieces. Features that were slightly out of alignment. A jaw that was fractionally lopsided. Teeth which made smiling a doubtful pleasure. A nose that was not quite straight.

The overall impression was of a face which had been taken apart and glued inexpertly back together. The same could be said of my mind, which Paul had also rearranged.

The difference was that I now felt I had the power to repair the emotional damage he had done me. I remembered the clients I had worked with, women who had been similarly disfigured by their violent partners. I recalled the anger I had felt on their behalf. Standing now before the full-length mirror I was seized by the bitter rage I should have experienced many months ago, and was appalled at the thinness of my body, my gaunt looks.

The bleeping ceased, but almost at once began again.

I picked up the phone, pressed the button and heard the familiar poison coming down the line.

'Where were you?' he demanded. 'Don't start playing silly buggers with me. You know your days are numbered, don't you? I can sense your weakness. I can finish you off any time I want to. I've done this before to women who have let me down. Ever wondered, have you Imogen, what happened to my wife?'

He could go on like this for twenty minutes; his voice was mesmeric. I felt myself weakening, just listening to him. So often in the past months I had tried and failed to once and for all slam the phone down on him. This time I knew that my sanity, my very life, depended on my actions of the next few minutes.

With a tremendous effort I closed my mind against him. I stood up on legs so weak they could hardly support me. I carried the mobile into the bedroom. As I moved I could still hear his voice, but only faintly. I sat down on the edge of the bed and gently placed the still-chattering instrument on the quilt.

With that single action I knew that I had begun to dismiss him. I clasped my hands tight together and still looking at the mobile I made one more tremendous effort to close my mind against the evil; and this time I succeeded. This was no longer personality disorder. This was madness.

He seemed to know what I was about. The voice from the phone became a shrill scream. I clenched my hands until the finger joints ached. I visualised my mind as a remote-controller of television channels. I simply pushed a button in my head and *banished him completely*.

Now think! I told myself. *Think* – this man is crazy. He is a dangerous, lethal, murderous madman. And now something weird was happening in the region of my larynx. The muscles and tendons in my neck began to tighten, my breathing grew rapid and uneven.

I snatched up the mobile, and the words burst from my throat like shot from a rifle. I hadn't planned what I would say, hadn't believed myself capable of speech. In a voice that was hoarse from lack of use I told him, 'Shut up, you crazy bastard! I know now what you're up to, and it won't work any more. You hear me. It's finished.' I balanced the mobile on the window ledge, tipped it gently with one finger and heard it crash into the paved yard.

I was trembling all over. I forced myself to watch from the window as the dark green car began to move slowly down through the network of lanes which led back into the town.

The pressure in my head increased, became unbearable. I fixed my gaze on the red winking of the tail light and as it finally passed out of view, the pressure eased. I felt a crawling sensation in my scalp; a sense of some foul and indescribable evil lifting and whirling away into the darkness of the beech woods.

I continued to sit beside the open window until twilight deepened into night. In control once again of my own mind, my own thoughts, I was able to begin to work out just how far I had veered from the reasonable, quiet, organised woman I had always considered myself to be.

I wanted to put all the blame on Paul, but the changes within myself had begun with my mother's move to the village of Ashkeepers. The dramas of her past life had affected us all, but I alone had been the one who could not accept that Nina was not like other people's mothers. That she was not, and never would be, the cosy, gossipy, demonstrative woman to whom I could tell all my troubles. Nina had her own style. She couldn't help the way she was, the way circumstances had made her, and to be fair I don't suppose I had ever been the sort of daughter she had dreamed of having.

In all those years we had been virtual strangers, but when

I really needed her – there she was, tender and concerned, a proper mother, giving me her full attention. You could say that Paul Mavsoni's fists, having battered me into submission, had brought out the maternal streak in Nina and cured me forever of my stupid pride.

There were other benefits if I cared to list them.

Niall, after years of indifference, unfaithfulness and blatant lying, now seemed able finally to come close, to confide his fears and hopes; to love me. My rearranged, unattractive face seemed actually to please him. When I was good to look at, he never said so. Now he insisted I was more beautiful than ever, and although this was a lie I could see that he believed what he was saying. And who was I to argue with him?

Nina

Her first spoken words in ten months were not what we had dreamed of. She came smiling into the kitchen that morning, which in itself was unusual. She wore the dark red velvet leisure suit and I noticed, belatedly, that her pudding-basin haircut had grown longer, so that her black hair now curled into her neck and over her ears. There was even a hint of healthy colour under the prison pallor of her face. She pulled out a chair and sat facing Niall.

'Oh my!' she said, 'that bacon smells wonderful. I feel really hungry this morning.'

I almost dropped the grill pan. So many improvements in so short a time? Niall and I exchanged warning glances which asked, 'What the hell has happened to her?' and a shake of the head which meant, 'Be careful. Don't ask questions!'

Astonishment kept us mute. Delight would come later. My fingers trembled as I laid extra bacon on the grill, halved more tomatoes, and cracked eggs into a basin. I was glad to be busy, to have my back turned towards her so that she could not see my tears.

I heard Niall's nervous laughter. Not knowing what to say, he muttered, 'You must have slept well. You're look-ing better.'

Her laughter sounded raw, her voice hoarse, and I realised that she must be feeling equally nervous and uncertain.

I slapped a loaded plate down before her, angled the toast

rack closer and refilled her coffee mug. I looked at the two bent heads, the embarrassed way they were pushing food around their plates.

'Oh, for pity's sake!' I yelled, 'let's not be so bloody British about this.' I leaned across the table and gave Niall a shove which almost had him off his chair. 'Forget the stiff upper lip act. She's *talking*, you great lummox! Well, don't just sit there mangling that bacon!'

In two great bounds he was beside her. He lifted her out of her chair and danced her around the kitchen. I wiped my eyes on a corner of my apron and looked towards the open kitchen door. An audience of three, grandfather, father and teenaged son stood grinning above their load of paint cans, brushes, and stepladders.

The decorators had arrived.

I didn't ask her what had happened.

It must have been something cataclysmic to have effected miracles of such proportions in so short a time, and I feared that any probing at this stage might send her back into that painful silence.

It was her suggestion that she should sit in the orchard while the gloss painting was in process. She was still weak and underweight and the autumn days were growing cooler, so cosseting would be in order. Niall hauled the waterproof cover from the hammock and carried out a garden table. I filled a Thermos with coffee and insisted that she wear a woollen jacket.

With Roscoe for company, and books to read, she was happily settled in fresh air and sunshine, her voice and her appetite restored. Immie had come back to us, not fully functioning, but nearly.

I almost waltzed my way back into the house, ridiculously grateful for the disruption caused by ladders and dust sheets, and the smell of paint. These were interruptions in routine which I was glad to deal with.

As I skirted the house I passed beneath Immie's bedroom window. I walked down the flagged path and my foot struck a small dark object and sent it skittering away into the bushes. I picked it up and found that it was Imogen's mobile, its plastic casing cracked in several places. I looked up at the window from which it must have fallen, or been thrown? The same window which gave a direct view of the top lane.

I found Niall in the home field. I handed him the mobile, telling him where I had found it.

'She was carrying it at supper time,' he said.

'She wouldn't have dropped it accidentally,' I told him, 'she was always clutching the wretched thing as if her very life depended on it.'

'So she must have deliberately thrown it out the window and smashed it.' Niall gave me a level look of satisfaction. 'You know what this means, don't you, Nina? She's broken her connection with him.'

'Hence,' I said, 'the miraculous change in her this morning.'

Niall put his hands up to his face and rubbed his eyes. He was even closer to tears than I was. I could see his shoulders heaving.

'It's over,' I said. 'Whatever it was, whatever hold he had over her, it's finished.'

Niall said, 'I should have put a stop to it myself, long ago.'

'How could you? We were only guessing it was him, and Imogen certainly wasn't telling.'

'I failed her. I should have gone down to Taunton and beaten the daylights out of him.'

'And been arrested for assault. Considering the state Immie has been in, what good would that have done?'

'Probably none. But I wouldn't be feeling so bloody guilty now.' He squared his shoulders. 'She owes me – both of us – some sort of explanation.'

'It's over, Niall,' I repeated. 'Only Imogen could end it, and that is exactly what she's done. I suspect that smashed mobile has more significance than either of us realise. Whatever was going on, it's better we don't ask questions of her. Let's be thankful for what we have. She's just eaten an enormous breakfast, she's recovered her speech, and she's sitting in the orchard. That is all we need to know.'

Come October, when the white mists lay in the hollows of Niall's river fields, and the Tone ran brown and shining through Taunton town, I would remember those over-optimistic words; and regret them.

Imogen

I began to read Barnacle's book at the end of September.

My head, released from Paul's domination, felt curiously empty, and inclined to drift away into dreams that lacked all meaning. What I needed was something gripping that would hold my concentration, and I knew from the way Nina brought me the book every morning, placed without comment on the tray which held a mid-morning snack of coffee and homemade biscuits, that she desperately wanted me to read it. But because she and Niall had this private arrangement that I was not to be pressured in any way, the repeated appearance of the book was as far as she would go. She had this strong conviction that we are all the end result of whatever ancestry we happen to have inherited. I had heard the theory from her many times. When I was a child I had this vivid image of all those ancient men and women, traipsing wearily before me, bestowing bits and pieces of themselves that I would rather not have, like this one's black hair and that one's ill temper. But it was always her father's family who were carefully resurrected by Nina, to hand on their doubtful attributes. Her mother's relatives were never mentioned. It was as if we had sprung from a single favoured line. From what I had already read of Barnacle's chronicles, the Lambtons' endowment was not altogether to be desired, and I wondered at my mother's persistence in forcing its details on me.

Well all right, there was the snob value of the Earl's daughter Pennina; if you are impressed by that sort of thing?

Having read about Pennina Lambton's various crimes, her kidnapping of her infant half-brother; her involvement in the murder of his nursemaid; not to mention her marriage of convenience to the Toll House keeper Ezra Lambton, and her shabby treatment of him, I could only hope she had kept her unpleasant genes to herself. Along with highway robbery and her deliberate casting of suspicion on a band of gypsies for the evils she had herself committed; she was not exactly the type one would have been proud to call grandmama!

I had dipped into early chapters of the book over a period of several months prior to my relocation in Taunton. I found it fascinating stuff, but could feel no kinship with the Lambtons.

I had reached the point in the narrative where Pennina had been condemned to hang or burn (or maybe both) for her many crimes; her sentencing watched from the gallery seats of the courtroom by her husband Ezra Lambton, and her one-time servant Georgie Barnacle and his gypsy wife Coralina.

On reaching this stage of the tale, it occurred to me that Pennina Lambton was at this time still childless. Since she was about to meet her end on a pyre or gibbet it seemed unlikely that Nina and I, and all those other Lambtons in between, could possibly have been descended from her.

But still there was Nina's daily insistence on presenting the book with the mid-morning snack; and with the whole house still reeking of white – with a hint of lemon – gloss paint, my only refuge was the orchard. I picked up the book that morning in a fit of irritation. My mother had placed a tooled-leather bookmark at the page where she obviously wished me to begin.

I was not even curious as I pulled out the marker. I nibbled on biscuits and drank coffee, and began to read.

BARNACLE'S BOOK. CHAPTER SEVEN

Pennina Lambton's execution had been ordered to take place

on the last day of April. The gallows and such viewing stands as were deemed necessary for the comfort of the populace, to be erected meanwhile on the green of Ashkeepers village.

The burning of witches had been forbidden by law since the year of 1735, and so the exact nature of Pennina's despatch had been carefully omitted from the fliers which were being distributed throughout the County of Somerset. But it was well known that in the isolated village of Ashkeepers hangings and burnings still frequently took place; a blind eye being turned by the judiciary. It had been the declaration made in court by her husband, Ezra Lambton, which had brought about Pennina's downfall. At the end of the trial, when the three had been exonerated from all blame, Ezra, Georgie and Coralina had been instructed to wait upon the judge in his private room in the rear of the Assize Court, where he would later 'have matters to discuss with them which would be to their advantage'.

Georgie had long since heard talk of the new Toll House to be built in Taunton. He had recently asked Coralina to leave her people, to abandon the Romany way of life, to live with him beneath a house-roof; all this in the frail hope that he might obtain the position of keeper of the Taunton turnpike. Now, standing before his lordship Sir Jeffery Roehampton, he could hardly take in the news he had hoped for, prayed for.

'North Town, Taunton . . . a tidy house . . . newbuilt . . . outbuildings . . . frequent traffic coming through . . . a need for two men and a strong boy . . . the position of head turnpike keeper to be taken up by George Barnacle . . . to be assisted by Ezra Lambton.'

George received the keys of the North Town Toll House from Sir Jeffery's own hand. His elation, and that of Ezra, knew no bounds. Hand in hand with Coralina they fairly skipped down the flight of steps that led from the Assize Court. But their joy was dimmed as they reached the street. Pennina Lambton, wearing leg-irons, a leather halter about her neck, was being led towards a wagon which would transport her to the Jail Lane prison.

Now, out in the street, they saw what had not been

visible within the court. Pennina, who was by this time no longer a young woman and, by her own admission to her husband, barren, was clearly in an interesting condition, her body ungainly and great with child.

North Town was an area of Taunton which was low-lying, damp, and dirty in all seasons. It was made remarkable by its many green and seething ditches, among which dwelt several hundreds of ducks, whose quacking and clacking could be heard from daylight till dusk. It was also a place famous for its fields of wild garlic, and the ferocious nature of its inns and taverns. The building of the new road and its accompanying Toll House had brought an increase of traffic and business to North Town, without improving the bad reputation of the place.

Ezra, Georgie and Coralina, following directions given them by an urchin, took the path which led past the Black Horse Inn, made a sharp turn at a corner, and found themselves standing before the turnpike gatehouse.

The single-storey house was built of the local golden limestone. The roof was of thatch, the windows small with leaded-glass panes. A number of outbuildings stood in a fenced space behind the house. Ezra and George began at once to plan for the house-cow they would keep, the pork-pigs and laying hens; a goat or two. They would also need to collect Ezra's furniture and livestock from the Ashkeepers' Toll House. This task to be carried out when they attended the execution of Pennina.

Meanwhile, they would be obliged to sleep on loose straw, and cooking would perforce be done out in the open, with a cauldron suspended above a fire of sticks, Romany fashion.

The turnpike was to open for business two weeks hence, and George and Ezra must become familiar with the town in which they would now be working and living; an experience which would be very different from the quiet isolation of their former habitation.

In the nature of men who consider their own affairs of

business to be of prime importance, they gave no thought to Coralina, set down as she was in a strange environment of bustling streets, rowdy taverns, and in the exclusive company of *gorgios*, with only a rare glimpse of her own kind when processions of flat-carts, ponies and donkeys wound their way through Taunton and out again, as the Romanies made for their summer *atchintans* in the Blackdown Hills. Already she was missing her parents, her sisters, the evening gatherings around the fire. She had lived her life in woods and forests, halting for short periods of time and then moving, always moving on, up hill and down dale through Somerset and Dorset. She had not thought how it would be to stay in the one place, daylong, nightlong, with only George and Ezra for company, and those two with their heads together, forever talking about tariffs and weights and measures, and the price of turnpike tickets.

It was a sparkling April morning when Coralina had fairly ached to be out with her own people on the white and winding road that led up to Buckland St Mary and the sweet shelter of the beech trees of Dommet Wood, when a familiar whistle brought her running from the house and into the fields where the wild garlic grew.

He was leaning against the slender bole of a silver birch tree. He did not run to meet her, but stayed, hands in pockets, as if it mattered not at all whether Coralina came to him, or remained beneath her husband's roof.

Her joy at seeing him, the fact that he had slipped away from the company even for an hour, and come to find her, brought tears into her eyes. She held his hands, looked up into his face.

'Ah, cousin,' she said. 'Ah, Silva. You can't know how good it is to see thee. What news of my father and mother, of my sisters?'

'Lina,' he said, using the name he had called her by when they were children, 'Lina – it breaks my heart to find thee in this stinking place. As for thy family, they are well but sad since you are gone.'

She loosened her hands from his grip and stared about her, as if seeing North Town for the first time; the hundreds of brown ducks quacking and splashing in the vile ditches, the low, foul mist that hung in wisps among the trees and hedges.

She looked back to the small squat house of yellow stone, with its many fences and heavy gates, and its three tall chimneys, and knew it to be her prison.

'George says we are fortunate to be here,' she said bravely. 'It is what he has always wanted, to be his own master. George has never been so happy.'

'And what do you want, cousin? What gladdens your heart?'

She took a step back from him, suddenly nervous of his power over her. It was many months since she had seen him, and in that time he had grown taller, his chest and shoulders broadened, a new alarming sureness in his voice, and in his manner. She studied the face which until now had been as familiar to her as that of her father, and a pang of fear twisted in her stomach. The high cheekbones, the deep-set no-colour eyes, the long-lipped mouth and jutting jaw were the same yet different. Frighteningly different.

He grew restless under her gaze. 'What is it?' he asked.

'You are no longer the boy I once danced with,' she whispered. 'What has happened to you?'

He laughed, a brief and ugly sound. 'The boy became a man,' he said, 'on the night we laid together, and on the morning after, when you would not own me.'

She turned away from him and looked back towards the house, fearful that George and Ezra might return to find her absent. She remembered the long black nights of winter in the great forest, the first nights of her marriage, and George's indifference, the bitter frost and deep snows, when he had turned away from her, had refused the warmth of her arms, of their shared bed.

'It was but the once,' she said. 'It should not have happened.'

'But it did.' He grabbed her wrist, pulled her round to face him.

'Tell me it meant nothing. Tell me you would sooner lie with your red-haired, red-faced lummox of a *gorgio* husband. Have you told him it was Silva who took your maidenhead? Silva who was man enough to be your first lover? But perhaps he knew that you were not a maiden? Perhaps he knew the signs?'

'No,' she murmured. 'I have not told him. He knows nothing at all of what took place 'twixt thee and me. I was his first woman, so he did not know the signs. He must never know, Silva! He is a good man, he is kind and gentle with me. If you ever tell – then I will call you "liar". No one would believe you. Especially my husband. I will never play the *lubbeny* again, with you or any other man.'

'Makes no odds,' he told her. 'I was your first, and that has made thee mine. You may live with him for the next fifty years, but it is Silva who owns your soul, and always will do.'

He looked so strange and wild that once again she feared him. 'Go,' she begged him. 'Go – and never come back. If he sees us together—'

She turned and ran towards the house, scattering the wild ducks, bruising the garlic bulbs beneath her bare feet so that their sickly odour rose in a cloud about her head. When George and Ezra returned she was skinning and gutting a fine pair of fat rabbits. She kept her head low and her fingers busy. She gathered from their talk that four days hence they would, all three, be travelling north to Ashkeepers village, to collect Ezra Lambton's furniture and effects. But principally to witness the hanging of Pennina Lambton.

Ezra hired two flat-carts and a pair of steady horses from a Taunton carrier named Pavey. They set off on the day before the execution was due to happen, the carts loaded up with straw and blankets, for they would pass the coming nights on the open carts. Coralina had packed cold roasted rabbit meat in vine leaves, and fresh baked bread in a wooden box. Ezra supplied three stone jars filled with good wine and a basket full of apples. The men were sad-faced and silent as they rode out of Taunton town. Coralina tried to comprehend their deep need to see the end of Pennina Lambton. It was as if they would not believe that she was truly dead until they had witnessed her hanging with their own eyes.

Pennina had deceived them both, then attempted to blame them for her own crimes. Yet, in their separate and different ways, both men had loved her.

Perhaps they still felt some affection for her? As they left the town behind them, and came on to the winding uphill roads that led to the north, Coralina felt her heart lift. Oh, but it was so good to be on the move, to breathe sweet air, feel the sun and wind upon her face. But for the grim faces of her companions, she would have started singing. Then she remembered her cousin Silva Lee.

She had known for a long time that he had loving feelings for her; she had been aware of his distress when she and Georgie Barnacle had married. She remembered how many times she and Silva had performed the love dance before the assembled groups of lords and ladies in their castles and fine houses.

Even then, when she was very young, she had sensed that the dance held significance for Silva, and none for her.

She had gone to him on that night in the snowbound forest out of loneliness and misery, seeking comfort as if she were still a child and he an older brother.

But as it turned out, it was her husband who behaved towards her like an older brother, and Silva her cousin who became for that one night, and with her consent, her first lover.

The memory shamed her. She took firmer hold of the slack rein and urged the horse along. She stole a glance at the young husband who sat beside her, his shoulders slumped, his head bowed. She loved this red-haired giant; trusted him with her very life. If Silva should ever tell Georgie about the enormity of her betrayal, she would slip a knife-blade between her cousin's ribs, find his treacherous heart, and halt its beating.

For when Georgie had finally come to her as a husband,

and laid with her on the 'bed of honour', his loving had been sweeter by far than the wild pain inflicted by Silva Lee.

As they came closer to Ashkeepers the paths and green trails which led to the village were crowded with traffic. Stagecoaches, plying their trade from Bath to Bristol, Exeter and London, were bringing the rich aristocrats and their servants to witness the shame of the Roehampton family. The artisans and small business people came with wagons, and pushing shabby carts. The poor walked barefoot, hoping for a day's employment, and for the satisfaction of seeing a dramatic ending to a wealthy woman who had become notorious in her own lifetime.

The gypsies were camped in a narrow lane, and as close to the village green as it was possible to be; their carts and bender tents stretched in a long line beneath the sheltering branches of beech trees. This particular lane had been a regular *atchintan* for generations of Lees and Lovells; Georgie and Coralina joined them now, introducing the *gorgio* Ezra Lambton as 'our bestest friend in all the wide world'.

There were tearful reunions and hearty handshakes. The horses were unbridled, fed and watered, and led into pasture. News was exchanged and the talk turned inevitably to the morrow's execution. Respect and sympathy were shown to Ezra as the wronged husband of Pennina Lambton, and as being the man who had spoken up in court for George and Coralina. Coralina wandered, seemingly without purpose, the long length of the lane. She hugged and kissed her sisters' children, greeted friends, and all the while her anxious gaze sought out Silva Lee.

A chance remark by her brother-in-law informed her that Silva was that day on his way back from a Dorset horsefair. That he would not, for all the world, miss the execution of Pennina Lambton.

He came when dawn broke red across the eastern skies. Coralina, lying deep in straw, her body curled close around that of her sleeping husband, heard the click of pony hooves in the stony lane, and she feigned sleep.

She heard the slap of Silva's bare feet as he approached the cart. He stood for a while looking down upon her and Georgie. He lingered so long that she became fearful that George would sense Silva's gaze and waken. She could feel her mind growing numb in his presence, and so great was Silva's power over her that even when he moved away her terror remained. She climbed down from the cart and slipped silently away to the fast-running brook at the lane's end; she splashed her face and hands in the cold sweet water. She had never yet, she thought, witnessed a hanging. She shook out her long black hair and began to braid it in a single plait. George and Ezra would be wearing dark clothes and black neckties. George had bought her a dress of plain grey cotton, which he said she should wear to show respect, her hooped gold earrings the only ornament he would allow. She looked forward to the day with mixed feelings of horror and excitement. As to Georgie's feelings she had no clue, save for the sadness of his eyes and face.

Beyond the brook she could hear men shouting, and the noise of hammering. She found a gap in the blackthorn hedge and peeped out through the frail white blossoms and leafless branches. The sun came up across the village green; she thought about Pennina, being dragged from her prison cell and gazing upon sunrise for the last time.

The tiers of wooden seating were already in place. A special viewing platform for the rich folk was at the very moment being completed.

The strength of the rope which hung from the gibbet was tested by a very fat man, among gales of laughter from his fellow carpenters. Away from Ashkeepers Green in adjoining fields, smoke from hundreds of fires rose up straight and blue on the still air. Women boiled water, brewed tea, fed their menfolk and children, suckled infants. Men looked to the safety of their tethered horses, and gossiped, hands in pockets as men do.

For these few hours the *gorgio* crowds would ape the lives of the gypsy wanderers, sleeping outdoors underneath the stars, cooking food on a stick-fire. Tasting a novel freedom away from their dull lives and stinking houses. Believing the cruel business of execution to be a great adventure for those who watched, instead of the tragedy it really was.

Coralina walked slowly back to her mother's fireside where George and Ezra sat with the rest of her family, eating fried bread and bacon, and drinking strong tea.

Silva Lee sat conspicuously apart from the main company of Lees and Lovells; still 'of them' but not 'with them', making plain his disapproval of their invitation to George and Ezra to take breakfast with the Romanies, thereby breaking the taboo that no *tatchi Romanes* should ever break bread and eat in the presence of the *gorgio*.

The execution of Pennina Lambton was timed to commence when the sun had reached its zenith.

George and Ezra donned their dark apparel, Coralina her gown of sober grey. Before taking their positions on one of the main public platforms they walked for a while among the dense crowd of spectators and those others who habitually sought to make a profit from a public hanging.

There was a mounting air of anticipation among the throng, as they moved between the sideshows and the stalls which sold cider and ale, cakes and sweetmeats. There were acrobats and jugglers, bare knuckle contests, cockfights, gypsy fortune-tellers, children selling lucky charms.

As the sun rose higher in the heavens, activity increased around the gibbet. When it came to the hanging of an aristocrat, the services of the executioner and his assistant were not enough. It required the presence of many officials of the judiciary, and high-ranking, bewigged gentlemen from London, to see an end to Pennina. The crowds were hard put to divide their attention between the diversions to be found on Ashkeepers Green and those to be seen upon the platform. A murmur, which grew into a roar, heralded the arrival of the hangman, and marked the start of the proceedings. Garbed from head to foot in black, deeply conscious of his own unique importance on this day of days, he mounted the steps like an actor who struts upon a stage.

A final rush was made towards the ranks of wooden seating. George and Ezra stood rooted underneath an old tree unable to bring themselves even when the chance presented itself, to move forward and claim a clear view of the gallows.

Coralina who, in any case, had planned to cover her eyes and ears when the moment came, was relieved to stand with them, beneath the budding horse-chestnut tree, prepared to hide behind its stout bole as soon as Pennina came into view.

What the three had not realised was that the path to the gibbet lay close to the tree. The prisoner was led, shackled and stumbling and near enough to touch, beside the place where stood her husband Ezra and her former servant, Georgie.

Coralina could not bear to look upon Pennina's face. What was impossible to ignore was the woman's condition.

She whispered to George, 'Surely they could show her mercy. At least allow the child to be born before . . .'

But even as she spoke Pennina groaned, swayed, and fell upon the path. The militia men who were her guards bent and pulled her roughly upright, but again she fell, the contortions of her body and her piteous cries terrible to witness. Coralina darted forward, pushing between the encircling men, and knelt at Pennina's side. Time and again the soldiers' hard hands thrust the gypsy back, but she would not be denied.

'Can you not see the child is coming?' she shouted. 'Are you men, or are you less than the beasts of the field?'

In the end, the sergeant of militia, himself not knowing what was correct procedure in the unprecedented situation, muttered, 'Let the *diddecoi* bide. Let her do what she has to.'

Coralina begged them to remove the leg-irons and the leather halter but they would not. She tore off the white apron worn over her grey dress, and placed it beneath Pennina's body. The shawl draped about her shoulders she laid to one side to receive the emerging baby.

And so the Lady Pennina Roehampton's son came into this world amid great agony and travail, delivered publicly by a gypsy woman beneath a chestnut tree on the green of Ashkeepers, and in the shadow of the gallows which awaited his mother.

The baying, yelping crowds on the observation benches behaved as if this unexpected drama were a part of the day's entertainment, specially timed for their further enjoyment and delectation.

Coralina wrapped the boy-child in her lace shawl, and placed him in his mother's arms, her hot tears falling on them both.

'Take him,' Pennina gasped. 'Care for him well. He has done no wrong. His father is a footloose rogue who will not own him.' Her head fell back and Coralina wiped the woman's face with the hem of the grey gown.

'I will love him as if he were my own,' she promised.

A few minutes later and the guards moved in; the sergeant learned over, once again prepared to drag Pennina upright. Coralina said, her voice filled with a bitter scorn, her face with loathing, 'You will not need the gibbet, sir! Neither will you need the hangman. Can you not see? Her soul has already flown her body. She is dead. She has cheated you all.'

They returned to Taunton that same evening, travelling throughout the chill April night, for none of them had the stomach to stay longer in that dreadful place. Ezra's furniture was loaded on to the spare cart, together with Coralina's cousin and her baby, a young woman called Jacinta who only days before had given birth to her first child. Since her husband had been taken by the *gavvers* for poaching on the King's land, and would languish for the next twelve months in Shepton Mallet Jail, Jacinta was more than willing to act as wet-nurse to the baby boy who was to be known henceforth as Peregrine Lambton.

Time passed. Months lengthened into years. Coralina bore a girl child, a beautiful wayward creature whose mane of red curling hair and bright blue eyes drew admiring glances from all who saw her. Peregrine, with his thick black hair and strange no-colour eyes, was not an easy child to love. He was quiet and withdrawn into himself, as if the circumstances of his birth, although he was too young to know about them, already weighed heavily upon his spirit. He was Ezra's constant companion, clever and quick to learn; he mastered with ease the tables of weights and measures, and scale of tariffs, imposed on all traffic which passed through the turnpike gate. He could reckon more accurately and speedily than Ezra and Georgie put together.

It was on a wild autumn morning of high winds and wide skies that Silva Lee came back into their lives. The children picked blackberries in the hedges around the Toll House, while Coralina fed and watered pigs and chickens. She had the Romany mother's anxiety for the children who wandered too far from the safety of their home. Her glance went out constantly to the bright red curls of Breda her daughter, and the tall thin figure of Peregrine Lambton. And so it was that she saw the approach of the man who had for some minutes watched them from the wooden bridge that spanned the widest of the ditches; saw him move slowly towards the busy children who were unaware of his presence.

There was something familiar about the tilt of his head, his lithe dancer's way of moving, that sent a shaft of fear through her body. She dropped the pan of buttermilk among the pigs, hoisted her skirts and began to run across the fields.

As she came up to them, it was plain to see that Silva had not yet spoken to the children, but stood some way off from the blackberry hedge, all his attention fixed on Peregrine.

He turned upon Coralina without even the customary greeting of one Rom to another. Knowing him as she did, she sensed the dangerous anger in him. 'Well – well! So you kept him well hidden from me, eh, cousin?'

Coralina caught her breath. 'Hidden,' she gasped, 'why would I need to keep him hidden? And why from you, pray?'

'Look at him, woman! Is he not my living image?'

Coralina stared, realising for the first time – seeing them together – that what Silva said was close to the truth.

She put a hand across her mouth, a superstitious horror seized her. What terrible curse was this, what magic had been worked here, that a child borne by Pennina Lambton, and left in the care of herself and Ezra, should so resemble the man who had been her own first lover?

It was Peregrine who, realising her presence, called out, 'Mama, Mama! Look – a whole basketful of berries!'

Coralina turned, relieved at the distraction, holding her hands out to the children. 'Go,' she told Silva. 'I have nothing to say to you.'

'Tonight,' he murmured, 'at fall of dark. Be here, or I shall come to find you. And that will surely set the cat among the pigeons.'

When the children asked later what the stranger had wanted she told them he was seeking the Black Horse Inn and had lost his way.

It was the night before Bridgewater horse fair, and the traffic was heavy through the turnpike. It was, she thought, the morrow's fair that had brought Silva Lee in this direction.

Coralina's thoughts were anxious as she went about her usual duties. There would be no rest for George and Ezra through the coming evening and night. She set out cold food on wooden platters, and left two flagons of cider ready for her hardworked menfolk. She settled the weary children in their beds, and all the time her heart was fearful lest Georgie should notice anything amiss.

She waited until full darkness had fallen before throwing a shawl about her shoulders and murmuring to George that two hens had been laying their eggs away in a distant hedgerow and she must perforce rout them out, and bring them home.

George, who was reckoning the tariff for three stallions and a pony, simply nodded her away.

She went down into the fields, disturbing the sleeping ducks which carpeted the damp grass. He was waiting for her beside the blackberry hedge, just as he had promised.

In the distance she could see the smoky lights of Taunton town. Music and singing drifted out from the open doors of the many taverns, and a great silver moon was rising through the willow branches.

She came up to him, her heart beating painfully inside her chest. Silva reached out both hands and gripped her upper arms. 'Now,' he said, 'now you shall tell me the truth! The boy is my son, of that there is no doubt. People say that the witch Pennina Lambton gave him birth. But I know different. You are his mother, Lina. He is thy child and mine.'

'No,' she cried, 'he may be thy child, but he is not mine. I was there at his birth, Pennina gave him into my care only seconds before she died.' Reckless now of any consequences, she said, 'Ask George. Ask Ezra. They stood by. They saw the baby born.'

Silva laughed. 'I have no need of asking. The boy has my looks.'

'True,' she said. 'But I had not marked it so until I saw the two of you stand together. Peregrine has a look of you, but that does not surprise me. The Lady Pennina had a fancy for young men such as yourself. Don't tell me that you did not know her.'

'I knew her. But that means nothing. I have known many women, but I have loved only one.'

All at once his mood changed. He grabbed her shoulders and began to shake her. 'Tell me true,' he shouted, 'you and I have had a child together, and that makes you my true wife.'

Fear rendered her speechless. Silva, always high-strung and given to black moods, had lost his wits altogether. She began to struggle and had almost broken loose from his cruel grasp, but it was in that very moment when she might have escaped him that he began to beat her.

Her absence from the house went unnoticed until the early morning hours when an exhausted George crept finally to his bed. He said nothing to Ezra, but lit a lantern and began to search the outbuildings and nearby hedges. He returned to the house, hoping that she might have come back in his absence.

He built up the fire and sat, head in hands, believing now that she had left him, altogether.

He had witnessed her longing looks that day as the gypsy tribes had come close to the turnpike but had not passed through it. They had gone with their horses down the green trails and rough tracks where no toll money would be demanded of them.

He had always feared this moment, the time when life beneath a house-roof became unbearable to her, and she would leave him. He had expected too much of her, and now she was lost.

He rose from the fireside, pulled on a jacket and returned to the hedgerows, seeking hoofmarks, the imprint of bare feet; any sign of her departure.

The early morning sky was the colour of skimmed milk; the still air disturbed only by the multitude of ducks. George walked slowly, up one hedgerow and down another, his gaze fixed on the marshy ground.

He found her lying in a bed of wild garlic, her head at an unnatural angle, her limbs splayed all ways, like those of a rag doll.

He knew that she was dead before he touched her.

There was a deep gash in her head where it had struck a sharp rock. Whoever had done this to her had rendered her face unrecognisable. But for the single thick braid of black hair, the hooped gold earrings, and his own wedding band of gold worn on her left hand, George could not have sworn on oath that this pitiful soul was indeed his Coralina.

The body of Silva Lee was found later that morning, dangling from the low branch of an oak tree. He had hanged himself with the length of twine he always carried looped on his belt, and which he used to tether ponies . . .

I sat for a long time in the sunlit orchard, caught between

past and present, experiencing all the emotions that Nina had intended I should. The autumn colours took my breath away. It was as if I were seeing them for the first time. But unlike Silva Lee, Paul Mavsoni had not hung himself from a tall tree. He was still out there, vengeful and cruel, with who knows what further mischief festering in his brain.

And, unlike Coralina, I still lived; able to point the finger and accuse him. I had the power to destroy him and he knew it.

When the sun went down behind the hills Nina came to find me. We walked back towards the house. I carried Barnacle's book. She said, 'You were reading for quite a time. Did you finish the tale?'

I knew what she meant. I said, 'I read the relevant pages. I made the connections.'

'I thought you might.'

Nothing more was said. I knew that she knew what had happened with Paul Mavsoni, and I was relieved that the knowing was sufficient, that she had no wish to talk about it.

From this day on, my mother and I would be able at last to deal honestly with each other. All I needed now was to bring my life back to some kind of normality. But I could no longer remember how that felt, or work out how it might be achieved.

It was Niall who suggested a shopping trip.

My hospital appointments were now monthly. Soon I would be discharged; there was talk of a return to work; for therapeutic reasons. I couldn't imagine going back to my office. I remained silent whenever the hospital people made the suggestion. For although I was looking and feeling better, I still clung to Niall and Nina, and the safe haven of Sad Acre.

It was in an effort to regain some measure of independence that I fell in with the plan that I should have a little spending spree in Taunton. Not that I needed anything. My wardrobes were stuffed full of the clothes I no longer wore. Perhaps would never wear again. I had a half-formed plan to buy heavy duty boots and a waxed jacket, and a couple of thick-knit sweaters. Just lately I had spent time with Niall in the sheds and fields, not being very useful, I admit; but I was learning.

The cattle market was already crowded when we arrived there. Niall bought feedstuffs, paraffin and thick socks. I made my purchases and stowed them in the pickup.

It was the first time in many months that I had made a trip that was not to do with hospitals and doctors. The morning was cold and clear. Already shop windows were decked out in tinsel and mock snow. A poster informed me that in Debenhams store I could visit Santa's Grotto. I thought about my grandson. I could spend a happy hour or two in the toy department.

Niall had appointments with the Inland Revenue and the accountant. He also had a dental appointment and needed a haircut. 'Will you be all right?' He put an arm round my shoulders. 'On your own for the whole day?'

'Looking forward to it,' I said. 'A visit to Santa, a long lunch and a rummage around Marks and Spencers. It's so long since I did those normal things.'

He looked doubtful, then smiled. 'Don't overdo it. Take it easy. I'll pick you up here at four o'clock.'

I wanted to say, 'Don't leave me,' but instead I watched him walk away. He turned and waved, and I waved back. When I tried to walk my legs were trembling so badly I could take only small steps. I made for the centre of town. North Street, as usual, was choked with traffic. The pavements were crowded with farming people, in Taunton for the market. I looked down at my boots and thick trousers, the fancy quilted jacket, a bit stained now and no longer pristine; the garment I had once thought in my ignorance to be required wear for the country. I thought, with satisfaction, that now at last I fitted in. I made frequent stops to look in shop windows; not that I was interested in the displays, but I needed to pause and catch my breath, and assure myself that I was not being followed. I looked back across my shoulder so often that the constant turning of my head sent me dizzy. By the time I had reached the Tone bridge, panic was fluttering in my throat, threatening to choke me. I leaned on the pale green structure of the bridge, and willed myself to remain upright.

The brown waters of the Tone, high from recent rain, ran fast and shining. Holding on to the handrail, I made my way cautiously down the steep steps to the Goodlands Garden Café.

I ordered chicken soup and a soft roll. The repair job on my teeth was as good as the skills of the orthodontists could make it; but still I was embarrassed to risk eating solid food in a public place. I crumbled the roll into the soup and glanced self-consciously about me. Nobody there was remotely interested in me and my infantile eating habits. Why should they be? Who did I think I was anyway? The soup lay warm and reassuring on my stomach. I leaned back in my seat and as my heart resumed its normal rhythm, my breathing slowed, the panic subsided and then was gone.

I was actually out on my own, minus my devoted minders; a woman window-shopping for Christmas presents, lunching in a café, no longer sick and dependent, but making her own decisions; living! And perhaps that should be enough for this particular day? I thought about Debenhams and Marks and Spencers, both of which would be hot and crowded. Better saved for another, less busy time. Trying to do too much, too soon, could be counter-productive. But my rendezvous with Niall was hours away.

His dental appointment was for two thirty. I could sit in the dentist's waiting room, read the out-of-date issues of *Country Life* and *Cosmopolitan*; watch the ghost-koi and shubunkins in the fish tank, and rehearse my excuses for being there. When he arrived I could explain how the streets had been cold, the shops too busy; no seats to be had in any of the cafés.

But Niall would know why I had sought him out. He would report back to Nina. They would feel guilty, believing they had persuaded me too soon to spend a day alone.

As I left the café a watery sun showed through the clouds. I began to enjoy the simple pleasure of walking among strangers. There were no curious glances at my changed face.

I looked exactly what I was. A farm wife, in town for a few hours. An unremarkable woman, who had no secrets.

I had turned into High Street, intending to stroll for a while in Vivary Park, when I saw Mary Grey heading straight towards me.

We had kept up our telephone contact, which was easier since I regained my voice. She rang me twice weekly, and had wanted to visit me at home, but I had said to wait a few weeks longer until I felt stronger.

And now here I was, with nowhere to hide.

The relationship had always been amicable but businesslike. She greeted me now with amazing warmth, holding both my hands, a smile of genuine delight on her face.

'Imogen! Oh, it's so good to see you. And looking so well. Are you on your own?' She glanced around, obviously expecting Nina or Niall to emerge from some nearby shop.

'Yes,' I said, speaking with more assurance than I felt, 'Niall has appointments, so I've been window-shopping.' I paused. 'You seem surprised to see me? I mentioned when you phoned that I was much, much better.'

'Well, yes. But Paul said you were just being brave. He's often in Accident and Emergency, as you know. He'd spoken recently to some of the doctors. They said in their opinion you would never recover—' Her face turned very pink. She put a hand up to her lips. 'I shouldn't be telling you this, Imogen. He's clearly mistaken about it all – but then he is about lots of things since you had your accident. It really shook him up you know, that such a dreadful thing could happen to you. He feels responsible for leaving the office early that evening, and allowing you to go into the car park on your own. He's said it over and over. You can't imagine the effect it's had upon him.'

I began to feel sick and dizzy. I said, 'Have you had lunch, or perhaps a coffee?' I fairly pushed her into Bath Place, and through the green-painted café door. The lunchtime rush was over. We shared a pot of tea, and Mary had a sandwich.

It was so much easier to talk to her face to face. Although to be truthful, I would have avoided her if I could.

To begin with we talked about work. I was now told that for two days in every week a replacement counsellor came to the office. A very confident young woman. She and Paul did not hit it off.

I winced at the unfortunate choice of words. Paul was managing the office. He was forever criticising Toyah, who argued every smallest point. Paul had even volunteered to work extra hours to catch up on the backlog of serious cases, in the hope of making Toyah redundant.

As Mary talked she glanced nervously at my lopsided features. At one point I saw her eyes mist over.

'We desperately need you back, Imogen. The atmosphere in the office is really awful. I'm thinking seriously of resigning.'

In the months we had worked together she and I had respected one another. But there had been no real warmth, no discussion of personal matters. I had never guessed that she would feel so concerned about me, or regret my absence.

She said, 'Oh, I'm sorry! I shouldn't be burdening you with my troubles. The past months must have been terrible for you. Such a horrible thing should never have happened – and to you of all people. As Paul keeps saying, if he could only discover who did it . . . But like I tell him, if Imogen can't remember, and the police can't find out, what earthly chance has he got?'

I wondered what her reaction would be if I leaned across the flowered china and said, 'Well, as a matter of fact – see this scar on my top lip. Paul's diamond-studded ring did that. He used his fists to break my nose and jaw. I no longer see properly from my left eye. You'll notice if you look closely how the eyelid tends to droop.'

But if I intended to accuse him, I should have spoken up long ago. I said, on impulse, 'I expect he's using my desk, my office?'

She smiled. 'Oh yes. Well, it's more convenient for him. But you'll be back soon, won't you? And no one will be more relieved than Paul to hand you back the reins.'

She was so artless, so genuinely concerned I could have wept. This was the effect he had on women. Mary Grey was happily married, but even she was not altogether impervious to his charm. She looked at her wristwatch. 'Must fly,' she said. 'It's been wonderful seeing you. We must fix up another meeting. You take care now!'

As she reached the door she called back across her shoulder, 'I'll be sure and tell Paul I've seen you. He'll be so pleased to know that you're out and about in Taunton again.'

After causing them so much anxiety it gave me great pleasure to answer Niall and Nina's tentative enquiries about my day. Not that they rushed to ask me. So great was our continuing pretence that everything was back to normal that nobody spoke about my solo run until we were eating supper.

My mother, while pouring cream over apple pie, said, 'Did you enjoy your day out?'

Equally offhand, I said, 'Very much. Didn't do any Christmas shopping, though. The stores were crowded.' I paused. 'Had lunch in Bath Place with Mary Grey. We met unexpectedly in the High Street.'

I could have laughed, but didn't, at their amazed faces.

For someone who refused steadfastly to have visits from her daughter and grandchild on account of her spoiled looks, this was indeed progress.

Niall's face was blank, his voice expressionless, when he asked, 'I suppose you were able to catch up on all the office gossip?'

'A temp comes in for two days each week,' I said, 'but nothing else has changed.'

Nina deftly turned the talk to other subjects, but I could see in her face the same fear that was haunting me.

When Mary, as she was sure to do, reported back to Paul that I was up and moving, lunching and shopping alone in Taunton, what would be his reaction? He was neither neurotic nor psychotic, but the personality disorder from which I was sure he suffered meant that his grip on reality was dangerously distorted.

This caused him to be unpredictable, lonely, isolated and frightened, with his aggression and hostility well hidden behind a façade of charm.

I should have reported my suspicions of his mental state long ago; but, without admitting to the world that Paul and I had been lovers, and that he was my attacker, what was I to do?

Coralina had never told Georgie about Silva Lee, and his persecution of her. Never told him that Silva and she had been lovers, if only for a single night. *And she had paid the price of that silence with her life.*

There was one person I could talk to; one person who knew the whole score from my point of view and could be relied upon to be discreet and sympathetic.

I needed to see Gloria. Urgently. While there was still time.

My behaviour that week was manipulative and rash. I began to make much of my new-found confidence, promising to drive myself in future; issuing Christmas invitations to all my family; phoning Primrose, in my mother's hearing, with exaggerated accounts of my improvement.

Thus when, on Monday morning, I announced my intention of making a second trip to Taunton and driving alone, there was not too much surprise or opposition.

'The stores,' I said, 'will be quiet on a Monday.' I brandished a long list of gifts to be bought. 'I'll call Mary Grey and arrange to lunch with her again. I would also like to drop in on Gloria. I've never properly thanked her for taking care of me that night. I might treat myself to a party frock while I'm in her shop. Something glamorous for Christmas.'

The delight they both showed made me cringe inside. Only recently I had believed that from this time on my mother and I would be able to deal honestly with one another. It was what I longed for, needed; but now and in the immediate future all

I wanted was to protect her. In the meantime I needed to find out more about Paul Mavsoni's past life.

I began to remember what Gloria had said about him. She was an acute judge of men. Streetwise, I think, is the word that sums her up. She had described him as being 'danger on two legs – dishy-looking fellah. Sinister type – quiet spoken. Blokes like him – they should carry a government health warning.'

I found it hard to imagine a circumstance or situation in which the two of them could possibly have met. Gloria was not the type of woman who would ever have required counselling; and her exotic, over-the-top style of speech and fashion would have set Paul's teeth on edge.

And yet? Even at the time I seemed to remember thinking that she could have said more about him, but deliberately chose not to.

But reflective thinking was no longer my strong point. The blows to the head and face had shaken up my ability to remember accurately.

There were days when I was no longer sure what I thought about anything at all.

I drove out of the farmyard on that October morning with a flourish of confidence I did not feel. But my nerve returned with every mile covered, and I pulled into a Taunton car park soon after ten with a sense of achievement. I walked to the Bath Place café and ordered cappuccino, spooning in the sugar in the hope of gaining back a bit of my lost weight. I felt a tide of wellbeing surge through my body. I was wearing jeans, a thick sweater and my new waxed jacket. With my short haircut and repaired face there was a risk that Gloria would not immediately recognise me.

I began to look forward to the visit, anticipating her welcome, her surprise at my recovery. I might buy another of her glamorous velvet leisure suits. The heating on Sad Acre, in spite of Niall's best efforts, was not equal to the draughts which whistled in beneath doors and at ill-fitting windows. I wandered out into the brilliant morning, breathing in the crisp air. Now that I had time to notice, I realised how attractive the town was. I looked down the long length of Hammet Street, lined on either side with ancient stone buildings which nowadays housed the local solicitors, the beautiful church of St Mary's standing at its end. A turn of the head and there was the archway of Castle Bow, and the Castle Hotel where I had spent an extravagant weekend. I remembered the night I had stood with Paul in the hotel car park, and how I had longed for him to kiss me. I thought I could smell the sachet of lemon verbena which had hung from the Range Rover's windscreen, feel the softness of the leather seats. I ran a finger down my lumpy jawbone and touched my drooping eyelid. It had all ended in tears, as such affairs deserve to.

I began to walk fast towards the Tone bridge. What I needed was an hour or two of Gloria's outrageous conversation; a dose of her unique style of counselling. Her normality in a terrifying world.

The window display consisted of a single black dress and a pair of golden sandals. I pushed open the door which set the bell jangling. The elegant lamp still burned in an alcove; music played softly from a hidden source. An expensive scent lay heavy on the overheated air. Of Gloria herself there was no sign.

I flicked through the rails of designer garments, not really concentrating. For some strange reason I was feeling nervous. I had a sense of being watched; gooseflesh tingled along the nape of my neck. When Gloria appeared in the archway which led into the café section I saw instant alarm in her eyes, and then a careful blankness.

'Imogen?'

'Yes,' I said.

'I wasn't expecting . . . I thought you were . . . ?'

'No,' I laughed. 'Rumours of my death have been greatly exaggerated.'

She came towards me and seized my hands. 'Oh bloody hell!' she gasped. 'Trust me to put my big foot in it. I didn't mean . . . Well you know I didn't. It was just . . .'

'The shock of it?'

'Yes,' she said, 'that's right. The shock – oh, but it's wonderful to see you.' She went to turn the door sign around so that it said 'CLOSED'.

'Come up to the flat. It's almost lunchtime. Soup and a sandwich?'

'Just soup.'

I followed her up the narrow staircase and into the long low room which overlooked the courtyard. I walked to the heavily barred window which gave a clear view of the bistro. I noticed Gloria's many security alarms. It would take an attack by the SAS to break into this place.

She called through from the tiny kitchen, 'So how've you been, then?'

'Improving,' I said, 'getting better every day.'

'I didn't visit,' she said. 'I phoned the hospital and sent flowers.'

'Yes. Thank you! How did you know that I love yellow roses?'

'Lucky guess?'

She rattled cutlery and china, and I moved back to the sofa. I remembered the last time I had sat here, my head ringing like a brass gong from the blows Paul had landed on it. My legs had buckled, my mouth had been filled with blood and smashed teeth. Gloria had spread towels across her pink linen sofa covers, and who could blame her?

The last time I was here I had been in no condition to take in the decor. Now I looked around the pretty pastel-coloured room. Pale walls and carpet. Watercolours, and yew wood cabinets which held collections of antique paperweights and oriental fans. I had imagined her taste to favour a Moorish setting, silk-hung walls and cushions on the floor. She set the tray down on a low table, handed me a napkin, a bowl of soup and a spoon, and seated herself in a facing armchair.

'Well – isn't this nice?' she said brightly, but the words and the tone did not match her anxious looks. If I had known her better I might have interpreted sooner that strained expression for what it signified. As it was I accepted her pallor, the way she picked at her sandwich, the thinness of what had been her voluptuous figure. If I considered the change in her at all, it was to dismiss it simply as Gloria overdoing some bizarre slimming diet.

Truth to tell, in the past months I had acquired the sick person's selfish habit of seeing no further than my own aches and pains. We talked for a while about my hospital treatment, then she said abruptly, 'The police. They never found out who attacked you?'

I said, 'No. I don't suppose they will. After all, I couldn't even give them a description.'

Her features sharpened, and all at once she looked much older. 'Why did you lie about it? Why did you say you had crashed your car?'

I stared blankly at her. I had forgotten about those initial lies. I said swiftly, 'I'd taken several blows to the head. I was punch drunk. Remember Mohammed Ali, the boxer?'

She didn't laugh. 'It's hardly the same thing. You hadn't put in half a lifetime being beaten up.' She paused. 'It was a fellah that thumped you, wasn't it? That bloke you thought had got you preggers?'

When I didn't answer she said abruptly, 'Come on, Imogen. You can tell your old pal Gloria. Remember all that we've been through together? Boots' family-planning counter? You throwing-up in my café loo?' She paused. 'By the way, I take it that you were never pregnant?'

I shook my head. 'Wishful thinking. Kidding myself that I was still young enough to be a mother.'

'But you didn't want it. You were terrified.'

I know.' I smiled. 'You're allowed to be unreasonable when you are menopausal.'

'Look,' she said, 'when a woman takes the sort of hiding you took, it's always – *and I mean always* – from a man she knows very well, a bastard she's been close to.'

I felt the heart turn over in my chest. She was stealing my

lines. Using the arguments I had used to battered wives in the days when I had been a marriage counsellor.

And she was right.

In fact she was coming so close to guessing at the truth that I no longer dared stay there. I rose, placed my bowl and spoon on the tray and said, 'I'd like to buy one of your leisure suits. Shall we go down and take a look? You told me once that I looked good in emerald—' Still talking fast, I went back down the stairs, swiftly made my purchase and left the shop, hardly pausing to thank her for lunch, or say goodbye. As I walked through the courtyard I glanced briefly at the bistro's steamy window, and just for a moment I thought I saw Paul Mavsoni's face, pale, with the sharply angled jaw and cheekbones, the long-lipped mouth and strange eyes.

I told myself that he could not possibly be in the bistro, spying on me; any more than he had been following me out on the street, or lying in wait in the bus station car park. It was Gloria's probing questions which had triggered my nervousness, and if I allowed my imagination to take over, all the progress of recent weeks would be undone. I had meant to tell her everything. But because of the fear I sensed in her I had told her nothing.

I put all thoughts of him from my mind and drove home to Sad Acre.

You may have noticed that by this time I was thinking of the farm in terms of 'home'. On that particular evening I was more than ever relieved and happy to be back there. I turned in through the white gate, and parked away from the house so that I might look at it, see it as Nina and Niall had always seen it. The soft blue dusk of the November evening concealed the cracked pink plaster and sagging thatch, and made the shabbiness charming. To save unnecessary use of the generator Nina continued to use oil lamps. The warm rosy light from their cranberry-glass shades spilled out across the driveway, and it came to me again as I sat there that my mother had made this house a home, in a special way she had never achieved when living in the city or in the Toll House in Ashkeepers.

And then there was Niall. I could just make him out as he came down the slope from the high woods, the dog at his heels, a heavy egg-bucket balanced on either arm. I could not see his face, but contentment showed in his slow, loping farmers' way of walking, in the relaxed lines of his body, silhouetted against the last streaky reds of the western skies.

I remembered the person I had once been, the way I had lived my life, the single-minded ambition which had driven me to the inevitable disaster which was Paul Mavsoni, and I was ashamed. I knew then that I would never return to my office. Whatever happened next, I had finally come home.

I pulled off my gloves and some peculiar superstitious impulse made me want to touch my wedding ring for luck. I ran the fingers of my right hand up and down the third finger of my left hand, only to discover that the gold band which had been in place for almost thirty years was no longer there.

Due to my weight loss the ring had been loose for many months. I remembered that while trying on the leisure suit in Gloria's boutique I had needed several times to push it back on to my finger. I would phone her this evening, to ask her if she had found it, and arrange to collect it in the morning.

I phoned several times, only to hear Gloria's recorded message of regret, and her promise to call back soonest. I announced over breakfast that I planned to visit the Taunton public library that morning, and to stock up on thermal underwear for all of us.

The least sign of increasing independence was greeted these days with approval. They had not noticed the absence of my ring, and since it would be back on my finger within hours I decided not to tell them how and where I lost it.

Before leaving the house I tried once again to contact Gloria, but without luck.

The first of the autumn gales was stripping the last leaves from the trees. My little car fairly rocked as it took the winds side-on when I reached the high road. The sky was a deep cold blue, the scudding clouds Persil-white. I was wearing my new leather boots, green corduroy trousers, matching sweater and waxed jacket.

For the first time I could remember, I felt at ease, comfortable, good about myself. Perhaps it had something to do with the fact that Niall and I now looked a matching pair; as if we belonged together. I drove into Taunton soon after nine, and then remembered that the boutique did not open until ten o'clock. I planned a leisurely coffee in the bistro. But as I walked into the courtyard I could see the OPEN sign showing on Gloria's door. I went in, picking up the half-dozen letters left on her doormat by the postman. I peered through into the coffee shop and called 'Gloria,' softly at first and then loudly. I waited, expecting that any moment she would appear in the velvet-draped archway that led up to the flat. It was possible that she had popped across to the bistro to buy croissants or warm rolls for breakfast. But she would never have left the shop unlocked for the ten or so minutes I had been waiting.

I laid the post down on a table which held an arrangement of fresh flowers, went through the archway and up the stairs.

I found her lying on the pink linen sofa. I was sure she was dead. No one could have sustained such terrible injuries and lived. Her face was unrecognisable, the bright red curls now flattened, black and matted with her blood. It was almost a replay of my own condition back in January, except that this time no one had bothered to protect the pale pink sofa covers. The shock did not immediately hit me. Cool and in total control, I dialled the emergency services. I described Gloria's condition. I said that I thought she was dead, but was not sure. I went back to the sofa and held her cold hand. I looked around the dainty room at the fragile lamps and china figurines, and saw that in spite of the violent attack, nothing was disturbed or broken. But for the bloodstained sofa covers, the room was immaculate as always. It was only then that I realised the assailant might still be in the flat. But I didn't think of him simply as the assailant. The man who had done this to Gloria was known to me. His name was Paul Mavsoni. It was only then that I began to fall to pieces.

The medical team took one look at me and, believing that it would help me pull myself together, ordered me into the kitchen to make strong tea. The kitchen decor repeated the dainty theme: all-white units and frilled blue and white gingham, with lots of green trailing plants and a breakfast nook built into a corner. The remains of a meal had congealed on the table: a casserole and two used plates, cutlery and wine glasses, two screwed-up table napkins. In the middle of the table lay my wedding ring. I picked it up and slipped it on my finger. While the kettle boiled I ran hot water into the washing-up bowl. I needed something, anything, to occupy my shaking hands.

I was just about to pick up the casserole dish and cutlery when a voice from the doorway said, 'I shouldn't do that, Mrs Donovan, if I were you. You could be destroying vital evidence.'

I dropped the dish back on the table. I recognised the policeman who had visited me in the hospital, and on Sad Acre.

I tried to lift the boiling kettle, to make tea, but could not. He took the kettle from me and poured water into a large white teapot. He dropped in a handful of teabags, then began to stir them with a ladle.

I said, stupidly, 'Wrong way round, Detective. It should be teabags first, water after. And you haven't warmed the pot.' I began to weep and could not stop. He led me to the breakfast nook where he sat me down on the gingham-cushioned bench. He poured tea into mugs, added milk and pushed a mug in my direction.

'I am told,' he said, 'that you found her?'

I tried to answer him and could not. A thick sob caught in my throat.

He walked to the worktop and brought back a sugar bowl. He dropped two heaped spoonfuls into my tea. 'Drink,' he ordered. 'Take your time. You've had a severe shock.'

Five minutes later I said, 'Yes. I found her. She was lying on a the sofa. She was cold. Dead.'

'Not dead. Not yet. She's in a bad way. The medics are very concerned at her condition. But you survived his attempt to kill you, hopefully she will be as lucky.'

'You think it's the same man?'

'Come on, Mrs Donovan. You don't need me to tell you that, do you? You've known who your attacker was all along.' He sent me a long look. 'If Mrs Beaufort dies . . .'

'It will be my fault,' I whispered.

'Let's look on the bright side,' he said briskly. 'She's a pretty tough lady.'

I could hear the medics as they struggled to carry Gloria downstairs.

'Damn nuisance,' said the policeman, 'these narrow stairways.'

'I want to go with her!' I stood up and made for the door, but he caught my arm.

'No,' he said, 'not now. She won't know you're there, and in any case I need you here to answer some questions.'

'You don't understand. When it – when it happened to me, she took me in, cared for me. I might have died without her. He might still have been following me that night. Planning to finish what he'd started.'

The detective began to slide used cutlery into self-sealing plastic bags.

'Who?' His tone was silky soft. 'Who are we talking about?'

'I can't tell you. What difference can it make now?' I could hear the rising hysteria in my voice. He labelled the bags then turned his attention to the wine glasses. 'He's still out there, Mrs Donovan. You know he is. Just give me a name.' He paused. 'There has to be a connection. She took you in when you were hurt, and eleven months later is herself done over.'

I turned the wedding band on my finger and shook my head.

'Why not?' he persisted. 'What hold does he have over you?'

Until now I had never voiced my greatest fear, not even to myself.

That morning, under extreme pressure, the words burst from me. 'He threatened my daughter. My grandson. Now, will you please shut up, go away, and leave me alone! He said if I named him he would do to them what he had done to me.'

He said, 'You know I have to catch him, don't you? If your family is in danger, there is all the more reason for us to apprehend him. You've just admitted that Mrs Beaufort probably saved your life. Surely for her sake you want to see this villain locked up?'

I sat, head bowed, terrified and mute. I watched as he stowed cutlery and glasses into a carrying-case. He abandoned his tough stance, and his voice was gentle. 'Look,' he said, 'I saw you in the hospital that night. You were in much the same state as Gloria Beaufort is now. The doctors thought brain damage at the very least. You have been lucky. She may not be.' He sighed. 'I know you're upset, in shock, and I can understand that. But if you had named him straight away, this second attack could have been avoided.' He refilled the tea mugs, added milk and sugar, and the small domestic actions made me see him for the first time as a fellow human, not a policeman. He was about my age, seriously overweight, dark hair greying at the temples; a good family man, the kind who mowed the lawn at weekends, who took his grandchildren to McDonalds and holidayed in Scotland. At that moment I could have trusted him, told him what he wished to know. But the bleeper sounded on his mobile, and a voice came through loud and clear. 'She regained a few minutes of consciousness, sir. I persuaded the doctor to let me see her and put one question to her. I asked her who had attacked her. The answer was, "My husband."'

The detective and I exchanged uneasy glances. I experienced a surge of triumph. 'Well, there you are!' I said. 'It was her husband, after all.'

'And why couldn't her husband and your attacker be one and the same man?'

'Not possible. Never. He isn't Gloria's type, neither is she his.'

'And what type would that be?'

I beat my clenched fists on the table-top. 'Let it rest, why can't you?' I stood up. 'I'm going to the hospital. I have to be with her.'

'So that you can persuade her not to name her assailant?' Again he sighed. 'You're being very foolish. He could be lying in wait for you. Those are lonely lanes you drive through on your way home. And have you considered that he might decide to attack your daughter and her child anyway? Have you warned them that they might be in danger? This man is out of control. Your stupidity could lead to murder.'

'No. I haven't warned them. I thought – if I didn't name him—'

'Right!' He was shouting now. 'This has all gone far enough. I want your daughter's name, address, and quickly! Mrs Beaufort was beaten up at least twelve hours ago. He could be anywhere by this time.'

I sat down. 'I know where he will be,' I said. 'His name is Paul Mavsoni. He's a creature of habit. Does the same thing every day at the same time.' I gave him the office address.

'I want it on record,' I told him, 'that you bullied me into giving this information. If anything happens to Fran and John . . .'

But he wasn't listening. He was already speaking to his inspector, giving him Paul's name and location, and then alerting yet another police force, setting in motion a procedure that would cause fear and anxiety in my daughter Fran, who had done nothing to deserve it.

I rode to the hospital in a police car. The portly detective took up more than his fair share of the back seat. He continued to ask questions.

'So how did you meet this Mavsoni?'

'He's a colleague. I'm his head of department.'

He gave a low whistle of surprise. 'So he's a social worker?'

'A professional counsellor,' I said. 'Marriage guidance, domestic violence, and so forth.' I flinched at the sound of his derisive laughter.

'Hmm. Typical. Blind leading the blind, you might say. Pot calling the kettle.' Once again I could hear the barely suppressed rage edging into his voice.

I couldn't argue with him. I was trying to control my queasy stomach.

'The trouble with you do-gooders,' he went on, 'you begin with the assumption that you know all there is to know about everything, but especially about human nature. You have the gall to sit in judgement, to tell others how to run their lives, how they've got it all wrong, and if only they will do what you advise, they'll live happily ever after. Crap!' he shouted. 'Bullshit! You and this bast—, this bloke, Mavsoni, neither of you are fit or able, in my book, to advise a toddler how to cross the road.'

I found my voice. 'You can't speak to me like that.' In my own ears the words lacked conviction.

'Oh, but I can,' he said quietly. 'It's high time somebody did. You still don't know what you've done, do you, with your stubborn criminal refusal to name him?'

We drew up at the hospital entrance. Three police vehicles were parked on the concourse, and two officers stood by the automatic doors. As the detective took my arm and helped me from the car I lost control completely, and vomited across his shoes and trousers.

I knew exactly what I had done wrong when they allowed me to sit at Gloria's bedside. In addition to the injuries that matched my own, he had also kicked her; in the ribs, the kidneys, the head and stomach. Tubes snaked from her nose and mouth, her breathing was assisted. After speaking those two vital words she had lapsed back into unconsciousness. I held her hand, stroked her fingers. I prayed, although I was not a believer.

To the nurse who brought me cups of tea I said, 'I really didn't think I would be allowed to stay with her.'

She smiled her cheerful smile. 'Poor soul has got no family,' she said, 'and the sergeant thought it would be easier to guard the two of you if you were together in the same place.'

Niall and Nina came in the late afternoon. The police had told them to bring me an overnight bag, since I would be safer in the hospital at present than in my own home. They looked drawn and weary, and I did my best to convince them that I was calm and in no danger and that Gloria was going to pull through because I would not allow her to do otherwise.

Nina smiled. Niall patted my shoulder. They left me with the worrying feeling that there was something very bad they had not told me.

The sergeant also came back late that afternoon. We talked in the nurse's room, drinking coffee and eating biscuits.

'So how are you doing? Stomach a bit better, is it?'

I felt my face redden. 'Sorry,' I said, 'about your shoes and trousers.'

'I pushed you too hard,' he admitted. 'Said things I shouldn't have. I'll send you the cleaning bill if it will make you feel better.'

I took courage and asked, 'Isn't this all a bit over the top? All this police guard. Keeping me here overnight. I'm surprised you haven't locked me in a cell "for my own protection".'

He gave me an assessing stare. He said, 'Are you really feeling stronger?'

My stomach flipped over. I set down my coffee cup, carefully and slowly. 'What's happened? It's Fran, isn't it? It's John?'

'No,' he said swiftly. 'They're safe. They're being well guarded. But I might as well tell you myself. Something else has happened.'

I knew by his face and voice that it was going to be awful.

It couldn't be Niall or Nina. I had watched them leave only minutes since. The sergeant said, 'Mrs Mary Grey? I believe you knew her?'

'Why yes. She works in my— what do you mean – *knew* her?'

'We went to your office intending to arrest Mavsoni. What we found were the battered remains of Mrs Grey.'

'And Paul?' I whispered.

'Gone. We tried his flat, but no luck.'

'So – so he's out there somewhere, anywhere?'

'Precisely.'

'He has a bungalow,' I said, 'near Dawlish. He told me it belonged to a friend, but I suspect it's his permanent home.'

There was a pause while this bit of information was passed on to the relevant police force. He slipped the radio back into his jacket. He said, 'They're fixing you up with a bed in a side ward. There will be an officer close by, so you can sleep easy.'

It was my turn for derisive laughter. 'I don't think I'll ever sleep easy again.'

'We shall catch him, you know! He's pretty distinctive-looking, wouldn't you say? Not too many six-foot-four, slant-eyed, black-haired blokes to be found in this bit of the world.'

'He could be miles away. He could already have left the country.'

'I wouldn't say so. Just think about it, Mrs Donovan. Paul Mavsoni still has unfinished business in these parts. He is, for some reason known only to him, carrying out a systematic purge of any woman who, according to his crazy reasoning, poses a threat to his safety.' He shook his head. 'We are dealing here with a mind that has lost its balance. We can only try to second-guess him, and that's not easy.'

He stood up and moved slowly to the door. 'If you think of anything else that might help us – like the reason why he might be doing all this?'

The side ward faced the double swing doors of Intensive Care.

The hospital mattress was hard, the pillows lumpy. From where I lay I could see the metal-framed chair and the black, nylon-clad knees of the woman police officer who was seated on it. I wondered just how much of a match she would be for Paul Mavsoni, should he decide to pay us a visit.

It occurred to me then, belatedly, that he was a familiar face around these hospital wards. Any member of staff who had not been forewarned would accept his presence without question. I left my bed, put on my dressing gown and slippers and sat down on the empty chair beside the policewoman. After I told her about my fears she straightway spoke into her radio. The sergeant's reply came loud and clear across the wire. 'Oh my God! So now she tells us! Ask the silly cow if there's any more vital information she's just happened to overlook?'

The girl gave me a questioning look and I shook my head. I wandered restlessly across to the swing doors, and peered through the glass panel. I felt useless, stupid, totally redundant. The sergeant was right. People like me served only to confuse and complicate the lives of others. The silly tears rolled down my face. I had set so much store by power-dressing; those expensive tailored suits, Italian shoes and Spanish leather briefcase said it all. When it came down to dealing with crises in my own life, I hadn't the brain cells of a wet hen.

I pushed open the door and returned to my vigil at Gloria's bedside. Nothing had changed. The coloured screens glowed and hummed, the nurses went silently about their business. I watched the deftness of their hands as they moved among the tubes and gadgets, monitoring, adjusting, watching for vital signs of recovery or deterioration.

These girls, these women, were the true carers of the world.

Something inside me died of shame as I remembered the pretentiousness of my own assumption of superiority. What was it the policeman had said?

'You have the gall to sit in judgement . . . to tell others how to run their lives . . . how they've got it all wrong. Crap!' he had shouted. 'Bullshit!'

I pulled my chair closer to the bed and began to tell Gloria about it. There was nobody else who would listen as she had. Her rough-and-ready advice had always been exactly right. I held her hand and thought it was less cold, less flaccid than it had been. I took courage from the slight change. I spoke softly. I said, 'Why didn't you tell me he was your husband? That first time, when I came shopping for a new dress – if I hadn't been so full of myself, so bloody snooty – I might have picked up properly on what you were saying. But I didn't, did I? And the irony is that listening to people is what I was trained for, latching on to the danger signals; and oh yes, you were flying red flags every time we met.

'I realised early on that you were an up-front sort of woman. What you would term an in-your-face, sod-the-consequences kind of gal. But I wasn't accustomed to honest dealing, to plain speaking. I come from a family of stiff upper lips. People who use words to conceal their thoughts and emotions rather than reveal them.'

I stroked her bruised hand. 'A strange breed of people, the Lambtons; the kind you would describe as "tight-arsed".' I struggled with tears and with the need to keep my voice steady, even though she could not see me, and almost certainly could not hear me.

'It's not easy,' I said, 'to get out of the habit of concealment, especially when you know that to speak your mind could cause mayhem. When people, seeing your distress even when you were a child, said, "Don't cry! You know I find other people's tears upsetting."'

I studied her swollen, misshapen face, and remembered how pretty she had been. And not just pretty. Piquant. Vibrant. Expressive. *Honest.* I touched my jaw, my droopy eyelid.

I said, 'Don't worry about a thing. The doctors here, they're like magicians. They *can* put Humpty Dumpty back together again. No problem for them. And speaking about the swine who did this to you, I know now that you did your best to warn me against him. Once you realised that he had been my escort on that first evening; the day I told you that I was in love, besotted with him, you explained how "all this in-love crap is an illusion. Watch my lips," you said, "there is *liking* and there is *lust*, and the sooner you admit that, the better you will feel."

'I don't know if you believed what you were saying. But thank you for at least trying to protect me. It didn't work though, did it? And here we both are – and I am so sorry – so bloody sorry.'

A nurse came to check on the machines that were keeping Gloria alive. Another nurse touched my shoulder. She said, 'You really ought to get some sleep.' She led me back to the side ward, handed me two tablets and a glass of water.

There was still Mary Grey to think about. I tried to work out what she could have known about Paul that would give him cause to kill her. But perhaps it no longer required the need to silence an incriminating witness? Perhaps he had reached a point where a wrong word, a wrong look, was sufficient reason for him to murder.

Imogen

It was three days after the attack upon her that Gloria stirred, opened her eyes and spoke my name. It had been an anxious time. I had left her bedside only to eat, sleep, shower and answer calls of nature. Advised by medical staff that it could be beneficial if I talked to her unconscious body, I told her stories of my childhood, read aloud the salacious items in the daily papers which I thought might stir her slumbering mind. I had started on *Northanger Abbey* when I looked up and found her watching me. Her beautiful violet eyes were the only part of her face that was still recognisable.

She spoke through swollen lips, badly bitten tongue and raw throat. 'Imogen?'

I leaned over, brought my face close to her face.

'I'm here,' I said, 'you're in hospital. You're going to be okay.'

'Was that you, reading to me?'

I nodded, full of relief and tears.

She raised the hand that was not attached to any machinery. She pointed at the book I was still clutching. 'That,' she said, 'is the most boring bloody rubbish I have ever heard.'

I laughed and cried both together.

Two nurses came running.

'She's back with us,' I cried, 'just as stroppy as ever.'

For the next two days she slept and woke, and slept again. But now the sleep was the healing kind. Within the week most of the monitors and lines had been removed. She began to ask questions. Her memory was patchy. I was warned to be careful; too much information too soon would not be good.

And so I prevaricated; dotted my answers with 'maybe's' and 'don't knows'. In the end she lost patience.

Still speaking with great difficulty she spluttered, 'For God's sake, Imogen, there's no need to spare my tender feelings! You should know by now that I don't have any. Can't you see? I need to be told exactly what happened.'

'So tell me, if you can, what you remember.'

She fell silent for several minutes, then she began, very slowly and with great effort, to reclaim her life.

'It was closing time and I was fed up. I'd had a browser in. Stayed for ages. No intention of buying. You know the sort. Pulling things out, pushing them back. Left the racks in a fine old mess, she did.'

She paused, moved her head and winced at the pain it caused her. 'I was straightening up, cursing to myself, when in walks Padraig. I hadn't seen him in months, and I certainly didn't want him coming round whenever the fancy took him. He was his usual revolting self, all smarm and charm. At the same time that he was trying to sweet-talk me, I was just finding out that my browser had helped herself to a few choice items. I could feel my temper rising.

'I said to him, "What do you want? If it's money, you're out of luck. I've just been robbed by some thieving bitch who—"

'He didn't let me finish. That had always been one of his irritating habits. He had to be in control, even in conversation.

'He said, "A coffee and a chat, that's all I'm asking. I've done something bad. I'm in terrible trouble."

'"I know you're in trouble," I told him. "You've been up to your old tricks. Don't ever think that I don't remember you and your little 'episodes'; you don't change, do you?"

'Even as I spoke I was discovering the loss of yet more small but expensive goodies. I remembered the woman's large shopping bag. I turned on Padraig. "You know the biggest joke of all? You as counsellor! Telling other people what to do, what their problem is.'

'The shock on his face made me laugh. "Oh yes. I know where you work. I also know what *your* problem is. *You're a nutter.* You need treatment. You should get your head examined. That spell you had in a secure ward – they should have kept you there – chucked away the key. How did you persuade them to let you out, by the way? Wouldn't surprise me if they're still searching for you."'

She fell silent and I put the drinking straw between her lips and held the plastic bottle while she drank.

'He looked so stricken that I felt ashamed. "Sorry," I told him, "I shouldn't have said that. You've caught me at a bad time." His lips began to tremble and I felt a right cow. "Look," I said, "I've a casserole in the oven. Come up and share it with me." '

She sighed. 'I was so full of my own troubles I didn't see the danger signals. His whining really got to me – I had forgotten to lock the shop door – I'd left the—'

Her head drooped and I was doubtful about letting her continue, but to stop her now could be even more risky.

'Take it slowly,' I said, 'we've got all day. I'm not going anywhere.' She raised her head and looked searchingly at me.

'Yes,' she said, 'I've been wondering about that. What are you doing here anyhow? You're not still poorly are you?'

I could hardly tell her that Paul had murdered Mary Grey. That the police believed Gloria and me to be in great danger. That Paul had disappeared. That he now posed a threat to my whole family.

I said, 'I still have one or two problems. More psychological than physical. Nerves and stuff. You know!'

'Tell me about it, why don't you,' she muttered. She closed her eyes and I thought she was asleep, but then she said, 'I can't believe I was so bloody stupid. How could I have forgotten what was most likely to light his fuse? He couldn't stand any hint of criticism, opposition. And if he even suspected you were laughing at him! We ate the casserole, had a glass of wine. I told him to go, that I was tired, that I needed to lock up, set the alarms.'

Once again she halted, and I could see by her expression that her full memory was returning. 'He was full of self-pity – as always, moaning on about his sad life. Oh my God,' she whispered. 'I actually told him to bugger off. I laughed in his face. I called him a poor pathetic Casanova. I told him his brains lived in his trousers. I remember seeing his fist come up, and the light catching the diamonds in that knuckle-duster ring. Then nothing.'

Her breathing grew laboured. Alarmed, I said, 'That's enough for one day. I shall have to call the nurse if you won't stop talking.'

'Just one thing,' she said. 'Who found me?'

'I did.'

'When? And where?'

I was saved by the arrival of the lunch tray. I spoon-fed her the same liquidised unappetising mush that had been my own diet when I was in her condition. But I was at least able to show her my repaired teeth and jaw, and to demonstrate my present ability to chew meat and eat apples, which is the acid test for all battered women whose faces have been rearranged. The effort of swallowing soup, followed by ice cream, was still enough to tire her. I also, having eaten egg on toast, fell asleep in the comfortable chair next to her bed.

As I opened my eyes two hours later, she began at once to question me.

'So when,' she repeated, 'did you find me? And where?'

'Upstairs. Lying on the sofa.' Having started, I thought it wiser now to tell her the whole story. I explained how I had arrived that morning to find the shop door unlocked, the OPEN sign showing, the music playing.

'That bastard,' she said, 'he left me for dead.'

I said, 'It could have been worse. He could have made sure that you were not found for ages! He could have dropped the Yale catch and locked you in.'

'He thought I was already a goner,' she insisted. 'All he could think about was a quick escape before another customer showed up.'

'Yes,' I said, 'that's how it would have been. He must have panicked.'

She attempted a smile, causing her lips to crack and bleed. 'What about my sofa covers?'

'A bit messed up, but I am sure they will dry-clean good as new.'

'Unlike *moi*. Take more than Sketchley's Gold Service to sort me out.' She again took a long pause. 'How would you rate my damaged looks,' she asked, 'set against your own?'

'A little more extensive,' I lied, 'but bruises and swelling soon disappear. And let's face it – you were more sexy and gorgeous than I was to begin with.' I touched her hand. 'It will take a bit of time, but you will mend, believe me.'

She moved her head a fraction, and grimaced. 'We're a right pair of sad bitches – you and me. What say we go gunning for him when we're both fit and able? He's done this before, you know. It's time he was stopped.'

'Good thinking,' I said. 'What do you suggest? Gun or razor?'

Her laughter sounded like rusty nails being dragged across tin, and then she fell asleep as suddenly as she had wakened, the smile still on her bruised face.

Allowing Gloria to talk, and filling the gaps in her memory had, I believed, been beneficial. But there was so much still unexplained.

I knew him as Paul. She knew him as Padraig.

He was not a widower, not even divorced, but still married to Gloria, although she did not use his name.

The backpacking son was a fictional touch, intended to add weight to the image he presented of a lonely, grieving widower and father.

I remembered his CV, his talk of previous employment, and the missing nine years which neither I nor head office had bothered to check up on. I wondered if the police had found out about the 'secure' ward. And why had Gloria, knowing what she so obviously did about his unstable history, his violent nature, not warned me more explicitly about the danger that he posed?

What was it about him that persuaded otherwise sensible and cautious women to protect him with their silence?

Even Gloria, tough lady that she was, had been tricked one final time into feeling sorry for him. Or perhaps she feared him, just as I had?

For if she had made mistakes, then so had I, and we both paid dearly for our folly.

The one who had least deserved to suffer, and who paid with her life, was Mary Grey. I had been asked by the detective if I knew of any reason Paul might have had to kill her. I could only say that it seemed to me his hatred for women was growing stronger with every beating; that sooner or later, never mind the degree of what he saw as provocation, murder had been a likely outcome. I was shown a silver-mounted, bloodstained hare's foot, which had been found lying under Mary's body, and asked if I could identify it. It was the lucky charm, the kitsch Christmas present I had given Paul; intended by me to be a bad joke, but received by him as a valued gift.

It hadn't brought him much luck, had it?

The smooth silver mounting had taken clear fingerprints. Prints which matched those on the cutlery and wineglass found in Gloria's kitchen, after that last meal they ate together.

Gloria was moved to the main ward and I went home.

Paul Mavsoni's Range Rover was found abandoned close to the estuary of Starcross near Dawlish. His flat had been searched; investigation showed that he possessed a valid passport and a sizeable bank balance. The passport was missing, and the bank account had been emptied on the day of Mary's murder.

A pile of neatly folded clothing was found close to the water's edge by a bird-watcher. I identified the white rollnecked sweater, the suit of green corduroy, the brown leather loafers.

The note found in his jacket was brief. 'No point in going on. Had enough.'

Remembering that afternoon in winter when we had watched the sun go down from that same spot, I felt a deep and aching sadness. I recalled his peculiar behaviour when the single magpie had settled on the Range Rover's bonnet. How he had gripped my arm and refused to allow me to shoo the bird away. Even then I had known his superstitious fears were abnormal, that his mind was troubled. But I did not believe he had drowned himself, and neither did the police.

Nina

We brought Imogen home on a cold grey morning in November. For almost a year we had made what Niall called 'the hospital run'. It was as much a part of our lives as the delivery of fresh eggs and bagged logs; and a routine we would be happy to relinquish. Immie looked well. She had regained some of her lost weight and her usual zest for life. Niall and I had feared that involvement with Gloria would set back Imogen's recovery by months, that her day and night presence at Gloria's bedside would stir up harmful memories of her own terrible experience. Each time we visited that intensive care ward we braced ourselves to find a collapsed and tearful Immie, begging us to take her home.

To our amazement, she seemed to thrive in hospital surroundings. She no longer complained about her own depression, or the pain she still suffered in her jaw and neck. Instead we were told of every slightest improvement in Gloria's condition. The fact that they were both under police protection was never mentioned. As the days passed I came slowly to realise that my daughter was simply doing the very thing she did best. She talked and she listened to Gloria with loving attention, and I was privileged to witness for the first time, and at first hand, the caring and compassion of a dedicated and devoted counsellor. Well, all right! I know what you are thinking. 'Patronising,' I had said. 'Unwarranted intrusion into people's private lives.'

But it all depends on the quality of the person who is doing the counselling. I should have come sooner to that conclusion. But I have never pretended that I am not opinionated and prejudiced.

Our neighbours, who had never quite known what to make of us, having learned of our troubles in the columns of the local *Gazette* viewed us with a mixture of sympathy and horror, and since we were more notorious than famous, a few of the more curious among them had edged closer, but not too close. Who could blame them?

In the soft fruit season there had been little offerings of strawberries and raspberries, brought to the kitchen door by Bob, and Silas. They refused to set foot across our threshold, although invited in. They peered fearfully across my shoulder, hoping for a glimpse of Immie. But since the attack on Gloria Beaufort and the murder of Mary Grey, our only visitors were policemen.

We were given their hotline number, told to be watchful. Niall bought a shotgun, ammunition and a licence to shoot. He taught me how to load and fire the gun. We had hours of target practice in the orchard. The shotgun hung from the lintel of the kitchen door, and we pretended that its purpose was to rid the barn of rats.

We were still, of course, a family under siege. Having Imogen home merely meant that now, although threatened, we were at least all together under one roof. It was Fran and her family who were most at risk. We were reassured by Immie that Mavsoni knew very little about them. Their names had never been mentioned in any TV or radio reports. To the best of her recollection she had never told him where they lived or what their surname was. Even so, police surveillance was a part of their protection; their door and window locks had been reinforced, and Fran advised not to leave the house unaccompanied. Our greatest sadness was that none of us had yet seen the new baby, a healthy ten-pound boy named Toby.

Joe continued to come each morning; the rattle of his bicycle wheels on the cobbled yard and his cheerful presence at the kitchen table confirmed that we were not totally pariahs.

In these weeks before Christmas we drew close to each other in a way that could never have happened in normal circumstances. We began to talk in the frank uninhibited way that hostages do to one another. Extreme tension and danger, we discovered, either closed people in upon themselves or opened the floodgates to confidences that would not otherwise have been given. We spent hours on the telephone talking to Fran and Mitch, to Primrose, and to Ashley and Angelique. We were visited at intervals by our detective, whose name was Henry.

And all the time life around us was going on exactly as usual. The tractor broke down and our detective sergeant, who had worked for a time in his father's garage business, took off his jacket, rolled up his sleeves and fixed it for us. Niall continued to deliver eggs and logs to surrounding villages. Ellie calved, five days late. For the whole of that anxious week I can truthfully say that we gave hardly a thought to the threat posed by Paul Mavsoni. Niall had built a shed especially for the confinement. We called it the maternity wing, and Imogen and I laid down fresh straw, filled the water bowl and forked hay into the rack, in anticipation of the event.

Ellie kept us waiting. She grew larger and more rotund by the hour, until we doubted that her short thin legs would take the strain. Immie and I, taking turns at carrying the shotgun, and looking like female homesteaders in an old-fashioned Western, walked down to the field many times each day between first light and dusk.

So great was our preoccupation with the little heifer that Mavsoni, despite the loaded shotgun, could have murdered both of us with no problem at all.

From time to time George, looking worried for quite other reasons, came loping across our fields to give us the benefit of a lifetime's experience of calving.

He examined Ellie's rear end and shook his head. 'Her'll be another week yet,' he informed us.

'In that case,' said Immie, 'she will have burst by that time.'

It was meant as a joke, but he did not laugh. 'You're not far out there, missus. Look at her, she's still eating like a good 'un, and that calf 'ull be gaining an extra two pounds for every day he's still inside, at this stage.'

Appalled, we could only gaze at one another. George ambled off, leaving us gawping at the munching heifer. Niall had also spoken lately about calvings he had helped at in his boyhood. Mention had been made of pulling-ropes and chains; of breach births and calves which presented upside down. Heifers which had died, and calves that were stillborn.

On the Saturday morning, inexperienced as we were in veterinary matters, it was obvious to Immie and me that something had changed overnight. Ellie no longer munched grass and hay. She was restless, pacing to and fro in the long grass that fringed the pond. Niall, who had other deliveries to make that morning, assured us that nothing significant would happen for hours yet. But, as Imogen said, he was a man, he had never personally given birth. What did he know?

Niall drove off in the pickup, telling us to keep in touch with him by mobile. He could, he said, be home within minutes if needed.

We began the daylong trek down to the field and back to the house, with never a thought for our safety.

Immie said at one point, 'This has got to go right for Niall! He's being all laid back about it, but this is his first calf from his own herd. It really matters to him.'

We were both aware of all that could go wrong. Ellie was very small even for a Dexter. The calf, if its mother's present girth was anything to go by, was a very large one. We had the vet's phone number written large on the kitchen blackboard. The worst that could happen was that we would lose both mother and calf. But even if the calf alone was lost it would be a bitter disappointment. We needed that calf, alive and kicking, for the sake of all our flagging spirits.

At five thirty in the afternoon Ellie's waters broke. Niall had not yet returned from delivering an emergency order of logs. Imogen pushed the mobile buttons with shaking fingers.

'She's started. Really started. Waters broke a few minutes ago.'

'Are you standing by her?'

'Yes.'

'Tell me what you can see.'

'What do I look for?'

'Two hooves and a mouth, perhaps a tongue. But whatever is showing, don't panic, I'm only half a mile from home.'

Immie held the storm lantern high above Ellie's rear. She said, 'Yes, I can just make that out. Two hooves and a tongue.'

'Is the calf the right way up?'

'I don't know,' she wailed, 'how can I tell?'

He had just begun to describe what she should be seeing when Ellie flopped down abruptly beside a blackthorn bush.

'Tell him,' I yelled, 'to get back here as quickly as he can. We're going to need some help, and soon! Ellie won't manage this on her own.' By this time it was completely dark, and I lit another lantern. The pickup came bumping down the field within minutes. Niall ran to the heifer, examined her and spoke gently to her. To us he said, 'She's having strong contractions, but this calf's a whopper.' As he spoke he began to unwind the expensive cashmere scarf that had been Primmie's last year's Christmas present to him. He rewound it about the partially visible calf and began, in time with the contractions, to pull very gently. To my relief the cruel ropes and chains lay abandoned on the ground.

Immie held aloft the storm lanterns.

I stroked the sweating trembling heifer.

Ellie groaned and bellowed while the soft scarf eased the black calf into the world. And then, with one almighty heave from Ellie, he popped out like a cork from a bottle, and I was young again, a visitor on Sunshine Farm, helping Jack and his brothers. I remembered the drill. I grabbed a wisp of straw and cleaned the bull calf's airways. I began to rub him dry while my tears dripped all over him.

Within half an hour he was on his feet and moving. In three

quarters of an hour he was sucking strongly. I had never known quite the same elation at any birth, either animal or human, and never will again.

The safe arrival of Henry seemed to be a sign, an omen of better times. Yes. We named our first calf for the detective sergeant.

Having settled mother and child in the clean straw of the lean-to, Niall could not bear to leave them. I suspected he might spend the night there. Immie and I took a Thermos of coffee and one of soup and went back to join him. We smiled and smiled, hardly daring to believe that something in our lives had finally gone right. The shotgun and its purpose was forgotten in the drama of that day and evening. I found it later, half-buried in the straw, and hung it back in place above the kitchen door.

Niall

Fatherless and motherless at the age of fifteen, there had been sufficient money to keep him at his boarding school for two more years.

He had wasted those years. Knew it, had always known it, but still felt no regrets. The distant relative, to whom ownership of Sad Acre had reverted on the death of Alice Donovan, had done his best by Niall, but the boy was not academically inclined.

Fin, his father, had put it more succinctly. 'Ye'll never make a silk purse out of a sow's ear, woman!' he had told Alice.

The boy Niall had liked this description of himself. After all, nobody expected great things from a sow's ear. Even then, all those years back, he could not stand pressure. He needed to freewheel, through schools, jobs, through women; he gravitated early towards bars and clubs, and betting shops. And now here he was, fifty plus, and his life come full circle, back where he started. At the age of fifteen he had not cared that Sad Acre Farm would never be his. If he gave it any thought at all, had any feelings about what might have been his inheritance, his only reaction had been one of relief. Farming was a hard discipline, a way of life. His father, by birth and inclination a wandering man, had been broken by it. Yet here was Niall, deliberately seeking responsibility in late middle age, tying himself down to fields and livestock. Sometimes he wondered about his father's early life, but speculation was pointless. Thinking back, now that he himself was no longer young, Niall believed that Fin's heavy drinking, his uncertain temper, was down to a deep inner sadness, and the frustration of a man who had tried and failed to fit a certain mould and way of living.

Niall, in his marriage, had been luckier than Fin.

He had not deserved Imogen, had never expected her to stay with him. His inner ear had always been primed to hear the final slam of the front door, and her car accelerating fast away from the house, suitcases crammed to the roof, with no forwarding address.

It had never happened.

But even though she had stood by him in all his excesses, had known him for the idle, feckless bastard that he was, he could never feel gratitude, never appreciate or admit her loyalty and yes, better face it, her forgiveness. Oh, they had sparred and griped at one another. But she was always there, the one constant in his world, beautiful, elegant, and icily controlled. And again, using his new ability to see through another person's eyes, he looked at himself as his wife must have done, and knew that icy control was the only option for a sensitive and faithful woman determined to stay married, no matter what. And she had been faithful. He had taken her fidelity as his due. His reaction to her affair with the rat Mavsoni had shaken him more than he would admit. For the first time in his life Niall no longer called the shots. Instead of being the sinner, he felt himself to be sinned against; and the worst of it was that he deserved it. The fact that he had altered radically in recent months gave him no satisfaction. Niall was not proud of those changes in himself or the way they had come about. A decent man should not have needed to first look upon his wife's smashed features, her poor mutilated face, before realising how much he loved her, needed her; could not live without her.

For a man not given to introspection, or even honest thinking where his own faults were in question, he had, he thought, come a helluva long way in the past year. There was still quite a way to go.

In his many affairs he had, without realising, learned a bit about women and their ways, their needs. Certain subtleties had penetrated his thick skull. He no longer felt the urge to lie just for the fun of it. In the long summer nights when the pain of her injuries prevented her from sleeping, he and Imogen had talked about their lives, their past mistakes and future hopes. They had made slow and gentle love, and he wondered how he could ever have threshed about with a stranger in lilac nylon sheets and considered the experience romantic. Immie's affair with Mavsoni and its horrific outcome was, as far as he was concerned, better not mentioned. He saw no point in resurrecting what was over and done with; there were adventures of his own that would not bear scrutiny. But later, in the first weeks of winter, she had insisted on talking about it.

'Who else,' she asked, 'can I tell? Nina is too old to be burdened with it, and it's not the sort of subject one discusses with one's daughter.'

As it turned out Niall learned a lot about his wife in those early morning hours of late November. He discovered how lonely she had been in that strange childhood, when Nina, mourning her kidnapped first baby, had failed to notice how desperately her second daughter needed to be loved. He began to understand how that same need for love had caused his wife to turn to Paul Mavsoni. Niall himself had done no better by Imogen. Mistaking her quiet undemanding ways for indifference towards him, and not seeing her coolness as being the protective mask she habitually wore, he had turned away, sought other comforts, like booze and women and gambling. He began to tell her about his own strange childhood.

He used words and phrases that were awkward in his mouth, since he had never spoken of such matters or allowed such thoughts to have houseroom in his head.

As he started to speak he watched her face, her eyes. Shyness made his tongue feel thick, his lips dry. And then, he thought, but she's a counsellor, dammit! She's been listening to people's troubles for years, it's what she's good at. He was unsure how much she already knew about him; how much she had guessed at.

Tell it all, he thought. Nothing to lose. Worst thing she can do is laugh. They were sitting in the large bed, propped up on pillows and drinking the strong hot coffee he had made. The grey morning light filtered through the rain that poured down the window. He said, 'I was born in this house. In this room. I never knew how my parents felt about me. They never said they loved me – never said they didn't. I don't know how they felt about each other. Their marriage was a mismatch. He was the wandering vagabond. She was the landowner's daughter. I was born too late in their lives. I can't believe I was anything but an embarrassing mistake. The conflict between them was all that mattered. They were fixated upon one another. Most of the time I felt as though I was invisible. When the violence became more than I could bear, I had my escape routes.'

Even as he spoke, memories of those secret places flooded him with feeling. In recent months he had wondered at his own longing to return here. Now he knew what it was that had called him back. Ladysmocks in April, growing thick in the damp hollows of the river fields. Primroses in great clumps shining like pale stars in the hedgerows. The secretive wild violets scenting the dark corners of the woodland. Skeins of dirty-white Canada geese flying low in autumn, honking over newly ploughed stubble. In winter, his booted feet cracking the ice that formed in the deep ruts of the lane. Snow that stood shoulder-high, its whiteness dazzling to the eye, magical stuff which, for a week or two, had changed a child's world. A circle of blackthorns, a shelter impenetrable to adults but accessible to a small boy; a secret hideaway to which he would run when life in the house became intolerable. But life in the house was different now.

Freed from his mother's penny-pinching grip, the rooms were warm and cheerful, the kitchen bright and welcoming, a place where people lingered. The echoes of anger and hatred that had bounced off his brain when he first came back here had faded now. He no longer met ghosts at every turn.

Sometimes he was seized by emotions he did not understand. All he could be sure of was that he would never return to his old, self-destructive ways. He had been given a second bash at life, and how many men could say that?

His bewildered brain, struggling to cope with this multitude of feelings, had actually succeeded in pushing Mavsoni to one side. Gone, he thought, but not altogether forgotten. Because of the attack on Gloria Beaufort and Mary Grey's murder, and the extent to which his family was again involved with the police, Niall needed to persuade himself that Mavsoni was dead, and that the suicide in Starcross marked the end of the nightmare.

Niall believed what he wanted to believe, although the detective warned him that he himself was certain that Mavsoni had faked his death, and was still in the district.

One of these days, Niall believed, a body would be washed up further down the coast, and that would be that. In the meantime, there were further calvings among the Dexters; Bonny the sow farrowed seventeen piglets. An opportunity had arisen to rent an additional fifty acres of woodland; and on being discharged from hospital, Gloria Beaufort was to come to recuperate on Sad Acre Farm.

The additional acres of woodland lay on rising ground on the far side of the river. It was a neglected mixture of hardwoods and saplings and impenetrable thickets. The land agent had mentioned a cabin built years ago by a solitary man who had fished the waters and communed with nature. On a day of gunmetal skies and no wind Imogen and Niall, led by Nina's dog Roscoe, crossed the stone bridge that linked Sad Acre to High Woods and began to walk the boundaries of their latest acquisition.

They found a gate almost rotted from its hinges, lifted it to one side and then stood silent, gazing into the dimness of the dense growth of brushwood, the hazard of fallen branches.

Niall felt the significance of the moment, the intimacy of it. The leasing of the woodland was their first joint venture. He intended to involve Imogen completely in its future uses. This place was to be about companionship, equal status; about love.

He turned towards her, held out his arms, and she walked into his embrace and buried her face against his warm neck. He felt the wetness of her tears slipping down beneath the thick wool of his sweater.

'It's all right,' he murmured. 'Whatever happens in the future nothing can touch us. I love you. Always did. Just didn't recognise it.'

The narrow winding path was almost obliterated by suckers and vines. A deep mulch of fallen leaves absorbed any sound their booted feet might have made. It was Roscoe, excited to frenzy by so many strange scents, who dashed repeatedly ahead barking his shrill bark, and then bounded back to them for reassurance.

As they penetrated further into the gloom his absences became more prolonged until finally they lost sight of him altogether. They pushed on through brambles, Niall whistling, Imogen calling. And then all at once the foliage began to thin, the light grew stronger, and they were looking at a small green-painted wooden shack which stood on a patch of recently cleared ground.

Roscoe, his small body rigid, stood stiff-legged before the cabin door and would not come when called; neither did he bark. The silent terrified dog unnerved them. Niall reached for Imogen's cold hand. They gazed helplessly at one another. He said, 'Something's spooked him. I should have brought the shotgun.'

Together they moved closer to the cabin. Niall reached out a hand and the door swung outwards at his touch. A camp bed was made up with a pillow and blankets. Rough shelves held a collection of plastic cups and dishes, and several tins of soup, baked beans, and corned beef. An opened waxed wrapper held sliced bread. There was a jar of instant coffee, one of strawberry jam, and an extra-large container of Mr Greedy's Chocolate Spread. The sight of the familiar child's treat was as clear as a fingerprint to Imogen; she indicated the container.

'He loves this stuff,' she murmured, 'he keeps a supply of it in the office.' There was no need for her to speak his name. They both knew who she meant. The scent of lemon verbena was strong in the cabin. She tracked its source to a sachet which was pinned above the camp bed. A few cobwebs, some dust, might have been expected in a place so rarely occupied. But every inch of the timber structure had been swept clean, the sleeping bag and blankets neatly folded as if for a military inspection. The signs of Paul's obsessions were unmistakable to one who knew him well.

Niall touched the kettle which stood on the primus stove. 'Still warm,' he said. 'He must have heard us coming.'

At the rear of the hut, half-hidden in a whitethorn thicket, they found a touring bicycle with panniers which held a waterproof cape and trousers.

'Oh clever,' said Niall. 'Nobody looks twice at a bloke on a bike. No number plates, no driving licence, no insurance.' They had been speaking softly, but it occurred to them now that their words might be audible to a watcher and listener. Niall picked up the nervous dog and gestured that Imogen should start walking ahead of him down the woodland path. It was not until they had crossed the river bridge and were back on Sad Acre that they risked further speech.

Niall halted, set Roscoe down and put an arm around Imogen's shoulders. 'You're quite sure it's him?'

'Yes,' she said, and with the admission came the full shock of what they had just witnessed. 'But how,' she asked, 'has he managed to stay hidden in there for all these weeks?'

Niall said, 'He hasn't. He'll have been constantly on the move. This time of year – plenty of seaside caravans and chalets closed up for the winter. A night here – a night there. Working his way gradually up the coast from Starcross. From the setup back there, I would say he's a bloke who's been on the run more than once in his life.'

'He'll have changed his appearance,' she said. 'Grown his beard back. Those cycling getups are like camouflage.' She paused. 'It's getting colder every day. He daren't risk a fire. How much longer does he plan to stay there?'

Niall said, 'Not much longer. Whatever he's planning—?'

'And now he knows that we know he's there—?'

Niall reached for the mobile on his waistband and then remembered he had left it on the kitchen counter.

Nina

I watched them walk away that afternoon, close together, hand in hand, across the yard and into the fields that led down to the river.

Sometimes in life what has appeared to be a hopeless situation begins to turn around, to come out right, and in circumstances and for reasons one would never have dreamed of.

I cleared away the remains of our lunchtime sandwiches and soup. The only problem on my mind was whether I should freeze what was left of the minestrone, or serve it up again for supper. I tidied the kitchen, folded some laundry, telephoned Fran about arrangements for their Christmas visit.

'So how are the parents?' she asked.

'In love,' I told her.

'With each other?' Her voice was light and mocking, but I could hear the undertones of pain. Fran had known more about her parents' problems than any of us had suspected.

I laughed. 'Very much with each other,' I told her. 'Lovebirds could take lessons from them.'

'In spite of all that's happened?'

'Because of it,' I said.

'I hear they have plans to start up a scheme for family farm-holidays?'

'They're just talking about it at the moment. But we have Gloria coming here to convalesce when she leaves the hospital, so we shall see how that goes.' We talked for a few minutes about the children, and promised to speak again soon. With the fate of the leftover soup still on my mind and undecided, I went back to the kitchen.

He was standing just inside the outer door. He looked changed but recognisable.

I knew at once who he was and why he had come.

I spoke with an authority I did not feel.

'Come in,' I ordered, 'and close that door behind you. Heating is expensive and this house is draughty enough already.'

To my surprise he obeyed, coming meekly in and pulling the door shut. I was acutely aware of the weapon which hung above the lintel. Keeping my gaze on his face I pulled out a chair, first making sure that it faced away from the shotgun.

'Sit down,' I commanded. 'You look absolutely frozen. I've got some hot soup on the stove. You'll feel better with a pint of that inside you.'

He sat down, looking dazed and surprised. 'Bossy old biddy, aren't you,' he said. 'Haven't I met you somewhere?'

'Not possible,' I said. 'I never go anywhere these days.'

I thumped a bowl of near-boiling minestrone down before him, and pushed a basket of bread rolls and a soup spoon in his direction. The cheeseboard still stood on the kitchen counter. I cut him a large wedge of Double Gloucester.

'There's some apple pie when you've finished that,' I told him. My hands were steady but my stomach churned and trembled.

He said, 'Are you always this welcoming to perfect strangers?'

'You're an experiment,' I improvised. 'I'm thinking of opening a farm-holiday business. You know, cream teas and bed-and-breakfast. Consider yourself my first guest.'

With his mouth crammed full of bread and cheese he was unable to answer. I poured myself a coffee from the still-warm cafetière, and sat down in a chair which placed him directly in my sight, and with a reassuring view of the gun; although much good it would do me, stuck up there on the wall!

He ate like a man who had not tasted hot food for many

weeks, then he paused, studied my face and pointed the soup spoon at me. 'Got you!' he said. 'You're the old girl who was spying on us in the car park!' He took time to gaze around the kitchen. 'Very nice,' he said, 'very *Homes and Gardens*.' His tone now changed from sneering to pleasant. 'Imogen has good taste, hasn't she? Pots of herbs on the windowsill, blue and white hooped china, bits of polished copper.' He nodded his approval. 'I like it,' he said, 'oh yes, I really like it.' He sounded like a prospective purchaser of the house rather than a murderous intruder.

'Apple pie?' I asked brightly. As long as I could persuade myself that this was a social occasion, and pretend that the man I was treating like a welcome guest was not the one who had beaten and left for dead his own wife and my daughter, and murdered an innocent colleague, then I might just survive.

But as if he read my mind he brought his fist down hard on the table-top, making dishes jump and my stomach turn over. Swiftly I slid the plate of apple pie towards him. He began to eat and I took the opportunity to study his appearance. He was dressed like a racing cyclist in one of those suits of stretchy, brightly-coloured latex material, striped blue, lime green and yellow. Topped by a long woollen sweater and grubby raincoat he should have looked ridiculous, but didn't.

I watched him, fascinated, as he shovelled the food into his mouth. I poured him a coffee. His eyes were red-rimmed as if he had not slept for a long time. His skin was grey with exhaustion and ingrained grime.

In my state of near-hysteria I was tempted to offer him a hot bath, since to place him in the bathroom, naked and soaking in hot water, would disable him at least until Niall and Imogen returned. He became aware of my gaze, read the terror in my eyes. He pushed his plate away. 'You know who I am?'

I nodded and he looked pleased, as if my recognition gratified him. He leaned back in his chair. He said complacently, 'They'll be back soon.' He began to sip his coffee. 'Wise of you to invite me in. I was coming inside anyway. I have more right to be here than Niall Donovan.' He slammed his cup into the saucer and I could feel the barely suppressed violence coming off him in great waves. He broke off a piece of the Double Gloucester cheese and began to chew it. 'I should have finished her off then, you know, when I had the chance. Getting involved with her in the first place was my big mistake.'

He was talking about Imogen. I studied his grimy fingers and the knuckle-duster ring he wore on his left hand. I thought about those fists smashing the delicate bones of her face, and I wanted to kill him.

I said, 'Gives you pleasure, does it, beating up women?'

He answered with deliberation, as if this were a serious debate in which he needed to score points. 'If we are using precise language here, and I think we should on a matter of such importance, then "pleasure" would not be the correct word.'

He steepled his fingers, looking quizzical, and I played along.

'So what terminology would you use, Mr Mavsoni, to describe your actions?'

He sighed and rubbed a hand across his face. I could see that the warmth of the kitchen and the hot food was making him sleepy. With an effort he shook himself awake; he looked towards the window, forgetting our discussion.

'Almost dark,' he said, 'so where the hell are they?'

I shrugged and stood up, but slowly, not wishing to antagonise him. I said conversationally, 'We used oil lamps to begin with, but just lately Niall put up a fluorescent strip here in the kitchen.' I moved slowly to the light switch, but he seemed hardly to notice. I flicked the switch and the room was flooded with the harsh light. I began to collect the dishes he had used, but this time my movements annoyed him.

'For God's sake sit down,' he shouted, and then in a low and charming voice, 'Do you believe in omens?'

It was then I decided that he was quite mad.

Niall

The light was fading fast as we crossed the field. We were walking at a smart clip, still talking about Mavsoni. I could hear the fear in Imogen's voice. 'He'll have been hiding in the woods,' I said, 'waiting for us to leave the cabin. He'll be packing his bags and on his way, now that he's been discovered. I'll phone the detective as soon as we reach home.'

The pale bulk of the house was just visible among the leafless trees.

Imogen said, 'There are no lights.' She sounded anxious. 'Not even a lamp in the kitchen.'

'Don't worry.' I told her. 'He'd never be stupid enough to go to the house.' But even as I spoke the fluorescent tube did its usual preliminary flicker and then sprang into full glare. I grabbed Immie's hand and began to run. 'Something wrong,' I shouted. 'Nina never uses that switch if she can help it, she prefers the oil lamp. You know how much she hates that strong light. She's trying to warn us.'

We slowed as we came into the yard. As we crept past the kitchen window we could see him seated at the table, the back of his head, the weary slump of his body. I turned the door knob very slowly and pushed open the ill-fitting door. At the sound of its high squeak he spun round in his chair and faced us. I glanced quickly at Nina and saw that she was very pale but quite unharmed. I stood beside him, looking down on the broad high cheekbones, the slanting no-colour eyes. I shrugged off my heavy jacket and draped it across a chairback. Behind me, just out of his sight, Immie was reaching upwards for the shotgun. As I seated myself, well away from him at the far side of the table, she pushed the gun into my hands. We both knew it wasn't loaded, but he didn't. I said, 'Hi Padraig! Well, fancy finding you here. It's been a long time. So what happened to the donkey?'

His face took on the expression of a petulant child. If our situation had not been so tense, I might have found him comic. But then I remembered what he had done.

He said, 'You weren't supposed to say that! Oh, you knew all the time.' He whined as if we were playing some child's game, 'You knew it was me.'

'No,' I said, 'how could I have known? A family counsellor called Paul Mavsoni is a far cry from a tinker boy who once saved my life. But you've got a memorable face, Padraig. I'm just amazed that the police haven't picked you up, long ago.'

Imogen spoke for the first time, and her voice was strong, contemptuous and cutting. 'Why have you come here? You must know the police are watching this house. Nobody believes that you drowned yourself in Starcross.'

He ignored her words, didn't even glance in her direction, and continued to lock his gaze on to mine. 'You know why I'm here, don't you, brother?' He leaned across the table. 'Take a good look at me. I'll tell you what you see and hear. You see Fin Donovan's body. You hear his voice. All right – so my mother was Romanian – there's a bit of her in me too. But that apart I'm Fintan's boy – just the same as you are.'

I stared at him, a sick fascination turning my stomach.

'No,' I whispered, but all the time I knew that what he claimed was true. The foreign mother accounted for his different eyes and facial bone structure, but in all other respects, he and I were a matched pair.

I stole nervous glances at Imogen and Nina. I could see by their stunned looks, the dawning comprehension in their eyes, that they were reaching simultaneous conclusions.

Both had heard the tale of my childhood rescue from the

bogland by the strange boy who had disappeared that same day. The word '*brother*' was sticking in my throat, and Padraig knew it.

He said, 'Happens in the best of families – the good son and the black sheep. Don't fret about it – *brother*! It's not contagious. Circumstances have turned me into a basket-case. You were the lucky one. You had a full-time daddy and mammy.' He waved a hand. 'And you copped for all of this.'

It was his confident assertion that I had been the favoured one that made me forget for the moment that this was the man who had beaten my wife and murdered her colleague. I was also surprised at his insight into his mental condition. I said, 'Is that what this is all about? You coming back to claim your birthright?' I shook my head. 'This farm belonged to my mother's family. It was never hers to dispose of. On her death it all reverted to a distant cousin. I have it on a five-year leasehold. So all your crimes have been for nothing.'

He continued to argue his case as if I had not spoken. He turned to Imogen. 'You never guessed, did you? It was pure chance that we were working in the same line of business. Mavsoni was my mother's name. When I saw the name Donovan on that seminar announcement I had an "intuition" that you were the one who would lead me to my long-lost brother. I have these "insights" you understand! I *know* things, and I am never wrong—'

'Well,' I interrupted, 'how bloody clever of you! Quite the latter-day Rasputin, aren't you?'

He nodded, obviously flattered by the comparison to the Mad Monk. But then he underwent another bewildering mood change, and became entirely lucid. 'You'll have to get out,' he stated calmly. 'I am not prepared to share the farm with you. You've done it up very nicely, and I am grateful for that. But you are in my debt. I saved your life, as you have admitted; and the law is on my side. I am Fintan Donovan's only legitimate son. And I can prove it.'

There was something gut-wrenchingly believable about the way he spoke.

'Shocked, aren't you,' he gloated. 'Guessed you would be. Who would have thought it of old tight-corseted Alice? But our papa was a regular charmer – something else we both inherited from him.' He paused. 'Ah, come on now. Don't look at me like that. We've the same blood in our veins, Niall, no matter how much you deny it. My Romanian mother might have been a gypsy – but I was the rightful heir. With her it was marriage – or on your bike, Fintan.'

I wanted to lay hands on Padraig, to do him damage, but there were things I needed him to tell me. 'How do you know all this? How could you know?'

He tapped the side of his nose with an index finger. 'Horse's mouth,' he sniggered. He pulled himself upright in his chair. 'I was here that morning, the day they killed each other. Saw it all. Heard it all.'

'Tell me,' I whispered.

'They were fighting. Top of the stairs. Alice knew that my mother and her people were camped up in the lane. There was always trouble between your parents when we were in the district. Alice believed that my mother was no more than an old flame of Fintan's, and Irena was happy to go along with the lie, just so long as Fintan was paying her well to keep her mouth shut. But Alice was a tightwad, she held the purse strings. He owed us a lot of hush money, and I had been sent down to the farm to collect.'

He paused to drink a mouthful of cold coffee. He looked so white and drawn I was afraid he might pass out before the tale was told.

'The front door was open. I stepped into the hallway. They were on the landing. "Not one penny more," Alice was shouting, "for your harlot and her bastard." Fin was drunk. He was hanging on to the stair-rail with one hand and punching her with the other. He was laughing. "You're wrong there, woman dear," he told her. "Time you knew the truth. 'Tis you that's the harlot, and your Niall that's the bastard. I married Irena, all right and decent in a Roman Catholic church, many years before I stood with you before the village parson."

'"That makes you a bigamist," she screamed.

'"And you a fool – *English* woman!"

'It was then that she pushed him, but as he fell he grabbed at her long skirts and they came rolling down the stairs together.

'I stood watching by the open door. When they stopped moving I went to them, but without needing to touch him I could see that my father's neck was broken; that he was dead.

'I knelt down by Alice, made to help her, but she called me "vermin" and said for me to go away, that she wanted no help from a dirty gyppo. She dragged herself to the rocking chair, and sat there – rocking. I sat on the floor and waited for her to die. The pain was in her chest, and I could see that it would kill her. It took quite a time, and all that while she was holding a great roll of banknotes in her left hand, clutching it as if it could prolong her life. When I was quite sure she was dead, I prised loose her fingers and took what was rightfully my mother's.

'We left the lane that same night. It was a great deal of money, and it changed our lives. We went to live in a small house, and I learned to read and write. I found a job, bought good clothes, and women were attracted to me. My mother died and I was on my own, and it was then that I began to think about my father's farm, this grand house and the land that went with it; and how I was Fintan Donovan's only true son.'

I said, 'But you never came back? All these years?'

He said, 'I was afraid to come back. I didn't know what had happened here when their bodies were found. I guessed the police must have been involved – someone might have seen me leaving the house that morning. But I never stopped thinking about it – about you – living here where you had no right to be.'

Loath as I was to touch him, I leaned across the table and gripped his wrist. His mind had a tendency to wander and I needed his full attention. 'I've said all this before, but you didn't take it in. So listen to me,' I said. 'Some things you should know. *I inherited absolutely nothing*. It was the distant relative to whom the property reverted on my mother's death who paid my school fees. I hated this place, wanted no part of it; made a different sort of life for myself in London. I married, had a daughter, and then a grandson, and suddenly saw myself, rootless, unhappy, and getting older, and I remembered Sad Acre. When Imogen's job brought her south I began to wonder what had happened to the farm. I found it virtually derelict, and the leasehold vacant. *You could never have owned it Padraig. Neither could I. It was never ours to claim.'*

I watched his face, saw the bemused haze clear from his eyes, and total sanity look out.

He said in a quiet voice, 'And this is the whole truth?'

'Yes. You can check with the Hammet Street lawyer in Taunton—'

'No. I believe you.' He loosened his wrist from my grip. 'You know what this means, don't you?'

'Yes,' I said, 'it means that all those years of your trying to trace me, of stalking my wife, of attacking her, and beating up your own wife, of murdering Mary Grey – it was all for nothing, it need never have happened. When the police catch up with you, you'll go down for life.'

He swayed forward in his chair looking pale and sick; and I thought that this time he must surely faint. But he fooled me; he lunged across the table and his hand snaked out to grab the gun. In one swift movement he was on his feet and making for the door. We heard his boots click across the cobbled yard.

I shouted to Imogen and Nina, 'He can't harm anybody with the gun. It isn't loaded.'

'Oh, but it is,' said my wife, who knows nothing about firearms. 'I reloaded it this morning.'

I recognised the approaching car by the rough sound of its engine. Jason's four-hundred pound bargain now lacked an exhaust as well as other vital bits. He used it lately only to drive between villages, but a vigilant policeman must have spotted his dangerous progress among the lanes, and both came through the farm gate, Jason at his usual reckless speed, the patrol car dangerously close behind him.

We stood, the three of us huddled together in the doorway, and watched it all happen faster than it takes to tell.

Padraig, his body bent low, the shotgun in his hand, ran fleet as a mesmerised rabbit towards Jason's headlights.

Jason, swerving violently to avoid him, hit the barn wall.

Padraig, still on his kamikaze course, headed straight for the patrol car, and was thrown up and over its flashing roof light.

We heard the thump of his body, the crack of the rifle, a shrill scream, and then silence.

The storm lanterns are kept on a high shelf in the kitchen. While Imogen and Nina did their best to illuminate the carnage I phoned the hotline number given us by Henry. Out in the yard I went first to Jason's car which was a total write-off. I felt sick as I wondered how I would ever find the words to explain his terrible death to his grandfather, Joe. I should have known better. As I opened the driver's door, Jason groaned, staggered out, and swore at some length when he saw what remained of his pride and joy.

Miraculously he had suffered only cuts and bruises. I persuaded Imogen to go with him to the kitchen, patch him up and make a pot of strong tea. Whatever might have happened to Padraig, it was better that she shouldn't see it.

Up by the farm gate the two patrolmen, badly shocked and possibly concussed, bent over Padraig. Even by the weak light of the storm lanterns, his injuries looked horrific. The spread-shot from the gun had all but destroyed his face; his limbs were at awkward angles as if several bones were broken.

Whatever he had planned when he made that crazy dash from the house, it could not have been this, and if suicide had been his intention, then he had failed. The paramedics, and later the hospital doctors, confirmed that although permanently lame, and blind in both eyes, there was no reason why Padraig, confined in the psychiatric wing of a prison hospital, should not live on for many years.

Niall

He was my brother.

In all that time, in the forty or so years since that morning when he pulled me from the bogland, he had known that we were close kin, but had made no move towards me.

The knowledge had festered in him.

'You were the lucky one,' he had accused. 'You had a full-time mammy and daddy.' And perhaps there was some truth in what he said. Looking back there had been a certain security for me on Sad Acre, a sense of belonging. Perhaps even warring parents are preferable to the wandering unsettled existence he had experienced in his early years.

I had it easy. Orphaned at fifteen, yet I was taken care of by a distant relative. I thought about him, learning to read and write in his late teens. Dragging himself up by his bootstrings, concealing his origins, struggling to attain the style of life, the education I had so casually rejected. The money he had taken from my mother was not stolen. Fintan Donovan had owed him that, and much more. But somewhere down the line something had turned sour in him. Just what and when I shall never know.

Perhaps, initially, it was that chance meeting with Imogen, the name Donovan, which had roused his curiosity, his subsequent enquiries which had led him back to Taunton and Sad Acre Farm?

There are whole areas, great slabs of his life about which I know nothing. When did the violence begin? And why?

Speculation is pointless, and yet . . . ?

Last week, two days after Christmas, I visited him in the prison hospital.

Death would be preferable to his present condition.

I sat at his bedside, knowing that he was blind, that he would never walk, never see, never leave this place, and in spite of everything I could not hate him. He had been my brother. All those years and we had never spoken.

He had a present for me.

Wrapped by a nurse in shiny Christmas paper, I found a faded green silk neckerchief, and a little pearl-handled pen-knife.

'Take it,' he said. 'You gave it to me. First gift I had ever been given in my whole life.'

He slipped in and out of consciousness, and the prison doctor told me that he would not live to see the New Year. The paramedics had been wrong about him, and all I can think of now is the wasted years.

Imogen and Gloria will recover eventually from the harm he did them. Immie and I attended the inquest on Mary Grey, who is gone forever. We took flowers to her funeral. Imogen spoke of Mary's kindness, her commitment to her colleagues and clients. An over-involvement which, although that point was not made, may well, in the end have cost her her life.

Imogen

Niall is still deeply disturbed, and only time will help the healing process. He conceals his pain very well, but I know what he is going through. We have all been offered counselling for post-traumatic stress syndrome, which we politely declined.

Our strength lies in the fact that as a family we are united and loving. We shall mend without outside intervention, because of our closeness and determination.

Christmas, which in the circumstances threatened to be another non-event, turned out to be happier than any I remember.

We held open house. Nina organised it all: decorations, large tree, a line of plastic dancing Santas fixed above the front porch, flaming pudding, crackers. The whole childish, glorious event.

I didn't know she had it in her!

They all came.

Gloria to convalesce. Fran and her family. Primmie, Ashley and Angelique. Joe and his wife, and their grandson Jason. Even Bob and Silas, those old enemies of Nina, dropped in on Christmas Eve, grinning broadly, and holding mistletoe above her head.

I was so angry when we first came here; my mind so narrow and closed off. I was so bitter about Niall, my mother, my whole life.

The future is down to us, although we still have one foot in the past. But already the wild orchids are blooming in the lanes, and our first lambs are skipping in the field.

Nina

The sign at the front gate says 'Sad Acre Guest House. Farm Holidays. Bed and breakfast. Children and pets made welcome. RAC and AA recommended'.

It's so easy to simplify one's life. All it takes is a few pen-strokes. I sold the Toll House in Ashkeepers to Ashley and Angelique. Advised by Monty Barnacle, estate agent, (who is fast becoming a valued friend) I invested the money from the house sale in Immie's and Niall's new venture.

We are fully booked already, up to and including next Christmas, with Gloria and Primrose as long-stay guests.

My great-grandsons, John and Toby, have taken to the farming way of life with as much enthusiasm as has Imogen, their grandmother.

As you will have noticed, I have been allowed to have the last word. But you probably guessed that I would. There have to be some privileges allowed us old folks!